T0162679

DRAGO'S JOURNEY

Through the Wormhole

Lewis S. Delameter

iUniverse, Inc.
Bloomington

Drago's Journey
Through the Wormhole

This is a work of fiction. All of the characters, names, incidents, organizations, and dialogue
in this novel are either the products of the author's imagination or are used fictitiously.

iUniverse books may be ordered through booksellers or by contacting:

iUniverse
1663 Liberty Drive
Bloomington, IN 47403
www.iuniverse.com
1-800-Authors (1-800-288-4677)

Because of the dynamic nature of the Internet, any web addresses or links contained in this book
may have changed since publication and may no longer be valid. The views expressed in this work
are solely those of the author and do not necessarily reflect the views of the publisher, and the
publisher hereby disclaims any responsibility for them.

Any people depicted in stock imagery provided by Thinkstock are models,
and such images are being used for illustrative purposes only.

Certain stock imagery © Thinkstock.

ISBN: 978-1-4620-0701-1 (pbk)
ISBN: 978-1-4620-0702-8 (clth)
ISBN: 978-1-4620-0703-5 (ebk)

Library of Congress Control Number: 2011904557

Printed in the United States of America

iUniverse rev. date: 05/05/2011

To my mother who never chastised me for day dreaming or story telling, but always supported me. And to my wife Lynne, who without her undying support, editing, and computer knowledge, this book would never have been completed.

I love you both bunches.

PROLOGUE

THE EARTH WAS DYING. The rapid climate change, pollution, senseless industrial accidents, and useless wars had combined to destroy half the world's oceans and large sections of the land mass. It had finally reached a point where even the most skeptical had accepted the fact that life on earth would only survive for a few more generations.

Consequently, the governments and scientists of the earth had joined together to form the New Interplanetary Space Agency (NIPSA).

NIPSA had developed a way to travel almost at the speed of light. In 2030 they had launched the first interstellar flight from the space station. The first ship was unmanned but had made it to the planet SBR375. While smaller than the earth, it met all the requirements for a habitable planet. In 2049, they had launched the first manned ship to the same destination. It too had been successful. However, the problem that affected both the Astronauts and scientists who made the flight was age. While they had perfected the cryogenics of keeping people alive, they still aged on the long flight. This affected their time for scientific research and development of the habitat.

NIPSA had finally come up with the idea to use children. This of course was met with much protest; both legitimate and bizarre. However, the earth was dying. The space program and travel to other planets had become the "new emergency" with the outcome being that they had finally decided to use orphans. Since the natural and manmade disasters had killed so many people, there was an abundance of orphans all over the world. Psychologists, physiologists, a multitude of other scientists, children's welfare groups, and governmental agencies had gone into overdrive to find and select these orphans for a hundred different reasons.

Finally, the first group of fifteen had been selected. The oldest was sixteen and the youngest eleven. They had been put through endless weeks of psychological, IQ and physical testing before being allowed to advance to the space station for more training while awaiting the long flight to SBR375.

Now the training was done, the ship was ready and they were taking off into space for a new beginning.

CHAPTER ONE

DRAGO HAD BEEN SITTING for over an hour listening once again to a lecture on what to expect when they finally made the trip. Looking around, he saw that the other kids were just as bored as him. They had been at the space station for over two months and had been through thousands of lectures and endless training sessions.

Drago was the youngest at eleven. They had found him at an orphanage in Puerto Rico. Whatever test and reasoning they had used; he would never be sure. As far as he was concerned, all that really mattered was that he had been selected. Now, he was ready to go. As he looked around again, he counted eight girls and seven boys including himself. I wonder why they picked more girls than boys he thought.

Suddenly, near the end of the lecture, the scientist in charge of their group appeared, leaned over, and whispered to their instructor. Standing back up, he cleared his throat to make sure he had everyone's attention. "Students," he announced, "the timetable for departure has been changed. Due to atmospheric conditions, we will now depart at 0600 hours tomorrow morning. Effective immediately, all classes have been canceled. Please report to the Med Bay Area for your final preflight medical exams. Afterward, there will be a brief Farewell/Good Luck Session, and then you will be allowed to retire to your quarters, do a final review of the personal items you are taking and prepare for your morning departure."

Immediately, all the children started talking excitedly. As they were led to the Medical Bay Area, there were a hundred different discussions going on. Drago heard the one girl, who seemed to be the oldest—she reminded him of Lucy in the Peanuts cartoon and seemed to be taking the lead in the discussions…. like she knew what was going on.

Her name was Naomi, and she had told everyone that she was from a

Christian orphanage in Haiti. Naomi had evidently gotten a good education at her orphanage; but just like Lucy in the Peanuts cartoon, she seemed to be a know-it-all with an opinion on everything. Drago wondered if maybe it was just the fear and nervousness that made her talk so much.

He knew that they were the first group of kids to do this, so nobody really had any idea what was going to happen. Some of them had been assigned to specialized training groups in preparation for their eventual assignments. The rest of them had been told that based upon their testing scores, they would be assigned to different groups once they got to the planet SRB375. All of them had been required to complete the basic training courses covering a wide range of topics that focused on survival and colony operations.

Sitting on his bunk after the final preflight medical testing and the Farewell/Good Luck session, Drago listened to the continuing talk among the group. Rashad, a black kid from a Brooklyn orphanage, who had the bunk next to him, leaned over and said, "I don't really care about all this talk. All I know is that I have eaten better and been better clothed than ever before in my life. Anything has got to be better than where I was. No more looking over my shoulder dodging gang recruiters, or being sent to another foster home, where the only thing they cared about was the check they received for keeping me."

Drago agreed. He had been given decent clothes and fed well at his orphanage in Puerto Rico. But the hours of loneliness and the countless interviews, where he had been rejected by first one couple and then the next was something he was glad to leave behind. To be going anywhere, to be a part of something was more then he could possibly have dreamed. Drago had felt for the last couple of years that he was destined to do something or be something different. He wasn't quite sure what that *something* was, but he was sure that this journey was his chance to find out.

In the morning at 0400 hours they started taking them in groups of two's and three's to prepare them for their cryogenic chambers. Once they were all in their chambers; the chief science officer, the navigator/engineer, and the pilot had one more meeting to discuss in-flight procedures before disembarking from the space station.

They were the only three adults going on this trip since the ship was totally controlled from NIPSA and there were already adults stationed on planet SRB375. The three had been selected from an elite group of applicants and would be staying on the planet with the others. They were on board primarily for emergencies, and would be entering the cryogenic chambers just as everyone else. Unlike the space kids however, they were scheduled for systematic wakes-ups to monitor the cryogenic equipment and to check in with NIPSA concerning the flight.

At 0600 hours, NIPSA initiated the flight and it took off from the space station. An hour into the flight after receiving the go-ahead from NIPSA Command and Control, the three adults entered into their chambers.

Three months later, the chief scientist and the pilot were awakened to go through the various in flight check point items required by NIPSA. After completing the required system checks and getting the okay from NIPSA, they returned to their chambers for another three-month period of cryogenic sleep as they hurled through space to their final destination.

CHAPTER TWO

Back at NIPSA Command and Control, the multitude of people watching over the monitors for each child and the three adults were pleased with how well everything was going. The NIPSA scientists and engineers assigned to monitor the ship's navigation and controls were also pleased. With all systems go and the journey well underway, everyone had settled into their daily monitoring routines and was beginning to relax a bit now that the first Ninety-Day Systems Check testing had been completed without a glitch.

Everyone had just finished with a round of applause and high-fives to each other when one of the scientists in charge of watching the universe through the Hubble telescope noticed an anomaly. He immediately notified his superiors and alerted the other scientists to a potential problem. Within seconds, everyone was refocused and attempting to verify the source of the anomaly. And what, if any affect it would have on the ship and its passengers.

At first, it appeared to be a blur on the telescope lens but closer inspection reveled that this anomaly was being caused by something happening in space.

The NIPSA engineers immediately began performing diagnostic testing while others reached out to their counterparts at various locations across the globe. One of the technicians tracking the spacecraft noted that the blur appeared to be directly in line with the spacecraft; while others started calculating the time and distance. Suddenly it became totally clear; the blur was not a piece of space fuzz that had landed on the telescope as many had hoped. It was a monster wormhole and before they could make any further adjustments, the ship entered the wormhole and disappeared from their screens. Warning bells sounded in the background of NIPSA's

Command and Control Center as the technicians desperately tried without success to reestablish contact. Other scientists and engineers were trying to determine if they could still track the ship's new path of travel.

Everyone was on high alert talking into their headset communication devices running their fingers over their computer keyboards like crazy.

All the top officials immediately came back from the conference room, issuing commands as they received reports by the second.

Finally, after many hours, everyone had to accept the fact the ship was lost. The science of interstellar flight and technology had advanced a great deal since man had first landed on the moon many years ago. Even though it had been hypothesized that wormholes existed as an erratic and unpredictable occurrence, they were still a thing of science fiction. All attempts to contact the ship's monitoring equipment had failed and no one had any idea where the flight was now headed; or, if it would even survive the trip through the wormhole.

With a heavy heart, the NIPSA Commander in Charge directed his staff to redouble their efforts in locating the ship then picked up the phone to notify the world leaders of the loss.

Meanwhile, aboard the ship everything was running normally. All the equipment kept functioning as it had been programmed to do. The only problem was in the navigation. The ship seemed to have momentarily lost the planetary signature directing it to SRB375. However, this contingency had been prepared for and the ship's automated navigation equipment automatically started trying to reacquire it. Should the navigation equipment fail to reacquire the SRB375 signature, it had been programmed to automatically readjust the destination flight pattern or find a similar planetary signature.

Within hours, the ship's massive computer program had crunched the numbers and found a planetary signature similar to their intended target. There was a slight difference in gravity, but oxygen and the other tangibles matched. Since there had not been any programming changes or alerts from NIPSA, the ship did not know it was in different galaxy. There was no need to activate the emergency cryogenic wake up procedures for the crew. It made no difference. The automated system readjusted the settings and headed for the new planet.

Six months later, the ship entered its landing orbit around the planet. As planned, the cryogenic equipment began the process of reviving the three adults so that they could start the pre-landing applications.

Coming out of a cryogenic sleep, one does not just awake and immediately get up. The process takes several hours as the equipment slowly shuts down while simultaneously monitoring the life support systems. Each person is injected with the necessary vitamins and other medications necessary to offset the prolonged sleep and ensure proper organ functions. As a final step, steroids are injected to overcome the muscle atrophy due to the lack of exercise, even though they had been electronically stimulated during the cryogenic sleep.

As the three adults had been going through this process, the ship had automatically gone into orbit around the planet. While orbiting, the ship had located a flat spot that resembled the predetermined landing coordinates and had made the necessary adjustments. It was then just a matter of maintaining altitude until the re-entry and landing processes began.

The pilot and navigator completed their wake up procedure first and went directly to the cockpit to start evaluating the landing procedures.

The Navigator/Engineer, Angelina first noticed the discrepancy. "Captain, you better check this immediately. My control screen is blinking with an alarm stating that there was a readjustment in the flight pattern and planet signature. None of these coordinates match the original coordinates that were programmed in the navigation system."

The Captain, just sitting down to his controls stated, "The landing procedure is already locked in. I don't have time to figure it out or take the chance on overriding the ship's controls. It appears that the whole landing procedure started ahead of the original schedule. We will have to let the ship land itself and hope for the best. Meanwhile, see if you can raise NIPSA while I check in on Doc, the medical officer to make sure he has everything under control in the Med Bay. Then we have to prepare for landing."

Just as the Captain was getting up to go check, the Medical Officer came into the control room;

"Captain something's not right. The chambers were not supposed to initiate the wake up procedures until we approached our landing orbit, but they have already started."

"That's because we are starting the landing process," said the Captain with a worried tone of voice. "At some point during the flight, something happened to cause a change of coordinates that we are still in the process of figuring out. Angelina is trying to contact NIPSA at the space station and the planet now. Take your seat and prepare for landing."

Just then, Angelina said, "Sir, there is no connection to NIPSA at the space station or on the planet. What's more, I checked the elements, flora, fauna, and life signatures that were stored in the data banks and I'm finding a slight difference. The oxygen levels are higher, nitrogen is about the same, gravity is lighter, and the flora and fauna of the planet are totally different. I did not get any internal matches. And most importantly, when I pull up the images of the planet on my screen, it's like nothing we have seen before."

Both the Captain and Doc looked at their screens. What they saw was totally different than they had learned about the planet SRB375. Just as they started to comment, the ship's audio/visual warning horns went off announcing, "Prepare for Landing."

Quickly strapping themselves in, they all watched their screens. Seeing an open plain before them with hills and what looked like trees in the distance. Saying prayers to their separate gods and crossing their fingers, they could do nothing but wait.

CHAPTER THREE

THE LANDING CAME so gentle that they were not sure it was done until the ship announced the landing complete. Unstrapping themselves; they all immediately turned to their computer screens to analyze the outside atmosphere and surrounding areas. Angelina activated the exterior cameras and recording equipment. Samples were being taken of everything. Probes had been deployed; including SAP's (Soil Analysis Probes) designed to test the ground they had landed on for microbes and mineral content.

The Captain immediately started checking to see if the landing had started any fires on the open plain before them. He noticed that the grass, for want of a better term, was melting rather then burning and that it almost seemed to put itself out. The Captain ran his hands through his hair, sat there for a moment then called for his crew to stop what they were doing so that they could figure out a plan of action.

"If I may go first," Doc said, "the children will be coming out of their chambers in about three hours."

"Is there a way we can slow down the process?" the Captain asked.

Doc quickly responded, "Not without going into untried territory. We could end up killing them all if we try to interfere with the process."

"Okay," the Captain said, "first we are going to need to come up with a plan on what we are going to tell them and what we are going to do when they come out of their cryogenic chambers."

"Second, Angelina, you need to begin analyzing the external monitoring reports. Run every test and diagnostic you can think of pertaining to our new environment. We have emergency rations for fifteen days, but we will need to go outside long before then. I know we are carrying a large shipment of plant seeds and animal embryos, but they were selected for the other planet. We will have to figure out if they will work here."

"Also, Angelina, please set up a permanent SOS signal beacon on every channel you have; maybe something will get out. Meanwhile, I will review the equipment and tool manifest to determine what we transported. The inventories will tell us what we have in order to survive."

"Doc, you have the tough job, figure out what we are going to tell these kids and how we are going to handle them. I never had any children. Other than being straight up with them like I was talking to the men and women under my command back on earth, I don't have a clue. Let's get back together in two hours to discuss—that gives us one hour to solidify our plans."

Drago was feeling the tingling sensation they had told him to expect when he was waking up. Next would come the needles and injections, some shaking of his limbs, coughing up fluids, and then finally, the capsule would open. This was the part he dreaded, lying there unable to move with the capsule cover just inches above his head. It was like being buried alive and his claustrophobia was riding him hard.

Finally, just when he was ready to try and smash the top, it opened. Sitting up was harder then he thought. Also, there was the light headiness and dizziness they had told him to expect. Finally, he felt good enough to slowly crawl out of the capsule. Standing on shaky legs, he noticed the others were in the process of getting out of their chambers, or were already out. The medical and science officer was there telling everyone to take it easy and get their feet under them for a moment. Then they were led into the open part of the cargo bay.

Some were already excitedly talking about going outside. Draco himself could not wait to have open sky above him again.

"Everybody please sit down on the floor," the Captain announced coming into the bay. "There has been a slight change of plans. The Medical Officer, myself and Angelina have discussed how best to tell you. After much discussion, we have decided to do it my way."

Drago found himself much disturbed by what the Captain was saying. Looking around he noticed Naomi was starting to cry. While the only twins aboard, Dana and Garrard from an orphanage in Europe were holding on to each other tightly.

"Sometime during our flight, something happened," the Captain said. "We have landed; successfully, I might add, on a different planet than the planned landing on SBR375." Immediately, there were gasps and questions and children talking all at the same time.

"Silence!" The Captain demanded in a raised voice which resulted in a hushed silence. "As the Captain, I made the decision to tell you. Both the Doctor, who has been involved with you since your initial training began, and Angelina who is a single parent, had advice on how to approach you with this news. However, I determined that the best course of action would be to treat you like any other adult under my command and be straight up in apprising you of the difficulties facing us—and, I expect you to behave like them." Pausing for a moment to make sure they understood the gravity of the situation, he continued. "Even though you are much younger and don't have the maturity or emotions to properly handle this, I feel that we are all in the same situation here. Our survival depends on all of us at every level. Should something happen to us adults, it will become totally your responsibility to survive. Consequently, I am going to tell you what we have done so far and how we are going to proceed."

"Anyone not following my procedures or endangering any of our party will be promptly punished at the appropriate level for the offense. Do you understand? Please demonstrate this by saying yes sir."

After everybody had acknowledged his or her understanding, the Captain continued. "First, let me tell you of what we have done and are doing at this point. One, we have set up a distress signal on every known band we have. Two, we have programmed the ship's exterior sensing devices to continually monitor and test the outside atmosphere, gravity, flora and fauna. Third, I will be reviewing each one of your files to help establish where you can be of the most use. As I was not a party to the initial selection and evaluation process, I will have to review each one of your dossiers to determine what areas of expertise you have and where best to use you. Over my career in the service, I have found that these reports can be influenced by not only the questioner but by the person being evaluated so they are not always exact in their determination."

"Now, I must inform you that both the Doctor and the Navigator have informed me that I have a habit of talking above people. If at any time you do not understand what I am saying or the words I use, please raise your hand and I will try to make myself clearer."

"Next, I also need to inform you that one of the most critical items facing us will be the food supplies. It was determined early on by the NIPSA scientists, that fifteen days of emergency rations would be more than sufficient to meet our needs should the ship miss our landing coordinates on SBR375. I have already started reviewing the manifest inventory records of food supply items, equipment, and materials. The good news is that there was a whole section of the Cargo Bay devoted to transporting seeds and animal embryos. The bad news is that we do not know how, or if, these seeds and animals can adapt to this planet since they were genetically engineered for SR375. It is one of the many things you will be working on."

"Oh! By the way, I forgot to mention the chain of command here. I am in charge. You will discuss any medical problems with the Doctor first. Our navigator, Ms. Angelina will help with both personal and emotional problems. Both will be available to help you, once you have been assigned your responsibilities. Only after going through them, and you feel that your situation has not been resolved will you come to me. Unless requested by me, you will need to request an appointment to see me. Do you understand? Please respond by saying, yes sir." After pointedly making eye contact with the assembled group to make sure they understood, the Captain said, "Good." He then continued with, "One of the first things I will be working on is determining who will be going outside. If we are going to survive, someone has to go out into to the environment and explore."

"Before I return to the control center to start reviewing your records, I will require two things of you; no, make that three. First, you must eat the prepackaged meal packets to help revitalize your system after the long cryogenic sleep. Second, I am requesting that each of you write down any of your interests or capabilities that you feel will help us all in our survival. Finally, I am leaving the Doctor and Angelina here to have an open discussion on what's going on and to answer any other questions you may have."

"I thank you for your time and I hope I have not misjudged my decision of treating you as adults in being candid about our situation. Try to look at this as an adventure and an exciting challenge, because I assure you, it will be." With that, the Captain turned and left the bay.

"Before you start asking questions," the Doctor said, "you must get your nourishment and eat what is supplied. If you will all line up, I will pass out the food and drink packets. Then you can sit back down and eat as we discuss our position."

CHAPTER FOUR

As the Captain went back to his control center, he turned on the video cameras in the bay area. One of the things he had discussed with the doctor and engineer was that they had to find out who in the group were leaders, what their talents were, who the whiners were, and which child would be best suited to perform the individual tasks they would need to perform if they were to survive as a group. Like he had stated, he had read a hundred evaluations, some good–some bad. Some evaluations were right on the money and described the person to a 'T' while others missed the mark and were totally wrong. Since these were children, he especially did not trust the evaluations. And, in order to survive, the three adults would have to make quick decisions on whom and what those talents were.

He chuckled to himself. The one thing nobody knew was that he was an orphan also. He always felt his experiences growing up were what dictated why he never got married or had any children of his own. He also laughed when he thought about the evaluations given him by the so-called experts and the experiences he had in various foster homes. They had said that he was a dreamer and spent too much time daydreaming. Early evaluations indicated he had a tendency not to follow up on projects. That he had difficulty being understood in communication; thereby not coming across as being very smart even though his IQ testing had indicated differently. When he turned eighteen and joined the Air Force, the structure and discipline allowed him to concentrate his abilities. When his testing scores kept becoming higher and higher, he was accepted to the academy. The rest was history.

Allowing himself still another moment to dwell on the situation, he smiled again. In spite of himself, he was excited. What a real adventure!

He had the opportunity not only to explore an unknown planet but also to build a future society.

A sudden dark thought crossed his mind. He realized that one of the goals the three adults had to make was to select and train their replacements. He was in his mid fifties; the Doctor was in his late fifties, only the Engineer was in her thirties. If this group was to survive, they had to establish a structure and train their replacements. He put the cameras on record so that he could discus the children's questions and discussion items with the Doctor and Angelina later. Then, with a heavy sigh, he grabbed the evaluation reports and started to read them.

As Drago sat down with his food, he was trying to make sense of everything the Captain had said. Many were now asking questions of both the Doctor and the Engineer. He listened, trying to evaluate both their emotions and their concerns. He noticed Naomi was no longer the know-it-all, but asked questions only about how they were going to survive. Dana and Gerard asked more scientific type questions about measuring air quality and the different types of testing equipment on board. Loren, a girl from the southern states and a tomboy through and through was asking about the different types of seeds and what type embryos had been transported. Rashad surprised him by asking what weapons and communication devices were on board.

The one thing he noticed with all of them being orphans was the fact that no one seemed to be concerned about their parents or families. Of course, many of them did not have any parents or families and those that did were most likely better off without them—otherwise they would have never been chosen for this journey. Still, Drago was surprised that there were really no hysterics. Everyone seemed to be more concerned and somewhat excited about what they were going to do—rather than what had actually happened to them.

After everyone had eaten and asked their questions, Angelina had handed out pens and paper so that they could write down their interests for the Captain to review later. Before leaving to meet with the Captain, the Doctor and Angelina had told them to relax. They were also given permission to view the streaming computer video of their new outside environmental surroundings. As soon as the adults had left the Gathering Bay, everyone jumped up and headed for the computer monitors. The excited shoving and jostling for a position directly in front of the screens quickly turned to them deciding to take turns. When it was Drago's turn, he immediately focused on views of the sky. It seemed like he had been closed in forever. Suddenly, he noticed that there seemed to be two suns and what looked like two moons. Turning the controls to look at the mountains in the distance, he thought he noticed some movement in the grass, but after watching intently for a few minutes, he did not see any more movement. After turning over the consol to Emir, who was from India, Drago decided that he was not nearly as interested in watching the live-feed computer videos as he was in actually being able to get outside. As Emir took his place in front of the consol, he mentioned that he really wanted to wait for nightfall to watch since he was into astrometry and wanted to see the stars. Drago told him about the two suns and possibly two moons he had sighted. After looking for a few minutes, Emir gave his spot up so he could look again that night. Bruce, who took Emir's spot, was from California. His whole interest was in checking out the accessibility of the computer programming. In his mind, Drago had already pegged Bruce as a computer geek and game player.

While sitting there quietly waiting, Drago continued evaluating everyone as he tried to guess where they would be best placed.

Rashad, he immediately placed as a scout and protector. Drago had met boys like him before when being transferred about. When you became an orphan, survival demanded that you rapidly learn how to protect yourself. Some of the ones like Rashad, who always seemed to bounce from one bad foster home to another, developed a warrior mentality. If you were lucky enough to gain their trust and friendship, they would protect and defend to the death.

Loren, he placed as the farmer. She seemed to be one who understood growing things and animals.

Dana and Gerard, he placed on the scientific end. He didn't know enough about engineering to understand how many different fields there were, but he knew they would be part of that group.

Bruce would be a natural fit for this group, because of his computer knowledge and interest.

He had talked with Matzo, who was from China, and Choi who was from Japan several times while they were completing their training back at the space station. Drago already knew that they both wanted to be architects since all they were interested in talking about was building design and the different types of structural supports used in construction.

Among the girls, he had already placed Loren and Dana. He had thought about Naomi more than once, and all he could come up with was the know-it-all Lucy character from the Peanuts Cartoons. He had not spent that much time with the other girls but felt he had to place them somewhere.

Natasha was from Russia, and was always friendly to everyone. He had decided she was one of those people that if you wanted something done, all you had to do was give it to her along with the proper instructions, and it would be taken care of.

Tani, from India was definitely a geek. She was into computers big time and would fit in with Bruce, Dana, and Gerard nicely.

Molly was from Japan and understood everything Matzo and Choi talked about when it came to buildings and infrastructure.

Margarita, also know as Maggie was from L.A. She was direct and to the point, yet seemed to have a shell around her. Drago put her in the same class as Rashad.

Sophie was from Louisiana, and had been paired with him a couple of times during their training sessions on Earth before they were transported to the space station. She was always going to the kitchen to help out. He instantly put her as the Cook. She could take plain institutional food and with this added here and that added there could turn it into a fabulous meal.

Satisfied that he had everyone organized into their proper place, he decided he would go to sleep and see what tomorrow would bring.

Meanwhile, the Captain, Doc and Angelina had been reviewing the tapes of the earlier discussion session along with the evaluation reports on all the kids. In reviewing the tapes they had noticed the same thing Drago had.

"You notice how none of them are really upset by the circumstances?" Doc asked. "Other than Naomi, who seems more concerned on how everything is going to work out, none of them seems to be exhibiting any sort of panic." Both the Captain and Angelina agreed, they had also noticed it.

"I think it says something about being orphans," the Captain said. "They are used to the circumstances of their lives changing all the time, and have had to learn how to adapt quickly. I think for the most part, you can judge their concerns individually by the questions they asked."

"For instance, Rashad's questions about weapons and communication systems put him on my list for being one of the first to venture outside. Loren's questions put her involved with the farm and embryos. Three or four definitely appear to be budding computer engineers and three of them have a definite interest in engineering and architecture. The rest, I'm not sure, we'll have to further investigate and judge. The one thing I did notice was that Drago did not ask a single a question. Instead, he seemed to be studying everyone else as they asked their questions."

Angelina said, "I noticed that also." "After reviewing the recordings a few times, he and Natasha were the only ones that did not ask any questions. Because of this, I took the liberty of pulling his file to see what his evaluators had to say. It was pretty interesting—they all stated that he seemed to go out of his way to fit in and didn't cause trouble; even though he seemed to keep to himself, he got along well with others. A couple of his foster parents described him as spooky and aloft."

"Humm," the Captain responded. "I think I've decided for the first trip outside that I want Rashad and Drago. But first, I want to talk to both of them individually. Doc, can you let them know that I would like them to meet with me for a few minutes before everyone beds down for the night? Also, it would be greatly appreciated if the two of you would take the comment and interest sheets with you and try to put some summaries together for me. Thank you and I'll see you tomorrow."

Drago half woke up when the Doc came to tell Rashad that the Captain wanted to see him. It seemed like he had just dozed of again when the Doc lightly shook him awake to tell him that the Captain wanted to see him too. Looking around, he saw that Rashad was back. Rashad looked at him and winked. Drago didn't know what that was supposed to mean, but he took it as a good sign. As the Doc was leading him to the Captain's Quarters, he noticed that Emir was at the computer looking at the night sky.

"Sit down Drago;" the Captain said. Draco sat, but couldn't help feeling this was like one of the orphanage counselors telling him to sit so they could tell him that another family had rejected him for adoption.

"Drago," the Captain said; "I noticed you did not ask any questions of the doctor or the engineer.

"No sir," Drago responded, "I was waiting to hear what the others asked first."

After looking at him for a moment, the Captain responded, "You didn't have any questions you wanted to ask?"

"Just one Sir, but I felt they couldn't answer it… that only you could."

"What question was that?" the Captain asked.

"When can I go outside?"

"Before we discuss that, I have another question for you," the Captain said. 'Why didn't you provide a sheet with your interests on it?"

"I didn't have any interests other than to get outside Sir."

"Well then, what were you thinking about all that time while the others were asking questions and filling out their interest sheets? I could tell you were listening and studying what everyone had to say." Drago hesitated; he wasn't used to sharing his thoughts with anyone, let alone the person in charge.

As Drago sat there trying to formulate an answer, the Captain spoke again. "Listen, Drago we find ourselves in a situation none of us have been in before. So a lot of the rules no longer apply. We are in a desperate situation and in order for us to survive as a group, we are all going to have to step outside our comfort zones. So please, tell me what you were thinking."

Again, Drago hesitated as he took in what the Captain had just said. "Well Sir," he finally replied. "I was thinking what areas I would put the others in if I was in charge and how I would use them if I was making the decisions."

It was now the Captain's turn to hesitate. "How did you make these determinations Drago?"

"I did it by applying what I know about some of them; others, I just have a feeling about and placed them based upon that feeling."

"How well do you know them?" the Captain asked.

"I only know Sophie from the training; I met the rest of our group class after we were picked for this assignment."

"Humm," the Captain mused. "Do you mind sharing with me what your decisions were?"

"I don't know sir," he replied. "I've never really shared my thoughts before, and don't want it to affect the way someone will be assigned."

"Don't let that bother you Drago. I need all the help I can get. I only know what I have read about all of you in the evaluation reports and I don't necessarily trust what was written. As I said before, our survival depends on us. We will make good decisions and bad, but we must make decisions. Also, we only have fifteen days of food, which means we must get out and find food for ourselves on a strange planet with absolutely no knowledge of what is out there. So please, share your thoughts with me."

Drago spent the next hour telling the Captain what he had determined and how he would use the different members of the group. The Captain interrupted him many times to further clarify Drago's thought process when deciding which members should be assigned to the different groups. At the end, Drago felt exhausted. He had never gone into detail like this about his thoughts before. Many times he had been questioned by the doctors and administrators along these lines, but he had always managed to keep most of his thoughts to himself.

"Okay," the Captain said. "Thank you for your input. I'll see you in the morning at 0400 hours with Rashad to go over some training and additional instructions." Drago was so exhausted by the day's events that he had to ask the Captain why he needed additional training and instructions.

"Because you and Rashad are going outside in the morning," the Captain replied. "Now go get some sleep."

Yes sir," Drago said.

Leaving the captain's quarters he could hardly control his excitement, his exhaustion had evaporated with the news that he was going to be allowed to go outside. How he was ever going to be able to go back to sleep was beyond him. When he arrived back to the bay, he noticed Emir was still looking out at the night sky. Looking around their makeshift sleeping quarters, he saw Rashad looking at him with a smile and shaking his head.

As he lay down, Rashad rolled over and quietly asked, "Are you going with me? The Captain said he was thinking about having you to go out with me in the morning."

"Yes," Drago said. "We're to meet with him and go over stuff in the morning."

"I can hardly wait," Rashad said. "Do you realize that no matter what, we will be the first people to step foot on this planet?"

"I hadn't even thought of that," Drago replied.

How he ever fell asleep with all the thoughts running through his mind he would never know. But the next thing he knew, Doc was there getting him and Rashad up. After checking their shot records, he gave them breakfast and took them to the Captain.

CHAPTER FIVE

"GOOD MORNING GENTLEMEN. PLEASE, sit down. There are many things we need to discuss before you go outside today. It will be well after nine o'clock, our time before you venture out." Both Drago and Rashad's chests fell as they realized that they would not be going out right away.

"First, you have equipment that you will need to become familiar with and learn to operate," the Captain said. "Doc and Angelina will be going over the types of samples and information we will need you to collect. This will not be a summer stroll in the park. This first venture out is for info and recon only. We must be able to establish boundaries before we can make extended trips out. How well you do today will determine our initial perimeters and the amount of time we can spend outside tomorrow and in the days to come. You will begin by meeting with the Engineer, Angelina. She will go over the communication and video cam devices, provide instructions on how to set out probes, and how you will need to collect the required samples we will use to determine the properties of our surrounding areas. Next, Doc will give you some first aid procedures to hopefully prepare you in case of emergency. Finally, you will meet again with me to go over some weapon training and to brief you on what I expect. Is that clear?"

"Yes, Sir," they replied in unison.

When they got to the Engineering Bay area, Angelina was already putting together their equipment.

"Sit down at the table gentlemen," she said smiling and then began explaining their equipment. "First and foremost, these are your communications devices. This little gizmo is an ear bug much like the ones you have seen people using with their cell phones back on Earth. Except, the really cool thing about this piece is that it doesn't need a phone. It will enable us to communicate with you directly from the ship's command center and between yourselves should you get separated." Angelina then gave them a stern look before reminding them, "Everything you say and hear in your surrounding area will be recorded for review later."

Drago elbowed Rashad and grinned when Angelina started gathering up the next device that she planned to show them. Drago wondered if Angelina already knew of Rashad's penchant for using swear words when he thought no adult was listening. Then Angelina turned back around holding what appeared to be some sort of Velcro headband and recaptured their attention as she continued to explain.

"This headpiece contains a built in web cam that feeds live streaming video back to the computers. It normally attaches to a helmet but since we don't have any helmets, I had to improvise." Angelina then instructed them to remove their shirts as she held up what appeared to be a couple of small flesh colored squares for them to see.

"These little round band-aide looking things are monitors that I am going to attach to your chests. They will send back readings about all of your bodily functions—heart beat, oxygen level, blood flow, and skin reactions. You do not take these off for any reason, understood?"

"Yes Ma'am," they replied.

Both Drago and Rashad got up out of their seats and stood there as Angelina attached the monitors to their chests then instructed them to put their shirts back on and sit back down.

"I am now going to run a test analysis of your bodily functions, this will only take a couple of minutes, but you will need to sit quietly without moving." While Angelina read the different monitoring equipment printouts, they both just sat there waiting for this part to be over. Finally, Angelina seemed to be satisfied that she had enough baseline information. She then turned to them and said, "Now, I want you both to jump up and down waving your arms until I say stop."

Just about the time their lungs were ready to burst and their arms felt as if they were ready to fall off, she told them to stop, walk around for a few minutes, cool down, then to sit back down and relax. While they were trying to get their breath back, she continued the monitoring until their heart beats and breathing was normal again.

"Okay, that should give me enough parameters to judge by."

Both Drago and Rashad breathed a sigh of relief as they watched Angelina turn from her monitoring devices. She then held up a vest with numerous pockets and pouches for them to see as she explained. "You will notice this tool vest has pockets that contain vials, collection envelopes, and different types of testing equipment. When you are outside, we will be observing everything you see through the web cams. If we see something we want you to collect, we will notify you over the communication device. You will notice all the pockets are color coded for different types of samples. Please take special note of the brown pockets. These pockets contain your weights." At this point, Angelina opened up one of the pockets and pulled out a thick piece of flat metal. She handed the piece to Rashad and continued with her explanation, "I have tried to customize the weights in these pockets to fit your individual height and weight. Trust me; you will need this since there is a gravitational difference between this planet and Earth."

The Lieutenant Engineer then stood back and watched as they proceeded to put on their vests, headgear, and inserted their ear bugs. When they had finished, she inspected them individually to make sure the equipment was functioning properly.

"Okay, now let's go see the Doc."

As they were walking to the Med Bay to see the Doctor, both Rashad and Drago were trying to get adjusted to their equipment. The weights felt uncomfortably heavy and getting the webcams adjusted on their headgear took some adjusting to before they found a comfortable fit.

The Doctor checked their vital signs, added a couple of emergency push-vials of snake and insect bite vaccines to their vest pockets along with some last minute first aid instructions. Said good luck and sent them on their way to see the Captain.

When they got back to the Captain's quarters, the Captain had what looked like two different types of rifles and some other equipment spread out on the table.

"You guys look ready," he commented with a smile. "But I have some more equipment for you."

Drago wondered to himself if he was going to be able to walk carrying all this extra stuff as he looked at all the different pieces of equipment laid out before them.

"These two rifles are two of the latest models from NIPSA's military-space arsenal. This one is a laser rifle; and, depending on the setting, it is capable of shooting a laser beam that will instantly burn and cut on contact." Rashad watched intently as the Captain ran a quick military style demonstration video touting the various applications and uses of the laser gun. When the video had finished, the Captain solemnly picked up the second rifle. "This is a subsonic rifle that fires sound waves at different levels of subsonic speed—both lethal and non-lethal. Once again, the Captain played another instructional video demonstrating the gun's proper use. At the end of this clip, the Captain informed them that he had pre-set the controls at a level that should destroy anything you see. He then continued pointing out his concerns by saying, "With the low gravity situation on this planet, these weapons are most likely twice as strong. You will need to remember to brace yourself before firing. Otherwise, the kick back may be hard enough to move you back an extreme distance." The Captain then picked up each of the weapons and showed them where the safety was located and how to disengage the mechanism. "You can figure out how to pull the trigger on your own." He then added, "I want you to understand this is against all known protocols. Under normal circumstances, I would not give weapons to untrained personnel at any time. It is only because we are in a totally unknown situation with limited options that I am even considering doing this."

"On this weapon belt are two regular grenades and two flash bangs; they make an extremely loud noise and a blinding flash. Finally, this is what we call a high sonic screamer. Depending on the setting, it will emit a high frequency sound wave that can paralyze or kill. You will need to add these ear protectors to your headgear. It is extremely important that you remember to insert the ear protectors into place before using the sonic screamer."

Drago noticed that Rashad was intently concentrating on every word and direction the Captain given them. He hoped Rashad understood more than he did, because he just wasn't sure he would remember everything.

"Now, most important of all," the Captain said. "You must not use these weapons in any way, shape, or form unless under the most extreme emergency and only then if I give you permission. Is that understood?"

"Yes Sir," they responded in unison.

"Now, please repeat what I just said. I want to make sure you understand."

The Captain appeared to be satisfied when they had finished repeating his instructions. "Gentlemen, please understand we are taking a serious risk in letting you fire these weapons in an uncontrolled environment. We have no idea how they will react when fired in this atmosphere or on this planet. You are carrying them for only the most extreme emergencies. Do I make myself clear?"

"Yes sir," they responded.

"Now, the Engineer has gone over and tested your communications devices and shown you how to operate each device?"

"Yes Sir," they responded.

"One last thing, you are only to go as far as the tree line which we show to be approximately, one and a half miles away. Upon reaching this tree line, we will give you further instructions about what you are to do based upon our observations."

"Finally, you both must understand that we know next to nothing about this planet. For all we know, the grass will jump up and eat you the moment you step out. A soft looking bunny type creature could attack you spitting poisonous venom. What I'm saying is, take nothing for granted. None of us know what is out there or what it will do. Understand?"

"Yes, Sir," they responded.

"Okay, let's go into the bay docking area and send you outside. Once down, we will do another preliminary check of your equipment. Until then, you will not move away from the ship. Only when I give permission will you move out. Do you have any questions?"

"No Sir," they responded.

"Okay, ready then, let's go."

CHAPTER SIX

As THEY GOT TO the hatch and the door opened with the ramp going down, Drago's heart was beating so loud he didn't think they would need any equipment to keep track of him.

The Captain gave them a thumbs up signal and wished them luck as they started down the ramp. As soon as they were on the ground, the ramp closed behind them. This gave them both a moment of fear, then Drago took a deep breath. After months of breathing recycled air, first at the space station then on the ship, this tasted wonderful. There was a light breeze blowing that waved through his hair and softly brushed his face that felt absolutely amazing. Also, he could actually see the whole sky rather than looking at it through computer monitors. Now that they were no longer enclosed in a metal machine, Drago's senses were kicking into overdrive.

Rashad must have been having the same experience because suddenly through their earphones they heard the Captain saying, "Today gentlemen, if you don't mind. Please test your headsets as instructed then move out in an orderly fashion." Both quickly confirmed that their communication gear was working properly.

As they started to move away from the ship, Drago realized that the weight of the gear was gone…almost to the point where it was nonexistent. When he took his first step it was more like gliding than walking.

Rashad, quickly falling into his position as scout, immediately informed the engineer of the gravity reaction. "Angelina, the gravity is almost lighter than expected. I am gliding rather then walking. I have enough weight to keep me down but it feels like if I pushed or jumped, I could soar across the ground."

"Please stop there," Angelina stated. "I want you to use a slight bit more pressure, flex your knees and push off slightly to see the affect."

Emphasizing her words firmly, the engineer said, "DO NOT push hard. Drago, you stand still and let Rashad make the move in case we need you to rescue him."

"Okay, Rashad on the count of three, I want you to flex and push off." The sound of Angelina's voice came through loud and clear as she counted. "One – Two – Three – Go."

Rashad did what he felt was a slight push. However, he found himself about six to eight inches off the ground and moving away at about five miles an hour. When he came down he was a good thirty feet from Drago.

"Hold it there," Angelina said. Within seconds, she was reading the monitoring devices. "According to the read outs, if you were to use a normal force for running or jumping, you would go approximately twelve feet in the air and cover a quarter mile in distance." They then heard Angelina say, "Captain, I suggest we bring them back onto the ship and add more weight."

"Negative," the Captain said. "It will give them a slight advantage if they have to get out of a situation in a hurry. Have Drago try it next."

Drago followed the instructions but being much smaller than Rashad, he flew about ten inches off the ground and went a good twenty feet past him. The Captain then directed them to stand still while the Engineer studied the print outs and made some additional calculations. In less than a minute, Angelina was reporting back to the Captain, "Drago has less mass than Rashad, but with similar kinetic energy, he will go higher and farther with less force. However, both of them have enough force to cover a quarter of a mile with minimal effort." At that point, Angelina spoke directly into their communication device instructing them to, "Go forward slowly and try to affect a gliding motion like skating. Do not be in a hurry."

Once again, Drago and Rashad started forward. Finally, after several slow motion attempts, they were able to develop a rhythm that was very akin to skating. The only thing they had to be careful about was lifting off the ground. They were concentrating so hard on maintaining the gliding motion that they were almost to the tree line before realizing it.

"Stand where you are," the Captain's voice instructed through their ear bugs. "Stop and look at your surroundings. Rashad you pan slowly left while Drago you pan slowly right. "

As Drago slowly turned to his right, he thought he saw a rapid movement in the grass. But after stopping to zoom in on the area, he saw nothing. As he continued to scan to his right, he heard the Captain issuing commands through their com devices.

"Look about you. Are there any small branches from the trees that you can bring back as samples? Is there any sign of water? Look for prints of wild life on the ground or possible scat."

"What's scat Sir?" Rashad asked before Drago could get the words out.

"It is poop, gentlemen. You are now on the scientific part of this mission. Look at every plant, bug, whatever. We will notify you when and of what type samples we want you to collect."

"Excuse me sir," Angelina said. "But Sophie says that the plant with the purple berries to the right of that small tree and bush looks a lot like Poke Sallie. Can we get a sample?"

"Okay," the Captain said. "Listen up men. Drago you will take the samples. Rashad you are the guard. Watch and look at everything. Protect Drago's back. Drago, move in slowly toward that plant."

"Sir, there is also a broken branch from a tree within ten feet of the plant."

"One thing at a time; Drago."

"Yes Sir." Drago responded.

"Drago, take the yellow pouch out of Rashad's belt. Pull off a couple of leaves, insert them into the pouch, and put it back on Rashad's belt."

"Got it," Drago said.

After removing the pouch from Rashad belt, he leaned forward and pulled several handfuls of leaves off the plant, inserted them into the pouch and reattached it to Rashad's belt.

"Look back at the plant," came the Engineers voice. "Notice how quickly the plant is replacing the missing leaves! Get that on camera." Both Rashad and Drago stood there with their mouths open in amazement as the plant sprouted new leaves along the stalk.

"Wow," Drago said. "I feel like I'm watching one of those time-lapsed educational programs the scientists kept showing us back at the space station."

"Okay gentlemen, move slowly toward the tree branch."

"I tell you Drago," Rashad said, "I feel like I'm doing ballet rather than scouting. If we move any slower it'll be dark before we get done."

"Stay within protocol Rashad," the Captain directed. "Move your webcam more slowly from side to side as you watch Drago. You're blurring the tape."

"Sir, I'm trying to keep us alive here. I'm afraid if I move too slowly, something will jump out and get us." Surprisingly, the Capitan did not reprimand him.

"I understand Rashad, but try to make a compromise."

"Yes Sir," Rashad responded.

Meanwhile, Drago had made it over to the small branch he had spotted laying on the ground earlier.

"Pick it up and put it in the green pouch on Rashad's belt," the Engineer said.

"Got it," Drago said.

Angelina's voice came back over the mike saying, "Hold it Drago, pan back to that bush to the right of the branch about five feet away. Good, now focus your webcam there and pan slowly left and right."

"Sir," the engineer said, "notice all the small bones on the ground around that plant?" Angelina's voice then came over their ear bugs, "Drago, stay away from that plant—it might be carnivorous."

"What?" Drago exclaimed.

"It might eat you," the Engineer said. Backing up, Drago kept a good distance away from the plant.

Suddenly, Rashad said, "Captain, Sir, I believe I see a glistening like water just past the first tree line."

"Focus your webcam on it," the Captain instructed.

"Sir, the Spectrograph shows it as being a type of liquid," the Engineer reported.

"Hold in place," the Captain instructed.

Rashad and Drago kept looking around, both on the ground and in the trees. Neither had been trained as observers. If they had, they would have picked up on the different movements that were not caused by the wind.

"Okay men," the Captain said. "I want you to both go forward slowly. Get a sample of that liquid, then immediately return to the ship. There have been enough investigations for one day."

Moving slowly forward, both were looking up, down, and around at their surroundings. The movement in the trees bothered them but neither was able to make out what was causing the leaves and branches to move. Finally, they reached the edge of the liquid just as the Captain's voice came back on line with instructions.

"Drago, take that glass vial out of your blue pouch and collect a sample. Immediately close it up after taking the sample and leave the area. Then, I want you both to head back to the ship," the Captain directed.

Drago removed the vial and gingerly lowered himself down to take a sample. As he finished and was corking the sample, Rashad suddenly yelled. The next thing he knew, there was a giant creature with big snapping jaws lunging out of the water after him. Jumping back in panic and momentarily forgetting about the lighter gravity, he found himself up in the middle of one of the trees nearly twenty feet off the ground. Grabbing a limb out reflex to hang onto to keep from falling, he found himself staring at a small animal covered in brown fur that immediately barked at him and ran away. Faced with his second shock of the day, he lost his grip and fell to the ground.

While Drago was flying through the air, he heard a massive sound and watched Rashad flying backwards about twenty feet in the air toward the ship. Even in his panicked scramble to hang on to limbs and branches as he fell through the tree, Drago realized that whatever the monster had been, Rashad had blown it to bits. After crashing to the ground, Drago was vaguely conscience of the fact that somehow, he was still holding on to the liquid sample vial as he inserted it into one of his vest pockets. As he sat there for a moment trying to catch his breath, he realized that he was also grabbing bits of the blown apart monster and stuffing it into one of the pouches on his belt. With his heart still pounding loudly in his ears, he scrambled out from under the trees and used all his strength to leap toward the ship.

Sailing through the air, he realized that he enjoyed the feeling. Landing about a quarter mile from the ship, he just flexed his legs and pushed off again. With tremendous luck, he came down within ten feet of the ship, and skidded to a stop, just before crashing into it. Looking around, he noticed Rashad lying next to the ship.

Drago quickly went over to him. Rashad looked up and said, "Damn, was that a trip or what?" Then, they both started to laugh not realizing that their laughter was releasing their nervous energy when they heard the sound of the Captain's voice coming through their ear bugs.

"Gentlemen, do you mind? I suggest you put your weapons on safety then use the ramp to come aboard for debriefing. Now get aboard!"

As Drago and Rashad came up the ramp into the ship, they expected everyone to be there asking questions about what had happened outside. However, the first person they saw was the Captain.

"Give me your weapons," he ordered. Then, the Engineer was there taking their vests with the samples they had collected.

"Report to the Engineering Bay," the Captain stated in a no-nonsense tone of voice. "We will debrief you there."

CHAPTER SEVEN

As Drago and Rashad walked into the Engineering Bay, they were surprised to see everyone else in front of computer screens. Dana, Gerard, and Loren were taking the samples, under the direction of the Engineer to different machines for testing and analysis.

Tani and Bruce were running computer programs and talking back and forth excitedly to each other.

Matzo, Molly and Choi were looking at the samples of the branch and comparing the information they had retrieved from the probes in the grass.

Rashad could contain himself no longer. The words came tumbling out in a flood. "Did you see that monster? Can you believe I blew him into a hundred pieces? Wow! Then I flew two miles through the air! What a trip! Man! I can't wait to out again. Drago do you hear me?"

Besides being totally caught up in his own thoughts and still coming down from the experience, Drago didn't get the chance to respond before the Captain issued new orders.

"Doc, you and Angelina meet with me in the Control Room. The rest of you gather what you can and set up in the Bay Area. We will all meet in about an hour to go over all the information gathered from this outing."

When Doc and Angelina joined the Captain, they sat down as the Captain said, "All right, let's take it one step at a time and review what took place and what everybody should be assigned to do."

"However," he said as he took his seat, "before we review the events of today, I would like to discuss what I read in the NIPSA reports on the children. Unfortunately, we only got the short form reports. I believe this was due to the fact that they were only were going to be on the ship with us and we supposedly didn't need all the evaluations on them."

"Consider yourself lucky," Doc said. "I got the full reports. Not only were they about a thousand pages long per child, but half the information was in jargon and abbreviations even I couldn't understand. I finally quit reading them and went to the short forms myself."

"Well, there had to be specific reasons NIPSA picked this group," the Captain said. "It is apparent that some of these children were selected to fit specific needs at the planet station. But for the life of me, I don't have a clue what they were selected for."

"I know this," Doc replied, "each child was picked from the highest test scores for the specific needs they had at the SRB375 station."

"If we only knew what those needs were," the Captain said as he turned to look at Angelina. "Moving ahead, let's discuss what happened today and what everybody has been assigned to do."

"Angelina, did the videos come out all right?"

"Yes," she said; "in fact, the one where Drago was attacked will make you jump out of your seat."

"It already did," said the Doc and Captain together."

Angelina then continued to explain. "As of right now, I have assigned different kids to different projects. Gerard, Dana, and Loren are looking at the materials from the pouches. They seem to be able to understand the functionality of the analysis equipment and have already started testing the samples. Tani and Bruce are reading the equipment manuals for Dana and Gerard and assisting anyone else who needs help assembling the scientific equipment. Molly, Choi, and Matzo were evaluating the tree branch and some leaves they picked from Draco clothes and comparing those to the ship's probe readings on the soil and grass."

"Maggy and Rashad are discussing the weapons while the rest are looking at the videos with the different computer programs available on the computer." Pausing for a brief moment, Angelina continued. "I have to tell you, these kids are something else. Oh by the way, Sophie's going through the remaining food supplies to determine if she can stretch a few more days out of the remaining supplies."

"Well now, that's one of the few evaluations I understood," the Captain said. "If she is half as good as her evaluator indicated in her report, we'll do fine. Doc, how does Drago and Rashad seem to be handling their emotions after the experience?"

"Rashad is fine; he can't wait to go out again. Drago seems to be okay; but as you already know, he pretty much keeps his thoughts to himself."

"Well, how do we go forward from here?" the Captain asked.

"We need to see how much these kids can really do with this equipment," Angelina said. "Also, I would like Bruce and Tani to go over the equipment list we had for the station and see what we can use."

"I can help out there," Doc said. "I'm familiar with a lot of the different pieces of equipment that the planet station would require."

"Okay," the Captain said, "let's go get the kids together and discuss where we go from here."

Walking into the bay area, they noticed all the kids were there discussing multiple things with each other. "All right, if I can have your attention please," the Captain announced. "Everybody settle down now." Everyone quickly sat aside their projects and stopped their discussions to hear what the Captain had to say.

"What we are going to do is discuss each group's findings—one at a time, then we will determine our next plan of action. First, who was reviewing the videos?" Everyone raised their hands. "Hold on," the Captain said. "Let me rephrase my question. Who did what in looking at the videos?"

Emir, Naomi, and Natasha stated that they had looked at the videos to observe what was going on around Drago and Rashad. They had also looked to see what plants, trees, and animals might have been picked up by the cameras without Drago and Rashad noticing.

"Okay, tell me what you noticed," the Captain said.

Naomi immediately said. "A great big alligator like thing almost ate Drago."

"We know," the Captain said, "what else did you notice?"

Both Emir and Natasha politely waited for the other person to say something.

Finally, the Captain said "Emir, we'll start with you. Tell me what you saw."

"Well, first Natasha and I just watched the video a couple of times. Then we started to notice different things.

"Please explain," the Captain said.

"Well, we noticed movement in the grass as Drago and Rashad walked toward the trees. At first, we thought it might just be the wind but then we noticed that the movement went in different directions. In some cases, it would stop then start again from the same place. Also, Natasha noticed that the plant with the bones around it had flowers that opened when Drago got close. We still want to try and get a closer look at the bones to try to determine what kind of animals they were. When Drago ended up in the tree, there was the one animal caught on the video that barked, but if you look closely, you can catch brief glimpses of other animals moving around on different branches. We thought we would try slow motion and maybe check with Bruce and Tani to see what other capabilities the computer has to look at the video in different ways."

"Well," the Captain said. "I'm impressed that you have done that in such a short time. Natasha, do you have anything to add?"

"No sir," she said.

"Wait a minute Natasha," Emir said. "What about what you noticed with Drago and the monster?"

"Oh I'm not sure, we can just let that go for now."

"Natasha," the Captain said, "we do not have the sort of time line that we can just let things go. I want all of you to know that whatever you think, or suspect you know, needs to be put on the table now. So tell me Natasha, what did you notice or think you noticed?"

"Well sir," Natasha said, "when we were looking at the video for the third or fourth time, I noticed that you could see the ripples of the monster coming toward Drago. When Emir and I looked at it again, we were surprised at how fast it was moving."

"Is that it?" asked the Captain.

"No sir," Natasha said.

"What else then?" asked the Captain patiently.

"Well sir," Natasha said, "I noticed that Drago, as he was getting the sample, was not looking out at the water but was looking down. Yet, just as the monster broke out of the water, Drago jumped back. Otherwise, the monster would have gotten him."

"Drago," the Captain asked, "did you see the monster at all?"

"I don't recall," Drago, said, "I just remember something made me jump."

"Also," Natasha said, "the second he jumped, Rashad fired, while the monster was still in the air."

"Okay," the Captain said as he turned to look at Angelina. "Make sure you have this in your notes. I think this will be one of the things that need further investigation." He then turned back to Emir and Natasha and said, "Thank you."

"Also, Bruce, Tani and Angelina, I want to know everything this on-board system can do in evaluating everything that is on this video." The Captain then turned to Dana and Gerard who were sitting quietly off to one side of the main group.

"Next, I would like to hear from Dana and Gerard."

"Well sir," Dana said; "we have been looking at the different samples they brought back."

"What do we have in the way of samples?" the Captain asked.

"We took the plant and water samples. We also have a sample of what looks like a piece of an animal but we're not sure where it came from," Dana responded.

"I grabbed that off the ground after I fell from the tree," Drago said. "It was from the monster."

"Good thinking son," the Captain said. "So Dana, tell me what you and Gerard have discovered from your investigations."

"Well, sir, some of the samples are still being processed and we won't have verifiable results for a while. Bruce and Tani had to help us figure out how some of the equipment worked. However, the good news is that Bruce came up with the idea to put some of the liquid sample through our on board water testing system. The first analysis showed it to be a better quality of water than the ship's recycled water."

The Captain turned from Dana and said, "Angelina, you and Doc make it your first priority to validate Dana and Gerard's findings. If Dana's findings are correct, we have overcome one of our biggest survival problems."

"Good work you two. When will you have the results back on the rest of your test samples?"

"We gave the tree branch to Choi, Molly and Matzo. The plant leaves have been through some analysis already, but we need to run some more tests to determine if this plant is edible."

Sophie interrupted saying, "its edible Captain."

"How do you know that Sophie?" he asked.

"Well sir, it looked like Poke Sallie, it felt like Poke Sallie and it smelled like Poke Sallie. So I took a piece and cooked it up the way I learned and it smelled just like the Poke Sallie I used to cook back home. So I took a bite and it tasted just like Poke Sallie. And seeings how I did it about two hours ago and I'm not dead yet, I figure its okay."

"Don't you ever do that again," the Captain said looking at her sternly. "We can't afford to lose one person of this group, and you do not experiment on your own, does everybody understand?"

"Yes sir," they replied.

"But sir," Sophie said, refusing to drop the discussion as she continued to push her point. "You already told us that we only got a fifteen day food supply. In the next thirteen days when we have used up all those supplies and don't have anything to eat, we'll all be out there trying stuff." With that, Sophie shrugged her shoulders and ended by saying, "I just thought I get started right away."

"Lord help us," the Captain said.

"Molly, Choi, and Matzo what did you find out about the branch?" asked the Captain.

"Sir," Choi responded; "we are studying it to determine if it can be used in building materials to develop permanent structures. We are also investigating the grass to see if it can be used in the making of bricks or adobe."

"And what were you able to find out?" the Captain asked.

"Well sir, it has some interesting characteristics just as the grass and leaves."

"What's that?" the Captain asked.

"We noticed that while it has a type of bark, neither the bark nor the branch really breaks. Molly found the same thing with the leaves."

"What do you think then Choi?" the Captain questioned.

"Based upon the testing we have conducted so far—all three, the grass, the branch, and the leaves seem to consist of, or partially consist of some type of rubber or plastic. In looking at the broken end of the branch, it seems it had died off rather than being broken off. We tried to cut off a small piece of the branch but were unsuccessful."

"What do you think this means?" the Captain asked.

"We don't know sir," said all three of them together.

"Excuse me," Emir said raising his hand. "If I may, sir, you said that anybody who had an idea or whatever should speak up."

"Yes Emir, please go ahead," the Captain said.

"My interest involves astrometry, and I have been studying the night sky. One of the things I've noticed is that this planet appears to have two moons. We have all noticed that there are two suns during the day."

"What are you getting at Emir?" the Captain asked.

"Well sir, if this is the case; their revolutions will have a great affect on the planet based upon Earth science."

"I still don't understand what you're getting at," the Captain said. "Please make it simpler for me."

"It could mean catastrophic storms Sir."

"What has that got to do with the trees and the grass?" the Captain asked.

"Well sir, in California, where they have earthquakes, the engineers continually tried to make structures stronger and more rigid to withstand the earthquakes. Those attempts failed, until they decided to make them more flexible, rather then rigid—when they did that, they found some success. I am thinking that maybe the plants have evolved that way here to help them withstand extreme major storms."

"I'll be dammed," the Captain said. "Why do I feel like the most ignorant person here?"

"Okay, Emir, your new project is to further expand on this hypothesis of yours. First and foremost, you need to determine when you think the next cycle of storms will occur."

"Now then, who is left that hasn't had a chance to give their report?"

"That would be us sir," Rashad said. "Me and Maggy."

"Okay, go ahead and tell me what you two have been investigating," the Captain said.

"We've been discussing the weapons, the effects of gravity when we use the equipment, and the best way to proceed when outside."

"So tell me your thoughts," the Captain said.

"Well sir, as far as the equipment goes, we would like to find out what is actually available. Also, can the cameras take infrared photos? What other capabilities do they have? Are there side arms available? And, while that sonic gun is awesome, we can't keep getting knocked back two miles every time we fire it. What kinds of controls are there on it? We also feel that there should be two scouts out there instead of one—whether operating as flankers or in front and behind. Finally, who's going to make the decisions in the field?"

"Okay, hold on a minute," the Captain said as he raised both his hands as protection from Rashad's flood of questions. "I can see you are thinking on the right track. As of now, you and Maggy are the team scouts. You will go with Doc, Bruce and Tani into the storage bays to find out what kind of equipment is available. I will give you the manifest sheets on everything that is on board. Also, Dana and Gerard will review these sheets and maybe go with you."

CHAPTER EIGHT

"Now, DRAGO WE HAVEN'T heard from you. What have you been up to?"

"Thinking sir," Drago replied.

"About what Drago?" the Captain asked.

"Well, I've been reviewing everything we did today and what has happened. Then I was listening to what everybody had to say."

"Did you come to any conclusions?" the Captain asked.

"Yes sir," Drago said.

"Well, tell us," the Captain said.

"First of all, I agree with Rashad and Maggy. We should have two scouts. I also agree with what they said about the weapons and equipment. And, I find everyone's discoveries very interesting, especially Emir's thoughts about why the plants on this planet have evolved."

"Have you come to any conclusions Drago?"

"Yes sir"

"Well," the Captain said, "are you going to share them with us?"

"I'm concerned sir; I don't want to cause any disagreements."

"Drago! Tell us your thoughts." the Captain demanded in exasperation.

"Well, I think we should plan our next trip outside for the day after tomorrow. That's gives us time to accomplish all the things we have already listed."

"Besides, Rashad and Maggy, I want to bring Loren along for her expertise on plants and animals with Natasha set up on the communication line." Drago still had difficulty boldly expressing his views and opinions with adults; but somehow, it seemed different with the Captain. He then took a deep breath and continued.

"I think our goal should be to find edible plants. I don't think we should be looking at animals yet—at least, not until we further understand the food chain here." After pausing for a second to make sure he still had the Captain's approval, Drago added, "The next day, I want either Dana or Gerard to join us to help with collecting samples. Finally, I think that other than finding a food source, the most critical thing on our list will be for Emir to figure out the weather cycle."

"I guess you have been thinking," the Captain said. "Alright, we will go with your plan. Consider yourself the squad leader. Rashad wanted to know who would be in charge outside, it is now you."

"Yes sir," Drago said.

"I hate to interrupt," Sophia said, "but dinners ready. And I won't have my meal go cold after all the trouble I went to fix it."

"I guess that ends the meeting," the Captain said. "After dinner you can go about what you were doing or relax. I'll see Doc and Angelina in my quarters after the meal."

When they sat down in the mess area, they were surprised by what was set out. Accustomed to eating form containers, they found the table set with dishes and bowls. They also smelled what smelled like fresh bread.

"Is that bread I smell?" several of them inquired as they walked into the mess area.

"It surely is," Sophia said. "I got fresh bread, beans, beef stew, and Poke Sallie Salad, for those brave enough to try."

"Where did you get all this, and how did you make bread?" the Captain asked.

"I went with Naomi into the bay where you said there were supplies for the station. I found wheat and beans for planting, dried beef and some other stuff. So, I put Naomi busy grinding up some of that wheat and I set about messing with the other stuff till it seemed right."

"This is amazing," the Captain said. Everyone else was busy passing out food and digging in.

"Awesome," said one.

"Absolutely delicious," said another as someone else said, "First real meal we have had since I can remember."

"Well," Sophia said in response, "You're my family and I'm always going to take care of my family."

Hearing those words, it suddenly struck everyone. As they looked around the table at each other, the realization hit them. This was the closest any of them had had to a real family in a very long time. There were tears in the eyes of some, smiles on the faces of others. The Captain stood up and raised his glass of water.

"To family," he said. "May we grow and prosper." To family they all toasted.

Later in the captain's quarters, the Captain, Doc and Angelina looked at one another, sat down and smiled.

"We're in it now," the Captain said. "What a group!"

CHAPTER NINE

LYING IN HIS BUNK that night, everything kept running through the Captain's head. The evaluations had done more to confuse him than help him in trying to determine which kids could do what and where to use them. What the hell was a physic profile anyway? He asked himself what tests and questions were they given to determine what? As he wondered to himself, he thought of Maggy's evaluation. Her evaluation indicated that she was not good in a group and resented authority—yet had leadership qualities. Where did that come from?

The other thing, these kids had jumped into looking into everything on the ship. He had no idea what some of them were talking about. Where was the panic? Where is the fear? They had adapted over night, and were questioning and looking into things to get answers he hadn't even thought of yet. Finally, he determined that he had to throw the book away when it came to organizing and being in charge. Nothing he had learned at the Academy or in Officer's Training School had prepared him for this.

Tonight, when Sophia had called them family, he not only saw how it affected everyone else, but knew it had affected him also. This was going to be his family from now until they were somehow rescued, which he doubted, or he died. As he fell asleep, his last thoughts were about how he had grown up in orphanages in upstate New York. Part French and part American Indian. He chuckled to himself as he thought of his mixed heritage and of the mixed heritages of all those aboard. What a group, he thought—no, make that family.

Lying in her bunk, Angelina was also thinking about the day's events, the group, and also about her own child. She had been raised by a single mom. Her father had left when she and her brother were babies. The only thing her mother had ever said about him was that, "He didn't want to be here. He left, that's it." She also remembered how her mother had worked three jobs. She always had neat and clean clothes for them to wear and insisted that they go to college. Every night, her mom read three new words from the dictionary to her and her brother. She taught them how to pronounce them, how to spell them, and what they meant. The next night, they had to be able to do all three correctly before being given new ones and going to sleep. Times had been tough, but there was always joy and laughter in the house. And, her mother was always encouraging them saying that there was nothing to stop them from being 'who' or 'what' they wanted to be in life—it just took hard work.

Just after Angelina graduated from high school, she found out she was pregnant. She didn't even tell the boy since she didn't really want him in her life anyway. It was just one of those things. When Angelina told her mom; she didn't freak out, she just said, "You have the baby. I'll raise it while you're in college, that's it." She attended Junior college first, both to get her grades up and stay closer to home and her daughter. Meanwhile, her brother had already spent two years in college in the ROTC Program. When he quit to join the Army, her mother had been devastated. A year later, he was dead, killed in action in another useless political war. She decided then that she would join the military just to make sense of it. When Angelina told her mom, she went crazy. After months of arguing about it, her mother finally relented and said she would give her blessing if Angelina would join the Air Force. According to her mother, the Air Force had better training and didn't leave their personnel on the ground where they could get shot at. Without pointing out to her mother that pilots and planes also got shot down, Angelina applied to and was accepted into the Air Force.

Her daughter was now in her first year of college. Her mom had raised her just like she had promised. While she knew it would be heartbreaking for both her daughter and her mom when they received the news, she knew they would survive and be fine. With that thought and tears in her eyes, she went to sleep.

Meanwhile, Doc was doing anything but sleeping. He was going over the manifest sheets showing the supplies and equipment destined for the station. There were lots of medical and testing equipment he was familiar with. He was also surprised by the amount of seeds and embryos that were being shipped. This would increase their survival odds greatly. There was also a lot of paramilitary equipment including remote controlled drones. He would have to get with Bruce and Tani to read the instructions. There was an MRI, Spectrometers, some portable isolation type labs that had to be put together, an Electron Microscope, and more. There were tools, dishes, pots and pans. He chuckled. Sophia would be pleased. How she had made tonight's meal he couldn't even guess. They might not survive, but they would be well fed when they went, he thought. With that he went back to making his list. He would have to involve some of the others to look at some of this stuff. He had been totally impressed with the way they had all accepted their fate and dove into the different tasks.

CHAPTER TEN

WHEN THEY AWOKE IN the morning, it was to the smell of cooking once again. Sophia must have been up early and started on breakfast. They all washed and used the facilities then sat down to breakfast.

"This morning there's Oatmeal—call it mush or gruel for you," Sophia said. "It will fill your belly and stick to your ribs and keep you going for the day. I found some sugar in the supplies to put on it. I also found they had bees in the bay for shipment to the station. So I swiped some honey from them without taking too much. Make sure you share. Also, there was some bread left over from last night so I made toast. Everyone gets one piece. Now eat up. I won't have anyone leaving my table saying they were hungry to start out the day."

The Captain, Doc and Angelina just looked at each other with wonder and amusement.

"Okay, listen up," the Captain said. "Today we have a lot of work to do. From now on at breakfast we will discuss and give out assignments. So while you're eating, I would like for Doc and Angelina to discuss the group assignments. If you have any comments, please raise you hand and wait to be recognized." As the Captain looked around, no one was raising their hands with questions. The only hand raising going on was between their bowls of oatmeal and their mouths. "Good, let's start with Doc."

"Well, last night I stayed up and went through the shipping manifests. There is quite a bit of equipment and supplies in there. If it is all right with Angelina, I have made a list of the people I would like to check out the various pieces of equipment."

"That's fine with me," Angelina said. "I too wanted to take people in there to check out what we have."

"I was hoping you were going to say that," Doc said with a grin. "There is so much stuff; I feel it would be more successful and quicker if we all got involved. I will read you the teams I set up and what they are going to be looking at. As back up, Bruce, Tani, Molly, Choi, and Matzo will be used to read and figure out the manuals that come with the equipment, Loren, Dana, and Gerard, you will be with me looking over the medical and diagnostic equipment. Sophia and Naomi will look at the supplies and foods stuff, with Loren helping with the embryos and seeds. Oh,—also the bees."

"Drago, Rashad, and Maggy will look at all the weapons and survival equipment. By the way guys, listed on the manifest are two robot-controlled drones. That should be fun."

"I'd like the Captain to go with Drago's group. I'll go with Dana's group and Angelina will go with Choi's group."

Emir raised his hand.

"Yes Emir," Doc said.

"What about me?" Emir asked.

"I knew you were going to ask that," Doc said. "You have a special assignment. In the cargo bay, there are a computer and some crates of equipment labeled atmospheric, weather and planet environmental analysis transducer. That my friend is yours alone—other than needing help with understanding the manuals; of course."

Emir's eyes lit up. He could hardly wait to get started and was hurriedly wolfing down his oatmeal.

"Before we all charge off to our various duties, I want to tell you all something" the Captain said. "It's now 0600 hours by my watch. At exactly 1200 hours, we will all meet back here for lunch and discuss your findings. Obviously, in the amount of time you have, you will not be able to review all the equipment. However, there is another reason. Today at 1300 hours we are going to start a new routine. We will all go to the bay area and then as a group, we are going to go outside."

There were audible gasps from around the table.

"We all need to get outside and start acclimating ourselves to this world. However, we will not be going out any farther than around the perimeter of the ship. I will set up a program so we can all get used to the gravitational affects, etc." The Captain watched as everyone excitedly discussed the opportunity to get outside for a few minutes then he turned to Angelina and said, "Please set up some controls to take outside with us so we can monitor the ship and keep an eye on the surroundings while we are outside."

"Yes Sir," Angelina said.

"Now," the Captain said, "the table is open for free discussion and eating. Enjoy. You have forty-five minutes before we have to get to work."

Everyone started talking at once, most of them asking Doc for copies of the manifest that listed their equipment assignments. Doc, prepared for such an event, had made copies with the various names along side the equipment.

As the group had not sat down in any order, they found themselves trying to lean over and look across each other to see their assignments.

"Hold it," the Captain said. "Everyone grab their food and move over next to their team. That way, we can all converse in a more orderly fashion." Suddenly everyone was moving around. They finally got settled and started to look over their lists.

"What's an MRI?" Loren asked.

"That's a machine that takes multiple X-rays and other computer graphics of anything living you send through it," replied Doc.

"Can it be used with animals?" Loren asked.

"That depends on the size of the animal," Doc responded.

"Oh Man! Doc, can I work with Rashad and Maggy on the radio controlled drones?"

"Along with everything else, you can Bruce," Doc replied.

"Naomi and I will need some help setting up a kitchen," Sophia said.

"Anyone and anything you need," the Captain said. "You, Sophia have been the first one to make this a home. And for that, we are all grateful."

"Here, here," Doc said as the others chorused him and added a round of applause.

Sophia actually blushed; then said, "Anything for family." Which quieted all again.

"Before you all leave to your tasks, I'd like to meet with Maggy for a moment," the Captain stated.

"What?" She asked.

"Please come with me to my quarters for just a minute," the Captain said, standing up and motioning her to follow him. Maggy looked at Rashad with fear and questions in her eyes.

"It's cool," Rashad said. "So far he's been a stand-up guy. He hasn't treated us like kids. Go ahead, you'll be all right. If you're not back when we start to leave, I'll come get you."

"You promise?" Maggy asked.

"For sure," Rashad said.

Reluctantly, Maggy got up and followed the Captain into his quarters.

"Please sit down," the Captain told Maggy. "Before you get all nervous, what I want to talk to you about is your evaluation report." This only made Maggy more nervous.

"Maggy, you should know by now that I like to be straight up with people." Maggy slowly nodded her head.

"Your evaluation is different than all the others on a couple of points and I felt it prudent that we discuss those points so there are no misunderstandings." Again, Maggy nodded her head.

"It says that you don't like authority and dislike discipline. First, I want to talk about the discipline. If we don't follow discipline both individually and as a group we will die. It's that simple. Second, as far as following authority goes, you must realize that we are in a situation none of us have ever been in before. That is why I'm always asking for everyone's input. But, I will make the final decision and that will be followed. Do you understand?" the Captain asked.

Maggy nodded her head in agreement refusing to look the Captain in the eye.

"No, that is not good enough. I need for you to look at me and verbally respond," the Captain said with authority in his voice.

"Yes sir," Maggy said weakly as she looked at the Captain.

"Now, there are just two more things about your evaluation you should know."

Maggy slumped even lower.

"First," the Captain said, "it recommends you for leadership and states that you have strong leadership qualities."

Maggy sat up straight, not sure she had heard right.

"Second, your test scores were higher than Rashad's; however, that is only for you and me to know."

That brought a smile to Maggy's face.

"Finally, I want you to know that whatever took place in your life before we landed on this planet does not count. This is a new beginning for all of us. You are part of this family. I need your input and talents to make us stronger and I am depending on you."

Without realizing it, Maggy had continued to sit up straight in the chair—like a load had been lifted off her shoulders.

"Yes sir," she said strongly. "You can depend on me."

"I already knew that," the Captain said. "Now, let's get back out there before they leave without us."

Maggy jumped up and headed out the door with the Captain. She wasn't sure what just had happened in there, but she had changed. One thing she knew for certain—even though the thought surprised her, she would die for this man. To fail in his expectations of her was inconceivable.

When they got back to the bay area, everyone was getting ready to go to the cargo bay.

"You just made it in time," Rashad said to Maggy.

"It wouldn't matter, Maggy replied; "you would have been lost without me."

Rashad stopped dumbfounded. In all the time he and Maggy had talked, she had stayed very serious and only seemed interested in what they were working on. Never had she shone any sign of camaraderie or friendliness. He followed as she led the way. When she asked him to give the copy of their part of the manifest to her, he did so without hesitation. What happened in there he wondered? He also realized he liked her this way. Besides, she was kind of cute in a rough way. Where did that come from he wondered, but his thoughts were interrupted by Bruce before he got much further.

"Let's look for the drones first," Bruce said. "I always wanted to fly one of those things."

"Okay," the Captain said. "But I think it's more important to find things we can use immediately tomorrow when we go back outside."

"I agree," Rashad and Maggy said together.

"Alright," Bruce said with disappointment in his voice, "but if we can locate them I would like to start working on putting them together. It's probably going to take a couple of days just to figure them out."

"That will give you something to do in your spare time," the Captain said grinning.

While the Captain's group was looking for the drones and the other equipment they had been assigned to investigate, Doc's group was excitedly listening to him. As he explained the functions of the different pieces of equipment, Dana, Gerard, Molly, Choi and Matzo were rapidly taking notes and marking the equipment containers with the additional info.

Emir suddenly interrupted. "Excuse me sir, but can you show me where the weather equipment you mentioned is located?"

"Right this way," Doc said motioning Emir toward the space where the weather equipment crates were tied down.

Emir's shoulders slumped with disappointment. For in front of him was a large crated box offering no clue as to what was inside. He looked back at Doc hopelessly.

"What do I do now?" Emir asked.

"I suggest you get a hammer or a pry bar and open the crate," Doc said.

As Emir looked around he noticed that many of them were in the process of opening crates. "Can I have a pry bar when someone is done?" he asked plaintively. Hearing this, the Captain looked up from what he was doing.

"Hold on everyone," he said. "We only have limited room in here. So we can't open all the crates at once and expect to set them up. I think we need to set some priorities as to which crates we open and where we are going to put the contents. I think we all need to take our lists and head back to the bay for a quick review of our priorities."

When everybody was seated, the Captain continued. "Now, the first priorities are food for survival, equipment that can help us determine what is outside and what protects us while we are outside. Since we have a limited amount of space on board, we are going to have to figure out where we are going to set up the different items being unpacked. Especially since we don't know how many pieces are in each crate."

"First, I suggest that any equipment that can be used to analyze plants or animals that our onboard computer can't facilitate, be opened up. Where do you and your group stand Angelina?" the Captain asked.

"The embryos and the plants and the bees have their own compartments along with onboard computer monitoring. The rest of the equipment is not essential at this time—unless we bring in live animals or whole plants."

"Good," the Captain said, "that helps."

"Next, any equipment that can be used in support of our exploration teams when they go outside should be unpacked. However, I believe this equipment is smaller and can be carried. Third, I want Emir's equipment opened and set up to tie in with our onboard computer system. I don't want to be surprised by any extreme weather."

"Finally, Molly, you, Choi and Matzo start designing layouts for the equipment we know about. Maggy what have you and Rashad found?" the Captain asked.

"As you already know, Captain, when we were going through the equipment, we found Bruce's drones; but it will have to be put together outside, since it is too large to assemble in here. However, we will need to study the manual some more to determine how to set them up and tie the controls into the ship's computer. Most of the other stuff was designed to be carried or worn." Maggy responded.

"Good. Bruce, I want that to be your first priority. Make sure the drone's controls are properly tied into the ships computer system."

"Yes Sir," Bruce replied.

"If it makes you feel better Bruce, Molly and her team can figure out a way to build shelters outside from the left-over crate material to house your drone." The Captain then looked around and asked, "Anything else?"

"Yes sir," Sophia said. "If you can give me some help I can set up a pretty good kitchen with what's here. The station people must have ordered a lot of kitchen equipment because Naomi and I found boxes of stuff. Also, I would like to know if Loren can bring back some soil when she goes out. With her help, I can plant some of these seeds."

"Since, we have another half an hour to go before lunch. I suggest everyone goes back to work on the priorities I just outlined," the Captain said. "Meanwhile, I volunteer myself to help set up the kitchen. Okay, people, let's move."

Forty-five minutes later, everyone was still involved with their projects when Sophia yelled, "Come to lunch now; or I'm throwing it to the pigs!"

"Do we have pigs?" Drago asked.

"I don't think so," Angelina responded as she continued inspecting some equipment next to where Drago, Rashad and Maggy were working. "It's a figure of speech. I heard my mother use it more than once when I was a kid."

"I guess we have a new mother," Rashad said.

When they all got back to the bay area, lunch was on the table. There were no new surprises. Lunch consisted of leftover stew and Poke Sallie salad from the night before.

"Don't nobody, complain now, you hear;" Sophia said. "We got to eat up all we got. Besides, I was busy setting up my new kitchen."

Since they were all hungry, they started right in helping themselves to the leftovers. As the Captain sat down with his plate, he noticed how they were now sitting in teams while they ate. Also, there were lots of different discussions about what they had found and what they were doing. Sitting back with a smile on his face, he could not help but think how this was like a million different Earth families sitting down to a meal. He felt good.

CHAPTER ELEVEN

As EVERYONE WAS FINISHING up with lunch, the Captain looked at Angelina and asked "Did you have time to set up that portable control for when we go out of the ship?"

"No, Captain I didn't. I figure I'll stay in the ship and then Doc and I can switch off later. If that is okay with you?"

"Did you discuss it with Doc.?"

"Yes, he was fine with it."

"Okay then," the Captain said.

"All right, listen up everyone. As I promised earlier, we are all going to go outside after lunch. Angelina will stay on board to monitor everything then switch out with Doc later. However, there are a few things that I want to go over first."

"All of you have seen the videos and heard about the gravity being less than what you were used to back on earth. Consequently, each one of you will be affected differently. Therefore, I want everyone to go out under the buddy system in teams of two. Which reminds me, did anyone find any rope or cable in the supplies that we can use to tie the partners together?"

"Yes Sir," Choi answered, "there was a lot of cable with connectors used to hold down the crates."

"Good," the Captain said, "please go get some pieces if you can. Twenty foot lengths with connectors would be ideal, but if that isn't possible, we can always cut them down to the size we need."

"My plan is to experiment a little and see how each one of you reacts, so we'll be taking turns. First off, I want Rashad and Drago to pick their partners, since they already have experience being outside the ship. The rest of you will need to pick a partner and line up. Okay everybody, let's do it."

It only took a few minutes for Choi, Matzo and Molly to gather up the cables, bring them back, and lay them out on the floor of the ship. For the most part, they had managed to find suitable lengths so hooking the different teams together would only take a few minutes.

"Okay," the Captain said. "Rashad, who are you picking to be your teammate?"

"I pick Maggy, if it's okay sir."

"Maggy, is that okay with you?"

"It's fine with me, sir."

"Drago, who's with you?" the Captain asked.

"I'd like Natasha with me, sir."

"Natasha?" the Captain asked.

She looked at Drago in surprise but answered, "Yes sir."

"The rest of you team up" the Captain said.

The final teams were Dana and Gerard, Sophia and Naomi, Bruce and Tani, Emir and Loren, Matzo and Choi.

The Captain said, "Molly you're with me."

Rashad led the way down the gang plank telling Maggy what it was like and how she would need to skate walk. Drago was saying pretty much the same thing to Natasha. However, the first thing both girls did when they got to the bottom of the ramp was to stop and breathe in the fresh air and feel the breeze in their face. They both stood there for a few moments just reveling in being outside again.

"I forgot how good the air tasted," Maggy said.

"And to be able to feel the sun on your face," Natasha said.

As the first group moved away from the bottom of the ramp and the others started coming down, everyone had much the same reaction. They had all forgotten how good it felt to be outside.

Now it will be harder to keep them inside, thought the Captain as he made a mental note to himself to make sure everyone got outside time now.

Rashad was laughing at Maggy who had always walked with a strong stride. Every time she tried to take a step, she went into the air.

"Glide," Rashad said. "Don't push so hard."

Meanwhile, Natasha glided across the ground like she had been doing it her whole life. Drago realized almost immediately that her ballet training gave her a definite advantage. In fact, she had just lifted herself and done a pirouette wrapping the cable around her and almost pulling Drago off his feet.

The Captain was directing from the top of the ramp trying to tell every one what to do. There was much laughter and giggling. But when Sophia and Naomi left the ground together and drifted about ten feet away he shouted for everyone to stop.

"I'm coming down. Let's do this one pair at a time."

Emir and Tani were headed down the ramp right in front the Captain and Molly. They had just stepped down onto the ground when Emir suddenly locked up as if he was in a trance. Tani couldn't move him and was calling for help. As the Captain stepped off the ramp with Molly, he too was struck into a deep immovable trance.

Doc, who had been standing next to the bottom of the ramp, shouted, "Everybody stop! Tani, Molly, do not try to move them. Is anyone else affected?"

Everybody shook their heads and replied no. However, Natasha suddenly got a strange look on her face and grabbed her head with both hands.

"What is it," Drago asked urgently?

"I suddenly have a strong buzzing in my head," Natasha said.

"All right," Doc said, "I want everyone to calmly go back up the ramp and re-board the ship. Rashad, you and Drago, stay here. Maggy, go on board and bring some weapons back so that you can stand guard. Let's move folks."

Doc then grabbed hold of the Captain and tried to move him but it was like he was made of stone. Going over to Emir, he found the same problem—it was if they had been glued to the ground. At that point, Doc untied Tani and Molly from their frozen partners and they were able to make their way back up the ramp holding on to each other. It took several minutes to get everybody else back up the ramp and into the ship; because some, in their hurry had popped up into the air and had to be brought back down by their partners. Finally, everyone was back on board but Doc, Rashad, and Drago with Maggy heading back down the ramp.

Suddenly, both the Captain and Emir dropped to the ground. Reaching over, Doc was able to lift up the Captain enough that he could half carry; half drag him back up the ramp. Rashad and Drago were able to follow suit with Emir—half carrying, half dragging him between them back into the ship and to sick bay as Molly stood guard.

Once they were in sick bay, Doc hooked up his equipment to start a complete analysis of their condition. After thirty minutes or so he could find nothing abnormal about their physical condition. It was more like they were in a deep restful sleep.

Meanwhile, everyone was anxiously standing outside sick bay waiting to see what happened and if the Captain and Emir were going to be all right. Angelina walked in and began asking Doc what had happened.

"I don't know," he said with a perplexed look. "It was as if they were locked in some kind of trance. We couldn't budge them—they were rigidly locked in place as if they were glued to the ground. Then suddenly they fell, and we brought them in here."

The doctor rechecked the monitors then continued with the same puzzled look on his face, "All their vitals are perfect. There seems to be a little more brain activity than normal, but I will need to run some more tests before I can tell what is causing it."

As Angelina bent over to look closer at the Captain, his eyes suddenly opened.

"Doc," Angelina said, "his eyes just opened."

Just as suddenly Emir's opened his eyes and started to look around with a slightly perplexed expression on his face.

With that, the Captain started sitting up wanting to know what the heck had just happened.

"Hold it," Doc said. "Lie back down for a minute. You and Emir need to just lie there and be still. We can talk this thing out after I have a chance to remove your monitors."

"I feel fine," the Captain said, sitting up again. "Matter of fact, I feel like I just had the best sleep of my life."

"So do I," Emir said.

"Well then," Doc said, "what say you tell us exactly what you remember."

The Captain winced several times as Doc removed the self-sticking monitors from his forehead and chest. Looking over at Emir he said, "I'm not sure how to explain."

Emir nodded quietly in agreement, dreading the moment when it would be his turn to have the monitors pealed from his skin.

Lets get up and go sit in the bay area with the others where we can discuss it," the Captain said getting up off the examination table and walking toward the door. As they walked out the door, everyone started asking questions of both the Captain and Emir.

"Hold it," the Captain said, "let's gather at the bay area where we can sit down and tell everyone at the same time." Quickly hurrying to their seats, they all sat and waited for the Captain to start.

"First, Emir, I don't know if we had the same experience. I'll try to explain mine and you can agree or tell us about your experience when I finish."

"Okay," Doc said, "tell us what happened."

"Well, when I first stepped on the ground I was fine. Then, when I stepped further out, I noticed a tingling in my feet. As fast as I noticed it, the tingling ran up my whole body. Then I was frozen in place."

"I felt the same thing," Emir said.

"What happened next?" Angelina asked.

"I'm not sure how to explain the next part," the Captain said, "but I'll try. It was like I was being evaluated by some unknown force—both physically and mentally, throughout every cell in my body. I suddenly had memory event flashes that went back through my life—all the way to childhood—including people I didn't recognize or hadn't remembered for years. After a few minutes, I had the feeling that I had passed the evaluation or judgment okay—but that there was still something yet to be determined. I don't know how else to explain it."

"Were there voices?" Doc asked.

"No," the Captain said, "it was just a feeling – but a very real feeling none the less."

"I too felt that way," Emir said. "However, the ending was different."

"How so?" the Captain asked.

"Toward the end, I felt I had passed whatever test had been given and that I had been accepted. Then, I saw the picture or vision."

"What vision?" asked three or four of them together at the same time.

"Can you remember?" Doc asked.

"Oh yes, it's clear as can be in my mind," Emir responded.

"Then tell us," Doc said.

"It's of a mountain," Emir said. "A particular mountain and there is a cave. I can't see inside the cave, but I can see clearly everything about the mountain. And, I feel a compulsion to go toward it."

"Wow," Bruce said, "this is like one of those space computer games, with monsters and witches and everything."

"Chill," the Captain, said, "we don't want to let our imaginations run away with us. Let's take time to figure out what happened here. Did any one else feel anything strange?"

No, they all replied in unison.

"Wait," Drago interrupted. "Natasha you said you felt a buzzing in your head. Remember?"

Natasha, who had been totally caught up in the story, listening with her mouth slightly open, was again caught off guard by Drago.

"I err, well, I felt something, but it could have been caused just by getting outside with fresh air."

"Tell us what you felt," Doc said.

"Well, it was like when you are in a big crowd and everyone is talking or whispering to each other at the same time. You can hear the buzzing without really being able to make out any of the words."

"Now that's interesting," the Captain said. "Anybody else?" he asked.

Angelina responded with "I didn't feel anything different while you guys were outside, but there is something else. I don't know if it coincides with the exact time when you and Emir went into the trance, but all the computers on the ship went off the grid. The system's alarm bells were ringing like some massive power surge had taken place. So much has happened since then that I have not had time to review the computer diagnostic print outs. However, I can say with confidence that everything came back on line about the same time the both of you collapsed."

"This gets more confusing and challenging by the minute," Doc said shaking his head in perplexity.

"All right," the Captain said, "let's all go back to what we were working on before we broke to go outside. We will discuss this further at the evening meal. Angelina, get on those prints outs and see if you can determine the cause. Emir, you and I are going back with Doc to the sick bay to see if his testing results can shed any light on our episode."

'Sir, excuse me," Maggy said.

"Yes, go ahead Maggy," the Captain responded.

"I would like to suggest that Rashad, Drago and I go back outside and work on our maneuvers. None of us were affected and I think we need to get better adjusted to the gravity and working together as a team."

"I see your point," the Captain said. "But I'd like you to use the cables as you practice."

"I think Loren should go too," Drago said. "She will be with us tomorrow and the more we work together the better prepared we will be."

"Makes sense," the Captain said. "However, as far as going out tomorrow, I will withhold judgment on that for now. We still need to figure out what happened today. It doesn't do us any good if one of you gets frozen out there, away from the ship. Okay everybody, let's get back to work, we still have a lot to accomplish and time is running short."

As everyone went back to what they were doing, Doc, Emir and the Captain headed back into the sick bay.

"I'll get the read outs," Doc said.

"Well, Emir, are you as confused with what happened as I am?"

"At first Sir," he replied. "But more and more, I feel that there is something that I need to do here. I'm not sure what it is, but I have been given some responsibility or task to achieve."

"And I have this feeling that I've been passed but that I will be watched to see how I perform or something," the Captain said. "What I do understand, is that this is a very real feeling."

"Here's the report," Doc said. "Everything is normal, except the brain activity. I wish we had the MRI equipment up and running. It would give me a much better idea of what is going on inside your brains and if there is something we need to be concerned about."

"Well, if this is all you have for now, I'd say Emir and I should go back and join the others."

"I'd like that sir; I still need to get my weather equipment uncrated and set up."

As they walked toward the Cargo Bay, Angelina came up to let the Captain know that she had the computer diagnostic print-outs ready for review. "Do you want to go over them now?" she asked the Captain.

"Okay," the Captain said. "Emir you go on to the bay, I'll be with Angelina for a while."

Emir, anxious to get back to his weather equipment, headed straight for the Cargo Bay. When he walked in, Molly, Choi, Tani, Matzo and Bruce yelled, "Surprise!"

"What?" questioned Emir as he realized that a large portion of his equipment had already been unpacked and partially assembled.

"Well," Bruce explained, "we decided rather than keep looking at different equipment and my drones, we would all work together and get certain pieces put together that we could use right now. After discussing it, we decided that after today, maybe you wouldn't be able to go out again. So we decided to set up your equipment first. We're about fifty percent complete, but with all of us working on it together, it makes it easier. Besides, I need to use the broken down crate material when we start putting together my drones outside."

Emir was so grateful all he could do was bow towards them in gratitude.

Matzo returned his bow and said, "Based on the diagrams, the platform for the equipment has wheels so it should be easy to move around once we get everything assembled. I'm thinking we should be able to set this up against the wall in the other bay by your bunk. Once we get everything set up and in place, Bruce should be able to tie your equipment in with the ship's computer. He's already started reading the spec files to determine how to best accomplish that."

While they were working, Sophia and Naomi went by caring arm loads of stuff. Sophia was humming to herself on her way to the Ships Galley, which she had named the kitchen.

Natasha, who was helping Dana and Gerard put together one of the pieces of equipment they were working on, looked up with a contented smile on her face as she watched Sophia and Naomi go by.

CHAPTER TWELVE

MEANWHILE OUTSIDE, RASHAD, MAGGY, Loren, and Drago were trying out various pieces of equipment and practicing moving about.

"I don't think the sonic gun is the weapon to take with us," Maggy was saying. "The kick back reaction could take one of us out of the area we're in. The laser, however, just has a small kick back to it that you can brace against your body."

"I don't know," Rashad said. "That sonic gun can blow the crap out of anything—the laser wouldn't have the same affect."

"What about the stun gun side arms?" Drago asked.

"They seem to be an advanced model of the old Taser guns used by the military and law enforcement back on earth," Maggy said. "But we have nothing to test them on. They have controls that go from low to high, but we have no idea what the affect would be. The good news is there is one for each of us. So each of us will have some sort of protection."

Loren, who had been practicing her gliding, asked about the rest of the equipment.

"Well," Rashad said, "we were able to determine with the help of Tani, that the head cams can take infrared along with the other normal stuff. Maggy and I decided to set one to record in infrared and the other three for normal."

Rashad continued bringing Loren up to date with what they had discovered. "We also found some recording gear we can add to our communicators. According to the instruction manual, they have the capability of recording different pitched noises that the web cams won't. Other than that, we have added flash bangs and some other grenade type objects to our belts along with a couple more pouches and a back-pack for you and Drago."

"There are still a couple of sample collection vials in the vest pockets, but we already know about the water and we didn't think it was necessary to go get more."

Maggie chimed in with, "Or see another monster."

"I heard that," Drago said.

"Me too," Rashad agreed. "I almost crapped my pants! Actually, we thought that we would go back to the tree line and then go either right or left around the water to see what we could find. Maggie and I also decided that on the way there, we would walk on both sides—about twenty feet out from you and Drago. Then, when we hit the tree line, one of us will go in front and the other behind. That way, we can protect you from the front and back."

Rashad continued, "Maggy and I don't think we should be cabled together but we have come up with an idea that we would like to try. If we each had a cable, we could throw it to the other, then the first one jumps while the other holds the cable allowing them to swing the person around. The second one then does the same thing. That would allow us to really cover some distance and get out of trouble fast if need be."

"Sounds good," Drago said, "let's try it."

First, Maggy and Rashad stood about 20 feet apart. Maggy threw Rashad her cable, which went easily through the air with the low gravity.

Next, Rashad said, "Ready?"

"Go for it," Maggy said, holding onto the cable with her hands. Rashad paused, and then jumped into the air. Maggy immediately pulled on the cable. It brought Rashad back swinging around and landing twenty feet away. But in doing so Maggy lost hold of the cable, causing Rashad to fall and roll across the ground for about another twenty feet.

"If you clip the cable to the belt around your waist," Drago suggested, "it will keep you from losing your grip and allow your hands to be free to use your weapons."

"Drago you never stop amazing me. As soon as I think you're not paying attention, you come up with a brilliant idea," Rashad said grinning. "Let's try it."

For the next hour, Maggy and Rashad then Drago and Loren practiced the swing retrieve, as they called it. As they perfected the technique, they found they could really cover some distance. More than once they found themselves a goodly distance from the ship, but they quickly returned the same way they went out.

"We have to think about this as a way to go out instead of just walking," Maggy said.

"I think we need to take our time going out," Drago said. "But I think it's the way to come back."

Meanwhile in the Engineers control room, the Captain and Angelina had been going over the computer diagnostic print outs.

"From what I can tell," Angelina said, "it seems like a massive energy surge. Why it didn't do any damage to the system I can't even begin to guess."

"Just what we needed," the Captain replied. "Another mystery." As he was commenting, he happened to glance over to one of the monitors that showed outside activity. Just then, he saw Rashad and Maggy about a mile from the ship. As he was about to yell at them, they came swinging back until they were just outside.

"Get them on the communicator, he told Angelina, and tell them to get in here now."

"Rashad, Maggy, Drago, and Loren, report to the Captain immediately," directed Angelina.

All four, who had been totally engrossed in what they were doing, immediately looked up to the ship and headed back. When they walked up the ramp, the Captain was standing right there to greet them.

"What the hell was that you were doing?" he asked.

"We call it the swing-retrieve," Maggy said. "We were trying to find a way to get us out of trouble quickly while staying in control. We decided we couldn't be always hooked together as that would cause too many difficulties."

The Captain was about to strongly reprimand them when Drago said, "It works Captain. That's all that matters. It increases our chance of survival."

The Captain looked at the four of them, shook his head and walked away muttering to himself.

"Give him time," Angelina said. "He worries about all of you and doesn't want to lose any of you. It's almost time for dinner. Go get out of your gear and wash up. Then we'll head to the bay area to see what everyone else has been up to."

CHAPTER THIRTEEN

ARRIVING AT THE BAY, the Captain noticed that there were multiple conversations going on. Everyone was talking about what they had found or accomplished that day.

"Good evening," the Captain said. "How is everyone?"

Almost immediately, three or four people started responding excitedly to his question at the same time.

"Hold it," the Captain said. "Let's sit down and wait for everyone else to arrive. Once the food has been served, then we will do the same thing we did earlier. Everyone will get their chance."

Sophia and Naomi, with help form Natasha started bringing out the food.

"Tonight we have kind of a Burrito," Sophia said. "I took some of the prepared food and added some stuff I found in the cargo bay. Then I ground up some of the corn seeds and made corn shells."

As they were passing around the food, Natasha went back into the kitchen and came out with some bottles and jars that looked like spices.

"I hope we're not in trouble," Sophia said, "but we found two crates that were marked '**Only to be opened By:**' one of them was for a head scientist named Rodriquez. The other one was for a Chief Scientist named Chang." While Natasha passed out the bottles and jars she had brought from the kitchen, Sophia continued. "When we opened the one for Rodriquez, it was full of spices, hot sauce, and seeds for plants like cilantro, basil and peppers. I figured he must be someone important who could order special. Meanwhile his loss is our gain," Sophia added with a grin. "The sauces and stuff really spiced it up and covered the bland taste of some of the food."

"Now, if I can talk first," Sophia said looking at the Captain, "I'd like to ask for a couple of things."

"Go ahead," the Captain said, reaching for his glass of water since the sauce had proved to be much hotter than he expected.

"I think we should take some of the wheat and vegetable seeds and try planting them. I was also wondering if we could bring in some of the soil to start seedlings—or try to plant them outside."

With that, Dana spoke up. "Excuse me Captain, but Gerard and I managed to get one of the spectrometers hooked up and running. Bruce tied it into the ship's computer system and we were able to analyze the soil, the grass, the Poke Sallie and have started analyzing the branch."

"What have you discovered?" the Captain asked.

"The plants and grass seem to resemble Earth plants; although, there are some differences. There was one substance common in all the samples tested so far and we suspect that substance will show up in the branch also."

"What's that?" Doc asked.

"It seems to be a compound not unlike plastic but different."

"Wait a minute, you said it was also in the Poke Sallie," the Captain said with some alarm in his voice.

"Yes sir," Dana said.

"How then were we able to eat it?" the Captain asked. "How did you fix it Sophia?"

"I just put it in a pan and boiled it," Sophia said, "just like I'd do at home. But now that you mention it, there was this substance that kept floating to the top. I just kept spooning off until the water was clear."

"What did you do with it?" Dana asked.

"I threw it down that sink like thing," Sophia said.

"That goes into part of the ship's on-board recycling system," Angelina said. "It continually reports all the liquids. We can run a quick analysis after dinner and see if the print-outs tell us anything."

"We have a problem testing the branch," Dana said. "It is too big for the equipment since our attempts at cutting it failed."

"What if we try one of our lasers?" suggested Rashad.

"That might work," Gerard said; "we can try it after dinner."

The Captain took another drink of his water and said, "Okay, I already know what Drago and his team were up to while they were outside. What else has been going on?"

"Well sir," Choi said, "we have managed to get a lot of the equipment identified. As a group we selected the pieces of equipment you indicated were the priorities. At first, we were not sure how much power we could use from the ship. But Bruce and Tani seemed to work it out and feel that we can operate the equipment we have started putting together without overloading the power grid."

"Sir, I should explain something I did," Bruce interrupted. "After checking the power grid, I released the outside solar panels."

"Oh my god," Angelina exclaimed, "with everything that's been going on, I totally forgot. That was one of the first things that I should have done."

"Well, the next thing I did was trickier and you may want to change it back," Bruce said. "I shut down the air filtration system and opened the outside air ports to let in fresh air. By doing that, I was able to increase the available power supply by another twenty-two percent.

Again, Angelina put her head down. "I haven't been doing what I was trained," she said.

"Relax," the Captain said. "We have all been adjusting to our circumstances here."

"I know," Angelina replied, "but protocols are protocols, and I haven't been doing my job properly. Tomorrow, if you don't mind, Bruce, I'd like for you to work with me so I can go over all the ship's on-board controls with you."

"No problem," Bruce said, "but I think it would be a good idea if we let Tani work with us too."

"Next," the Captain said as he looked at Emir.

"Well sir, they got my equipment hooked up and Tani got it tied into the ship's controls. We moved everything into the sleeping bay close to my bunk. I plan to start studying the sky tonight and hope to have some answers by the day after tomorrow."

After Emir had finished with his update, Matzo informed the Captain that his team had completed the layouts needed to make sure the equipment would fit the available space. He concluded with, "You just need to decide which pieces of equipment you want us to set up first."

With that, the Captain said, "I'm sure you got everyone's input as to what they wanted. Doc, Angelina and I will go over it with you tomorrow."

"Good meal Sophia. Matzo, if you can give me a copy of your layouts, I will review them now. The rest of you may go back to what you're doing," the Captain said as he stood up and headed to his quarters.

Everyone started moving away from the table—most getting up with their dishes and taking everything back to the kitchen galley to help with the clean up.

CHAPTER FOURTEEN

NATASHA GOT UP AND walked over to where Drago still sat preoccupied thinking like he was most of the time. "Excuse me," Natasha said. "Drago, can I talk to you for a minute?"

"Sure," he said, "what's up?"

"I wanted to ask why you wanted me to be on the communications with you."

"First, can I ask you a couple of questions?" Drago responded with a question of his own.

"Okay," Natasha replied.

"These might be kind of personal for you to answer, but please try as best you can," Drago said.

"I'll try," replied Natasha.

"Have you ever met someone for the first time and been able to immediately tell what they were thinking or what they were like?"

"Sometimes," she said.

"How about if someone passed you in a crowd and you felt you knew exactly where they were going and what they were thinking?"

"Yes, but I thought it was my just my imagination and something I like to do."

"The other day when we all went outside, you mentioned a buzzing in your head. Did you notice anything else?"

"What do you mean?" Natasha asked with a perplexed look on her face.

"Did you feel or think what I was thinking when Emir and the Captain froze up?"

Natasha looked down at her hands, trying to cover her sudden embarrassment to Drago's question. "I'm not sure what you mean," she said.

"I think you do," Drago said.

"I'm not sure I want to talk about it," Natasha responded.

"I thought so," Drago said.

"What do you mean?" Natasha asked.

"I felt you in my head," Drago said.

"What!" Natasha exclaimed.

"Chill," Drago said. "These things we're talking about—I have been having these feelings since I was a little boy. I accepted it a long time ago; however, I have also learned to be cautious with it." Drago confided quietly to Natasha, "I read some books on it and the best I could come up with is that it is some sort of psychic talent. Now, will you please tell me what I was thinking or what you thought I was thinking?" Drago requested earnestly.

"You thought it was the planet itself that caused Emir and the Captain to be frozen in place," Natasha replied.

"You're right," Drago said.

"Do you think that's what also caused the buzzing in my head?" Natasha asked.

"I'm not sure," Drago said. "I am anxious to see what they can get out of the print outs before I say anything more."

"Is this why you want me on the communicator?" Natasha asked.

"Yes," Drago responded nodding his head, "that way I'll have someone who can pick up outside thoughts along with me."

"Drago, do you think what we do is wrong? Sometimes, I feel like I'm invading someone's personal life."

"I know what you mean," Drago said. "That's why I said you have to be cautious."

"Good night, Drago."

"Good night, Natasha."

Sitting alone with his thoughts once again, Drago kept having the feeling that something dramatic was going to happen again tomorrow but he couldn't put his finger on it—just that something was going to happen. He did feel it concerned Loren though, and this bothered him. Go to bed; he told himself; tomorrow will be here soon enough.

As he headed for his bunk, he noticed that Emir was at his computer equipment looking at the night sky.

CHAPTER FIFTEEN

THE NEXT MORNING AS they were again eating their oatmeal, they discussed their plans for the day. Everyone was pretty much continuing with what they had already started. Bruce asked Angelina how long she thought he and Tani were going to work with her on the ship's control systems because he really wanted to get started on the drones.

"Hopefully it won't take more than three or four hours," Angelina replied.

"Oh….." Bruce groaned with some disappointment.

"Is your team ready to go, Drago?" the Captain asked.

"Yes sir, I think we have it pretty well planned. Rashad and Maggy have worked out what equipment we need to take with us when we go out and they have set up one of the head cams to record on infra-red. That way, we will be able to pick up the heat readouts of things we can't easily see. Maggy was able to find backpacks for each of us and Angelina fitted Loren with a belt that has pouches for collecting samples since we are focusing on finding edible plants today."

"Sounds like you have thought it out," the Captain remarked. "Doc, if you will keep an eye on them while Natasha maintains the communication devices, I'm going to spend some time with Emir. Just let me know when they go out." the Captain said then dismissed everyone with, "All right everyone, have a good day and stay safe."

Drago got together with Loren, Rashad, and Maggy. They gathered their equipment, and made sure that every thing was working, connected the cables around their waists; and announced that they were going out.

When they got to the bottom of the ramp, Drago again felt the sense of relief from the confinement of the ship. It was another perfect day with a gentle breeze that invigorated.

"Let's go back to where we found the lake," Maggy said. "But don't get too close, we can decide which way to go from there."

"Do you want to do our swing retrieve going out?" Rashad asked.

"No," Drago said. "I want to see what the infra red camera picks up in the grass on the way out. We can get there pretty quick just by gliding."

"Okay," Rashad said, "let's move out."

Again, they were quickly at the tree line. Moving slowly toward the water, they stopped when about fifty yards away.

"Well," Maggy said, "which way should we go?"

"I think we should go to the right, Drago said; "the lake seems to turn in there."

"I agree," Natasha said, over their mikes.

"Why do you think that?" Maggy asked.

"Err... I don't know;" Natasha said. "It was just a thought."

"Wait," Drago said. "Natasha what did you see?"

"I just felt that you should go to the right," Natasha said.

"Ok, let's go that way," Drago said.

This time Maggy took up the rear guard and Rashad took point like they had agreed.

"Loren," Rashad said, "There are a bunch of plants ahead on the right that looks like they have berries on them. We'll move that way."

When Loren and the rest of the group got close to the plants, she noticed that there were animal droppings around the plant. "We will need to gather the scat," Loren said. "I am going to pick some of the berries and take a couple of the smaller branches and twigs that have fallen off."

Rashad, who had moved in front said, "Hey you guys, it looks like the lake curves away to the left and, there are wet lands up ahead on the right."

"We'll move that way next," Drago said.

"Let's take our time," Loren said. "I see three or four plants that look somewhat familiar. I want to get some samples of them too. I also think I need to focus my head cam closer to the ground so that we have some video of these foot prints around the berry plant."

"You'd think we would have seen some animals by now," Maggy said. Rashad agreed, but also noted that there could be several reasons why they hadn't seen any animals by pointing out that they might be too small or too fast to see because of the lighter gravity.

As they moved towards the wetlands, Loren continued to take samples of plant material while directing Drago to pick others. So far, they had gathered about ten or twelve different plant samples. Using the lasers, they had managed to cut off some pieces when suddenly, Loren exclaimed in a hushed voice while pointing to their left, "Oh, look over there! It looks like some animals next to that large rock underneath those bushes."

"Be careful," warned Drago and Rashad at the same time. But Loren had already unclipped the cable from her belt and was moving in that direction. She stopped just short, waiting for the others to catch up to the point where they could see a large animal lying on its side with what appeared to be two small cubs moving around next to it.

"Everyone stop!" said Drago in the same hushed voice Loren had used earlier. "Don't go any closer till we check out things."

"The mother doesn't seem to be moving," Loren said quietly.

"How do you know it's the mother?" Maggy asked.

"You can see the cubs trying to nuzzle," Loren answered.

"Oh—right," Maggy said.

"I'm going in closer," Loren said.

As she moved in and squatted down a few feet away, the two cubs made growling noises and moved closer to their mother. As she was kneeling down and reaching out to them, Loren suddenly froze up just as Emir and the Captain had before.

"Don't anyone move," Drago commanded in a whisper loud enough for the others to hear. "We'll wait this out, till she comes out of it."

Meanwhile back at the ship, the Captain who had been working with Emir heard the computer alarm bells and warning beeps go off. As he quickly made his way into the command center, he asked what was going on.

"It's happening again," Angelina said.

Bruce and Tani, along with Angelina and the Captain watched helplessly as the computers went hay wire. Suddenly just as fast as it started, everything stopped and everything went back to normal.

"Check on those outside, now," the Captain ordered.

"They're okay," Natasha said. "This time it was Loren who froze up, but she seems to be fine now."

Unlike the others, Loren had not fallen over when she came out of the trance. "It's okay now," she whispered to the cubs, not to the others. The cubs quit growling and came towards Loren's extended hand, sniffling closely then licking her fingers. She reached down and picked them up saying. "It's okay Zena, you too Butkis. It will be all right. I'll take care of you."

"What the hell is going on?" The Captains voice came through their ear bugs.

"It's seems as though we have two new animals added to our group," Drago answered.

"You could get infected," Doc said. "Don't touch those animals."

"Too late," Drago said, "Loren already seems to have them under control."

"Head back now," ordered the Captain. "And don't bring those animals into this ship until we can test them."

"How?" Angelina asked.

"I don't know," the Captain said, "ask Doc."

"Before we come back I want to get some samples of those plants over there," said Loren, gently putting the two cubs in her back pack.

"Does anyone remember that I am the one who is supposed to be in charge?" asked the Captain in an exasperated voice.

"Yes sir," they all said together.

After Loren had gathered some of the plants that were in the wet lands, they started back.

"Can you bring back the corpse of the mother for examination?" Dana asked. Who, like everyone else had run to the computer screens to see what was going on when the computer alarms had sounded.

"No," Loren said. "Leave her. She'll go back to the planet."

"Where did that come from?" Drago asked.

"I just know its right," Loren responded.

"Well, I suggest you use your swing retrieves and get back to the ship at once," the Captain said.

This time when they got back, everyone but Emir was outside waiting for them. Only the Captain remained on the ramp to ensure he didn't get frozen again.

"Let's see them," everyone was shouting.

"Hold on a minute," Loren said, "you'll scare them." Taking off her back pack, she gently reached in and took the cubs out. "Alright come up one at a time—slowly and I'll introduce you." Maggy who was the closest came forward and held out her hand.

"Zena, Butkis, this is Maggy," Loren said.

Both cubs went up and sniffed her hand. Suddenly, Zena started jumping around and acted like she wanted to play with Maggy. Maggy reached out and Zena rolled on her back to have her belly rubbed.

"She likes you," Loren said.

"How did you come up with their names?" Maggy asked.

"They told me," Loren said.

"How?" Maggy asked.

"I don't know," she said, "they just did."

One by one, they came by and were introduced. The pups were polite but didn't behave like Zena did with Maggy until Natasha met them. Then Butkis went up and just lay down next to her licking her hand.

"It looks like Butkis picked you," Loren said. But Natasha was lost in thought looking into Butkis's eyes as if they were privately communicating.

CHAPTER SIXTEEN

"ALL RIGHT EVERYONE, LETS get back inside," the Captain said from the ship's ramp, "I want all the plants to be unloaded and analyzed. Loren, you can stay outside with the cubs until Doc can do some tests."

"No sir, I'll come on board," she replied. "The cubs are fine with Maggy and Natasha."

"Okay," the Captain said. "Let's go everyone."

Sophia said, "Naomi and I'll be right there. We have to finish up first."

"Whatever," the Captain said curtly as he headed back up the ramp mumbling to himself about no one listening to him any more.

Once inside, they started emptying the packs and pouches to see what they had.

"Rashad, run your infra reds through the computer program and see what you come up with. Also, get me still pictures of the mother animal and run it through some analysis," the Captain ordered.

"Right sir," Rashad responded.

"Angelina, do you have any more information on the shut down?"

"We're looking at a couple of the anomalies now sir," replied Angelina.

"Good, let me know as soon as you have something."

"Loren, I want to meet with you. I want you to tell me what you felt when you froze up."

"I'd like to hear this also," Drago said.

While the Captain, Drago and Loren went to the Captain's quarters, everyone else unpacked the pouches or went back to work. Dana and Gerard particularly had a handful of things they wanted to analyze.

Meanwhile outside, Maggy and Natasha were happily playing with the cubs. Doc had examined each of the cubs, took some swabs for later testing, ran a scanner over them, and had gone back inside to analyze the information.

When Drago and Loren got to the Captains quarters, he had them sit down. "So tell us Loren, exactly what you felt and thought while you were frozen."

"Well sir, I was thinking about the cubs and was reaching for them when I froze. It felt like something or someone was checking me out like you said. But I kind of thought, don't worry, I won't hurt them. And the next thing I knew, I was able to move again."

"This is getting more interesting all the time," the Captain said. "What's your opinion Drago?"

"I'd like to talk to Natasha first," Drago said. "Then I want to meet again with Emir. I'd also like to see what Angelina and Bruce found out before I give you my opinion."

"Okay, I'll wait, but I have to be honest with you, I'm running low on patience."

Sensing they had been dismissed, Drago and Loren headed back to the bay where everyone was busily working on their various projects.

The Captain decided to just stay out of the way and wait till dinner to hear out what their investigations and testing had revealed. Then, he changed his mind and went into the kitchen to see what Sophia and Naomi were up to.

"What's up ladies?" the Captain asked.

"Well, we planted some of the seeds outside and we just finished planting some of the same seeds in the small containers sitting on the counter over there." Sophie said as she washed off her hands. "When me and Naomi finish cleaning up our mess, we were going to take them over to Dana. I believe they set up the growing equipment in her lab."

"I'll go with you," the Captain said.

When they walked into the lab, Dana and Gerard were discussing the tests they had performed, while Tani was looking through a microscope.

"So guys, what have you got?" the Captain asked.

Dana looked up from her notes and responded with a satisfied look of accomplishment on her face. "We have cleared about six plants for consumption, as long as you wash off that plastic like compound first. The berries seem to be fine. Right now, we're testing the plant samples Loren gathered just before they returned to the ship. One of those samples looks an awful lot like rice. We'll know more shortly, Tani is looking at it under the microscope right now."

"You give me rice," Sophia remarked enthusiastically, "and I can make a bunch of things–including wine."

"I'm not sure we need wine," the Captain said, "but that's sounds like good news."

"Captain, may we speak to you please," Matzo requested.

"Yes, what is it?" the Captain said.

"We've been going over the videos," Matzo said, "and I think we have some interesting things to show you."

"Let's go look," the Captain said.

When they got to the computer, Choi was already there looking at something.

"What have you discovered?" the Captain asked.

"Oh, good day sir, I was just rechecking something I noticed earlier. Let me set it back to the infrared images first, sir. When we run the infrared, you will notice that there are quite a few small heat sources. Our analysis shows them to be small animals weighing three to four pounds each with the ability to move extremely fast. There are a few that appear to be bigger, but the majority of them are small."

"That's a possible food source then," the Captain said. "Were you able to obtain any information from the video shots taken of the mother animal? Or, do you need more time to review them?"

"Yes sir, let me pull them up for you." When the images came up on the computer screen, the Captain studied them closely.

"It almost looks like some type of wolverine," the Captain said. "Except, it looks like it would be much taller and longer."

"The computer says it weighs about 160 pounds, sir. Plus, its eyes are in the front which means she was a predator sir."

"Too bad we couldn't get samples of her stomach to see what she had been eating," the Captain remarked. "What else do you have?"

"Well sir, we have some good videos of the area they walked through. And, there are a couple of other things we have seen that are very interesting."

"Show me," the Captain directed.

"Look at this section," Matzo said. "This is when they had reached the lake and were beginning to go around. If you look in the background you'll notice there are what seem to be fish jumping on the lake."

"Play it slower," the Captain directed moving closer to the screen. "Yes,

I can see what you mean. Try to get some stop action on them for a closer look." He then asked, "What else were you looking at when I came in?"

"Well sir, I was going back over the videos section by section, rechecking everything in slow motion when I thought that I noticed something in the trees," Choi responded.

"Let's look at it," the Captain said.

Choi ran the video through then stopped. "Look there, in the trees to the right," Choi said. "See that shape on the dead branch on the second tree on the right?"

"Can you zoom in?" the Captain asked.

"I was just about to do that when you came in, sir."

"Please elaborate," the Captain said.

As they zoomed in and readjusted the video clip, they could see a shape about six feet tall, sitting on the branch. As Choi readjusted the focus, they could see it was a large bird shaped animal. Choi finely tuned the clip some more and they could see it definitely was a bird with a hawk like beak. The computer estimated a wing span of twelve feet.

"That's a big bird," the Captain stated.

"It really is," Choi said.

"This has been a big day," the Captain commented. "About the only thing left, is to see what Angelina and Bruce were able to figure about the second power surge and the shut down. Let's go see what kind of answers they have come up with."

Walking out to the bay, they saw everyone was still working away. Then they went looking for Angelina and Bruce in the engineer's room. Walking in, the Captain could see they were engrossed studying the print outs.

He overheard Bruce say, "I'm telling you Angelina, that is where it's coming from."

"But that's impossible," Angelina exclaimed with disbelief.

"Maybe on Earth," Bruce said, "but we don't know what's possible here."

"Excuse me," the Captain said, "please tell me what you think is or is not impossible here."

"Well sir, we have been running every analysis we can on the computer and Bruce thinks it has something do with the planet itself."

"Show me how you came to that conclusion Bruce."

"Well sir, I really can't—except that the computer shows that the electrical vibrations seem to come out of the ground and vibrate up. Sorry, I can't give you anything more definite than that."

"Alright, I will accept that hypothesis for now but will reserve judgment until we have more facts. Let's go see what the others have come up with." When they returned to the bay, every one was still working.

"Where's Drago?" the Captain asked.

A couple of them looked up from their tasks and indicated that they thought he had gone back outside to see Natasha.

"Okay, what is going on with you guys?

Everyone had something to say, so he went back to his old stand by and said, "Let's wait till supper, and we'll talk it over then."

CHAPTER SEVENTEEN

MEANWHILE OUTSIDE, DRAGO HAD gone up to Natasha who was sitting with Butkis in her lap.

"Hey Natasha," he said; "How's it going with Butkis?"

"He's just wonderful," Natasha said, "but his attention span isn't real long; he is a still just a cub, you understand."

As Drago stood there watching Natasha pet Butkis, he said, "I wanted to ask you what you felt or saw, when Loren froze up today."

"I'm trying to pay more attention to what I am thinking and feeling about those sorts of things. So today, when Loren froze up, I tried to focus on everything that was happening around me and I felt the same buzzing. It was not as intense and it didn't last nearly as long as before—but there was something else too. I felt that there was another presence watching us. I tried to lock on to it, but it slipped away. Whatever it was, it was definitely concentrating on Loren."

"Humm," Drago said, "I wonder what that was all about?"

Suddenly, Zena jumped up from the spot she was laying and took off toward the grass. Butkis immediately jumped off Natasha's lap and followed.

"What's going on?" Drago asked.

"I got the thought about food just before Zena took off." Maggy responded.

"Butkis had the same thought," Natasha said.

Both cubs had taken off in a streak, disappearing into the high grass. The three children ran forward into the grass, but could not see anything. Suddenly, they heard a high squeal and a tussle with a few moments of growling and grunting. Then a few moments later, both cubs came out, licking their chops.

Zena immediately went to Maggy, sat down and started grooming herself. Butkis walked over to Natasha and tried to wipe his muzzle on her.

"Stop it Butkis," Natasha said, "go wipe your face on the grass." Butkis promptly started wiping his muzzle back and forth on the grass groaning with pleasure. When he had finished, he stood up and moved over to Zena. Content, both cubs curled up to take a nap.

"Let's go inside," Drago said, "it's almost time for dinner."

"We haven't got the go ahead from Doc yet," Maggy said. "I mean—to let us bring the cubs inside."

"I'm not worried," Drago responded, "let's go."

Picking up the cubs, they headed up the ramp. When they got inside, no one paid any attention to them. Everyone was busy talking about the stuff they had been working on all day.

Sophia suddenly called out, "Supper's ready, come and get it."

As they all sat down, the normal amount of conversation was going on. Meaning that, there were at least ten different conversations going on at the same time. No one noticed that Maggy and Natasha had sat down with the cubs in their laps sleeping peacefully.

"Well, I can hardly wait to start tonight," the Captain said. "As soon as Sophia and Naomi serve the food we will go ahead and begin our discussions. Let's go from left to right as I am sure everyone will have something to say."

Emir, who was seated to the Captain's left announced, "I believe I have figured out some of the atmospheric and weather conditions," he announced.

"Go ahead," the Captain said.

"The best I can figure is that the moons reach full at different times. However, there is one time that they both reach full at the same time."

"What does that mean?" the Captain asked.

"My predictions and computer analysis suggest it will be a time of extensive and strong storms."

"How extensive?" the Captain asked.

"According to the computer, these storms will equate to a Level Five hurricane back on earth," Emir responded with a serious look on his face.

"When will this take place?" the Captain asked.

"My best prediction is that they will start approximately six months from now—give or take a couple of days variance."

"At least that gives us a little time to prepare," the Captain replied as he considered Emir's prediction. "Do you think this type of weather event is something that reoccurs on a regular basis?"

"It seems to take place about every twelve months, Earth time," Emir replied. "But this planet seems to be on a sixteen month cycle rather than a twelve."

"If this occurs with regularity..." Gerard commented with a thoughtful look on his face then added, "I wonder if this has any thing to do with the plastic compound in the plants?"

"That would make sense," Molly said. "Rather than develop structurally strong, being able to bend with the wind would make their survival chances better."

"Interesting point," the Captain mused.

"It really does make sense," Choi said. "The trees would have a better chance of survival if they could bend rather then break during a Level Five hurricane. I wonder if that is why all the plants and the grass have that placidity in them?"

"We have to remember," the Captain said, "that we are dealing with something we know nothing about, with this planet, it's ecosystem—everything—so anything is plausible."

"That ties in with what we have discovered so far," Dana said. "Many of the plants that Loren brought back duplicate plants on Earth, except for some small differences and the plasticity. Once we washed the rice like plant down, there was basically no difference between it and the rice grown back on Earth."

"That's good news," the Captain replied. "We can live on rice forever. Many civilizations have already done so. What we haven't found is meat or poultry. However, based upon what Matzo was able to get off the videos, it looks like there are fish in the water."

"Zena and Butkis seemed to find some meat type animals that they ate for dinner," Maggy said.

"What do you mean?" the Captain asked.

Maggy told him what they had experienced outside when the cubs took off.

"Where are the cubs now?" the Captain asked.

Both Maggy and Natasha looked uncomfortable.

"In our laps sleeping," Maggy said quietly.

"What?" the Captain exclaimed. "Did Doc give you permission to bring them inside?"

"I'm sorry," Doc apologized. "I got wrapped up in other things. But, by the best I can tell, all the tests I ran proved negative for any diseases we know about. They're fine."

The Captain shook his head and said, "When are you guys going to start following protocols?" Then he proceeded to ask what else had been going on with their investigations.

"Well," Natasha spoke up suddenly getting a burst confidence. "I noticed the buzzing again when Loren froze up, it was not as strong as it was with you and Emir, but it was there just the same. And, I also noticed something else… There seemed to be another presence that was concentrated on Loren. I couldn't place it, but it felt real."

'We found a bird in the videos," Choi stated. "It seemed to be watching Loren."

"I didn't feel it like I did the cubs," Loren said. "Where was it at?"

"We have pictures of it in the trees to your right," Choi told her.

"I've got to see them and go back," Loren said.

"Take it easy," the Captain said. "You'll get back, but let's take our time. Now, no more excuses Drago. I want to know what you think is going on."

"Well sir, I have listened to what everyone said concerning the plants and the videos, what Loren had to say about her experience, and what you and Emir said. I also heard what Bruce and Angelina had to say about the print outs. And, I talked to both Loren and Natasha after today's incident."

"Today, if you don't mind Drago," the Captain said with a bit of exasperation in his voice.

"Well," Drago said, "I've come to a conclusion."

"What's that?" the Captain asked.

"Well sir, I think it is the planet itself, sir."

"What?" The Captain exclaimed.

"I think the planet itself is controlling what goes on and who it accepts to be here. I think the part where you were 'frozen' was when the planet was checking you and your intentions out. Just like with Loren, the minute the planet felt she was not a danger to the cubs, she was released from her frozen state."

"Earlier, you said you felt you were still being checked out; whereas, Emir felt that he had been approved and given a vision. That vision is a guide for us. What it means, I'm not sure—but I feel it's a guide."

"I also think everyone else is safe from the frozen stasis. However, based upon what Emir said, if he gets back on the ground, he will be forced to head toward that vision."

Everybody including the Captain sat in stunned silence. Drago's revelations had forced everybody to think about what it meant.

"You know," Emir commented. "It's been suggested by many scientists that the Earth tries to heal itself; especially since all the natural catastrophes had increased."

"What happens if that's the case and it rejects any of us?" Naomi questioned.

"I'm not sure what to say," the Captain responded. "However, if Drago is correct and that is the case, there is little we can do about it.

Seeing the affect his statement had on everyone, the Captain added, "Tomorrow, I want everyone to stay in the ship. We have too many things we need to complete."

Pushing back from the table, the Captain looked at Sophia and said, "Good meal again Sophia. I don't know about the rest of you, but I'm going to my quarters. It's been another exhausting day." Then he got up and took his dishes to the kitchen. The rest slowly got up and did the same. There was an unusual quiet about them as they thought about the night's discussions.

When the Captain lay down on his bunk that night, sleep would not come easy. He thought about all the discussions and what they had discovered. He kept running possibilities through his mind but could not come up with answers. Finally, he thought of a plaque he had once seen in Ted Turners office back on Earth. "Lead, follow or get out of the way," it read. Well, he told himself, it was up to him to lead. Maybe something will come to me tonight, he thought as he finally dozed off.

CHAPTER EIGHTEEN

AT BREAKFAST THE NEXT morning, everyone seemed subdued and unusually quite. None of them seemed to have gotten a good night's sleep, even Doc and Angelina had circles under their eyes. Everyone was sitting there eating their morning Mush, as they had decided to call it, when in walked the Captain.

"Good Morning everyone," he said jovially. "I hope you had a good nights sleep. I've come up with a plan for today's activities that I want to go over with you."

The group looked up from their bowls with some hope in their eyes.

"First," he said, "I've changed my mind about everyone staying inside today. Since we don't have any satellites on board, I want Bruce, Matzo and Choi to go out and put the drones together. If were going to follow Emir's vision, I want to be able to see what's ahead."

Bruce immediately sat up straighter with excitement lighting up his face.

"Also, Maggy and Natasha, I want you to take the cubs outside and see if you can teach them to fetch. If there are animals out there that they can eat, maybe we can too."

"Rashad, I want you and Tani to go over every video. I want a complete report on everything seen from the monster, to the things in the trees, to what the infra red clips reveal to us. If we can get good info on this, and Maggy and Natasha can teach the cubs to fetch, we may have a way to get some meat. Dana, Gerard, Sophia, Naomi, and Loren, I want a complete break down on all the plants you have. Emir, I want to go over everything you've been studying on the planet. Doc, you and Angelina move between the groups to see how you can help. Drago, you're with me. We're going to review the findings of each group; in detail, one at a time. Any questions?"

No sir, they replied in unison. But you could see the gloomy looks had disappeared from their faces and the weight had been lifted off their shoulders as they all had direction in what to do.

"Good," the Captain said. "Enjoy your breakfast, then we will all get back to work."

Once again, talk around the table picked up.

As the Captain got up he said, "Drago, when you and Emir finish up, I'll meet you at Emir's computer station."

Walking into the kitchen, he said, "thanks again Sophia, good breakfast."

"I'm hoping the seeds and plants we planted yesterday will grow," Sophia said. "It will improve the meals and maybe we won't be stuck with oatmeal mush everyday."

Going back through the bay, he noticed everyone was getting up and going about their business. When he got to Emir's computer station, Drago and Emir were already in deep conversation.

"Okay men; tell me what's up," he said.

"Well sir, we were discussing the planet's rotation, the two suns, and the longer daylight hours versus dark times."

Emir continued, "Judging by the atmosphere, there should be large bodies of water on the planet. You already know about the lighter gravity, and the air has a slightly higher oxygen content than we had on Earth. All and all, it seems to be a highly habitable planet. However, I am worried about the storms. My analysis indicates that they will be highly volatile."

Emir then continued with, "I would also like to have the drones working so that we can see more of the planet. There should be various types of animals, birds and plants. We seem to have landed in a grass land, close to one edge. I believe the grass lands continue in what I'm calling the South."

"That's a good question," the Captain said. "Which way is North?"

"Well sir, the planet's axis is about six degrees different than that of Earth's, so if there are Polar Regions, they would seem to be smaller."

"Okay, I have a question for you," the Captain stated. "Which way does your vision say we should go?"

Emir turned without hesitation and pointed in the direction that Drago and his team had gone, only more to the right.

"When we get the drones working, that is the direction we will send them," the Captain stated. "Until then, I don't want you going outside Emir. It seems to have a stronger hold on you and I don't want you frozen in place again or walking off in that direction."

"I thought about this last night in bed," Drago said. "My guess is that we'll all get judged or receive some sort of direction before this is over; however, I don't feel any hostility form the planet, it's more of a curiosity thing. How about you and Emir?"

"No, I didn't feel hostility," the Captain said. "But I got the feeling that if you weren't wanted here, you would be gone."

"There's one other thing Captain," Emir commented. "When I went over the readings this morning, it showed that we had rain last night."

"Really, where?" the Captain asked.

"Well, that's the surprising part, sir. It only rained over the garden that Sophia and Naomi planted yesterday."

"If we follow the train of thought that the planet is running everything, then it would seem that it wants to know what's growing," commented the Captain.

"This could get spooky," Emir said.

"Until we know for sure, I think its best we think in those terms and try not to do anything that upsets it," the Captain said. "I think we should go see Sophia and Naomi and find out what they planted."

Walking in to the kitchen, they saw that no one was there.

"Now, where could they have got to?" the Captain asked more to himself than to Drago or Emir. Just as they were about to leave, Sophia and Naomi returned to the kitchen.

"Wow! Captain. We were just going to come find you," Sophia said.

"Where have you been?" the Captain asked.

"We went outside real quick to water the garden. You'll never guess what happened," Naomi said.

"The garden got rained on last night," the Captain said.

"Yes, how did you know?" Sophia asked.

"Emir already told us. He pulled it off his computer print outs this morning."

"Did Emir tell you what else happened?" Naomi asked, kind of snottily.

"No," the Captain said, "why don't you tell us."

"No, this you have got to see for yourself," Sophia said.

With Emir staying inside the ship, the Captain and Drago followed Sophia and Naomi out of the ship and down the ramp. When they got to the bottom, Sophia led them around the ship to the other side where they had planted the garden.

"See," Sophia said.

"Well, I see that some of the plants are maybe two inches tall and some are about ten inches tall. So, what?"

"The ones you see that are about two inches tall were the seeds we planted yesterday. The ones that are about ten inches tall were seedlings when we planted them yesterday."

"Are you sure?" the Captain asked.

Both Sophia and Naomi gave him a looked that said volumes.

"Okay, I believe you," the Captain said.

"Let's go back inside and get with Dana, Gerard, and Loren and see how the plants they are growing inside are doing."

Going back up the ramp, they told Emir about what they had discovered.

"Excuse me Captain, but I want to go back to my computer equipment and look at something."

"Sure," the Captain said.

The rest continued on into the bay where Dana and the others were working. When they got there, they found everyone working away.

"Hey," the Captain greeted them, then questioned, "how's everyone doing?"

"Hi sir, we're just going over our findings again," Dana said.

"How are the plants doing that you planted in the soil, from the outside?" the Captain asked.

"About what you'd expect," Dana said. "We only planted them yesterday, so the seeds will probably take a week or so to come up." "The seedlings are about the same."

"That's interesting," the Captain said.

"It makes sense if you use what we discussed, about the planet being in charge," Drago said.

"What do you mean," the Captain asked?

"Well, these plants may be in the same soil, but they're inside the ship where the planet can't feel them"

"What are you talking about?" Dana asked.

"Well," the Captain said. "Do you remember Drago's discussion last night about the planet?"

"Yes," Dana said, "Gerard and I talked about it all last night. But we doubted whether a planet could have that much control over everything. It would have to be sentient, and we don't understand how that could be."

"Well," the Captain remarked, "we have learned two things this morning that seem to give some validity to that thought."

"What?" Dana asked.

"Hold on a minute and let me tell you," the Captain said.

After going over what Emir had discovered and what Sophia and Naomi had shown them earlier, Dana, Gerard and Loren sat there in stunned silence.

"We have got to go see, right now," Dana said excitedly. "Get the equipment Gerard, we're going outside."

"Hold it," the Captain directed. "First, tell me what information you have come up with."

"The plants all seem edible, even though they all show signs of plasticity like we said before," Dana explained as she was gathering equipment and heading outside.

"Oh," she said, stopping for a minute. "We think that the only way the animals can digest the plant material is if they have two stomachs. That way they can break down the plants before digesting them." And with that, Dana and her group were out the door.

"We might as well go outside too," the Captain told Drago. "We can check on Bruce and his group and see how they're coming with the drone."

As Dana and her group were coming down the ramp, she saw Maggy and Natasha playing with the cubs.

"Loren!" Natasha yelled over, "we can't get the cubs to do anything but play with the ball we made and tear it up. How do we teach them to retrieve?" she asked.

Loren, who was hurrying behind Dana, responded by saying, "Why don't you just ask them."

Maggy, who was retying the ball they had made out of cloth, looked up at Natasha.

"Okay," Natasha said, telling Maggy to take the ball and put it about ten feet away. "Hang onto Zena, and I'll try to tell Butkis what to do."

"No, you should ask him," Maggy said.

When Maggy had finished repairing the ball, she took it ten feet away and placed it on the ground. Then she came back and sat down holding Zena in her lap and said, "Okay try it."

Natasha picked up Butkis and holding him in her hands, looked him in the eye and thought, "Butkis, go pick up the ball and bring it back to me please." Butkis started to wiggle and Natasha set him down. He immediately ran over to the ball, picked it up and brought it back, dropping it at Natasha's feet. His stub of a tail was wagging as he gave out a sharp bark like sound. Natasha picked him up and was telling him what a good cub he was as she scratched his belly.

With that, Zena jumped off Maggy's lap, went over picked up the ball and brought it over to Maggy.

"Okay, Maggy said, "I guess we have to rethink how we train them."

"Maybe the next time we get the thought they're hungry, we can ask them to bring some back," suggested Natasha.

"That's a good thought," Maggy agreed.

Meanwhile, the Captain and Drago had walked around to where Bruce and his group were putting together the drone. He was surprised by how much they seemed to have accomplished in a short period of time—and by how big the drone was.

It stood on the ground on its three wheels about ten to twelve feet long and about four feet high. Bruce and Choi were hooking things up while Matzo seemed to be going over the manuals with pieces and parts laid out in front of him.

"How's it going?" the Captain asked.

"Pretty good," Bruce said. "It looks like we might have it completely assembled by tonight. The most important thing is that we've got the solar batteries out charging. We hope they'll be fully charged by the time we're done."

"What can you tell me about it?" the Captain asked.

"We know it has GPS capabilities and it has four different cameras. They can be set up in two or three different modes, all with zoom capabilities. It can also be programmed to automatically adjust itself in flight without someone running the controls to keep it on line. Additionally, it has equipment that checks the air quality and a few other things we haven't figured out yet," responded Bruce proudly.

Matzo then interjected, "According to the manual it can achieve speeds of 120 miles an hour or fly at a low speed of just 20 miles and hour. With the batteries fully charged, it should have a flight time right around six hours depending on what equipment is being used at the time."

"Bruce is going to set it up so the cameras will feed directly to the ships computer, so we can view what the cameras see real time," Choi said. "Although, there was one thing I didn't see. According to the manual, the drone has the capability of having some sort of armament hooked up to it; however, there was nothing in the crates that looked anything like guns."

"That could be with the other arms equipment that Rashad and Maggy were going through. I'll ask them when we get back," the Captain said.

Then he added, "It would be helpful, or at least make me feel a little better to know that we could use it for defense if need be."

He then turned to Drago and said, "Okay, let's go back and check out how Natasha and Maggy are doing with the cubs. It should be close to lunch time."

Walking back to where Maggy and Natasha were with the cubs, the Captain could see that while Natasha was teaching Butkis to do all sorts of tricks like rolling over, Zena just lay beside Maggy and seemed uninterested.

"Ladies," the Captain said, "How is it going?"

"Well, Loren told us to just talk to them and it seems to be exactly right," Natasha said. "If I look at him and explain what I want and then think it, he seems to pick it up right away."

"What's with Zena, Maggy?" the Captain asked.

"I tried to tell her about rolling over and sitting up, but the mental thought I get back is 'whatever for?' She seems content just to stay beside me. However, both of them retrieve easily, when we ask them to," Maggy explained.

"That's great," the Captain said. "Now see if we can get them to bring back one of those animals that seemed to be in the grass that they eat."

"Natasha came up with an idea on that," Maggy said. "When they're ready to eat again, we'll try to get them to bring one back."

"It will be interesting to see if that works," the Captain said.

"Something else we noticed," Maggy said. "You know how dogs back on earth, after they take a dump, take a few steps away then scratch the ground with their hind paws like they are trying to cover it up before they finally walk away? Well, we noticed when these two have to go; both of them dig a hole first. When they have finished doing their business, they completely fill in the hole and cover it up; making sure every thing is buried—more like cats do back on earth."

"We'll have to ask Loren about that," the Captain said. "I don't know what that means."

"Alright Drago, lets go back inside, I'm hungry. I'll call out to you guys if lunch is ready," the Captain said.

That proved to be unnecessary; as they were approaching the ramp, Naomi came out and yelled, "Lunch is ready. Come and get it!"

CHAPTER NINETEEN

WHEN EVERYONE HAD WASHED up and was seated, the Captain asked Dana and Gerard what they thought of the garden.

"I don't know what to say," Dana responded in a perplexed tone of voice. "There's no question that the plants out there are growing at a much faster rate than the ones in here."

"What all did you plant?" the Captain turned and asked Sophia.

"We planted lima beans, wheat, corn, potatoes, green beans and peas. We also found some coffee beans that we planted along with a couple different types of squash and melons—including watermelon. We had more seeds, but we were afraid to put them all out in case they didn't grow in this soil."

"Well, everything appears to be doing fine," Dana said. "However, we didn't find any melon plants. Although, now that I think about it, we did notice some plants at the end of the rows that were kind of brown and wilted."

"If that's the melon plants, I wonder why they weren't allowed to grow?" The Captain wondered out loud to no one in particular then turned to Sophia. "What kind of seeds and plants do you have left, that you have not planted?"

"We have tomatoes, some lettuce plants, red and black raspberry, some strawberry plants, onions, radishes, and some peanuts," Sophia said.

"I think you should take some of each and plant them," the Captain said. "If they're going to be rejected; we will still have some we can grow inside."

"Excuse me Captain," interrupted Emir. "I have a theory on why the plants are growing so fast."

"Okay," the Captain said, "let's hear it."

"Working on the assumption that we discussed earlier and going over my weather charts, I made an educated guess that the storms are coming in six months. Maybe, the growing season is close to the end."

"I'm not sure I understand what you are telling me," the Captain responded.

"Well sir," Emir said, "we don't know what time of the year it is here or what the seasons are. If we're close to the end of the growing season and we're going into fall or winter or whatever the season, and if what we suspect is true about this planet…." Emir let the statement hang there for a minute before continuing with, "It would want to grow these crops faster to see how they fit in. Or, it could just be that is the way things grow on this planet."

"Just what we needed," the Captain said. "Another mystery."

"Sir, I have a problem with the theory that the planet is running everything," Dana said. "Based upon everything I know about science, it just doesn't add up."

"I understand how you feel Dana. But please remember we know nothing about this area of the universe or how things work here. We have to keep an open mind. Right now, it seems that something or someone is in control and it's not us." The Captain then turned to look for Angelina and Doc.

"Angelina and Doc, we haven't heard from you in a while, what have you been up to?"

"Well," said Angelina, "I've been going over and over the computer diagnostic print outs trying to determine exactly what happens when someone is frozen. So far, all I can determine is that there are electromagnetic currents along with some sort of a higher level electric current involved. There also seems to be multiple colored beams radiating through the affected person while they are in the frozen state, but I have no idea what they are or what they represent. Especially since the colors change as they radiate through the affected person."

"Are the colors different for different people?" the Captain asked.

"I didn't check that," Angelina said, "but I'll get on it right after lunch."

"Talk to me Doc," the Captain said.

"I've been monitoring the ship's life support systems and I don't like what I'm seeing on the recycling of the waste and water systems. Based upon what I heard about the rain last night, I'd like to suggest that we set up some water barrels or something to catch some fresh water for our use or to put into the system."

"Also, I would like to run some additional tests on everyone; especially, the people that have been frozen. I need to determine if there have been any adverse affects to their physical make up. In fact, I think it's important to test everyone at least once a week for now," Doc said in conclusion.

"Okay, we can make that happen. I'll be your first guinea pig," the Captain said. "The rest of you schedule some time to get checked out or I can set up a schedule."

"I have one already prepared," Doc said, "with you being the first one on my list."

"I guess that settles that," the Captain said.

'Sir, I would like to make a request, if I may," Dana said.

"Yes, what is it Dana?"

"Well, now that we have the MRI working, I'd like to put the cubs through it to see about my two stomach theory."

Immediately, both Natasha and Maggy yelled, "No Way!" in defiance to this suggestion.

"Besides," Natasha said, "they are meat eaters, not plant eaters"

"Also," Maggy added, "there is no way you can keep them still while they go through that machine."

"I thought we could sedate them," Dana said.

"You have no way of knowing what sedatives to use or how it will affect them," Natasha challenged.

"Hold it! Everyone calm down," the Captain said. "There are good points to both sides of this."

Maggy was fuming and using all her control not to jump across the table at Dana.

"I have an idea," Natasha said. "We were going to see this afternoon when the cubs get hungry if they would retrieve one of the animals for us. If they do, we could use that for the experiment."

"I'm willing to wait for that," Dana stated, "especially since they are probably plant eaters anyway."

"Good, I'm glad that's solved," the Captain stated.

Both Maggy and Natasha breathed a sigh of relief.

CHAPTER TWENTY

AFTER LUNCH, EVERYBODY AGAIN went back to what they were working on.

As he got up, the Captain said, "Doc, do you want to do those tests now?"

"I'd like to get started right away," Doc said.

When they got to the medical lab Doc asked, "Captain, did you happen to notice the reaction of the cubs when Maggy and Natasha got excited?"

"No I didn't," the Captain said. "What happened?"

"Well, from where I was sitting, I could see both of them. When the girls got excited, both cubs arched their backs and drew back their lips exposing some pretty scary teeth. Both of them looked ready to pounce at a moments notice."

"We will have to talk to the girls about that," the Captain stated. "That behavior is similar to how dogs react back home when they feel their master has been threatened."

"This is home," Doc reminded him as he started hooking up equipment to the Captain.

The test took longer than the Captain had anticipated and he was just about to tell Doc to stop, when Doc announced, "Just one more, Captain and I'll let you go."

"Sorry Doc, I was beginning to get impatient, it's been at least three hours."

"Yes, but you have to remember, you are the first one. Once I set up some standards based upon your evaluations, I'll know what to look for and it should go faster. Besides, the kids seem to be doing just fine without you there every minute."

"That's one of the things that bothers me, Doc. I can't help thinking that they are still just kids."

"I know; it concerns me too. I keep waiting for a major melt down in one of them. But then again, you have to admit that these are special kids."

"Yes," the Captain said, "but kids just the same."

After leaving the med bay, the Captain decided he would spend the rest of the afternoon with Bruce and his crew working on the drone. At least it was something he knew about. Plus, it would be fun to help put together.

The rest of the day went by without incident as the Captain and Bruce's crew worked on the drone assembly while everyone else kept busy doing what they were doing.

CHAPTER TWENTY ONE

It was almost supper time when Natasha noticed that she was picking up thoughts about hunger from Butkis. She asked Maggy, who said she was picking up the same thoughts from Zena.

"Let's let them eat first; then, when they come back, we can ask them to get one for us," Natasha suggested.

"Good idea," Maggy agreed.

With that, Zena jumped up and ran into the grass with Butkis right behind her. Both Maggy and Natasha were amazed at how fast the animals could move. She and Maggy were still discussing how fast they could run in the low gravity when the cubs came back out of the grass licking their chops.

"Well, Maggy, how do you want to do this?"

"Let's try to ask both of them to go get one and bring it back to us."

"Okay, let's try," Natasha said in agreement.

Both girls held the cubs up and tried to mentally express to them what they wanted. Setting the cubs down they watched to see what would happen. At first, both cubs just looked back up at them; then turning around, they walked off into the grass.

A few moments went by before Maggy and Natasha heard growling. There was a sudden squeal, and then Butkis came out of the grass, dragging an animal twice as big as him with Zena walking at his side. When he got to Natasha, he let go, sat down and wagged his stub looking up at her with a grin on his face.

"Good boy," Natasha said, petting him and scratching his ears.

Meanwhile, Zena walked over to Maggy, half heartedly accepted her thanks and started preening herself.

"The thought I just got from Zena was, why can't you do this for yourself?" Maggy said.

"She definitely has an attitude," Natasha noted.

"Yeah, but that's what I like about her. It's like she knows exactly who she is and what she wants, when she wants it. She seems to be very confident about who she is—almost as if she is some sort of royalty within her breed." Maggie said as they both looked over the animal the cubs had brought back to them.

"Look," Maggy said pointing, "one of them bit it thought the throat to kill it. It also looks like they hamstrung it first."

"It looks a lot like a big ground hog or gopher," Natasha said.

"Whatever," Maggy said, "let's take it in to Dana and she can have all sorts of fun dissecting and testing it."

"Good idea," Natasha agreed. "I'm hungry anyway."

As they were walking back to the ramp, the Captain and Bruce's group joined them. They all were excited and wanted to look at the animal. When they went aboard, Maggy took the cubs and Natasha took the animal into Dana.

"Here you go Dana," Natasha said, "one plant eating animal ready for testing."

"Look, Natasha; don't be so upset with me. I'm just trying to figure out things here too."

"I know," Natasha said. "I'm sorry, but the thought of Butkis being experimented on was something I couldn't handle."

"Well, we don't have to worry about that now do we?" Dana said.

"This will keep until after dinner. Let's get washed up and go get something to eat."

When they got to the bay, they noticed everyone else was already there. Just then, Sophia and Naomi entered with the food. Sophia looked around and noticed that they were all there too and said, "My, my, I always heard it was a good sign when everyone was waiting for supper."

"What's for dinner tonight?" Rashad asked.

"Well today, me and Naomi opened that Mr. Chan's crate. With the stuff he had in there, along with that rice like plant, we have made you some garlic chicken and rice—only there's no chicken. So dig in. If you like it, we'll see if we can't send someone out to get more of the rice tomorrow."

"Captain," Rashad said, "Tani and I have gone through all the videos today and we thought we'd put on a show here at dinner tonight, if it's okay with you?"

"Fine," the Captain said.

Tani and Rashad got up and turned all the computer screens in the bay toward the table.

"We'll start with the world famous shot of the monster going after Drago."

With that, the screen showed Drago bending toward the water. Here, Tani put it into slow motion so everyone would get the full effect as she began her narrative of events.

"Now, if you watch closely, you'll see what Natasha said appears to be true. As the monster starts to come out of the water, Drago suddenly jumps." Tani clicked her computer screen again and said, "Here, we have the only two still shots of the monster before Rashad blew it up."

Everyone stopped eating for a moment and looked at the screens.

"According to the computer, it's approximately twelve feet long—including the tail. It's about three feet wide and when standing up is two feet high. While it looks similar to an American alligator or crocodile, there are differences. Note it has two rows of teeth. Also, the tail is shaped more vertical like a fin."

"That's too bad," Sophia said; "I could eat some good old gator tail."

"What? You eat gator tail?" exclaimed Naomi.

"Heavens yes girl, its good when cooked right," Sophia replied. "The boys back home would go into the swamp to catch small ones just to cut off their tail and bring it home for supper."

Changing back to the subject, Tani continued on. "Also, notice that this creature has four feet, but they are webbed without claws, more for swimming than walking on ground. My guess is it's not that comfortable leaving the water and walking on land. But I don't know for sure. Finally, from these shots, you can see it appears to be a blood and bone animal." Tani paused for a few seconds as the video clip showed the creature being blown to bits and pieces by Rashad. Tani continued as once again, everyone cringed as they watched.

"Next, we have some more interesting shots. These were recorded when Drago landed in the tree. Because he was only there about forty-five seconds, we have made these into a still slide show. The first slide just shows the tree Drago lands in."

Taking a pointer, Tani went up to the main screen and said, "If you look closely here, you'll see what looks like berries or some sort of fruit or nuts in the tree. Going to the next slide she said, "here we have a good picture of the furry animal in the tree. If you look closely, you can also see the back of another one retreating."

Everyone was looking at the animal.

"It doesn't look like a monkey," Dana commented. "Nor does it look like a squirrel."

"It kind of looks like an animal I saw in one of the National Geographic books at the orphanage," Natasha said. "I think they called something like a Timor."

"You'll note it definitely has a prehensile tail," Tani said continuing. "Also look at the eyes—they seem very large, which might mean it is a nocturnal animal."

"Or it might mean its eyes bugged out, when it saw Drago," Rashad wise cracked with a grin.

Everyone giggled.

"Next, I want to show the same shots in infra red and then some computer enhanced imagery."

"The first one is infrared," Tani took her pointer and pointed to the center of the animal's stomach. "The animal seems to have a pouch, like a kangaroo. If that is true, it makes it a mammal that raises its young in the pouch. Oh wait; there is one more thing I wanted to show you back in the normal shot."

Switching the computer back, she again pointed out. "Notice those fruits or berries or nut like things hanging off the branches in the back ground?" Then, going back to the x-ray type slide, she said, "I don't know what this program is called, but it shows the make up of the plants and animals with different colors."

"We're not interested in the animal here. We already know it is a flesh and blood mammal, but if you look right here"….she said using her pointer again. "You can see a difference in the colors in the make up of the tree. I believe this area to be a nest in the tree made by the animals."

"Earlier today, I reviewed the videos of the tree animals several times. There wasn't much to work with, but I wanted to check out their teeth, to see if they could chew through the plastic barrier…" Here, Tani switched back to the still shot of the animal. "It not only has some formidable fangs—but check out its claws. They appear to be quite capable of digging and slashing into the tree," she said as she looked at everyone around the table.

Tani concluded with, "I believe that's it for this particular video.

However, we can take a quick look at the infrared videos from Maggy's camera the other day. These video slides positively show that there are warm, living animals running through the grass around you, as you were walking."

"We brought one in for Dana to look at," Maggy interrupted.

"Wow, how did you catch one?" Tani asked. "They appear to move really fast on the videos."

"We didn't," Maggy said. "We sent Zena and Butkis after them and they brought us one back."

"I'll begin testing it in the morning," Dana said.

"Try not to cut it up too bad," Sophia said. "I might be able to make a meal out of it."

Finally, Tani said, "We have also reviewed the videos from Rashad's head cam when they went out all the way, to what we're calling the rice paddies. Besides verifying that the rice paddies are large, we were also able to pick up more infrared readings on small animals in the area. However, this is the prize Gerard mentioned earlier when he said that he thought he saw something sitting in a tree that looked like a bird. We were able to zero in on the object. Even though the zoom didn't quite get us close enough, the computer was able to take the pixels and make a picture of what the animal looked like up close."

Tani paused for a moment then asked, "Is everybody ready? You're going to be surprised when I pull this up."

Everyone stopped eating and turned their attention to the screen as Tani pulled up the next picture. They were amazed to see a giant hawk or eagle like bird sitting on a branch.

"Based upon the computer read outs," Tani continued, "this bird is approximately six feet tall and has a wing span of twelve feet. You can also see that it has formidable claws. Using the standards of a hawk or eagle from back on earth, it should have eye sight capabilities of up to fifteen miles. This is a big bird. It could pick up anyone of us and take us back to the nest to feed its babies."

"Wow!" said Bruce. "That's as big as our drone!"

Meanwhile, Loren had got up and walked up to the screen, starring at the image. Finally, she turned around and walking back said, "This bird will be mine."

The others looked at her like she was crazy.

"I don't think you will be going on any bird hunting trips in the near future," the Captain told her as she took her seat.

"Tani, Rashad, thank you," the Captain said. "Great job. Now we at least know what we need to look out for and we also learned some more about our environment."

The Captain then took a sip of his water and added, "I think it's time for me to lay out the plan for tomorrow's activities."

"First, Bruce, Matzo, Choi and I will finish up with the drone assembly and then do a test run in the morning. Since I'm sure it will take a while to get use to the controls, I'd like to spend the rest of the morning running test flights. If all goes well, we should be able to send it out on its first mission tomorrow afternoon."

All the boys grinned in anticipation, particularly Bruce who chimed in with a firm, "You can count on us, sir."

The Captain then continued. "If one of you will put out the second set of solar batteries so they can be charging, we will be able to replace the ones from our initial test flight."

"I already set out the solar batteries today," Choi said. "I had the same thought since I knew we wouldn't have the second drone put together."

"Good work," the Captain told Choi then looked over to where Rashad was sitting. "Rashad, Matzo found that the drone is equipped with mounting brackets for armaments, but there were none in the crate. Could you go through the equipment manifests and the crates first thing in the morning to see what you can find?"

"Yes sir," Rashad responded.

"Sophia, you and Naomi, along with Doc, need to see if you can locate some containers suitable for collecting water. If Emir's assumption is correct, the rains will come again tonight on the garden and we need to collect some fresh water."

"Dana, you'll be working on the animals tomorrow, so I'd like to borrow Gerard."

"Okay sir," Dana said winking at Gerard. "I suppose I can make do without him for a little while.

"What I want to do tomorrow is send out two groups instead of one. One group will go with Rashad. This group will be Drago, Natasha, Gerard, and Loren. The second group will be under Maggy's command and will consist of Molly, Tani, Naomi and Choi." The Captain then continued with, "I want the different groups to practice the swing retrieve, and get familiar with the equipment, as each group will have different responsibilities. Bruce, you and Matzo will be practicing with the drone."

"Okay everybody; let's enjoy the rest of our dinner. Get a good night's sleep, and I'll see you in the morning."

After dinner, Sophia, Naomi, and Doc went into the bay and started gathering up containers to collect water in. Rashad and Gerard helped them carry the containers outside and put them around the garden.

Molly, Tani and Choi were still sitting at the table excitedly discussing the trip outside tomorrow. As the Captain got up to head to his quarters, Angelina came up to him.

"Excuse me Captain," she said. "I have a favor to ask."

"What's that?" the Captain asked.

"I want to go on one of those teams tomorrow. I haven't had much of a chance to get outside or get used to the planet."

"Good idea," the Captain said. "You can go with Maggy's team."

"Thank you Sir," she said, and then hurried back so she could tell Molly and Tani.

The Captain's last thoughts as he was laying in his bunk that night, were that tomorrow should be an exciting day.

CHAPTER TWENTY TWO

THE NEXT MORNING, OVER their meal of mush, the Captain laid out his plan.

"As I indicated last night, I plan on working with Bruce and his group this morning so that we can get the drone flying. While we are conducting our test flights, I expect the other two groups to go out and practice their swing retrieve maneuvers and bring the new team members up to speed."

"Now for the team assignments, Maggy, your team will be responsible for gathering and bringing back the plants we have already determined to be edible."

"Yes sir," Maggy responded as she squared her shoulders and sat up a bit straighter.

"Rashad and Drago's group—you guys are to explore further out around the wet lands. However, the first thing I want Rashad to do is look for that drone armament we talked about yesterday."

"Any questions?" the Captain asked.

"No sir," Rashad answered for his group.

"Good."

"By the way," Doc said, "I took an early morning walk outside, and Emir was correct. The rain came again last night. Most of the containers are full. I'll need some help bringing them in this morning, if I could have a couple of volunteers."

Two or three readily volunteered.

"Good," the Captain said. "Enjoy your breakfast, and then we'll get to work."

When they had finished, the various teams headed out for their assignments.

"I can't wait to try the Sling Around," Molly told Maggy as they collected the gear.

"The what?" Maggy asked.

"The Sling Around—you know, where you tie yourself to someone else and sling each other around."

Maggy chuckled. "Well, that's a better name than swing retrieve."

As the Captain, Bruce, and Matzo got up to head for the drone, the Captain looked over to Choi and said, "I hope you don't mind being reassigned to one of the other groups today, Choi."

"No sir, I'm excited. I knew it didn't take three of us to run the drone. I'm sure with Bruce running the controls and Matzo watching the computer it will be fine. Then he quickly added, "Ahh, especially with you there to help Captain."

Doc, Rashad, and Gerard had helped Sophia and Naomi bring in the water containers and Doc had gone back to the Med Bay to review the Captain's test results from yesterday.

Rashad was busy going through the equipment crates to see if he could locate the armament parts for the drone.

Meanwhile, Gerard went to see his sister. "Hey Dana," he said.

"Hey, brother mine."

"Listen, you don't have a problem with me going out with the group, do you?" Gerard asked.

"The sister part of me does. I don't like you being away from me, especially when I can't see you and see what's going on. On the other hand, as a scientist, I'm glad one of us is going out."

"Well, you can watch us on the computer. Plus, you know that we can communicate in our special way."

"I know," Dana said, "but you know I'll still worry."

"That's what big sisters are supposed to do," Gerard replied grinning because they both knew that Dana was only three minutes older than him. "I've got to outside now and learn the equipment," he said as he turned to leave.

"Go ahead; I've got to get to work on this animal."

Already outside, Maggy had her group lined up in front of her as she said, "Alright everybody, listen up. I want Molly and Tani to be one team, Choi and Naomi will be the other team, and Angelina, you'll be with me." Everyone quickly shifted around to stand next to their partners as Maggy had instructed.

"We're going to practice the Sling-Around as Molly calls it. But first,

I want you all to practice gliding and jumping again. Tie up with your partner and we'll practice that for a while. Then we'll take turns with the Sling-Around."

Drago had Gerard practicing with Loren since she had already been out and was used to the equipment. Then he sat down next to Natasha so they could talk about what they were going to do. Suddenly they all stopped as they heard a loud noise and realized it was the drone.

Bruce and his group had started up the drone engine as the Captain called off items on the preflight check list. Everyone watched as the drone started to move across the ground. The next thing they knew, it was in the air. As the drone took off, they all came running over to watch. Bruce was there with the controls in his hand acting just like he was playing a video game. Meanwhile, both the Captain and Matzo were glued to the computer screen. They all watched as Bruce flew it through the air taking it though different manures.

"All right Bruce, hold it steady," the Captain instructed. "We want to try out the different cameras, and check out the different readings."

Everyone continued to watch for a little while then lost interest and went back to what they were doing.

Sophia was coming out of the garden, humming to herself. As she went by the Captain, she said, "We got blossoms on the plants, Captain. It looks like we will have some stuff shaping up in a couple of weeks."

"Great Sophia," the Captain responded keeping his eyes on the computer screen.

Meanwhile, Molly and Tani were having the best time, slinging each other about. Molly had actually tired to perform a flip while in the air. Gerard and Loren were more serious, but were making progress.

Butkis had left Natasha's side and was running excitedly back and forth between the ones practicing with the Sling-Around, while Zena sat placidly watching Maggy and Angelina.

"Relax," Maggy told Angelina. "You're too stiff. You have to have flex in your knees when you land and you're not really jumping hard enough."

"Easy for you to say," Angelina said. "You're a lot younger. I'm worried about breaking bones."

After all of them had been practicing for a while, Drago called everyone from both groups together and said, "We need to sit down and discuss exactly how we're going to organize this trip. I want us all on the same page, so if something does come up, we are prepared to handle it."

"Always the thinker," Maggy said, pulling Angelina back to the ground.

As they gathered around Drago and sat down, Rashad came out of the ship with some equipment and went over to the Captain.

"Sir," he said, "I think I have found a couple of guns for the drone. One is a sort of stun weapon and the other is a laser. I also found one that looks like the sonic gun I carried, but I didn't think that it would be advisable to try it with the recoil I experienced, so I left it."

"Good," the Captain said.

"Bruce, bring the drone back in. Land it where the grass was burned out on our landing. That will make it easier for both landing and take off."

"Aye, Aye Sir," Bruce said, grinning.

Turning the drone and bringing back to the ship went well, but the landing was a little bumpy. Twice the drone jumped up into the air and Bruce had to bring it around again. Finally, it was on the ground safely stopped.

"I guess I'll have to work on the landing. It's a little tougher than I thought," Bruce admitted.

"Okay, let's check it out," the Captain said. "Rashad, you get with Matzo and see if you can figure out how to attach the weapons. I want to check how much battery power we used up."

Meanwhile, as they were doing that, Drago and his group continued discussing their plan for that afternoon.

"I want to get as many plants as we can," Loren said.

"We also need to pick a bunch of that rice plant to bring back," Drago added as he remembered Sophie's request. "Maggy, your group will be the gathers. I also think everyone should carry a back pack. Loren, our group will go farther out and explore past the wet lands if we can. However, we will need to stay in communication with Maggy's group at all times—just in case any of us run into trouble."

"I have printed pictures from the computer showing different type plants from Earth. I thought having some examples might make it easier to identify any similar plants we might find here." Loren said as she started passing out the pictures to both groups.

After finalizing their plans, Drago said, "I'll go over the plans with Rashad when he gets free. Oh, by the way, Maggy you and Natasha need to figure out what to do with the cubs. We can't take them with us."

Both Maggy and Natasha looked at each other but before either of them could come up with an answer, they heard the Captain's voice announcing that it was time for everyone to stop for lunch.

Chapter Twenty Three

Going into the bay, everyone started sitting down while discussing what they were going to do that afternoon. Drago sat next to Rashad so that they could go over what he had discussed with the teams. The Captain was going over the flight conditions and controls for the drone with Bruce and Matzo while the girls discussed their sling around maneuvers.

While they were talking, Doc came in and said, "Captain, I'd like to see you after lunch to discuss the tests I took yesterday."

"It will have to wait till after lunch. The two teams are going out; plus, we are launching the drone on its first, real flight. I'll get with you tonight." Then the Captain added, "However, I would like for you to be on the computer watching both teams today if you would?"

"Sure," Doc replied as he sat down.

"Are both teams ready?" the Captain asked.

"Yes sir," both Maggy and Drago replied.

"Although, there is one thing I think I need to add to our equipment," Drago said. "We need some type of canteen or bottles to carry water in. I think we need to start thinking in terms of survival; in case we can't make it back to the ship."

"Good thought," the Captain agreed.

After lunch, the teams went outside. Drago had gone over the plans with Rashad—both were a little uncomfortable with the teams breaking up but knew that it was necessary.

Rashad and Matzo had quickly installed the weapons on the drone. Bruce and the Captain had decided to test them before flying the drone on its mission. So the teams would be heading out before the drone.

Natasha and Maggy were still trying to figure out what to do with the cubs. When Sophia passed by on her way to check out her garden again, she overheard their conversation and volunteered with, "I'll take care of them."

"I'm not sure they will stay with you," Maggy said. "They're pretty attached to me and Natasha."

"Wait here a minute," Sophia said turning to go back into the ship. She came back out a couple of minutes later holding something in the palm of her hand. "Bring them to me." Maggy and Natasha brought the cubs over.

"Hi babies," Sophia said looking down at the cubs. "You babies want to stay with me?" With that, she reached her hands out giving them both a small piece of what she had been holding in the palm of her hand. Both cubs immediately wolfed it down and licked their chops while jumping around Sophia looking for more. "Alright babies," she said, "you come with Aunt Sophia and she'll take care of you." She turned and started back up the ramp with both cubs jumping around her feet and following her back into the ship.

"That was really sickening," Maggy said. "I thought Zena was more dignified then that."

"It kind of hurts me too," Natasha agreed.

Initially, both teams stayed together until they got to the wet lands. When they got there, Maggy and her group started to collect the rice and other specimens, while Drago's group continued around the wet lands. Before splitting up, they agreed that Maggy's group would wait until Drago's group returned and that they would all head back to the ship together.

As Drago's group headed toward the wet lands, Bruce and the Captain's team had finished with their testing and were in the process of starting the take-off procedures.

"We have about four hours of flying time," the Captain said. "Let's keep some in reserve and fly out for about an hour then turn and come back. I want to head in the direction that Emir feels we should go. Going out, I think we she should fly at top speed as some of the ground has already been covered. Once we get past the wet lands, we will slow down and turn all the cameras on. When returning we will fly over the open plains and try out the guns."

"Okay," responded Bruce and Matzo as they programmed the flight pattern in the computer and sent the drone into the air.

When it flew over the heads of the two teams, it was about a 1000 feet in the air and at full speed.

"Okay, reduce the altitude and slow it down," the Captain said; watching the monitor. "Start all the cameras. Maintain altitude at about one hundred feet with a speed of about forty-five miles an hour. The high speed cameras should be able to pick up everything at that speed."

On the ground, Drago's group had come to another semi-plain type area. This seemed about a half mile wide before going into another area of trees and brush. As they were just entering the tree area, there was a sudden movement in the grass and a bird like animal started to run for the trees. Before he knew what he was doing, Drago had pulled his stun gun out and fired at the fleeing animal. Hitting it straight on, the bird dropped in its tracks.

"Go Wild Bill Hitchcock!" yelled Rashad excitedly. "Did you see that? The fastest gun on the planet!"

Drago was embarrassed and explained that it had happened so fast that he hadn't thought about it—he had just drawn his stun gun and fired.

Going over to the bird, Loren said, "We better tie its feet and wings down before it wakes up or it will take off on us. And, I'm sure Dana would want us to bring it back alive."

"Your right," Gerard said. "I just told her and she said exactly that."

"How did you tell her?" Rashad asked.

"We always talk to each other like that," Gerard said.

Getting some string and rope out of their backpacks that they had found on the ship, they tied the bird up including its beak.

"I don't know how long it will be out," Drago said. "See if you can find a branch or something we can hang it from to carry back." "That way, if it wakes up we can just stun it again."

Loren said, "It looks like a cross between a prairie chicken and a turkey." Lifting it up, she said, "It feels like it weighs about twelve pounds or so."

"I'm getting hungry already," Rashad said. "Let's see if we can find some more."

"You can look around," Loren said, "but I see bushes with berries on them over there that I believe it was eating at. I want to get some samples of those."

While Drago and Rashad looked for more birds, Gerard sat guard over the one they had caught. Loren unhooked her cable and moved about twenty feet away to gather the plant and berry samples she had seen. When she got there and began picking some of the berries, she also noticed that under one of the trees close by, there appeared to be nuts lying on the ground under them. After picking the berries, she moved over underneath the trees and gathered some of the nuts.

Hearing some whooping and yelling from Rashad, she started back to where Gerard waited for them. Suddenly, she had the feeling she was being watched. She looked around but did not see anything. Continuing to look over her shoulder, she quickened her pace. Just as she got back to where Gerard had stationed himself to watch over the captured bird, Rashad and Drago came out of the bush grinning from ear to ear. They each had another bird with them.

"Wait till Sophia see these," Rashad said. "I can feel a big meal coming up."

"With three of these, I think we better head back," Drago said. "It's going to be hard enough getting them back before they wake up. To go further ahead would only cause us more difficulty."

Natasha, who had stayed behind with Gerard said. "I get the feeling something is watching Loren."

"I got the same feeling," Loren said, "but I couldn't see any thing."

"I get the feeling whatever it is; it is really interested in you Loren," Natasha said.

Looking around but unable to locate whatever was watching Loren, Natasha shrugged her shoulders as they headed back to meet up with Maggy's group.

Chapter Twenty Four

About the time they saw their team mates walking back, the first bird came out of its stunned state and started to flop around. Rashad was in the process of pulling his stun gun out of its holster when Drago yelled.

"Stop! Move away from the bird Gerard. We don't want to stun Gerard along with the bird."

The commotion alerted the others, who had been sitting around talking, since their back packs were full. They immediately got up and went to meet the others. When they saw the birds, they got excited.

"Wow, Sophia is really going to freak out with the birds and what we got today." Maggy said.

"What do you mean?" Drago asked.

"Well, we had filled up our packs and were sitting around, staying back from the lake but looking at it. We kept seeing what looked like fish jumping," and then Molly mentioned, "It's to bad we don't have fishing poles. We might catch some fish."

"We looked around but we couldn't find anything to use. Besides, we were afraid to get too close to the water because of the monster," Maggy explained. "Anyway, while we were sitting around talking about it, Tani had taken some of the reeds and weaved them into a basket."

Then Angelina said to us, "If we could make some fish traps or baskets and somehow get them into the water, maybe we could catch some of the fish."

"So we decided to try it. "We attached the baskets to one of the cables and were getting close to the water when I thought I saw movement by the shore. Afraid it might be another one of the water monsters; I pulled out my stun gun and fired at it. What happened next freaked us out. It wasn't a monster; it was some of the fish feeding in the shallow water close to the shore. When I fired my stun gun, it knocked them out and they came to the surface. So we took the baskets and the cable and threw it out. Catching some in the basket we brought them to shore, so we now have six fish in our packs."

"Well this food trip turned out better then we planned," Drago said. "Sophia is going to go crazy with all this food."

"Not until Dana checks it out," Gerard warned them.

"Right," Drago said. "Let's head back"

The trip back was uneventful except when the birds woke up and had to be stunned again.

While they were on the way back, Matzo and the Captain had been watching the flight of the drone. After it had flown past the wet lands, they had watched on the screen to see another line of trees and a forest. Once it had passed over the forest, there were more plains. Then they had come upon what looked like the beginning of a jungle.

"Notice how quick the land changes," the Captain pointed out to Matzo.

"Yes sir, it seems as if it was almost laid out this way. There shouldn't be a jungle that quickly after the forest."

As they talked, a large river came into view. "That's a big river," the Captain said.

"According to the computer it's approximately two miles across," Matzo said. "And look Captain; on the other side, there appears to be another rain forest."

After flying for another half hour or so the drone was still flying over the rain forest. The Captain checked the time.

"How much time do we still have in the batteries?" he asked Matzo.

"We could go another half hour and still have enough to get it back to the ship," Matzo replied.

"Let's not take a chance," the Captain said. "Bruce, adjust the video camera resolution to record as far as they can in the distance for fifteen minutes then turn the drone around and head it back to the ship."

"Aye, aye," Bruce said making the adjustments.

After fifteen minutes, Bruce turned the drone around and was heading back to the ship as he had been instructed. The drone was still flying at a slow speed at about fifty feet. It had just got close to where Drago and Maggy's group had joined up, when suddenly the drone was rocked, and Bruce yelled out in surprise.

"What the Hell was that?"

Matzo, looking at the monitor exclaimed with alarm and fear in his voice, "Something large just attacked the drone. It looked like a bird but was so big in the camera it's hard to tell."

"Bruce, take it up to a higher altitude, kick it up to maximum speed, and get it out of there now!" the Captain shouted.

Matzo yelled, "It's coming back again! It's a really large bird and it can fly!"

Bruce turned the drone straight up and put the power to it. When it hit a thousand feet, he leveled it off and under full power headed back to the ship.

"The bird seems to be dropping back," Matzo said. "I can see it turning around and heading back to the tree line."

"Thank God," the Captain said with relief. "Cancel the gun test and come straight back."

Ten minutes later, Bruce was bringing the drone in for a landing about the same time Maggy and Drago's groups were approaching the ship. The minute the drone landed, the Captain and Matzo ran over to it to see if there was any damage.

Looking it over, Bruce said, "I don't see any damage Captain."

"Neither do I," the Captain agreed.

"I found something," Matzo said; "from the rear of the drone."

Both the Captain and Bruce went to the back expecting to see some damage; however, when they got there Matzo was removing something from the tail section. Turning around, he held up a large feather. "Well," he said, "I guess we have something else for Dana to analyze."

As they were looking at the feather, they heard shouts from the returning groups. Turning around and heading for them, the Captain could see what looked like large birds hanging from cables over their backs. As they got closer, they took them from their backs and laid them on the ground. The Captain could see that they were in fact birds of a variety he was not familiar with.

"It looks like you had a successful outing," he said. "Too bad you had to kill them."

"They're not dead." Drago said. "Just stunned so we are going to have to figure out how to keep them penned up when they wake up."

"Hey," Bruce said, "we never used the crates to store the drone in since it was too big. We just put some of the tarps over it that was used to tie down the crates. Then we just lashed it down with cables to the ground."

"All right," Drago said, "we can make some pens for them."

"Okay, let's see the birds," Dana said, striding down the ramp.

"How *does* she do that," asked Maggy?"

"I told her," Gerard said.

Walking over to them, Dana looked over the birds, then asked, "Where are the fish? I want to see them too."

"What fish?" the Captain asked.

"That's another story," Maggy responded grinning.

Choi and Molly walked over to the crates and started discussing how they would go about building a proper pen.

Dana said, "It looks like you have two females and one male. If one of you can re-stun them, I can run an MRI on them. That way, I'll only need to dissect one of the females which would leave us with a possible breeding pair."

"What about the fish?" Tani asked "Can you check one of those out first, so maybe we can have some for dinner tonight?"

"All right," Dana said agreeing. "I can do that."

"That sounds like a good idea, I wouldn't mind having fresh fish for dinner," the Captain said. "But if that is going to happen, I suggest we all get back to work."

"Matzo, you, and Bruce remove the video cards from the cameras and get them into the computer. Also, make sure you change out the batteries and put the used ones out to charge."

"Aye, aye," Bruce said.

"It looks like we'll have something to watch, with dinner tonight. The rest of you just chill or help Molly and Choi build the bird pen. I'm going in to see Doc."

Maggy turned to Natasha and said, "Let's go see what the cubs are up to." Nodding to her, Natasha followed her into the ship and back to the kitchen. When they got there, they saw that both cubs were sleeping on a bed Sophia had made for them out of one of the tarps. They didn't even wake up when Maggy and Natasha came in.

"Well, they seemed to have been able to survive without us," Maggy commented looking down at the sleeping pups.

"Them babies did just fine," Sophia said.

"We have some news for you," Maggy told her. "How would you like to have some fresh fish or maybe a turkey-bird to make for dinner?"

"What you talking about girl?" Sophia asked.

"We brought back some fish and captured some birds that look like a cross between a turkey and a prairie chicken."

"Where are they at?" Sophia asked with excitement in her voice. "I'll start fixing them up right now."

"Dana has them," Natasha said.

"Oh no!" Sophia exclaimed. "Dana gave me what was left of that animal the cubs caught. After testing it, she said it was okay, but there was barely enough scraps left over to feed the cubs. However, I tasted some and it and it tasted kind of like pork."

"You cooked some and gave it to the cubs?" Maggy asked in dismay.

"No, I didn't give them any of the cooked part. It was only about two bites full I fried up."

"No wonder they're sleeping," Natasha said, "you probably fed them all day. You're only spoiling them."

"You can't spoil babies," Sophia retorted.

"Well, the good news is that Dana said she would check out the fish first. If they pass her inspection, she will bring them to you to fix for supper."

"What about the birds?" Sophia asked.

"Oh, they're out there building a pen, for them right now."

"They're alive?"

"Yeah, we just stunned them," Maggy answered grinning.

"Let's go see them," Sophia said.

"You go," Maggy said. "I'm going to get the cubs up and make them get some exercise. I get the feeling if we leave them with you any longer, they'll become too fat to hunt for us."

"Humph!" Sophia said as she headed out to see the birds.

Grabbing up the cubs, Maggy and Natasha followed her.

Chapter Twenty Five

"What a day," the Captain was saying to Doc, as he entered the medical lab. "There never seems to be a dull moment around here."

"That sounds interesting, tell me what happened," Doc said as he picked up the Captain's medical folder. "I've been locked up in here all day going over your results."

"Well, other then catching some fish, capturing a couple of turkey like birds and the drone being attacked by a giant hawk, nothing much really happened today," the Captain informed him with a straight face and in a deadpan tone of voice.

"The results can wait. I want to hear everything."

For the next hour, the Captain went over everything that had happened that day concluding with what everyone was trying to get accomplished before dinner. As he finished up with the story of day's events, he asked, "so what about the tests?"

"There's really nothing new, but I would like to run an MRI. I think that would help me better evaluate what caused that brain activity we talked about."

"Okay," the Captain said, "but we will have to check with Dana. Right now, she's running all sorts of fish and birds though it."

"Hopefully, she cleans it each time she uses it," Doc replied. "Let's go see the birds, I could use a breath of fresh air."

Getting up and heading out of the med bay area, Doc remarked to the Captain. "Oh by the way, I put some of the water into our recycling system. The rest, I put in the cooler for drinking water. I had some, it's quite tasty."

When they got outside, they saw that the team had completed the pens and were trying to figure out what to put over the top to keep the birds from flying out.

"There are still some tarps in the storage bay," Bruce was saying, as they walked up. "I'll go get them."

Sophia was leaning over petting the birds crooning, "Oh my pretty turkey-birds, you're going to make some fine eating."

At that moment, one of the birds came awake and started flopping around. Caught unaware, Sophia fell back on her butt, much to the amusement of the others.

"You'll be the first one I cut the head off of," Sophia told the bird, getting up and brushing herself off.

Drago stunned the bird again, just as Bruce was returning with the tarps. After putting the tarps in place, finishing the door, and making sure there seemed to be enough air holes in the pen, they took the restraints off the birds and put them inside their new home. Satisfied that the birds were safely contained, Sophia went back inside to see Dana about the fish.

As the Captain looked around, he saw everyone sitting around in different little groups talking to one another. Rashad was telling Maggy something about Drago being Quick Draw McGraw with Natasha and Maggy a few feet away playing with the cubs. The rest were just sitting around talking about the day.

When Sophia got to Dana's lab, Dana said, "I knew you would be here soon. As far as I can tell, the fish are fine. They do have a lot of bones though," Dana warned.

"How many are there?" Sophia asked.

"There were six," Dana said. "But I pretty much destroyed one of them. I don't know if you can feed everyone on just the five remaining."

"Let me take them back to the kitchen and see what I can figure out," Sophia said as she grabbed up the remaining fish and headed back to her kitchen.

Meanwhile, Matzo along with Emir had uploaded the video onto the computer screen so that they could review it.

"I think we should wait till dinner and everyone is here before we go over the videos," Matzo said.

"Alright," Emir said. "But I feel so left out of everything, not being able to go outside and just looking at a computer all day."

"Maybe we can get the Captain to let you try again. At least, let you see the birds we brought back."

"What birds?" Emir asked.

Feeling sorry for him, Matzo sat down and said, "Let me tell you what happened today."

Finally, everyone drifted back into the bay for dinner. When they sat down, the Captain asked Matzo if the videos were loaded into the computer.

"Yes sir," he said. "Emir helped me."

"What were you able to get from them?" the Captain asked.

"Well," Matzo replied, "we decided to wait for dinner and let everyone see them at the same time. That way, we can review them and pick what we want to look closer at since it will take quite a while tomorrow to go over everything."

"Fine," the Captain said. "As soon as dinner is served, we'll start the show."

Suddenly, they all smelled something tantalizing as Sophia and Naomi entered the bay carrying food.

Sophia announced with aplomb. "Tonight, we're having my version of a cat fish stew. Not that I think they were catfish, mind you, but there wasn't enough to fry up for everyone. So I made a stew with a white sauce. You might want to spice it up a bit by putting some of Mr. Chen's hot sauce in it."

Naomi spoke up at that point saying that she and Sophia had decided earlier in the day to use some more of the wheat to make fresh bread. As she uncovered the tray allowing the steam to rise from the warm bread, Sophia said, "Enjoy, I hope you like it."

There was complete silence around the table. The videos were totally forgotten about as everyone concentrated on eating. The only words you heard were. "This is great." "Please pass the hot sauce and can I have some more please."

Only after everyone had eaten and soaked up every scrap with their bread and were sitting around in complete contentment, did Bruce ask, "What about the videos?"

"Right," the Captain said. "Emir, you want to start the show?"

"Okay," Emir said. "We can start with the drone videos first, then we can look at the head cam videos."

With that, he hit some keys on the computer and the video began. The cameras hadn't been programmed to start recording until the drone reached the tree line; so as everyone sat there watching, the drone flew in just above the tree tops. It was now showing the trees. It then went past them, showing the jungle, followed by the rain forest. The drone flew over the rain forest then turned around and headed back. Everyone had started losing interest when suddenly, a large object completely blocked out the camera. The next few seconds showed the drone shooting up into the sky. Then just as suddenly, the rear camera video shots showed the bird.

"Stop it there," the Captain directed. Emir immediately paused the video.

"Look at the size of that thing!" Bruce exclaimed. "It actually kept up with the drone for awhile."

Everyone was looking on in amazement, when Loren said, "It was protecting its territory. It thought the drone was another bird flying into its territory."

The Captain looked over at her and asked, "Why didn't it attack when we first flew over on the way out then?"

"Were you flying at the same altitude?" Loren asked with a questioning look on her face.

"No," Bruce responded. "We were at about a thousand feet going out. Coming back, we varied the flying altitudes between fifty and a hundred feet."

"Then you were high enough going out that it didn't feel threatened," Loren said.

"You're probably right," the Captain agreed. "We will need to keep that in mind the next time we send the drone out."

"Emir," the Captain said, changing the subject. "Can you back it up to where we had the camera focusing long distance and see if you can bring any of those shots into focus?"

"If you'll give me a moment Captain, I'll have to fast forward the video to that spot; then have the computer refigure and develop the pixels for us."

"Okay, please do that," the Captain requested.

"Well," Rashad said, "I don't know about anyone else, but I've got food coma and it was a long day. I'm going to bed."

Me too, came a chorus from around the table.

"Can I get someone to help put out the containers again before you all head to bed?" Doc asked.

"I will," Drago volunteered. "I want to see what the video looks like when Emir gets it done."

"Count me in too," Natasha said.

While everyone else headed to bed, Doc, Drago and Natasha got up and went about gathering up the containers then headed out to the garden.

Matzo stayed with Emir and the Captain to see the videos. When Drago and Natasha had finished helping Doc set out the containers, they went back in and sat down to see the video.

Emir was still working on his computer so there was nothing on the screen yet. Doc came in and joined them as they were talking about the day.

"Finally," Emir said. "Ready Captain."

"Good," the Captain said in anticipation. "Let it roll."

Emir hit a few keys on his computer then said, "I have taken the video up to the time the cameras started recording long range, then the computer will start zooming in and readjusting the pixels to give us the clearest picture."

As they watched intently, the screen showed the long range blur again, then the computer began to clear up the picture. First, they could see the end of the rain forest. Then what looked to be another plain. As the computer made the final adjustments, they were looking at mountains. And in the mountains, they could see caves.

"Is that the same mountains and caves you see in your vision Emir?" the Captain asked.

"Close, but not the same," Emir responded.

"If you look closely, you can see that there's a plateau in front of the cave," Drago mentioned.

"There is no plateau in my vision, just a path leading to the cave" Emir explained. "However, this video proves that there are caves in the mountains," then added, "and I feel it's the right direction."

"Judging by the time it took the drone to fly there, it would take us months to get there on foot," Drago said.

"According to my studies, the last place we want to be when the storms come is sitting here out in the open on these plains," responded Emir.

"We need to start making plans for that," the Captain replied. "How much time do we have remaining?"

"About five and half months," Emir replied.

"Okay, we will need to sleep on this. We will discuss this again in the morning," the Captain replied. "It's been a long and eventful day. Let's all go to bed. Good night."

CHAPTER TWENTY SIX

AFTER A FITFUL NIGHT'S sleep, the Captain walked into the bay for breakfast with the others. "Good morning everyone," he said, "I hope you had a better nights sleep then I did."

As Sophia and Naomi were passing out the breakfast mush, the Captain announced. "Yesterday, after dinner a few of us continued reviewing the tapes with Emir. After he finished programming the computer to reconfigure and adjust the pixels for us, we noticed that there were caves in the mountains. Unfortunately, those mountains are on the other side of the rain forest and jungle. This means it would take us—even with the reduced gravity, about six months to get there. Based upon that information, we need to start preparing for the storms Emir has predicted. As of right now, we will be forced to try and ride out the storm, here on the ship exposed to hurricane force winds."

"My plan is this. Bruce, you and Matzo will need to take the drone out on another reconnaissance mission. Only this time, I want you to go in the other direction. Your objective is to determine how far these plains really go or if there is a suitable location somewhere closer that can provide us with temporary shelter from the storms."

Bruce and Matzo both responded, "Yes sir."

As the seriousness of what the Captain had just said started to sink in, he continued lining out the assignments.

"Drago, Maggy, Rashad, Molly, and Choi, I want you to scout out into the tree line and rain forest. I don't want you gathering food or anything else. Your mission is to determine what is out there and if there is a place that could provide us shelter from the storms.

Other than Emir, everyone else is to work around the ship or will start gathering the food we will need to survive during the storm. Now, enjoy your breakfast, we have another big day ahead of us."

"Excuse me Captain;" Sophia interrupted. "I have a surprise for you this morning."

"Really?" the Captain questioned.

"Yes sir, it is a special treat for you only, because there is not enough for anyone else." With that, she presented him with a plate with two brownish eggs on it.

"I found these this morning when I went to check on the garden and look in on the birds." Sophia told him with a proud smile on her face; then added, "So you get the first two sir."

The Captain looked at the plate with the eggs on it. For some reason this gave him the feeling that they were going to make it. Slowly, he took his fork and cut into the eggs. With every eye at the table on him, putting the fork full in his mouth, he slowly chewed savoring the first bite.

"It needs a little salt and pepper," he said. "Other than that, it tastes like an egg—a little bit of an earthier taste, but an egg none the less."

"We need to get more birds," Bruce stated, "both for eating and for the eggs."

'How did you get them?" Tani asked.

"Well, you all know how Drago got the first one; the other two were much simpler." Rashad responded as he warmed up to the story telling. "Drago and I spotted some feeding, but when we approached, they took off and flew into one of those low trees. At that point, we just stunned them and they fell out."

"Reminds me of how we use to hunt turkeys," Sophia said. "You get there early in the morning when they're still sleeping in the trees and you just sneak up and hit them with a stick."

"Alright, we'll try to get some more today," Molly, said.

"I'm finished analyzing the first bird," Dana said. "You can have it for cooking now, Sophia. I tried not to chop it up too bad."

"Great," Sophia replied. "I've got some more good news. The vegetables in the garden are growing fast. We should be able to harvest some in about three to four days."

"Good," the Captain replied. "Emir, I want you and Tani to break down and analyze everything you can off those videos. The rest, like I said, will be gathering food. Then the Captain looked at Doc and asked, "how did we do on the rain water collection last night?"

"We filled the containers up again. In fact, the water you're drinking this morning is from the containers."

"I can taste the difference," two or three replied.

"Which reminds me," Doc said. "Dana, I need to use the MRI this morning."

"Okay," Dana said. "What do you need to run through?"

"The Captain," Doc replied.

Everyone looked at the Captain, with questioning looks in their eyes.

"It's just a routine test, but, one we have put off for a couple of days now. There is nothing to worry about; besides, I'll be testing the rest of you also. With all this running around you have been doing lately, I've let you slide on your check ups."

"Emir, you'll be next."

At that point, Angelina spoke up stating, "Captain, I want to work with Emir's group today. There is a lot of information to go over on those videos."

"Fine," the Captain replied as he took another bite of his eggs.

"After breakfast, I'll go over what I want Drago's group to look for, then I'll report to you Doc," the Captain stated. "Now, if you guys don't mind, I'm going to finish these eggs."

After breakfast, everyone set out on their duties. The Captain, who was meeting with Drago's group, instructed them to go into the tree line as far as they could toward the rain forest.

"I want everyone to have their head cams on with the primary objective of getting as much information as possible on video. We have to prepare for further exploration of the rain forest or possibly having to live out in it during the storms. However, I will not be able to make that decision until we have more information. Does everybody understand?"

"Got you Captain," Rashad responded.

"Okay, I'm off to see the Doc."

"We'll need to take the back packs just in case we see something to bring back," Drago said. "I also think we should take the sonic blaster. I'm not real comfortable heading into those heavy trees or the rain forest without being prepared to take on anything that might come at us."

"I'm with you," Rashad agreed. "Molly you carry a stun gun, Choi you carry the laser, Drago, you're fine with that stun pistol. Make sure everybody has their ear bugs in and cables on."

"I want to add Natasha to the group," Drago said. "She has a way of seeing and hearing things that the rest of us don't."

"We agree," responded both Rashad and Maggy together.

"I'll go get her and let the Captain know of our decision." Drago said as he turned to go find Natasha.

Meanwhile, the food gathering group was trying to figure out the best way to gather as much as they could and bring it back.

"Why don't we make some sacks out of the tarps," suggested Sophia. "That way, when we stun the birds, we can put them in a sack. With this low gravity, we should be able to carry a lot without it being that much of a burden."

"Good idea," Loren agreed, then added, "We can also carry more rice and plants that way."

Naomi and Sophia went back inside to get some tarps. They returned with a couple large pieces of the tarp material and a pair of scissors Naomi had borrowed from Angelina's office supply crate. Within a few minutes, the group had made carry-sacks out of them.

"With these carry-sacks and the back packs, we should be able to collect plenty," Loren said.

They quickly adjusted their back packs and carry-sacks fitting them over the rest of their equipment, adjusted their cables and head gear then headed out toward the tree line.

Meanwhile, Bruce and Matzo had reinstalled the charged batteries and were getting ready to put the drone in the air. When they had finished the final preflight check list, Matzo commented.

"After take-off, let's maintain altitude at a thousand feet going out over the plains. We know there are some animals in the grass, but I think if we fly high and fast we can cover more ground. That way, if we see something of interest, we can drop down and check it out. It should also give us more flying time."

"Works for me," Bruce said. "Let's fly."

CHAPTER TWENTY SEVEN

DOC HAD FINISHED RUNNING the Captain through the MRI. "Okay, Captain, it will take me a while to go over all this information so you're free to go."

"Do you want me to send in Emir?" the Captain asked as he was getting redressed.

"Not right now, no. I want to make sure I know what I'm looking for first. I'll come find you when I'm ready for him."

When the group going out to gather the plants got to the tree line, Sophia said, "Show me where the birds were."

"Hold on," Loren said, "let's get the rice, then pick the plants and berries first—that way we won't have a bunch of birds flopping in sacks lying around all afternoon."

"All right," Sophia said, "I guess that makes sense."

After about three hours of picking and gathering, Loren looked around and noticed that everyone's back packs and carry-sacks were pretty full.

Figuring they had enough, she stopped and announced, "Okay, let's go back to where the birds were first sighted." When they got to the area, Loren said, "Let's leave the packs here. How many of us do you think should go looking for the birds?"

Naomi volunteered, "I'll stay with the sacks, you and Sophia go for the birds."

"Alright," Loren agreed, "we'll call you to bring the sacks when we get some."

"Okay," Naomi replied as she looked around for a comfortable place to sit down and wait.

Loren and Sophia headed off into the brush. They had gone about fifty yards when Loren raised her hand. "Do you hear that? It sounds like clucking."

Sophia stopped and listened, and then she too heard the clucking noise.

"It sounds like it's coming from that direction," Loren said, pointing. The two of them had started creeping through the brush toward the clucking sound when suddenly, they came to an open space. There in front of them was a flock of the birds feeding underneath some bushes.

"Okay," Loren whispered," how do we do this?"

"Let's put the guns on full stun and just sweep it though the flock," Sophia suggested. "I'm not sure how good of a shot I am anyway."

"Okay, on the count of three," Loren whispered quietly. "One—Two—Three!" Then they both stepped out and aimed at the flock while sweeping from side to side with the stun gun. Some birds had taken off when Loren and Sophia had jumped out of the bushes, but there were four or five lying stunned on the ground when they stopped.

"Yeah!" Sophia yelled, "Naomi, bring the sacks."

Naomi jumped up when she heard Sophia yell.

"Where are you?" she yelled back.

"Over this way," Sophia yelled.

Naomi worked her way through the brush eventually coming to the opening a little way from where Loren and Sophia were gathering up the birds. As she started over to them with the sacks, she saw something in the grass. Stopping and looking down, she saw that there were four baby chicks lying there. She took the sacks over to Loren and Sophia, then went back over to the baby chicks and gently picked them up and put them into her backpack. When they had completed putting the birds in the sacks and returned to where they had left the other sacks, the girls realized that they now had four sacks of plants and three sacks of birds along with their backpacks.

"What do we do now?" Naomi asked.

While the sacks were not that heavy, they were quite cumbersome. Since there were only three of them and seven sacks, it created a problem, even with the low gravity.

"Okay," Loren said, "let's do this. The three of us will drag these sacks back to where the clearing starts. Then we'll take turns doing the Sling-Around, each time carrying a couple of sacks. We'll leave one person with the sacks, then I'll come back for the other. We continue slinging each other with the remaining sacks until we get all the way back to the ship."

"This ought to be interesting," Naomi said.

It almost worked out the way they planned. First, Loren and Naomi took two sacks and did the sling around twice on to the grass. Then, Loren went back to get Sophia. Carrying three sacks, they slung their way back to where Naomi was waiting. They then realized that there were still two sacks left behind. So Loren and Sophia slung back together, got the last two sacks, and returned to Naomi. They continued this way until they got all the way back to the ship.

When all three were there with the sacks, Sophia said, "I'm about slung out. I need to sit down for a minute."

About that time, the birds started coming awake in one of the sacks and began flopping all over.

"Stun them!" Sophia shouted.

Loren promptly pulled her stun gun and shot it at the whole bag. "I think we need to put them in the pen now," Loren said as she put her stun gun on safety and re-holstered.

While the birds were somewhat stunned, the tarp must have reduced the affect, because they were still half awake. It was a struggle to get the birds safely in the pen with the other two, but they managed to accomplish it without any escapes. After the birds were secured, Naomi had gone to her back pack and taken out the baby chicks, opened the pen gate just enough and added the baby chicks to their growing flock.

"I gathered some of the seeds and berries they were eating," Sophia said, "when we were gathering. We will also need to put some water in the pen for them to drink and some of those seeds for them to eat."

"I'll get it," Naomi volunteered. "I've taken care of chickens before."

"Okay," Sophia responded, "you are now the official Turkey-Bird Lady. You can make sure that they get fed and watered everyday."

While they were waiting on Naomi to return, Loren and Sophia sat back down to rest for a few minutes before getting back up to take the sacks of plants and berries into the ship. Within minutes, Naomi came back out carrying some containers with water in them. As she was putting the water in the pen along with some of the food, she noticed one of the birds had a broken wing.

"Hey, Sophia! I think one of the birds has a broken wing; it must have done it flopping around in the bag."

Sophia got up and looked in the pen. Then she purposely pulled her stun gun from its holster and shot the bird with the broken wing. Dodging all the birds flying around, Sophia grabbed the stunned bird and brought it out of the pen.

"Do you think you can fix it?" Naomi asked.

"Yup, I sure can," Sophia replied as she expertly broke the bird's neck. "Now, we'll have two birds for supper."

Loren chuckled as she watched Sophia head for her kitchen carrying the dead bird. "Come on Naomi; help me get these plants into the ship."

CHAPTER TWENTY EIGHT

MATZO AND BRUCE HAD watched the girls unloading the birds into the pen while still flying the drone. In the three hours they had been watching the live cam feeds from the drone, they had seen nothing but more and more open prairie land. The drone pretty much flew itself, and they were bordering on boredom.

"Let's bring it back," Bruce suggested. "I don't think we are going to find anything out this way other than more of the same."

"Yeah, I believe you are right. It would take us months just to cover that amount of ground even if there was something there," Matzo replied. "Turn it around and bring it back by a different route, so we can check out new areas rather than what we have already been over."

Bruce made the adjustments and Matzo set up a new grid on the screen.

"Well, the good news is that we're going to have meat for supper tonight," Bruce said.

"I was just thinking the same thing. I wonder how Sophia is going to fix it?"

As they sat there looking at the miles and miles of open grass land, they were both thinking about supper that night. Two hours later, with the drone about an hour out, Matzo lifted bored eyes to the screen once more.

"Hey, Bruce, turn the drone to the right. It looks like something dark on the edge of the screen."

Bruce gently banked the drone in that direction. With the drone still flying at about thousand feet, they could just make out what looked like a dark cloud, moving across the plain below.

"Drop down to a hundred feet," Matzo directed. "Let's see what this is."

As Bruce adjusted the altitude controls and the drone dropped down, the picture became clearer. What had looked like a cloud was actually a large herd of buffalo sized beasts.

"Get all the cameras focusing this," Bruce said excitedly as Matzo started adjusting the controls.

They flew over the herd for about three miles then circled the drone back over the herd.

Excitedly, Matzo said, "Let's head back to home base now. We need to share this information with everybody."

"Roger that," Bruce said. Still thinking about supper, he added, "Did I just see steak medium rare on the hoof?"

"I believe you did," Matzo replied with a big grin on his face.

Meanwhile, Drago and his group had been anything but bored. Getting to the tree line had not been difficult, even though the big bird sitting on a branch in the distance had caused a bit of apprehension when they first noticed it watching them. But Natasha had assured everyone that it was just watching and not interested. So they had moved on.

The problem was the rain forest itself. Their cameras were picking up infra red images of animals everywhere, some big, some small. They had nervously stopped to discuss it several times, but had then decided to move on. Fighting their way through the thick ground brush and foliage was sapping everyone's energy. They had all tripped and fell numerous times even though they had been using the laser for the last hour just to cut their way through foliage. To make matters worse, it was hot and steamy and they were all sweaty.

Finally, Drago said, "Stop, this is fruitless. All we're doing is wasting our energy trying to fight our way through this. It's just too dangerous when we can't even see four feet in front of us. I suggest we turn around and go back. Emir will have better luck looking at the images from the drone than we will trying to find anything in here."

"Agreed," they all said.

"At least going back will be easier; we won't have to cut our way back through," Maggy said.

They had turned around and were heading back when Drago noticed that the brush foliage was already growing back in places. He mentioned it to the others who also agreed.

"Let's hope it doesn't grow back too fast," Maggy said. "I don't want to have to cut our way back out."

They had about another hour to go before they would be back to the tree line, when suddenly Rashad yelled; "Ouch!"

"What happened?" Drago asked.

"Something fell out of the trees and hit me on the head." Looking around the ground, he reached down and picked up a round object. "Well, well, this could be why the melon seeds Sophie planted didn't grow." Rashad commented as he held up what definitely looked like some type of small melon. "The planet already had some."

They all looked up but could see nothing in the dense foliage.

"I've got an idea," Rashad said motioning for everyone to move over closer to one of the tree trunks. "Move over there, I'm going to try something." As the others did as they were told, Rashad borrowed the laser from Choi, raised it up, and shot it into the trees moving it around. The next thing they knew, melons were falling from the sky. After the last of the melons had fallen to the ground, the group moved away from the tree trunk and picked them up.

"There seems to be three or four different kinds," Molly commented.

"Okay," Drago said, "let's put the ones that didn't get busted in our packs and get out of here. I need to see daylight again."

When they finally made it back to the clearing at the tree line, Drago called for a halt so everyone could sit down out in the open and cool off for a bit.

"I know this," Rashad said as he continued to watch for any danger signs in the foliage behind them. "If the Captain thinks we're going to go through a jungle, across a river, and traipse across another plain to make it to the mountains and the caves, he has another thing coming. It would take us years to get there."

As they sat there, Drago looked over at Natasha who seemed to be in a daze. "Natasha, are you all right?"

Slowly coming out of a trance like state, Natasha said, "Yes, I'm fine."

"What were you doing?" Drago asked.

"I was communicating with that hawk. It's right over there watching us." They all looked to where she was pointing and saw the giant bird, sitting in the tree.

"He could take anyone of us back to feed his family," Rashad said in a low tone of voice.

"It's a she, not a he," Natasha replied. "She has been sitting here the whole time we were back in the jungle."

Knowing that Natasha had a talent to hear or sense the thoughts of both humans and animals, Drago asked, "What did she say?"

"All I could get was an image of Loren," Natasha said. "It seems to be fascinated with her."

"Good," Maggy said. "Does that mean it will let us go?"

"It's not interested in us," Natasha responded with a puzzled look on her face.

"Well, I suggest we head back to the ship before it changes its mind," Rashad stated getting to his feet. "Besides, if the others found those turkey-birds, we may be having chicken and dumplings for dinner tonight."

The thought of food got them all moving again as they got up and headed back to the ship. When they got back, almost everybody was outside talking to each other.

"What's up?" Maggy asked.

"We got birds," Naomi announced proudly.

"We got steaks," Bruce added with a grin.

"Well," Rashad said not to be out done, "we brought the melons," reaching in his backpack and taking one out for everyone to see.

The Captain was just coming down the ramp to see what all the commotion was about and heard the jumble of back and forth conversation about birds, steaks, and melons.

"Whoa! What in the world is going on?"

With that, everyone started to excitedly tell him all at the same time again.

"Okay! One at a time…the short version, please. You go first Loren."

"We got the plants and captured some more turkey-birds."

"We found a melon tree," Rashad said.

Not to be out done, Bruce said, "And, we found steaks."

"What do you mean steaks?" the Captain asked.

"Well, not really steaks," Matzo said.

"They're steaks on the hoof," Bruce replied. "We spotted them on the drone's cameras."

"Okay," the Captain said, "we'll do this the usual way. Everyone go get cleaned up and head to the bay, it should almost be time to eat."

They all walked in talking excitedly. As they sat down, they could all smell something delicious coming out of the kitchen. Just then, Naomi appeared with a white cloth wrapped around her waist like an apron. Coming to the end of the table, she announced.

"Tonight's special is a baked turkey-bird stuffed with berries, rice, and other things Sophia put in there. Along with this, we have rice and gravy made from the broth. For your drinking pleasure, we have an excellent vintage of clear sparkling water."

With that, Sophia, Dana, and Gerard came out of Sophia's galley with large serving trays of food.

"I think I'm going to pass out," Molly said as she took a deep breath savoring the aromas.

The talking ended. All you could hear was groans of enjoyment and pass this or pass that please. There was no thought of discussing the day's events. Everyone, including the Captain was engrossed in eating.

As everyone sat there after they finished eating, the Captain said, "all right lets talk about what happened today."

"I'll go first, if it's okay with you," Drago stated. "Our adventure today was probably the least exciting and uninformative."

"Go ahead," the Captain replied.

"Well sir, we made it all the way to the rain forest; however, once there, we didn't accomplish much. The ground cover and the foliage was so thick, we had to cut our way through. The only thing we saw was more brush and foliage. Although, our cameras did seem to pick up some animal shapes moving around when we switched them over to infrared. Hopefully, we will know more after Emir downloads everything to the computers. We did notice that the plants we had cut with the lasers had started to regenerate immediately. Also, I would state that the rain forest does not offer suitable shelter from the storm. That's about it, except for Rashad discovering the melons."

"Tell me about finding the melons," the Captain requested.

"Well, the idea kind of struck me," Rashad said grinning. "So I borrowed the laser from Choi and shot it up into the trees. Then the melons came raining down," Rashad replied, whimsically.

"I hope we don't have to wait for Dana to test them, so we can eat one right away," Sophia said.

"We test first; then eat," the Captain said.

"All right girls, tell me about your day. We'll save Bruce and Matzo's reports for the end," the Captain stated.

"Well," Sophia stated, "we went back to the tree line and started to gather plants. Loren thought it would be better to gather the plants first, then go looking for the birds. Good thing too, or we would have had an even more difficult time getting everything back. Our carry-sack plan worked out pretty well. The only problem we had was that there were too many sacks to bring back at one time, so we had to make more than one trip."

"So how did you get the birds?" Rashad asked. "Did they fly into the trees like last time?"

"No, we snuck up on them though the brush, when we heard them clucking," Loren replied. "When we peaked out through the brush, we could see them feeding under some bushes, so I had Sophia quietly move next to me. Then on the count of three, we jumped out together and just sprayed our stun guns back and forth. We ended up getting five birds. When Naomi came to help us, she found the baby chicks."

"So that gives us a total of seven birds and four baby chicks," said the Captain.

"Err, ah, no sir," Sophia replied. "One had a broken wing from struggling in the sacks. You ate it for dinner."

"An honorable sacrifice," the Captain said with a satisfied look. However, do I understand there were only three of you and you left one behind with nobody guarding?

"There were only three of us," Loren stated.

"That is not a legitimate excuse, the Captain stated. "No one or group goes out without the proper amount of people and protection. Does everyone understand?"

"Yes sir," they replied in unison.

"So now, Bruce, you and Matzo tell us about your flight today and where you found the steaks."

"We didn't really find any steaks sir, that was just an expression," Matzo replied.

"I realize that," the Captain said; "please continue."

"Well sir," Bruce continued, "we had been flying for about two hours at a thousand feet and top speed. We saw nothing but miles and miles of plains. Then, Matzo and I decided to turn around and come back by a different route. Again, we flew over miles of plains, but then, about a mile out, Matzo saw something at the edge of the screen. So I redirected the drone back toward it and low and behold, we came upon some animals on the screen. I circled the drone around and dropped to a hundred feet. We then flew over the length of the animals and took close ups with the belly camera."

"From what we could tell, the animals kind of resembled a buffalo like creature—but different. We flew over them for about forty-five minutes, with all the cameras going."

"I would estimate the herd size to be about two miles long by about a half mile wide," Matzo added. "We should be able to learn more after everything has been downloaded on to the computer."

"It sounds like our meat problem might be solved," replied the Captain. "All in all, even though we didn't find shelter, I'd say it was a successful day."

"Anyone else have anything to add?" the Captain asked.

"I do," Doc said. "I need to discuss your MRI results with you tonight. Also, I'd like to bring up an important health matter."

"Go ahead Doc," the Captain said.

"As you know, we have recycling equipment on board for water and waste. The addition of the fresh rain water we have been collecting has helped clean up the system. However, the ship has no provision for cleaning clothes; even though you brought some extras." Crinkling his nose and sniffing the air for emphasis as he pointed looked around the table, he continued. "Based on the aroma around some of you, I'd say that it's time to do laundry. With that thought in mind, I took the time to make up a batch of liquid soap in the lab today and I have set aside two large containers of fresh water. You can pick someone, or you can all do your own, but you need to do it first thing in the morning."

"On another note, I'll need to see Emir for testing in the morning," Doc concluded.

There were groans around the table when he finished.

"I've never had to wash clothes before," Rashad said.

"Me either," Bruce and Matzo chimed in at the same time.

"There is not that much to it," Naomi said shrugging her shoulders. "I've been doing it my whole life." Then she noticed everyone looking at her and smiling. "Oh no, I've got the birds to feed and water; plus, I have to help with the garden. I don't have time to do everyone's clothes."

"I'll feed and water the birds," Molly offered.

"I know something about gardening," Choi stated.

"I can take some cable and make a clothes line for you," Matzo offered.

"Please, Naomi," they all asked together.

"You got to be careful with them birds" Naomi stated, "They can get spooky and start flying around. I don't want no more broken wings. Plus, you'll need to look for eggs."

"I'll do that," Sophia said. "I'll even throw in an extra surprise at breakfast…just for you."

"Okay, okay," Naomi said, "I give up. I'll do your clothes."

"I'll help you," Natasha offered. "I've done clothes before."

With that decided, everyone headed off to their bunks for a well earned rest.

Chapter Twenty Nine

The Captain and Doc remained sitting at the table for a few minutes before heading back to the Med Bay to review the Captain's test results.

Walking into the lab he asked, "Find anything Doc?"

"That's what I wanted to go over with you. As I stated before, all of your test results were within normal ranges, but I wanted to do an MRI."

"After spending a few hours going over the print outs from the MRI, I found a strange anomaly." Putting some negatives on his board, he pointed to a spot on the Captain's brain. "See that?"

"Yes," the Captain responded.

"That is not normal," Doc replied. "It shows activity in a part of the brain that usually doesn't show that much activity."

"Can you tell what it is Doc?" the Captain asked with concern in his voice.

"Actually, I asked Dana to help me because she's very good at reading these. But the only thing we could come up with is that it is an abnormal amount of activity. It does not appear to be cancerous. It's more like electrical impulses." Doc explained.

"What do we do now?" the Captain asked.

"Nothing," Doc replied. "I'm going to run the same tests on Emir in the morning and see if it shows up in him, other than that, I'd like to check you every couple of days and see if there has been any change."

"That doesn't exactly make me feel very comfortable Doc," the Captain stated.

"I understand, but right now, I don't have any other answers."

"Then I'm going to bed," the Captain said. "This is just one more thing I get to worry about."

The next morning when they all showed up to sit down for breakfast, the Captain couldn't help but notice the wide assortment of clothing. Maggy appeared to be wearing an abbreviated toga made out of one of the tarps.

Seeing the Captain look at her, she said, "I didn't have anything left so I made this last night." "Please do my clothes first," Maggy asked Naomi; who was just sitting down.

"I don't know, I kind of like your new outfit," Rashad commented with a smirk on his face.

"You would," Maggy retorted. "By the way, are those shorts or underwear you have on Rashad?"

"What's for breakfast?" Rashad asked, trying to change the subject.

Sophia was just coming into the bay with Dana and Gerard helping her. "I've another little surprise this morning, Sophia announced. "I dug up a few young potatoes and along with some left over turkey-bird from last night; I scrambled some eggs and made a bird hash for breakfast."

"What no mush?" Bruce exclaimed. "I was just getting used to that stuff."

"I can take yours back and bring you some mush if you'd rather," Sophia said with mock sincerity as she reached for his plate.

"No, no that's alright," Bruce said quickly.

"Where's my surprise?' Naomi asked; between mouthfuls.

"Wait till you're done, then I'll go get it."

As everyone was finishing up, Sophia got up and went back to the kitchen. Returning, she had something on a dish that had a towel over it. Going over to Naomi, she set it down. Removing the towel with a flourish she said, "This is the only melon Dana had time to check out and approve for consumption last night. I hope you enjoy it."

Everyone around the table looked over at Naomi's dish. On it, Sophia had arranged five melon slices. They were brownish green on the outside but the insides were a reddish pink like watermelon.

Naomi reached down, took the first slice, and bit into it. With the juices running down her chin, she looked up and smiled, "This is really good. It's like the sweetest watermelon I ever tasted."

"Wait! Stop!" Rashad exclaimed. "I'll do the laundry! Just give me a slice."

Naomi looked up and smiled. "Well, I can only eat another slice, so that leaves three. I'll give one to Natasha, because she said she would help me and one to Dana who has to test all this stuff so we can eat. The rest of you can draw straws for the last slice," she said handing Natasha and Dana their slices.

Both girls bit into their slices and gave out groans of delight.

Rashad jumped up and ran into the other bay coming back with twelve pieces of straw-like stems from the plants they had brought in.

"Hold it," the Captain said grinning. "I believe you are three short. What about me, Doc and Angelina?"

Rashad ran back for three more. Upon his return, the Captain said, "Give them to me Rashad. I'll make sure there is only one short straw."

After fixing the straws, the Captain held out his hand, covering the bottom. "Who goes first?"

Rashad reached out and grabbed the first straw before anyone could answer. It was long. He sat down with disappointment.

One by one, the rest drew straws until only Angelina, Doc, and the Captain were left. Angelina drew first. It was long. That left only the Doc and Captain to draw. Doc stood up and came over. After studying them for a second, he reached out and pulled a straw. It was noticeably shorter then the rest. The Captain opened his hand showing the remaining long straw.

Doc then went over to where Naomi was sitting and with quiet dignity, lifted the last slice from the plate. With a dreamy smile on his face and closed eyes, he bit into the melon.

"Wonderful," he said. "Just wonderful."

Everyone had started getting up to leave the table when the Captain said; "Hold up everyone, I still have to give out today's assignments."

'Emir, you have to go with Doc for some testing. Bruce, Matzo, Tani, Angelina, Rashad, Maggy, and Drago, I want to review the videos from yesterday."

"Naomi and Natasha are working on clothes."

"Dana, you Gerard, and Loren keep checking out the food supply." Choi, you, and Molly have the birds and the garden to take care of. I'll be with the group looking at the videos."

"See you all back here for lunch."

Gathering the group together that was going to review the video, the Captain said, "Okay, we have the head shot webcam videos from the two teams that went out yesterday and we have the video from the drone. How do we split this up?"

"I'll take Maggy, Rashad, and Drago," Angelina said. "That way, I'll be able to ask questions as we review the webcam videos. Afterward, they can watch the videos from the drone, with the rest of us at lunch."

"Okay, that means you, Bruce, Tani, and Matzo will be reviewing the drone video with me," the Captain stated.

Outside, Naomi and Natasha had already begun on the clothes. Naomi was washing and scrubbing while Natasha rinsed and hung them out to dry on the clothes line.

Doc was in the process of giving Emir his battery of medical tests. "You won't have to go through as many as the Captain did; however, I do want to put you through the MRI. Let's go see Dana," Doc said getting up.

Meanwhile, Bruce and Matzo had fast forwarded through most of the video. It just showed the continuing plains even though the infra red showed small animals in the grass. When they got to the part of the video showing the herds, they put it on slow motion and set up the computer to analyze.

"They are quite large," the Captain noted.

"According to the computer, they average around 1200 pounds each." Matzo replied.

"Can you zoom in on the back of the herd?" Tani asked. "It looks like there are some other animals following the herd."

Readjusting and switching to another camera they were able to see that in fact, there were other animals following the herd.

"Those look just like the cubs, only bigger," Bruce noted.

"The computer shows them at around 300 pounds," Matzo replied.

"Look," Tani said pointing to the screen. "Two of them are attacking that one straggler."

They watched in fascination as one of the animals ran up and bit hold of the animal's snout, while the other went to the back and hamstrung it. Within seconds, the animal was on the ground. Instantly, two more of the wolverine like animals attacked, one getting the throat of the beast, the other gutting it.

When the animal was completely down and dead, the one wolverine let out a barking, yelping type sound. Within minutes, there were small cubs coming out of the grass. The adult animals let the cubs eat first. In fact, two of the adults stayed while the other two adults went on the hunt again.

"It looks like there are eight cubs," Matzo said. "I wonder if they belong to the two teams or if they belong to a group that is still out hunting?"

"There are all sorts of animal packs back on earth that behave that way," the Captain said. "Matzo, can you determine how far the herd is from us, and which way they seem to be heading?"

"Yes sir," Matzo replied as he typed in a command on the keyboard. "The computer confirms that when the pictures were taken, the herd was about fifty miles out from us and headed in a North West direction, which means they are heading slightly toward us. Their rate of speed is about ten miles a day."

"I'd like to be able to get one of those animals for food," the Captain said. "That much meat would feed us for quite a while. Somebody, get Rashad and Drago in here, I want them to see this video clip."

In response, Matzo stood up and went to get Rashad and Drago.

"When Rashad and Drago arrive, I want them to look at this video," the Captain continued. "Make sure they pay particular attention to the herd animal size and the animals that are following them."

Within a few minutes, Matzo returned with both Drago and Rashad who sat down to watch the video. Drago was curious about the Captain's intent. After viewing the video, Drago requested a second review before asking about the herd's location. When Matzo informed him, he sat there quietly pondering the situation.

"I want to get one of those animals for food," the Captain repeated. "I don't want to bring any back here to raise." He then stood up and started pacing back and forth with his hands clasped behind his back. "As I see it, there are several issues we will need to resolve. It will take us at least an hour to get a team to the herd location using the Sling-Arounds. We will also need to figure out how to separate one of them from herd and kill it. I don't want to use the guns on the drone. We haven't tried or practiced with them yet, and I don't want to take a chance of hitting some of the team. You will also have to butcher it and bring the meat back, which will be very heavy–even with the lower gravity. And most important, you will have to accomplish all this without getting attacked by the wolverine type animals or the herd animals."

'Shooting it will be the easy part," Rashad responded. "I can use the laser and shoot one of them either in the heart or head."

"Looking at the animal and being an avid western reader, I would think the heart is just behind the front leg. That's where they always shot the buffalo in the books and movies I watched growing up," the Captain said. "The problem is how you are going to be able keep up with it and shoot if it's running? Even using the Sling-Around, you might be up in the air as it comes by. Also, it would be extremely important that you don't shoot your partner while slinging. Drago, what do you think? You've been awfully quite over there again."

"I was thinking sir. It will take three teams of two each. When we get the beast down, one team will move in to butcher the animal while the other two teams stand guard with their stun guns to protect."

"I didn't hear how you were going to get the animal to where you could shoot it safely," the Captain responded.

"Well sir, I think that will be the easy part—depending on how good Bruce and Matzo are."

"Please explain," the Captain said motioning for Drago to continue.

"Well, Bruce and Matzo can use the drone to buzz the herd. When one separates from the herd, they should be able to direct it to where the teams are lying in ambush, when it gets within range they shoot it. Then two of the teams stand guard while the other team butchers it. That also gives us three teams to carry back the meat."

"You always seem to amaze me," Rashad said.

"I suppose you have figured out who should be on the teams," the Captain stated.

"Yes sir," Drago replied. "One is Rashad and Maggy. Molly and I will make up the second, and Sophia and Loren will be the third."

"I understand the first two, but I don't quite get Sophia and Loren," the Captain queried.

"Because they both know how to butcher meat," Drago responded. "We certainly know that Sophia and Loren worked on farms. I'm sure they'll know how to cut it up."

'So much for that," the Captain said. "We'll have Bruce and Matzo find the herd in the morning. Get set and tell the others so they can be ready for tomorrow."

"Now, Drago, did you find anything interesting on the other video clips?"

"Not really sir. The infrareds show many life forms in the rain forest. Angelina and Tani are trying to sort them by size and figure out what they are, but that's about it except a lot of video showing trees, brush, and foliage."

Chapter Thirty

Doc had finished with Emir and sent him back to the others. He then went looking for the Captain. Seeing him walk into the bay, Doc asked, "Captain, can I see you back at the Med Center?"

"Sure, let's go," the Captain replied.

Once there, Doc opened the file containing the MRI results on his computer screen.

"All of Emir's tests came back normal; with one exception," Doc reported to the Captain. "But look at this. That is the same spot where your brain showed unusual activity. However; it would appear that the spot in Emir's brain is almost twice as active."

"What does that mean?" the Captain asked.

"Your guess is as good as mine," Doc replied shaking his head. "I have no idea other than it doesn't seem to affect either one of you. It will be interesting to see how the rest of the group tests out. I'll set up a schedule for bringing them in one at time, then let you know what the results are. By the way, isn't it about lunch time?" Doc asked in conclusion.

"I believe you are right," the Captain replied. "Isn't it interesting that the thing I was worried about the most—feeding us, has turned into the one thing that we all look forward to."

"You have to admit that Sophia can take old shoe leather, leaves and rocks and somehow make a meal," Doc said as they headed for the Gathering Bay.

The others were walking in as they arrived. Emir was discussing what he had seen on the videos with Matzo. Drago and Rashad were starting to tell Molly, Maggy, and Loren about tomorrow's hunt. While Angelina and Tani were discussing the computer generated results from the infrared video.

Just then, Naomi walked in wearing her head waitress gear and announced,

"Today's special consists of a chicken like salad. Dana has inspected an assortment of plants that were brought back and issued her seal of approval. Sophia has mixed those along with some fresh vegetables from the garden to produce an excellent salad. Oh! By-the-way, another bird has been sacrificed. The remainder will be served with dinner tonight."

With that, Dana, Gerard and Sophia began setting the plates down.

"I made kind of a vinaigrette dressing from some of the stuff we had, I hope you like it because I don't have anything else," Sophia stated.

"Are these tomatoes in the salad?" Molly exclaimed.

"Yes, from our very own garden," Sophia replied.

"Once again, you have out done yourself," the Captain stated; putting a fork full in his mouth.

After lunch Drago came up to the Captain and said, "Excuse me sir, I've been thinking about the plans we made for tomorrow and I'd like to make another suggestion."

"Go ahead," the Captain, replied.

"I'd like to add another team. "I think we should add Choi and Natasha as a back up team. They can stay about half way back with additional sacks and be ready to help out in case of an emergency."

"Good thinking, I like it," the Captain agreed. "Get with them and let them know."

The rest of the day was spent with Angelina and Tani working at the computer analyzing the infrared shots. Emir had finally found the time to review the video while working on his weather analysis. Gerard was checking out the garden with Sophia and Naomi. Drago's group was finalizing their plans for tomorrow's hunt while Doc was testing Dana.

As Drago's group finished up, Natasha turned to Maggy and said, "Have you seen the cubs lately?"

"No," Maggy replied. "In fact, we didn't take them out hunting last night. I completely forgot about it."

"So did I," Natasha said. "Let's go find them."

They looked around outside but could not fine any evidence of the cubs. Going into the ship, they were just wondering where to look when they ran in to Sophia as she was coming back from the garden.

"Sophia, have you seen the cubs?" Natasha asked.

"You mean my babies? I sure have, they were taking a nap went I went out to the garden."

Walking into the kitchen with Sophia, Maggy and Natasha noticed both cubs were sleeping on the bed Sophia had made for them.

"Look at them," Maggy said; "they're getting fat and lazy." Reaching down, she shook Zena awake. Meanwhile, Natasha was waking Butkis. Waking up, both cubs ran to Sophia wagging their stubs.

"Do Aunt Sophia's babies want a treat?" she asked the cubs. Both immediately started to spin around in place making a barking sound.

"Stop right now," Maggy ordered. "You're ruining them. They're getting fat and spoiled and they'll forget how to hunt."

"Nonsense," Sophia replied matter of factly. "I already told you that you can't spoil babies."

"Wrong," Maggy said, grabbing up Zena. "No more food scraps, they have to hunt for their supper."

Natasha grabbed Butkis and the two of them took both cubs outside. Butkis was happy to see Natasha and was playfully running around her. Zena however, was miffed with Maggy and was sending her thoughts of her displeasured temperament.

"I don't want to hear it," Maggy told Zena. Who immediately sat down and turned her back to Maggy. "Okay," Maggy said, "if you want to become fat and useless, lying around the kitchen all day, I guess Natasha and I can take Butkis and maybe find another cub to replace you."

"I'm a much better hunter than Butkis," Zena sent back.

"Well, I thought you were the smarter of the two," Maggy said. "But now I just see you lying around on the kitchen floor waiting for hand outs because you're to fat to run."

"Hunpft!" Zena sent back. "I do miss the gush of fresh warm blood when you catch one of the creatures." Here she used a name for the small critters that Maggy didn't understand, but Butkis picked up the thought as he too thought how good it tasted. Both Maggy and Natasha looked at one another swallowing with difficulty at the thought.

Zena got up and looked at Butkis as if to say let's go, then they headed out into the tall grass to hunt. Zena looked back and sent the thought to Maggy. "Do you want one too?"

"Yes, Maggy sent back, have Butkis bring one for Natasha also."

Both girls waited. A short time later, they heard the growling and snapping, then the sounds of the cubs eating. Finally, both cubs came out dragging one of the critters each.

"Oh! You are the best!" Maggy said to Zena lavishing her with praise; which Zena, despite herself responded to by wagging her stub.

"You too," Natasha told Butkis. "I know you're going to grow up to be the best hunter yet."

Both cubs lay down and contentedly started to clean themselves while both Natasha and Maggy watched every bit as content as the cubs.

Meanwhile, Doc had finished testing both Dana and Gerard and was looking for Loren, who was scheduled next. Coming back into the Med Bay, he saw the Captain and asked if he had seen Loren.

"No," the Captain responded. "She is probably outside with Drago's group getting ready for tomorrow's hunt." Doc turned around and went outside where Drago's group sat around talking.

"Hi," he said, "have you seen Loren?"

"She was here awhile ago," Drago answered then added, "when we finished going over the details, she said she had something to do. I thought she was going to see you."

"It looks like she took her head cam, belt, and ear bug," Molly noted looking over the gear they had sat aside when they finished practicing. "Maybe you can get in touch with her that way; or, you can always track her with the GPS."

"No need," Doc said turning around. "I'll go back inside and look for her first. She could be waiting for me at the Med Center by now." With that, Doc headed back into the ship. Back at the Med Center, there was no sign of Loren. After checking in the kitchen and then with Dana, he went back outside to where Drago was.

"Alright," he said, "see if you can locate Loren on her GPS."

Drago took his pad out of his belt and turned it on. "It shows her at the tree line," he said perplexed.

"What is she doing there?"

"She's gone to see that hawk," Natasha replied. "I told you there was something between the two of them."

"We better go check on her," Drago said getting up. "Come on Rashad, let's go."

"Hold it," Doc advised. "I think we should let the Captain know first."

After notifying the Captain, Drago and Rashad headed for the tree line. When they got within site of Loren, Rashad started to yell out to her but Drago caught Rashad's arm and said, "Hold it. Let's see what they're doing. She doesn't seem to be in any danger."

As Drago and Rashad watched, Loren moved up closer to the tree where the hawk was sitting and sat down on the ground beneath it. She kept staring up at the hawk, which was looking down at her. Neither moved or made a sound. After about twenty minutes or so, Loren stood up. When she did, the hawk flapped its wings and took off, as Loren waved goodbye.

Turning around she was surprised to see Drago and Rashad standing there watching her.

"What was that all about?" Drago asked.

"We were just talking," Loren replied.

"You and that bird?" Rashad questioned with disbelief. "I didn't hear you saying anything."

"Her name is Aria—we were just getting to know each other. I told her I had to return to the ship and wouldn't be able to come tomorrow, but that I would be here the day after."

"She understood all that?" Drago questioned.

"Yes," Loren replied.

"And you understood her?" Rashad asked.

"Yes." Loren replied again.

Starting back, Rashad suggested they try to get a couple more birds to replace those they had eaten.

"Okay," Drago agreed. "Just give me a minute to let the Captain know what we are doing, and then we'll go." After notifying the ship, they started heading to the same place as before.

"Wait a minute," Loren said. "I don't think it's a good idea to keep taking birds from the same flock. Let's go over to where we saw those other berry bushes and see if there are any of them over there."

"Good idea," Drago responded heading in that direction. When they got there, they did not see any birds but they did hear some clucking so they followed the sound to what looked to be a small clearing just on the other side of some bushes.

"Let's only take one a piece since we didn't bring any sacks with us," Drago whispered to Loren and Rashad. Nodding their agreement, all three moved quietly forward. When they got past the brush, they could see this was a bigger flock than the other one. Drago silently pointed to the three birds that were feeding closest to them. Using hand signals, he pointed to each of them, then the bird they were to stun.

Nodding in agreement, Rashad silently mouthed the words, "one-two-three." Moving in quickly, they scooped the stunned birds up and headed back to the ship. All three had gone out without their sling-around cables so they had to glide as fast as they could to get back before the birds woke up. They had just made it back to the ship and were putting them in the turkey-bird cage when Rashad's bird woke up, struggled for a second then broke free. Before they could stun it again; Zena ran up, jumped into the air and grabbed it by the neck shaking it as she came back down to the ground.

"It looks like we're going to have another turkey-bird for supper," Rashad said grinning.

Maggy and Natasha, who had been coming over to find out what all the commotion was about, had arrived just in time to see Zena capture the fleeing bird.

"Good girl Zena," Maggy said as she bent down patting her on the head and lavishing her with praise.

"You have to get them before they get too far off the ground," Zena sent back to Maggy. "Maybe Sophia will be pleased and she'll give us some," Zena added as an after thought.

"You're incorrigible," Maggy said picking Zena up and hugging her.

Going into the ship to take the bird to Sophia, they ran into the Captain.

"I need to speak to you alone young lady," he said sternly to Loren pointing toward his quarters. Loren, looking sheepishly followed the Captain into his quarters.

"Just what did you think you were doing?" the Captain asked as he pointedly stared down at Loren. "No one goes out on their own without asking or telling us where they're going. You could have been killed in any number of ways. What were you thinking?"

Loren, who had never heard the Captain raise his voice before, sat there in stunned silence with tears starting to run down her cheeks.

"I took my com unit and my belt," she said hesitantly.

"Not good enough," the Captain said gruffly.

"I'm sorry; I had to go see her. I knew it was wrong, but she has been calling to me and I knew she wouldn't hurt me," Loren explained in her defense. Wiping the tears from her face and taking a deep breath, she continued. "Her name is Aria. She is the leader of a large flock of them— they all have different ranges, and when she heard about us from one of the others in her flock; it was her job to come find out about us. For some reason, we can understand each other and I told her I would meet her the day after tomorrow again," Loren blurted out almost hysterically.

"Whoa, slow down," the Captain said. "You exchanged all that with this bird?"

"She's more than that," Loren said defensively. "She's the Queen of the Tashi's. That's what they call themselves. In their language, it means Protectors of the Sky."

"All right, enough," the Captain said in an exasperated tone of voice. "That is too much for me to absorb at one time. However, this does not excuse you from going out by yourself and not telling anyone. You are hereby forbidden from meeting with Aria again until you can find someone to go with you *and* we are all aware of when you're going. Do I make myself clear?"

"Yes sir," Loren replied with relief. For a minute there, she had thought he was going to forbid her from seeing Aria again.

"Now, go wash your face and go back to the others," he said in a dismissive tone of voice.

Loren left quickly, going back to the bay.

Everyone was there waiting for her. The questions started coming like crazy from everyone at the same time. All, that is, except for Natasha. As Angelina was telling everyone to be quiet and let Loren tell them what had happened. Natasha walked up to Loren and asked if she had spoken with her.

Loren, surprised by the question answered, "Yes I did. Her name is Aria."

"Sit down and tell us the whole story," Angelina directed, leading Loren to a seat.

After being interrupted with questions at every statement, Loren finally finished her story. When she finished, she looked over at Natasha and asked if she would go with her the day after tomorrow.

"Of course," Natasha replied.

While they were all discussing Loren story, Naomi showed up in what had become a meal time ritual.

"Tonight," she announced, "we have chicken and mashed potatoes, with a salad tossed in red berry sauce and melons for desert." With that, she turned and went to help bring the food out of the kitchen.

If there was one thing they all could agree on, it was that the food was great. Even Maggy and Natasha could forgive Sophia from spoiling the cubs, when they ate her food.

"Tomorrow's going to be a big day," the Captain announced. "So I want every one in the ship on standby in case anything goes wrong." Then he added, "I don't think I need to go over anyone taking solo trips from the ship."

"For the rest of dinner and through desert I'd like to see the computer print outs that Angelina and Tani have been working on."

With that, Angelina reached down and picked up a folder. Reaching inside, she started passing photos to the Captain.

"Tani had the computer take the information and try to develop figures of the animals form the videos. Even though they were taken from the infrared settings, I think you are going to be surprised by the results."

The first pictures she passed the Captain showed many different types of birds and animals that looked like what Drago had seen in the trees.

"These next ones are a little more interesting," Angelina said pointing as the Captain started passing the computer generated photos around.

The first one the Captain looked at resembled a wild boar or pig, only bigger and with large tusks. The next one resembled a giant saber tooth tiger. The computer had estimated it at around four hundred pounds.

When that picture got to Rashad, he exclaimed, "Wow, I'm really glad we turned back when we did. I'd hate to run into that thing!"

"Last but not least," Angelina said, "the really big guy." The photo she handed the Captain along with the size reading that went with it froze the Captain in his place. While it resembled an extremely large gorilla, it had massive fangs and claws instead of teeth and paws. When the Captain passed the photo around, it was met with total silence.

"That's most of them," Angelina said. "There are plenty more small animals both in the trees and on the ground, but I felt these were the most impressive."

"If there ever was a time I wish the computer was wrong, it was looking at that monster," the Captain said. "If anyone had any doubt or hesitation about obeying my rule of not wondering off to investigate things on their own without letting anyone know, this picture should really drive that point home."

"It wouldn't even fit through the MRI," Dana exclaimed.

That relieved the tension somewhat as Rashad half remarked under his breath, "If you want a specimen of that, you'll have to get it yourself."

As Sophia served the melon slices, she noted that this was the last batch, and that she could use some more of those melons.

"You should have asked before we saw those photos," Rashad replied. "I don't need melons that bad if I have to get close to that thing."

As they were finishing their desert, the Captain announced that he'd like to meet with Angelina and Doc in his quarters when everyone was done.

With that, everyone started picking up their dishes and taking them to the kitchen. A few more came back to look at the pictures again while they talked about their day.

Meanwhile, the Captain, Doc, and Angelina went to his quarters. When they got there, the Captain said, "I don't know about you two, but this is almost getting beyond my control. We can't seem to have one day without something dramatic happening." With that said, he brought out one of the things Sophia found in Mr. Rodriguez's special container. "I have been saving this bottle of Tequila for a special occasion. This may not be a special occasion, but I am making an exception. Do you care to join me?"

"Here, here," Doc replied.

"Oh yes, please," Angelina said. "I know you have been doing a lot with these kids, but working with them on the ship's computers and the equipment—they make me feel as though my Magna Cum Laude from Harvard and graduating at the top of my class from the Air Force Academy was nothing. Tani, Bruce, and Emir do things with that computer that I didn't even know it could do. And, what's worse, they just take it for granted!"

"Well," Doc said, "after I finished testing everyone today, I can confirm that everyone has the same brain activity in the region we have been talking about. Also, I found that Dana and Gerard have this other place on the other side of their brains showing activity I've never seen before. I think it has something to do with that twin telepathy they have with each other. Natasha shows a high level in that same area; but has an unusual amount of brain activity on the other side as well. Loren's is the same, but not quite as strong as Natasha's. And, Drago's brain scan reminds me of pictures I saw of Einstein's brain, which they still have at the Smithsonian. In conclusion, I'd have to agree with you. These kids go way beyond what I'm use to looking at."

As the Captain poured them all a good four fingers in the glasses that he had gotten from the kitchen for just such an occasion, he remarked. "You should have to deal with them all day every day. I just hope we can keep it together long enough to see them grow up." Then, raising his glass, he said, "Salud."

"What do you think about that deal with Loren today?" he asked after they had sat there for a few moments lost in their private thoughts.

"I got to hear the story first hand—right after you had the little 'chat' with her in your office," Angelina said.

"I only got bits and pieces of it from the others," Doc commented. "About the only thing I can add is—amazing."

"It's just one more mystery on this planet," the Captain said then continued with, "I'm really starting to believe that the planet is running things and just watching to see what we do next."

"Aria, Queen of the Tashi and protector of the sky. Suddenly everyone talks to the animals," the Captain concluded as he shook his head and finished his drink.

Chapter Thirty One

The next morning after breakfast, the Captain gathered everyone. "All right, as we discussed, Bruce and Matzo will be running the drone. They'll send it out first. When they locate the herd, Drago and his group will move out to intercept it."

"We'll notify Choi and Natasha, when to drop off and wait at the half way point." Drago stated.

The Captain nodded his head in the affirmative then continued. "Bruce, you and Matzo look for an opportunity to separate one of the beasts from the herd. When you do, notify Drago where to set up the ambush. I only want two of you to shoot. The rest will stay behind. I don't want anyone being hit in a cross fire. I suggest one aim for the head, with the other aiming for the heart. When the beast goes down, the four of you will immediately go on guard surrounding Sophia and Loren as they butcher it. As soon as you get the meat in the sacks, you sling back, picking up Natasha and Choi along the way."

Having finished laying out his plan, the Captain asked, "Does everyone understand?"

"Yes sir," they replied.

"Okay, I want everyone else on the screens watching this. You are to have your equipment ready, in case we need to go out and rescue anyone. This includes you, Doc. Have your medical equipment ready," the Captain directed.

"All right Bruce, let's launch the drone."

Bruce and Matzo set up and launched the drone. All eyes were on the screens as they went searching for the herd. Thirty minutes later, they picked up the edge of the herd on their screen. Turning the drone slightly, they flew over the herd following in the same direction.

"The herd is about an hour out by sling time," Matzo reported. "I'll put the drone on high altitude circling until you get close. Set your GPS on this location."

Doing that, Drago's team got their equipment together.

"Okay, follow me," Drago said starting to sling around with Molly. The rest followed in somewhat of a line. Sophia and Loren had a little trouble getting started, but finally got into the swing of it with everyone else.

After what seemed like two hours, their arms were getting tired from slinging and several had bumps and bruises from falling upon landing. They were all grateful when they heard Matzo direct them to stop where they were over their head phones.

His voice came through loud and clear saying, "You're about a mile away on the north side of the herd. That's lucky, because they are turning away from your direction. Stay put and Bruce will buzz the herd trying to separate one."

Bruce dropped the drone down to about fifty feet and began to buzz the side of the herd. At first, they didn't seem disturbed; but then, suddenly they were running.

"Holy Smoke!" Bruce exclaimed. "They can really move! Drago, your team is going to have to move to keep up. I separated one group of about ten from the rest of the herd. I'll try to break one off from the smaller group, but you're going to need to move more to the East." Drago's team started to move in the direction that Bruce directed.

Suddenly, they heard Matzo's voice coming through their ear bugs excitedly saying, "There's one breaking from that group to the right. It's headed right towards Drago's group!"

Next, everything happened so fast that Matzo and the people watching the screens couldn't warn them about it. Drago and Molly had just landed. Rashad had landed and was in the process of slinging Maggy around. When she landed, the beast was right in front of her—not twenty feet away coming at a dead run.

They all gasped as they watched Maggy jump high in the air firing her laser at the beast, as she soared over its head. Drago was simultaneously firing his stun gun at the animal hoping to stop it. When she landed behind the beast, Rashad immediately pulled her cable slinging her back toward him. Maggy landed back beside Rashad and turned to face the animal that had dropped to the ground.

"Drago, what do we do now?" Rashad asked. "How do we know if it's dead?"

"Shoot it in the head one more time," Drago said. "Then we will approach slowly with our guns ready to fire again if need be." Rashad did as Drago had asked, but as they began to get closer, they could see that there was no need... Maggy's shot had just about cut the animal in two.

"I believe its dead," Rashad said. With that, the others came forward.

"It looks like you have done half our work for us," Sophia said to Maggy. "You cut it from stem to stern."

"Post your guards," the Captain's voice ordered through their headsets.

Immediately, the four took up places around Sophia and Loren as they went to work. They had finished the butchering and were putting the last of the meat in the sacks when Matzo's voice came through in a quietly warning tone.

"Drago you have a couple of those wolverine type animals moving in on your right."

"Rashad, Maggy, check out the right hand side," Drago commanded.

As Rashad and Maggy moved over beside Molly and Drago, they were continuing to look about, trying to see the animals.

Matzo said, "They're about fifty feet in front of you now."

"Okay," Drago said, "let's just spray the grass with our stun guns and hope we get them; otherwise, they'll be too fast for us."

They started spraying at movement in the grass in front of them from left to right.

"Got one," Matzo said; as he instructed them to shoot more to their left.

Doing so, Drago and Molly concentrated their fire.

"Got the other one," Matzo said.

"Good," Drago said, "hurry up packing the meat. We need to get out of here before their relatives show up."

"We're sacking the last," Loren said.

"Start hooking your sacks up, and let's go."

The sacks were heavier then they had thought they would be. Their sling around distance going back was much shorter than going out. It was a relief when they made it to where Natasha and Choi were waiting.

Redistributing the weight by splitting up the sacks between the partners, they started making better time.

CHAPTER THIRTY TWO

WHEN THEY FINALLY GOT back to the ship, the six of them fell to the ground exhausted.

"I don't think my heart can take many more adventures like that," the Captain said.

"Yours!" Maggy exclaimed. "How would you like to hit the ground, and face twelve hundred pounds of animal charging down on you?"

"What you did was amazing!" Angelina said hugging Maggy.

"Amazing, my butt! That was pure fear! I just jumped as hard as I could and remembered to shoot at it as it went by. My only thought was to get out of its way before being run down!"

"You would never have guessed it watching the screen," Dana said with new found respect in her voice. "It looked like you knew exactly what you were doing."

"Tomorrow, I'll take credit for it being part of the plan; today, I am still shaking," Maggy responded grinning.

"Well, let's see what you brought back," the Captain said.

Opening the sacks, they saw they had about 800 pounds of meat.

"Good job," the Captain said. "Dana, please take a sample back for testing. Everybody else will need to help Sophia take the rest of it and put it in the make-shift freezer she made from the cryogenic chambers."

"Not all of it," Rashad corrected. "I'm looking for barbeque ribs tonight!"

"To do that properly, we need to grill them," Sophia said. "The microwaves won't make good ribs. Besides, the microwaves are not big enough for a rack of ribs."

"No problem," Rashad said. "Molly, Choi, and Matzo are our building engineers. You got the rest of the day to make a fire pit and grill."

The three of them got together and started talking, then they went into the ship to find something that could be used to build a grill.

"The one thing we haven't done yet is build a fire on this planet. How do we know the small branches we have will burn?" Drago asked. "Plus, I don't think we have enough for a fire."

That started another discussion with the outcome being that Rashad and Maggy would go back to the tree line and look for branches and dead tree limbs.

"Make sure you wash out those sacks when you're done," Doc directed. "We may have to use them again and I don't want any sickness caused by bacteria from blood left in those sacks."

After taking the meat inside, part of the group took the sacks around to the back of the ship to wash and clean them out

When Rashad and Maggy got to the tree line, they found very few branches. Looking around, they couldn't find any dead tree limbs either.

"This doesn't look good," Rashad said.

Maggy nodded her agreement and said, "We could use some of the brush but it would take an awful lot of it to keep a fire going."

"Let's see if the branches we found will burn," Rashad suggested. "I know we can cut them with the lasers, but they don't seem to catch on fire when we do." He then laid one of the branches on the ground and adjusted his laser setting on the controls to low. After directing his laser beam on the branch for a few seconds, all he had managed to do was melt some of the grass around it.

"Even the grass won't burn," Maggy said. "Put a piece over against those stones and try with a higher setting."

Rashad took two of the branches and laid them on top of the stones. Stepping back, he turned up the laser and kept moving the beam up and down the branches trying to start a fire.

"It's not working," Maggy said disappointed. Walking over, she bent down to pick up the branches. "Yipes! These are hot!" Kicking one away with her foot, she bent back down to touch it after a few minutes. "This branch isn't hot now," she said. Rashad walked over and bent down holding his hand above the branch on the rocks.

"Wow, this is really hot." He too kicked the branch off and when he touched it, it was cold. "What the heck?" he said perplexed.

Maggy, meanwhile had gone over to the rocks and held her hand above them. "Rashad it's the rocks, they are still extremely hot."

Rashad went over and held his hand above the rocks. "You're right. The rocks are really hot."

They stepped back and sat down.

"Let's think this out," Maggy said. "If the rocks can generate that kind of heat, they can cook the ribs. Let's see how long it takes before they cool down."

"While we are waiting, I can go look for another bird to capture."

"No," Maggy disagreed. "Help me start gathering rocks to take back while were waiting for these to cool."

They filled up both their back packs with rocks, the largest being about the size of a softball. When they went back to check on the heated rocks, they found they were still hot.

"What do we do now?" Maggy asked. "Do we wait until they cool, or do we go back?"

Looking around, Rashad said, "The grass around them has melted away about six inches; other than that, it doesn't seem to be spreading."

"I know, but we can't leave a fire behind. Let's dump our canteen water on it." She then proceeded to pour their water on it. Immediately, there was a hissing sound and steam arose from the rocks.

Jumping back, Rashad said, "We could make a great sauna with these."

Pouring the rest of their water on the rocks, Maggy held her hand just above, then slowly lowering her hand, she said, "they have cooled down quite a lot, to the point where they are just barely warm now. I think it's safe for us to head back now. Without the lasers to heat them up again, I don't think they will start any fires."

Shouldering their backpacks, they headed back to the ship. Upon arriving, they noticed that Molly, Choi, and Matzo were building a grill out of something.

"What are you doing guys?" Rashad inquired.

"At first, we had a hard time finding something to make a grill out of," Matzo explained. "We couldn't use the crates because they would burn and the containers we use for water and stuff are all made out of plastic. While we were looking around, trying to find something that would work, Molly noticed that air grill up there would make a great grill top."

"When we started taking it down, Choi noticed that the duct work for the grill was made from stainless steel. After further investigation, we realized that the first section of duct was only about four feet long. We checked with Angelina and she said it wouldn't cause a problem with the air venting system so we took it apart and brought the grill cover out here to make the grill out of. Our problem is how to cut it up, then fasten it together."

"I can show you how to cut it with the laser," Rashad stated. "Also, you can weld the pieces together on a lower setting."

"Did you find any fire wood?" Molly asked.

"No," Rashad answered shaking his head. "But we may have found something better."

"What's that?" Choi asked.

"Hot rocks," Maggy said dumping her backpack out on the ground. "When Rashad and I first tried to get the branches to catch fire, we only succeeded in melting the grass. So we put the branches on some rocks lying nearby. We still couldn't get the branches to catch fire but we noticed the rocks got hot—really hot. At that point, we filled our backpacks with these. Then it was just a matter of pouring the water from canteens on the heated rocks and waiting long enough for them to cool down before we came back."

"I wonder if it will work for grilling?" Matzo asked.

"Trust me;" Rashad told him. "They get hot enough. I just don't know how we can control the heat."

"Let's finish putting the grill together, then we can go check with our Master Chef," Molly said. "If any one knows how, it will be Sophia."

When they got to the kitchen, they saw Sophia chopping away at the meat with what looked like a small wood axe. Seeing them walk in, Sophia sat the axe aside and wiped her brow.

"Whew! I found this in one of the equipment crates that was supposed to go to the other planet and thought it would make a good meat cleaver."

"You know," Rashad said, "there are some hand held lasers in the equipment locker that might make cutting easier, I'll go get you one."

"We came in to ask you to check out the grill and to find out if you can cook over hot stones?" Maggy asked.

"Heavens yes, I've put pigs in the ground with hot coals and rocks. I've even cooked fish over hot rocks."

"Then you need to check out our new grill." Maggy said.

When Sophia got outside, she made a big deal of looking over the grill. She shook it to see how steady it was as she walked around it checking out their work.

"I think this is pretty good," she said. "But you need to add a shelf for the rocks and make some kind of opening to put them in." As Molly and Choi went back to work on the grill, Sophia asked, "Where are the rocks?"

Maggy showed her the rocks they had brought back.

"Take one and heat it up for me," Sophia directed.

Maggy took one the size of her fist and set it down on a bare spot on the ground. She then took her laser gun and held her beam on the rock for about a minute before stopping.

Sophia reached her hand down close to the rock and said, "Wow, that's too hot to cook with—ribs have to cook slowly."

"We poured water on them to cool them down when we were in the woods," Maggy told her.

"How bout if you don't heat them as long?" Sophia asked.

"I don't know," Maggy responded. "How hot should they be?"

"It has to be hot enough to cook the meat; but not too fast, if we start cooking in the next thirty minutes or so, it will take the rest of the day to cook this much meat."

"Okay, while you get the ribs ready, we will experiment with the heating up the rocks," Rashad said.

After experimenting for a while, they found if you heated the rocks up for about a half a minute they reached what everyone guessed to be the right temperature. However, they also found out when they made them too hot, they could sprinkle water on them to reduce the temperature just as Maggy and Rashad had done back at the tree line.

Going in to get Sophia, they found her mashing tomatoes from the garden into a bowl.

"Choi, would you mind getting me that hot sauce and the powered mustard from the boxes we opened? It'd also be a big help if one of you would go get me some honey comb from the bee hives in the lab."

"What are you doing?" Molly asked.

"I'm trying to make a sauce to put on the ribs," she explained. "Only, I just don't have what I'm used to, so I am experimenting."

Choi returned with the hot sauce and the powered mustard and let Sophia know that Rashad was getting the honey.

Sophia started adding some of the hot sauce to the tomato paste along with the dry mustard then added some water and started mixing it up.

"I wish I had some brown sugar," she said wistfully.

When Rashad came back with the honey, he said, "boy that smells good, can I try some?"

"A volunteer taster was just what I was looking for." Sophia said dipping a spoon into the sauce and handing it to Rashad who grabbed it eagerly and put it into his mouth. Suddenly, beads of sweat broke out on his forehead as he started slapping his chest and yelling for water.

"Still too hot," Sophia noted with a clinical tone of voice as Rashad gulped water trying to cool his mouth. "Guess I need to add some more honey and water." She then winked at the others as she watched Rashad with a grin on her face.

"Molly, would you go get Dana? I need to ask her about some of the plants we've collected so far and what flavor they might add to the sauce."

When Molly came back, she had some leaves Dana had given her.

"She said to try these. Dana told me that this one is a lot like cilantro and the other one is similar to basil."

"Okay," Sophia said. "Now, the rest of you get out of my kitchen. I have to stop what I'm doing and make lunch. Naomi, will you help me make the salad for lunch?"

While lunch was good, everyone was looking forward to the ribs. They talked about the day's events and then went back to their work. Naomi finished cleaning the kitchen while Sophia prepared the sauce and got the ribs ready for the grill.

As Sophia headed outside with the platter of ribs, she yelled over to Maggy and Rashad who were still experimenting with heating the rocks. "Okay, who's going to watch the fire while Naomi and I prepare the side dishes?"

"I will," Maggy volunteered. "When do we start?"

"Right now," Sophia answered. "If we do it right, everything should be ready right about dinner time."

Maggy heated up the rocks as Sophia laid out the ribs on the grill top.

"That sizzle tells me it's a little too hot," Sophia said. Maggy then sprinkled some water on the rocks until Sophia thought it was the right temperature.

Setting the rest of the ribs on the grill, Sophia started putting the sauce on them. When she turned them over to put the sauce on the other side, some of the sauce dripped off onto the rocks. Suddenly, there was a terrific aroma in the air, and everyone started coming out of the ship asking what it was that they were smelling.

Sophia chased them all away while letting them know that dinner would not be ready for another six or seven hours.

The Captain, who had been reviewing the information that Emir had brought him, suddenly sat up. "What's that I smell?" he asked as he headed for the outside. Walking down the ramp, he went over to where Maggy and Sophia were standing. "The smells are killing me," he said.

"Well, you have got a few more hours to die before you can eat," Sophia replied. With that, the Captain turned and walked back into the ship grumbling to him self.

Throughout the rest of the day, people were constantly coming out to see how the cooking was going. This was the first meal they had cooked outside and the first beef like meal they had had since they had been on the planet.

The Captain, back in his quarters was going over Emir's report when he came upon a note Emir had jotted to one side that indicated his findings could be plus or minus thirty days. This could be a major change in their plans, the Captain thought. They would have to speed up finding a place to weather out the storms described by Emir. He was still going over the reports and trying to develop a plan, when hours later he heard Naomi come through the ship shouting.

"Come and get it! The food has been set up outside."

The Captain got up and walked into the bay to see everyone but Emir heading outside.

"We have a spot set up for you at the top of the ramp," Naomi told Emir. "I'll bring you the food myself."

When the Captain got outside, he saw that someone had spread the tarps over the ground and Sophia had set up a buffet. Everyone was lined up getting their food then going over and sitting on the tarps like a picnic. God Bless Sophia, thought the Captain, she is the glue that keeps us all together.

Getting in line, Sophia put some ribs on his plate. Next, he saw that there was salad and beans and at the end of the line and there was more of Sophia's sauce for putting on the ribs.

Sitting down with the others, he could hardly wait and started eating the ribs right away. "These are really good," he said.

"Good? These are great!" Rashad said, putting more sauce on his ribs.

Once again, it was completely silent as everyone dug into their dinner. My idea about discussing business over meals seems to have not completely succeeded thought the Captain as he continued to eat his ribs.

"There's enough for seconds tonight," Sophia announced, "so help yourselves." With that, three or four promptly got up and went back for more.

Upon everyone finishing, Doc remarked that tonight he would be going to bed with an over full stomach.

"I'm not going to worry about storms or abnormal brain activity, or anything. I am just going to sleep like a baby."

Several agreed with him.

"Not till we clean up," Sophia said. "This stuff has to get back in the ship's galley and get cleaned up."

"We also need to put out more containers, for the water," Doc said.

With groans, the group got up and started picking up and cleaning up. Maggy and Rashad went with Doc to put out the containers. Even Emir went to bed early that night.

Maggy was the last, making sure the stones were cool before she went to bed. Then walking up the ramp, half a sleep, she headed for her bunk.

CHAPTER THIRTY THREE

THE NEXT MORNING WHEN everyone got to the bay, the Captain announced that before they ate, they needed to discuss the upcoming storms. "Emir's information suggests that we may not have the time we thought we had to make ready for the storms. As you all know, there is nothing the other way across the plains. I think we are going to have to head into the tree line or rain forest for safety."

"Why not go to the caves?" Drago asked.

"Based upon our discoveries, I haven't been able to come up with a way to get us there safely before the storms start occurring; however, I am open to suggestions."

"I know a way," Drago replied confidently.

"Go ahead," the Captain said, "I'm all ears."

"We take the ship and fly there," Drago replied. "I'm sure we have enough fuel. Not only did you tell us that we arrived here earlier than at the planet we were supposed to land on, but we should have had enough fuel to maneuver on the planet once we got there."

The Captain put his hands over his face and put his head down. "I'm no longer qualified to lead this group," he said in exasperation. "I never even thought about using the ship and I am the pilot."

"Sometimes, you can't see the forest for all the trees," Doc said. "Besides, you've have had a lot on your mind to think about since we landed. I think we can forgive this little lapse."

The others around the table also supported the Captain. He was feeling a little better, if only because they could now have a plan.

Just then, Sophia came in and said; "I don't want my food getting cold. We have fresh eggs and I cooked up some of those critters Zena and Butkis brought in, that taste mighty like bacon. I suggest we eat now and worry later." With that, she started serving the food.

After breakfast, the Captain gathered Doc, Angelina, Drago, and Rashad to begin discussing the plan to fly to the mountains.

While they were talking, Loren came up and said, "Captain, if it's all right with you, I'll take Natasha and go see Tashi."

"All right," the Captain replied, "but I want you in full gear and I want someone on the screens watching you."

"I can do that," Tani volunteered. "I'll be on the screens anyway."

"Fine," the Captain replied.

Getting back to his discussions with the others, the Captain asked, "What do you feel our major obstacles will be in making this move?"

"Well, there is one thing for sure," Doc replied, "we have unpacked a lot of equipment that took up a lot less space than before."

"We will also take up more room when we harvest the garden," Angelina stated.

"Plus, the drone will no longer fit unless we dismantle it," Rashad chimed in.

"We also have the birds and the cubs," Drago said.

"And the fresh water containers," Doc added.

"Okay, let's start with Choi engineering the space we have and figuring out what will fit and how."

"Doc, can you get with Sophia and Naomi after we finish our discussion and see how much food we will have from the garden harvest? I think I also want to see Bruce and Matzo to discuss the drone. Let's get them in here too," the Captain said to no one in particular.

Rashad volunteered, "I'll go get them."

When they returned, the Captain asked about breaking the drone down.

"I don't think that is that feasible," Matzo stated. "While it can be done, we risk damaging parts that we can't replace. Besides Captain, I feel we should fly to the mountains again and try to get more detailed video for analysis."

"If we fly at a high altitude at full speed, we should be able to get closer," Bruce stated. "We also need to get a better look at the landing area for the ship."

"Good point," the Captain replied. "Go ahead and set it up. Fly out there today so we can get a better idea of what were facing." With that, Bruce and Matzo left to get the drone ready.

"The rest of us need to start looking everything over and checking with the others to see what we might have missed," the Captain stated getting up and heading towards where Dana and Gerard were working.

During the time the Captain had been having his discussion, Loren and Natasha had made it to the tree line. Aria, was sitting on her usual branch preening her feathers as Loren and Natasha walked up and set down beneath the tree.

"Good morning," Loren said. "I have brought a friend, her name is Natasha."

"I see she can also hear me," Aria sent back.

"Yes," Natasha replied respectfully.

"Tell me more about your flock. I'm unfamiliar with your kind," Aria requested.

To any casual observer, it looked like the small group of three; the one great bird and the two girls were just sitting there, looking at each other. Tani had checked in on them a couple of times, but as far as she could tell, there was no movement.

Meanwhile, Bruce and Matzo had gone through their standard system check then took the drone up heading toward the mountains. Their plan was to fly at a high altitude and top speed, not using any of the equipment so that they could extend the life of the batteries for as long as possible.

The drone had been in the air for about two hours when Matzo remarked that they were about an hour out. "I'm starting all the cameras on full zoom."

"I'm fighting a little head wind," Bruce stated.

"We're getting great feed back," Matzo said, "I'm transmitting the video directly to the ships computer."

Over the next half hour, they kept the drone high, and then Bruce brought it down to lower altitude, putting it on level with the largest cave.

"Bring it around when you get closer so we can see the size of the plateau," Matzo said. As Bruce got within 100 yards of the mountain, he swung the drone around, flying parallel with the plateau.

"It's large enough to hold the ship," Matzo commented. "The computer is indicating that the plateau is about a quarter mile wide by about a mile long, but it curves around the side of the mountain so it may go farther," Matzo observed while still keeping his eyes on the computer screen. "Can you bring it back around and fly as close as you can to give us a better shot of those caves?"

As Bruce was maneuvering the controls trying to bring the drone in closer to get a better look at the caves, both he and Matzo failed to pay attention to the flying time.

When Matzo remembered to check; he said, "Bruce we have a problem. We don't have enough flying time left on the batteries to bring the drone all the way back."

"How far can we get?" Bruce asked.

"According to the computer we might be able to make it across the rain forest." Matzo replied with concern in his voice.

"What should we do?" Bruce asked.

"I'm thinking maybe we should land it and leave it on the plateau," Matzo stated.

"That would solve the problem of transporting it back there later," Bruce replied. "Call into the Captain and inform him of our decision."

"Right," Matzo said.

When Matzo called in, Tani who was still monitoring the exterior computer screens answered.

"I'll get the Captain on."

When the Captain got on the headset, Matzo explained the problem and, what they were going do.

"I wanted that video," the Captain said, "but I don't want to lose the drone in the rain forest."

"I set up the drone to live feed all the info from the cameras directly into the ships computer," Matzo replied. "We won't lose anything."

"Okay," the Captain said, "do your best and set it down easy."

Matzo got back to Bruce, "we got the go ahead and because we're not going to have to fly the drone back, we have about forty-five minutes to select a landing spot."

"I'd like to try and land in front of that big cave," Bruce said. "That way, maybe we can maneuver it into the cave for protection."

"Good idea," Matzo agreed.

Ten minutes later, Bruce informed Matzo that he was going to try and land. Matzo watched his computer screen with anxious anticipation as Bruce brought the drone around and gently set it down then taxied up to the front of the large cave.

"I have lots of room on both sides, shall I take it in?" Bruce asked Matzo.

"Give it a shot," Matzo replied.

Bruce slowly guided the drone into the cave, going in just past the tail before he shut it down.

"I'm going to run the cameras on infrared for a minute or two to see if we can pick up any thing inside the cave."

"Affirmative," Bruce responded as he nodded in agreement.

When they finished, both Matzo and Bruce headed back up the ramp and into the ship.

"It's done." Bruce reported. "We managed to get the drone just inside the cave."

"We are now going to get with Angelina and have her pull up the video," Matzo said.

"Have her put it up on the main screen so we can all see it," the Captain instructed.

When the video came up, they were joined by some of the others, including Emir. As the zoom shot taken directly looking at the cave came up, the Captain asked Emir if it was the cave he had seen in his vision.

"No it's not," Emir said shaking his head. "Something tells me it's further around to the right and not that close."

"The cave almost looks big enough to hold our ship," the Captain stated as he continued watching.

"According to the computer," Angelina said while running a comparison analysis, "if you can head it in, you could get about 15% of it into the cave."

"Okay then, ignore that plan," the Captain stated. "Pull up what information you have about the cave itself; please Angelina," the Captain requested.

"The infrareds that Matzo got show the cave to be fairly large and deep; however, it also shows a lot of minerals in the cave. The analysis indicates that part of the cave may have been volcanic at one time–so it is definitely a natural cave."

"Okay, show me the landing area on the plateau," the Captain requested.

"There's plenty of room for the ship," Angelina reported. "It's about a quarter mile wide and plenty long enough."

"How high is the plateau?" the Captain asked.

"About three hundred feet above the plain," Matzo replied.

"Okay," the Captain said making his decision, "Bruce, you and Matzo can help Choi figure out what kind of space we have to use for our trip."

Then he got up and headed to the storage bay. As he walked by Tani, he paused long enough to inquire about Loren and Natasha.

"So far they haven't moved a muscle but they seem to be having a deep, nonverbal conversation with Aria." Satisfied, the Captain continued on to where Choi was working.

"How's it going Choi? Do you think we are going to have room for everything?"

"I don't think so Captain. I figured we can move all the unopened crates together and even stack some of them; however, with the equipment that we uncrated and put together, plus the water containers, we are just not going to have enough room. And, I don't have any idea what to do with the birds."

"We can always butcher them, but I'd rather not," the Captain said. "They are too valuable as a continuing food source."

"I also haven't started calculating the amount of space we'll need for the food harvested from the garden," Choi continued.

"We need to go take a look at that garden," the Captain said; then added more to himself than Choi. "I haven't looked at it lately to see how it is coming along." As he turned and headed into the kitchen with Choi following along behind, he called out, "Sophia, lets go look at your garden."

"Okay," Sophia agreed with him. "I was just getting ready to go out and collect some stuff for lunch anyway."

Walking outside and around the ship, the Captain was surprised by what he saw. The corn was six foot high, fully tasseled out and looked ready to be harvested. The small wheat patch also looked like it was ready and the tomato bushes were covered with tomatoes, as were the beans.

"You can't see the potatoes or the peanuts," Sophia said with pride, "but they're also ready to harvest."

"How much do you think we have here Sophia?" the Captain asked.

"I think when we get everything harvested we'll have about ten to twelve bushels of corn, most likely five to six bushels of beans and about a hundred pounds of potatoes. I'm not exactly sure what the take will be on the peanuts since they were started late. And, we'll have about another five or six bushels of tomatoes. However, we are going to need quite a bit of room for the wheat. I can reduce it some by grinding it down, but that is going to take time."

"We're going to have a problem," the Captain said as he tried to visualize the space it would require to store all the harvested produce.

Shaking his head, he admitted to himself, Choi and Sophia, "We just don't have enough room for everything."

"Can we make more than one trip?" Choi asked.

"No, we just don't have that much fuel," the Captain replied. "The ship was not scheduled to return after it landed. It was designed to be broken down with the parts being reused in the planet's habitat. I think we are going to have to figure what we can leave behind."

Going back into the ship, the Captain checked on Loren and Natasha again.

"They just got up;" Tani replied to the Captain's question. "It looks like they're getting ready to come back."

Everyone was heading into the main bay area getting ready for lunch. As they were sitting down, the Captain explained the space issues and problems with the lack of room. While everyone was talking, Sophia and Naomi started serving lunch. Then about mid-way into the meal, Loren and Natasha showed up.

"How did it go?" Maggy asked.

"It was amazing!" Loren replied excitedly. "Besides sharing a lot of information and us being able to understand each other, I think she likes us. Oh by the way, she did warn us—the storms will start in five weeks and we need to get off the plains."

"That falls within my estimate, Captain;" Emir stated.

"Okay, Loren, you and Natasha missed the first part of our discussion; but the truth of the matter is, we don't have enough room for everything. My first impression is that we need to leave behind some of the food, since we'll need all the equipment when we get there. We can finalize everything over the next couple of days. But first, I think we need to concentrate on harvesting our crops to and determine how much space all that produce is going to require."

After lunch, a couple of groups broke off and started organizing the different pieces of equipment. The rest helped with the clean-up then went outside with Sophia to start harvesting what they could. It would take another day to complete it.

Loren and Natasha were discussing the day they had as they helped pick the vegetables.

"I think Aria really likes me," Loren was saying. "I wanted so bad to stroke her feathers."

"I believe so too," Natasha agreed. "You didn't notice, but there came a time when the two of you were communicating and I was just a bystander."

"She is beautiful don't you think?" Loren asked.

"Yes, she is," Natasha, replied in agreement. "When she was showing us where her nest was, do you think it was the same mountains we're going to?"

"I don't know," Loren replied, "there were quite a few of her kind there and it looked like it was higher up in the mountains. Did you notice how Aria kept using the term *"she"* when discussing her world, like there was someone else in charge?"

"Yeah, I couldn't quite figure that out," Natasha replied.

"I want to go back tomorrow."

"I think we had better help around here before we take off again. There's a lot that needs to be done," Natasha advised.

The rest of the day, through lunch and past dinner they all were working on getting the ship ready. There were crates to move and tie down. They also had to secure the water containers since they felt these were the most important. Since none of the video clips taken by Bruce and Matzo when they were flying the drone had shown any water sources.

The next morning after breakfast, they went back out to complete harvesting the garden. When they had finished picking all the vegetables, Sophia suggested they leave some seeds and plants behind to reproduce voluntarily in the garden, in case they should ever return to this spot again. When they were complete, they had quite a few bushels of food. Naomi had started grinding down the wheat to help reduce the size needed to store it, but they still didn't have enough room. And, they hadn't done anything about the birds.

When they got back together at lunch, the Captain said, "Okay, let's discuss where we are and what we are going to do from here. According to Emir and Aria, we need to leave tomorrow for the mountain. That will give us a couple of weeks to prepare for the storm once we get there. Angelina, let's start with you."

"Well, Bruce, Tani, Choi, and I have been studying the ship's schematic drawings and the instructional manuals on how to dismantle the ship. We're concerned, that once on the mountain; we will have to move the equipment from the ship into the caves. As you know, the ship's power is supplied by solar panels. These panels were designed to be removed and set up independently of the ship."

"Meaning we will have to install the panels outside on the mountain itself," Choi added.

"We are also concerned that the ship will not make it through the storm—since it will be exposed on the plateau," Angelina continued. "This means that we will not only have to find a place to set the panels that is protected from the storm; but we will also have to remove the cabling from the ship and run it into the caves somewhere in order to supply the power. Not knowing the cave's make-up, the sooner we get there and get started the better off we will be. Additionally, we have to unload and move all the equipment inside the caves. I will also want to install some recording equipment at this site to determine the strength of the storm; and I will bury a responder here that continues to put out a beacon signal in case anyone ever finds a way here to look for us."

"That gives us a tremendous amount of work to accomplish after we get there," the Captain stated. "What else needs to be done before we leave?"

"Well sir," Matzo replied, "we don't have enough room for all of the harvested food. And, I still haven't figured out what to do with the birds."

"I hate leaving the birds behind," the Captain stated, "as they are a continuing source of food."

"I have an idea," Drago said. "We can put them in the cryogenic chambers since we won't be using them to just fly up to the mountain."

"That might work," Matzo agreed.

"So, we still have all that fresh produce that we haven't been able to find a storage spot for… I hate having to leave anything behind because we don't know what will be available when we get to the mountain," the Captain stated. "It's too bad we can't tie the sacks of food onto the ship and drag them behind us."

"If we had time, we could shuck the corn, it would help," Sophia said. "but we just don't have enough time."

While she was making this statement, Loren was excitedly talking to Natasha.

"What's your idea?" the Captain asked Loren.

"I'd rather not say just yet, Captain. But I request permission for Natasha and I to go out again to talk to Aria."

"Fine," the Captain responded. "Just make sure you're back by dinner time as we will be preparing to leave first thing in the morning, food or no food." With that, Loren jumped up, grabbed Natasha's hand, and hurried out of the ship.

"What are you going to do?" Natasha asked.

"Wait and see," Loren said. "I need to talk to Aria first."

When they got to the tree line, there was no sign of Aria.

"What do we do now?" Natasha asked.

"I'm going to try and call to her," Loren said. Closing her eyes and concentrating, Loren formed the image of Aria in her mind and mentally called out to her. A few minutes went by where nothing happened. Then, just as Natasha was ready to give up, Aria soared into view and landed on the limb just above them.

"You called out to me?" Aria asked of Loren.

"Yes," Loren replied. "I need your help."

"Tell me," Aria said.

While Loren sat there sending her thoughts to Aria, Natasha could do nothing but wait since she was not picking up any of the conversation.

Suddenly, another hawk flew in and landed on the tree limb next to Aria.

"This is my sister Shia," Aria introduced her sister to the girls. "These are the little ones I told you about."

"They can hear us," Shia stated, "and I can hear their thoughts as well."

Once again, Natasha was left out of the discussion. After about forty-five minutes, Loren stood up as Aria and Shia flew away.

"Okay," Natasha said. "Tell me what that was all about."

"Wait till we get back to the ship," Loren said, "I need to figure out a couple of things before we tell the Captain and the others my plan."

"Why can't you tell me now?" Natasha demanded.

"Please wait," was all Loren would say and would not talk about it any more.

When they got back to the ship, Loren went immediately over to where Choi, Matzo, and Molly were working. After a few minutes of discussion, the three of them headed off to do something.

By this time, Natasha was visibly upset by being left out of the conversation. She was still standing there with her arms folded across her chest looking very perturbed when the Captain walked up to her with a puzzled look on his face.

"What's going on Natasha?"

"I don't know Captain." she retorted. "Loren won't discuss it with me."

"What did Aria say?" the Captain asked.

"I don't know that either," Natasha replied, "I was left out of that discussion too."

Mystified, the Captain went up to Loren and said, "Okay, what's going on?"

"If you'll just give me a little more time to see what Choi and the others find, I'll let you know," Loren replied heading off in the direction of the others.

Finally, after everyone else had sat down to dinner, Loren, Molly, Choi, and Matzo returned. Smiling among themselves, they sat down at the table.

"Okay, before any food is served, I want to know what's going on," the Captain stated in a stern voice.

"We'll let Loren tell you," Choi said. "It was her idea."

"Well," Loren stated, "when you mentioned earlier about tying the sacks to the ship and dragging them in the air behind us, I thought why not get Aria to fly them to the mountain for us? She's big enough to carry the weight if it is distributed correctly. That's why I wanted to go back to see her—to ask her if she would help.

"At first she didn't understand what I was trying to ask her. When she finally did understand, she wanted to know why she should grant my request."

"What did you answer?" interrupted Natasha.

"I told her that her flock and mine were meant to be together."

"What did she say to that?" the Captain asked.

She was quite for a moment and then said, "*She* finds this to be acceptable."

"Who did she mean by '*she*'?" the Captain asked. "It sounds as if it means someone other then herself."

"I believe so," Loren replied, "Natasha and I noticed it when Aria used it before in our talks."

"So what is the idea?" the Captain asked impatiently.

"Well, next she called in her sister Shia, to discuss it with her."

"Her sister, Shia?" the Captain exclaimed. "I'll never get this figured out. Just tell me the plan, please Loren," the Captain demanded.

"Okay. When we got back, I asked Choi to see if there was enough material left over from the tarps to make a harness. Then we could attach the sacks to Aria and her sister so that they could fly the food up to the mountain between them. Choi and Molly came back and said there was enough material and are designing them so that Aria and Shia can carry the food to the mountains for us." Loren concluded with, "Aria said that she and her sister Shia will be here in the morning."

"They're coming here?" the group all asked in surprise.

"Yes," Loren replied. "We'll work on the design tonight, but we won't know if it will work until we try to fit it on them in the morning."

The group sat there in stunned amazement. Just then, Sophia came in with Naomi, Dana, and Gerard loaded down with food.

"I figured we may as well carry as much food inside as leave it behind," Sophia said "Tonight we have grilled bird, corn on the cob, mashed potatoes, fresh bread, and a salad."

The Captain couldn't help thinking, "the condemned man ate a hardy meal" as he helped pass the plates around.

CHAPTER THIRTY FOUR

THE NEXT MORNING AFTER a light breakfast, everyone still being full from last night's dinner, they started preparing to take off. Dana, Gerard, Sophia, and Naomi were tying down the food stuffs. Then they went outside and stunned the birds one at a time, brought them back inside and placed them in the unused cryogenic chambers.

Bruce, Tani, Matzo, and Emir were going over how they were going to take everything apart when they got to the mountain. Meanwhile, the Captain, Angelina, and Doc were preparing the ship for flight.

Outside, Choi, Molly, Natasha, and Loren were waiting for Aria and her sister Shia. They had decided to make two harnesses for the birds so they could carry the sacks between them and had prepared the sacks as best they could. Molly had made slings to go around them out of some of the straps from the ship. Choi had taken and removed some of the seat harnesses to make them adjustable.

Suddenly, Loren shouted, "Here they come!" Looking up, they could see the two birds flying toward them. "Go tell the others; but remind them to stay in the ship as we don't want to scare them."

The two birds landed on the ground in front of Loren.

"Thank you for coming," Loren said to them.

"Where is the rest of your flock?" Aria asked.

"I had them wait inside since I did not want to frighten you with a lot of people," Loren replied.

"Bring them out," sent Aria with a chuckle. "We are not afraid."

Natasha called to the others and explained what Aria had said. They started coming out one at a time. As they headed down the ramp, Loren introduced each of them and told the birds a little about them.

Both Molly and Choi bowed when introduced, and to their surprise,

Aria and Shia bowed back. When they got to Doc and Loren explained what he did, Aria asked for more information not understanding what Loren had said.

Finally, Loren explained, "If you were to break a wing, he could make it well again." Aria looked at Doc closer.

"Interesting," she sent back to Loren.

Last out was the Captain. When Loren introduced him to Aria and Shia, Shia sent the puzzled thought, "but he is male."

Aria followed up with, "Our males do not lead; their minds seem to be limited in their thoughts."

Loren told them that among human flocks, both male and female lead.

"Interesting," Aria replied as she looked up to see Emir standing at the top of the ramp. After studying him for a minute, Aria bowed her head toward Emir.

"Greetings Communicator, *She* said you were among this flock."

"Greetings Aria, Leader of the Tashi," Emir replied formally.

"Now what the devil does that mean?" the Captain asked out loud.

"You will learn in time," Aria replied, "when *She* is ready for you to learn".

The Captain looked up in shock for Aria had spoken directly to his mind. He stepped back and bowed. "If you'll excuse me Aria, I must prepare my ship for the flight."

Aria bowed in reply.

Everyone went back to their duties talking among themselves about meeting the Tashi.

Loren, along with Molly, Choi, and Natasha started to spread out the harnesses as Loren explained to Aria and Shia how they worked.

"Come over and put the harness on them," Loren directed Molly and Choi.

They approached very slowly and looked at Aria and Shia to see of it was all right.

"Go ahead," Loren said. "They understand."

As Choi approached Aria, she lowered her head to make it easier to fit the harness. Putting it over her neck and running it underneath her breast, he hooked it to the straps that went to the sacks. After Molly had done the same with Shia, they had the birds move father apart to give their wings room, making a sling like carrier between the two birds.

"I've adjusted it so the sacks hang about ten feet below their bodies," Choi said, "to give them as much freedom as we can."

"How much weight do you think they can carry?" Molly questioned Loren.

"I don't know, I was going to ask Aria if they wanted to try them first before we put the food in the sacks."

Aria sent back the thought that it wasn't necessary. "I will tell you when we think there is enough."

So they began putting the vegetable containers in the sacks. After about half of the gathered produce had been placed in the sack, Aria said, "I believe that's enough for the first trip. We can come back for the rest. Okay, Loren, climb in."

"What?" Loren exclaimed. "You want me to fly with the sacks?"

"Who do you think is going to empty them when we get there?" Aria pointedly asked as she looked at Loren.

"I hadn't thought about that," Loren replied nervously.

"Then climb in," Aria directed. "Let's be off."

Hesitantly, Loren climbed into the sack. Without any further notice, Aria and Sha took off together throwing Loren down in the sack. With the sling hung between the two birds, Loren was able to stand up by holding on to the straps and peek out. They were about 100 feet in the air.

"Oh, this is trilling," Loren, said to Aria. "It's just like flying."

"It is flying," Aria responded; pleased that Loren was enjoying the experience.

They were at the mountain and landing in front of the cave much sooner than Loren expected. The landing was a little bit bumpy, as the sacks hit the ground with a thump when the birds landed.

"We will have to work on that," Aria sent to Loren as she was getting out of the sacks. Loren unfastened one side of the harness and began to drag the containers of food out. When she was done, she refastened the straps and informed Aria.

"Okay, get back in," Aria said. "If we try to fly with the empty sack between us, it will just get caught up in the wind and drag on us." Without hesitation Loren climbed back into the sack, trilled to be flying again.

Meanwhile, back at the ship everything was ready for take off. The Captain walked outside to tell Molly, Choi, Natasha, and Loren to get aboard. When he got outside, he noticed he didn't see Loren.

"Where's Loren?" he asked perplexed.

"She flew off with Aria and Shia," they replied in unison.

"What?" the Captain exclaimed. "You mean she sat on one of them and flew?"

"No," Natasha said, then explained. "She flew in the sack with all the produce. Aria said that one of us had to be there to unload the produce when they got to the mountain."

"That girl and her friend Aria are going to give me a heart attack yet," the Captain said with exasperation. "All right, the rest of you get on board. We are leaving right now."

"I'll stay and wait for Aria to come back," Natasha said, "someone needs to be here to help load the rest of the food."

The Captain looked at her a minute and shook his head again.

"All right, the rest of you get on board. Natasha you'll need to get way over there and stay out of the way of the jets backwash when we take off. The food is on its own."

Natasha agreed, moving to where the Captain told her. Within minutes, the ship was taking off. Natasha moved back farther as she could feel the backwash and the dust flying. Within seconds, the ship was airborne and headed toward the mountains.

As Natasha walked back over to the food, she suddenly realized that she was all alone. Shaking off her fear, she said to herself, "Well, if nobody comes back, at least I'll have plenty to eat."

On board the ship, the Captain sat in the cockpit with Angelina going over the controls.

"I have the GPS location locked into the ship's computer, Captain."

"Good," the Captain responded, "but for this distance, I'll be flying it manually rather than letting the computer take command. Let's hope I remember how."

"What happened to Loren?" Angelina asked.

"Oh, she got another ride," the Captain stated nonchalantly.

"What do you mean, she got another ride?"

"Never mind, I'll explain later, we need to concentrate on getting this bird up in the air." the Captain chuckled at his own play on words.

Meanwhile, Natasha was beginning to get impatient and a little worried. She had watched until the ship had completely disappeared in the distance. Looking around, she noticed that a few of the food packages had toppled over so she straightened them back up then sat down to watch the sky for Aria and Shia.

The ship was flying at about five-hundred feet when Angelina exclaimed, "I can't believe what I'm seeing! Is that Loren flying in the sack between the two birds?"

"Don't even ask," the Captain replied.

Natasha finally caught sight of the two birds returning. With relief in her heart, she watched them come in to land. They hovered for just a minute above the ground then gently lowered the sack down. After the sack had touched the ground, both birds landed.

Climbing out of the sack, Loren yelled, "What a trip! It's so amazing, wait till you see Natasha."

Natasha, who had been anxious to see them return, had not thought about flying in the sack. She and Loren quickly loaded the rest of the bundled vegetable packets into the sack.

"Okay, climb in," Loren directed Natasha as she excitedly jumped into the loaded sack. Natasha climbed in much more slowly and lowered herself, sitting down in the bottom. Almost immediately, Aria and Shia lifted up, flapped their wings, and took off again.

Loren was standing up holding on to the straps for support and shouting for Natasha to get up. "You have got to see this Natasha!"

However, Natasha remained sitting in the bottom of the sack with her eyes tightly shut. "No that's okay, I'm fine where I'm at."

Meanwhile, the ship had reached the plateau, the Captain turned the ship parallel with the plateau and brought it gently to the ground, moving forward slowly to get as close to the cave as possible.

As he shut the down the ship's engines everyone started clamoring to get outside.

"Rashad, you and Maggy get on your equipment and check out the area and cave. The rest of you can just wait until they give us the okay," the Captain stated.

As everyone eagerly waited to get off the ship, the Captain warned them about going in to the cave and wandering about. Rashad reported that the cave was big and deep but they could see nothing without going further back into the cave.

Forty-five minutes later when they arrived at the mountain, Loren could see the ship was safely set down on the plateau. Finally, coaxing Natasha up to see them land, Loren was waving at Maggy and Rashad already out of the ship and standing on the plateau.

"Alright, the rest of you can leave the ship now," the Captain informed them.

As the rest disembarked from the ship, they saw Aria and Shia heading to the plateau with Loren waving excitedly from the sack. As the two birds gently set down the sack and landed, they all went over to see Loren and Natasha getting out.

"How was the ride?" Molly asked.

"I don't know," Natasha responded as she stepped out on wobbly legs thankful to have solid ground beneath her once again. "I didn't open my eyes till we got here."

"It was absolutely wonderful!" Loren exclaimed. "I can't wait to do it again!"

As they started emptying the sack, Choi and Molly removed the harnesses from Aria and Shia. Loren went up to Aria and said, "I can't thank you enough for helping us. Flying with you was the most glorious thing I have ever done in my life!"

"I too enjoyed having you fly with me. We will have to do it again sometime after the storms have passed," Aria replied.

"I'd love that," Loren enthusiastically agreed.

"You are closer to my Aerie now. It will be easier to see you. I wish you well through the storm." With that, she and Shia rose to the skies and flew away.

CHAPTER THIRTY FIVE

"ALRIGHT," THE CAPTAIN SAID, "Let's get some light into the cave and see what we have. Rashad, you and Maggy go inspect those other smaller caves. Angelina, you stay at the computer. The rest of us will check out the cave and start figuring out how we are going to move stuff in."

Maggy and Rashad moved out to investigate the smaller cave openings as everyone else entered the main cave. They had only gone about fifty feet inside when the Captain called everyone to a halt.

"We're going to need better lighting in here before we go any farther. These head lamps just don't give us enough light."

Heading back to the front, they were still discussing how to get more light into the cave when Doc said, "the only big lights we have are in the medical lab. But I'll need those in case of an emergency."

Matzo and Tani had gone back on the ship and were looking around. Coming back through the kitchen, Tani asked how much of the ship was going to be dismantled.

"Almost all of it," Matzo replied.

"What are you going to do with the stainless steel panels that form the kitchen?" Tani asked then added that she was thinking that they could be used as reflectors to shine sunlight into the cave.

"Great idea," Matzo replied. "Let's get Bruce and Choi in here to help us."

Meanwhile, Rashad and Maggy were standing in front of the second cave.

"I'm not picking up any life forms from the infrared readings," Maggy said.

"Okay," Rashad said. "Let's go in."

This cave opening was about twenty feet wide and maybe twelve feet high. Going in, they could tell it was also deep. Moving their head lamps around, they saw nothing but open cave.

As they cautiously moved forward, Rashad suddenly stopped and whispered, "do you hear that? What is that sound?" Maggy stopped and cocked her head listening.

"It seems to be coming from up ahead."

"All I can see is blank cave walls," Rashad said.

As they got closer, Maggy pointed and said, "That wall looks like an outcrop of some kind. There seems to be a space around behind it." Moving slowly, they went around the outcrop and beamed their lights into the area.

"I can't believe this!" Maggy exclaimed in amazement. As they stood there looking at a room about fifty feet wide by about a hundred feet long. Along the back wall, a small waterfall was flowing into a pond about thirty feet by twenty feet. Walking closer they could see that the one end the pond spilled into another, smaller pond that had steam rising up from the top of it. When they reached the edge, Rashad reminded Maggy that Angelina had said that caves could be volcanic. As they looked down into the water, they noticed there was a glow. Walking around the edge, they saw that this too spilled out over a shelf and into a hole in the floor then disappeared.

"Well, this looks like it's going to be my room," Maggy commented. "I've always wanted a bath and sauna together."

"You and everyone else," Rashad replied grinning.

Going back the way they had come, they looked into the back of the cave. Satisfied that there was nothing there but the back of the cave, they turned and headed back out.

Rashad said, "Let's hope the last cave has something just as exciting."

The last cave opening was much smaller, only ten feet wide by eight feet high. Checking the infrared again, Maggy assured Rashad there were no life signs inside this one either.

As they stepped inside, both of them immediately felt that this cave was much cooler than the other two had been. They could also see it was only about fifty feet deep by fifty feet wide. When they got to the back wall, Maggy said, "Shine your light over here by mine."

"What is that? Rashad asked.

"It looks like a mini cave in the floor," Maggy replied. When they had both lights shining down into the hole, they could see it was an ice cave. As they stood there marveling at the multitude of colors reflecting back from their head lamps, Rashad commented. "I'd say this pretty much proves Angelina's analysis was correct in that these caves could be volcanic. That's the only place you'll find ice caves."

"Let's go back, I can't wait to tell the others what we found," Maggy said.

Reaching the main cave, they saw that Matzo, Bruce, and Choi were setting up some sheets of stainless steel on some hand made tripods. As they got up to them, they realized that they were moving the sheets around trying to capture the sunlight and send it into the cave. Inside the cave, Tani and Molly had two more sheets—with Choi adjusting his sheet towards Tani who in turn was directing hers toward Molly's.

All of a sudden, they got it right and the whole cave seemed to light up. It was much larger than they had originally thought. Just then, the rest of the group walked into the cave, looking about them.

"We need to design how we are going to set this up," the Captain stated. "We'll leave everything else in the ship today while we figure this out and start moving things tomorrow."

"I'll volunteer to stay in the cave tonight," Maggy said.

"Yeah right, Rashad said. "I'd better stay with you just in case."

"Okay, what's this all about?" the Captain asked raising his eyebrow in an inquiring look. "What did you two find in the other caves?"

"Nothing but a water fall, a hot tub, and an ice cave. Other than that, there's not much to report," Maggy responded.

"A hot tub?" All the girls chorused together. "Can we take a bath?"

"You'll have to draw straws," Rashad said grinning.

"Hold on," the Captain said. "You mean we have fresh water inside the caves? That's great news!"

"We didn't taste it," Rashad answered, "but it looked clear and clean."

"I'll be glad to collect some samples for you Captain but I will probably need to take the girls with me—just to make sure I am doing it correctly," Maggy said winking at Molly and Tani.

"Not so fast young lady, we need to go back into the ship and bring everyone else up to speed."

When they got back to the ship, they all gathered around in the main bay. While they were sitting down, Sophia came in and asked what they had found.

When Rashad told her about the ice cave; she immediately said, "Great, we need to take the meat to the ice cave now while it is still frozen." Rashad and Maggy got up along with Naomi and headed back to the kitchen with Sophia. They took the meat out of the cryogenic chambers and turned them off, which made more room for the birds.

"Choi, how fast can you come up with a design for everything to move into the cave?" the Captain asked.

"Well, there's a lot of room, so it's more about doing a working layout than trying to fit everything into the space. Plus, the other two caves give us a lot of different options to work with." Then he continued, "I think the first thing we should do is find a place to set up the solar panels and feed the cables into the cave."

"How long will it take to dismantle them?" the Captain asked.

Choi considered the Captain's question for a moment, then answered, "I think it will take at least half a day to dismantle with at least another half day—maybe longer to get them set back up."

"Bruce, you and Choi see if you can find a spot to set them up," the Captain directed as he looked toward Bruce and Choi. With that, Bruce and Choi went outside to start looking over the mountain.

Standing there looking up, Bruce said, "I guess we're going to have to climb up there." Looking around, he found what looked like a good spot to start.

This was one time the lack of gravity really helped, as they were able to climb easily. The mountain itself was rocky and provided plenty of places for hand holds and foot grabs. When they got to the summit, they still hadn't found a good place to position the panels. Looking around, Bruce moved to his right and noticed there was a little cut away in the mountain.

"Come over here and look at this Choi."

As they both looked down into the cut out, Choi said, "It looks big enough and the cut out should provide some protection. Let's see if we can get down there." Working their way down into the cut, they started discussing what it would take to fit the panels into the space.

"Look here," Choi said pointing. "There's a hole going down toward the cave."

"We couldn't be that lucky," Bruce said coming over to where Choi was standing. Looking into the hole, they couldn't see anything. It was too far down and dark.

"Do we have anything we can drop in to see if it makes it down to the cave floor?" Looking around, Choi found a rock about the size of a small ball. The rock had a distinctive orange color to it that they thought they would be able to recognize if it made it to the cave floor.

"It's going to be tough to get the panels up here," Choi remarked as he looked around again.

"Yeah, we will have to have someone up here and try to pull them up, without breaking them." Bruce agreed as they worked their way back to the summit and started down the other side. When they got down, they noticed that the drone had been pushed back outside the cave.

"I wonder if it will fit in the other cave?" Bruce asked. "We don't want to leave it on the plateau with the storm coming."

When they got back to the ship, they noticed everyone was busy moving stuff out of the ship and into the cave.

"What's going on?" Bruce asked.

"Well, there's equipment and stuff we can move into the cave and kind of leave in the center till we decide where to put it." Matzo responded. He then asked, "Did you find a place for the panels?"

"We think so," Bruce answered, "but it won't be easy." He then asked Matzo, "Can I borrow your head lamp? Choi and I need to look at something in the back of the cave."

"Sure," Matzo replied, handing over his head lamp.

As Bruce and Choi went to the back of the cave, they left the area where the light from the panels reflected. Letting their eyes readjust for a few minutes, they started looking around the floor for the rock. As they moved further back, they notice it seemed lighter toward their right. Going around an outcrop of rock, they found themselves standing in a small spot of daylight. Looking up, they could see a large hole on the upper right hand side of the ceiling. Further to the left, they could see a smaller hole with light coming through it also.

"Wow," Choi said as he looked at the beam of light filtering in from outside. Suddenly, Choi reached down and picked up their orange rock. "I can't believe we were the first ones to notice the light filtering down through the ceiling like this."

"This will work," Bruce said. Walking back to the front of the cave, they shared their news with the others. Molly wanted to go back and look at the back of the cave area right away. Grabbing Tani's hand, the two of them followed Bruce and Choi back towards the back of the cave. Getting to the back of the cave they at first didn't see past the outcrop—then going forward they finally saw the light coming from around the outcrop.

Turning the corner around the outcrop, they found themselves in a brightly lit area.

"This will work much better than having the reflector sheets outside where they are exposed to the storm. Plus, we can set up a more permanent light source this way without having to worry about taking them down when the storm comes," Tani said.

When they got back to the front of the cave, they noticed everyone had gone back into the ship. Going back up the ramp, they realized that it was lunch time and everyone was sitting down to eat. Bruce and Choi took turns telling the Captain about what they had found.

"How difficult is it going to be to get those panels up there?" the Captain asked.

"It's going to be real tough," Bruce replied. "There are outcroppings and lots of areas where we won't have much room to maneuver. Plus, I don't know if we have enough equipment to make some kind of pulley system. The good news is that there is a hole that drops down into the cave that's big enough for us to run the cables through."

"The other good news," Tani added, "is that there is a larger hole letting in sunlight that will allow us to move the reflector panels inside to reflect the sunlight without them being exposed to the storm."

Just then, Sophia and Naomi entered with the food. Today, they were having a kind of stew made up with the leftovers from the night before. There was also salad and more bread.

"We need to get those birds out of the chambers," Sophia remarked. "Besides making a mess of them, they're starting to flop around inside and they'll hurt something."

"We knocked down the crates we had made their holding pen out of back at the landing site so that we could bring them along. We can set it back up right after lunch," Molly offered.

"We don't have enough time to start taking down the solar panels this afternoon; besides, I want to charge up whatever we can on the ship," the Captain said. "I also think we need to move whatever we can without hooking any thing up and kind of take it easy the rest of the day."

"I'm taking a hot bath," Maggy said with a dreamy look on her face. "It's been forever."

"Us too," echoed the other girls.

"Let us know when you're done," the Captain said, "and the men will go next."

CHAPTER THIRTY SIX

THEY HAD FINISHED MOVING all the equipment that wasn't connected to anything and were looking around the cave.

Bruce commented, "I think we need to set up the power source first—but that means some of our computers will be down when we make the switch. I also think we need to build some sort of work stations or cubicles."

"We have to separate working quarters, living quarters, a kitchen, Doc's medical area, Dana and Gerard's work area, plus yours and Angelina's. That's a lot to figure out," Choi added. "We'll have to do a lot of planning to make it right."

"We have to do it fast," the Captain, responded, "we don't have much time before the storm."

They were still discussing how everything should be set up when the girls came back.

"That was wonderful," Molly said. "I feel half human again."

"You guy's have to try it; it feels really great," Natasha confirmed as she ran her fingers through her wet hair.

"We will later," the Captain replied." "Right now we're trying to figure out the logistics of getting the solar panels up on the mountain and getting all the equipment and the cave set up where it's livable."

"Getting the solar panels up, is not a problem," Loren, stated.

"How's that?" Bruce questioned.

"I'll just call Aria and ask her to fly them up. I'm sure she won't mind."

"Now, why didn't I think of that?" Bruce commented.

"If you get the panels ready, I'll call her."

"It will take us a while to get them ready," Choi told them. "We'll also need to have enough cable ready to lower into the cave."

Later that afternoon, they had finally completed removing the solar panels and cabling from the ship. They had tied the panels up and already had them in a sling when Choi told Loren they were ready for her to try to call Aria.

Loren went outside and concentrated on calling Aria. Like the last time, she waited a few minutes without hearing anything. Then, suddenly she felt Aria's presence in her mind.

"She's on her way," Loren informed them. When Aria arrived, they were outside waiting to see her, enjoying the sight of the large bird flying in and landing.

"Greetings," Aria said upon landing.

"Greetings Aria," Loren replied bowing. "I'm really pleased to see you again."

"How can I be of help?" Aria asked.

Loren explained what they needed. Within moments, Aria was hooked up to the sling, lifting the solar panels into the air. Bruce had already climbed up, and was standing there with Matzo waiting to unfasten her. As she flew up to Bruce, she hovered momentarily while they grabbed the panels, then she lowered them to the ground. Bruce then unhooked the panels from the sling so that Aria could fly back to the plateau to pick up the second load of panels and their supports. When Aria had completed this, she returned to the plateau and Loren.

"Thank you once again," Loren said gratefully. "As much as we appreciated your help, I enjoyed seeing you more."

"I enjoyed seeing you too," Aria responded. "However, before I go, I would caution you. If you plan to stay in these caves, I suggest you find a way to close the openings. The winds are very strong along with water and frozen water. I will leave you now. If you need me, feel free to call." With that, Aria took to the skies and flew off over the mountain.

"I miss her already," Loren said then added, "Isn't she just wonderful?"

Back on the mountain, Bruce was waiting for Choi, Matzo, and Molly to climb up with the additional tools and equipment that would be needed to install the solar panels. When they arrived, they started discussing the best way to install the panels. The cut in the mountain allowed them to be set down a little and not mounted on the side of the mountain itself. While they had prepared the frames for the panels, they had not determined how to attach them. They first fed the cable down the hole to get it out of the way. Then they set the panels on their frames. After adjusting the panels to get the maximum sunlight, they took a break to study the problem of attachment. There was no way to bolt them to the mountain, since they hadn't taken any bolts from the ship. Molly finally suggested they go get a laser and try to melt the frames to the rock. When Molly returned with one of the laser guns, they set it on low, but while it melted the frame, it did not burn into the rock. Adjusting the setting to high and aiming the laser beam at the rock, Molly started burning around the frame. The result was that the rock started to melt, allowing the frame to settle into the liquid rock. Molly finished burning around the frames then stopped to allow the stone around the frames to cool. When they tested the panels for sturdiness after the rock had cooled, the frames had successfully hardened into the rock.

"That should do it," Bruce said. "Let's go back down and check if the cable made it all the way down to the cave floor."

When they returned to the cave and went to the back, they could see the cable coiled on the floor.

"All right," Bruce said, "we need to hook up the cable to the batteries and attach to the computer grid. Let's get everything we need in here and start hooking it up."

As they worked together getting the batteries set up, Rashad, Maggy, and the Captain were discussing how to close up the openings to the caves. Maggy was saying that they didn't have enough material to close up all the openings and make some kind of doors for them. She then added that they would need to figure out how they were going to get to the other caves for food and water.

"Yeah," Rashad said, "we've moved all the food supplies into the cave with the ice cave. Sophia says it's like a natural refrigerator in there. She has also wrapped up all the meat and put it in the ice cave itself. We'll need to be able to get in there to get the food and supplies."

"It's too bad we don't have a way to get in and out of the caves without going back outside," the Captain stated.

"Wait, that gives me an idea," Rashad said. "Seems like I read something in the manual for the sonic gun indicating it could be used to excavate rock. I didn't pay that much attention to it at the time, but now that I think about it, there is an excavator setting on the gun itself. Let me go find the manual and read up on it—if we can make a passage through the rock from one cave to the other, we'll only have to close up the front openings."

With that, Rashad and Maggy went back into the ship to find the manual. When they got inside, they noticed that Doc, Angelina, and the rest were taking everything apart.

"We have to get as much in the cave as we can," Angelina told Rashad. "Whether we have it hooked up or not—if the storm destroys the ship, we won't be able to replace any of the missing parts."

Rashad told them they were looking for one of the manuals. Dana and Gerard have been gathering all the manuals and putting them in a crate to move inside, Doc informed them. Going back to where Dana and Gerard were, Rashad told them what they were looking for.

"We haven't packed those yet," Dana said. "Look over there in that pile," she said pointing.

Rashad found the manual and quickly thumbed through to the excavation section. Giving it a quick read, he told Maggy, "It says here that they use both the laser and the sonic gun. Let's get both of them and go back to the waterfall cave to see if this really works." Agreeing, Maggy grabbed up one of the lasers, while Rashad got the sonic gun and the manual, then headed for the waterfall cave.

When they got there, Maggy asked, "Why this cave first?"

"I think we should try and go from this cave into the ice cave first because there is more room for error. Also, this cave doesn't require that big of an opening." Moving to the back side wall of the cave, Rashad said, "I think this is where the two caves meet. We need to go look and try to figure out if this side lines up with the other cave."

With one standing at the opening to the waterfall cave and the other in front of the ice cave, they tried to figure out if they lined up correctly.

"It looks right," Maggy said, "but we're going to have to move some of the supplies to the other side to make sure they're out of the way." After moving the food supplies in the ice cave, they again checked to see if the walls lined up.

"It looks like there's about twenty feet of rock between the caves," Rashad commented then added, "That's a lot of rock to remove. Let's read the manual again and see what happens when we use the sonic gun." Reading the manual, it stated that the rock would crumble and fall out; this meant that the rock would be in the waterfall cave. It also explained how to cut an outline with the laser and then use the sonic gun to excavate the rock.

After they had read it through a couple more times to make sure they understood the process, Rashad said, "There's nothing left to do but try it." Maggy got the laser and approached the wall.

"How big do I make the opening?" she questioned.

"Make it about eight feet high by about four feet wide," Rashad replied. "You will also have to make it curved at the top—that will give it more strength according to what we read."

Maggy stepped up to the wall, putting the laser on full strength she started cutting the outline. They couldn't tell if the laser went all the way through but decided they could use it again after removing some of the rock.

Rashad then stepped up and setting the sonic gun on the lowest excavator setting, he pointed it at the bottom of the opening that Maggy had outlined and pulled the trigger.

A small circle of light appeared on the rock about four inches in diameter. At first nothing seem to happen; then slowly, small pieces of rock started falling out of the wall onto the floor.

After Rashad had removed about three inches along the bottom, he said, "Okay, I'm going to turn it up two settings and see what happens. Make sure you stand back."

Rashad adjusted the sonic gun to a higher excavator setting, pointed toward the base of the wall, and pulled the trigger. The first thing he noticed was the gun pushing against him, making him have to adjust his stance by putting one foot further back to off set the push. This time, the circle was about sixteen inches in diameter and larger chunks of rocks immediately started falling away from the wall. It was making a hole about two feet deep and Rashad, now that he had the feel of it was slowly moving it back and forth removing the rock.

"Hold it a minute," Maggy said.

"What?" Rashad asked. "I was just getting the hang of it."

"Yeah, but look" Maggy said pointing at the rubble. "We are going to have to remove some of this rock, it's piling up on the ground in front of the opening, and we won't be able to get past it." Looking around, Rashad saw she was right. If he kept it up much longer, there was going to be too much rock to let them continue.

"I think I need to go back to the ship and get some volunteers to help remove the rock as we go."

Rashad agreed, then set the gun down and began moving rock out of the way while Maggy went back to get some of the others to help. When she got back to the ship, the first person she saw was the Captain. After explaining her problem to him, the Captain went around gathering up the people he felt could be relieved from what they were doing.

Going back to the cave, he had Angelina, the twins, Doc, Molly, Natasha, Naomi, and Sophia. When they got there, Rashad explained what he was doing and what was needed. Once again, the low gravity helped and they were able to move rocks of large sizes without much difficulty. Alternating between Rashad excavating, the group removing the rocks, and Maggy outlining the opening with the laser again, they finally broke through to the cave to the other side. Maggy then smoothed out the rough edges with her laser while everyone else removed the remaining rock and debris. They now had an arched opening about four feet wide by eight feet high going into the ice cave. As everyone, stood back to admire their handy work and let the rock cool down, Sophia noticed that their new doorway was letting the cold air out.

"We'll have to hang a tarp or something over the opening to keep the heat out."

"It will help when we close up the front opening," Rashad stated.

Hearing that, the Captain said, "While we are all here, let's start piling the rocks into the opening and close it up."

With a groan, everyone started moving the rock over to what was now the exterior opening.

"I've have an idea," Molly said. "When we fastened the solar panels to the rock face up on the mountain, we were able to melt some of the minerals in the rock to weld them together."

With that, Maggy cautioned everyone, "Be careful not to touch the hot rocks." Then she stepped up and began to laser the rocks together along the bottom of the opening as the others took turns stacking the rocks one course at a time. Slowly but surely, they were able to meld some of the rocks together. Finally, a couple of hours later they had managed to completely close the opening from the outside. Exhausted, they all set down in the waterfall cave.

"Are we going to have to do this again for the other two caves?" Natasha asked.

"I'm afraid so," the Captain responded nodding his head. "Unless you can come up with a better idea."

"We looked at the other two caves earlier. They don't appear to be as far apart," Maggy said, "but the openings are larger."

"Well, we still have some rock left," said Rashad looking over at the remaining pile of rock. "But I don't think we will have enough to close up those openings—even if we combine what we have left over here and use what we cut from the new opening."

"Can you cut the opening between this one and the main cave closer to the front, so we don't have to haul the rocks as far?" Gerard asked.

"It looks like it," Rashad responded. "Also, if we cut from this side, we can move the rocks into the opening, that way we won't have to move them twice."

"What about the drone?" Molly asked. "If we close this up, we won't be able to fit the drone inside."

"Humm, good point," the Captain said as he stood up. "Let's go back to the ship and discuss this. It should be getting close to lunch time anyway."

"Not with me here moving rocks it isn't," Sophia noted. "It will take me and Naomi at least twenty minutes to throw a cold bird salad together."

"Cold salad it is," the Captain replied. "Let's go back."

Arriving back in the ship, they saw that Bruce, Matzo, Tani, and Emir had pieces of cable and parts of the ship lying all over the place as they diligently took everything apart.

"Is my kitchen still intact?" Sophia asked as she stepped over the parts and cabling laid out on the floor.

"Sure is," Bruce responded. "We were saving it for last so we wouldn't miss any meals, but sometime this afternoon we were going to start on it"

While Sophia and Naomi headed back to the kitchen to prepare lunch, the rest sat down and began discussing how they were going to completely dismantle the ship. They would also need to relocate all the pieces and parts from the ship to the caves before they closed up the openings. They were still bouncing ideas back and forth when Sophia and Naomi brought in lunch and called the rest of the group to join them.

As they passed the plates around, the Captain asked if anyone had figured out a plan of attack to accomplish everything that had to be done.

"Well, we know how we are going to seal up the water fall cave," Rashad replied.

"And we pretty much figured how to hook up the power," Bruce added.

"We have most of our equipment ready to move," Dana stated.

"That leaves only a hundred things to figure out and get done in the next four weeks," the Captain added then looked over to Drago. "Drago, what have you been up to?"

"I've been walking around looking at things and thinking."

"Okay," the Captain responded. "I'm starting to get used to you and your thinking. Tell us what you've figured out."

"Well sir," he replied, "I think I have it all—except what we are going to do with the birds."

Everybody sat there waiting in anticipation, knowing that Drago went far beyond them when it came to thinking things out. His mind seemed to work in five or six different directions at the same time.

"Okay," Drago said. "The first step is to get everything in the cave. That means dismantling the entire ship. Once we get everything into the cave, we can concentrate on closing it up. If we move Sophia's kitchen into the waterfall cave, it will allow her to be close to a water source both for cooking and clean up. Most of the equipment is stainless steel; so it shouldn't rust, but I would still recommend that we install a tarp or some sort of barrier between her kitchen and the water fall. If you can leave room to run a vent near the closed up opening, we can set up the grill for cooking, allowing it to vent outside."

Drago then continued. "In the main cave, if you make an opening close to the front of the cave, we can place the drone just to the left of it. Sorry, Bruce. But you Matzo are going to have to remove the wings and associated cables and controls for it to fit."

"Across, on the other side of the cave, we can set up a storage area. There, everything we have removed, but don't have time to install can be stacked and sorted. This will leave the rest of the cave available for setting up the various areas."

"In the far back, where Bruce and his group dropped the cables from the solar panels, we set up the main power generation area. This is also where we will need to set up most of our computers. That same area has the larger opening that reflects sunlight off the reflector panels Tani and Molly set up to provide lighting. However, we will have to provide cover for the hole to keep out the weather and allow the light in at the same time. For this, I made some measurements and discovered that we should be able to use the glass from the cock pit. Even though this glass has a protective coating on it, if we install it over the opening, I believe it will let enough sunlight in to accomplish what we need."

"For the large opening to the main cave, I went under the ship and measured the large panels of the skin. There seems to be enough to almost complete the opening. Using the ramp door and hydraulics from the landing gear, we should be able to manufacture a door that opens and closes with the least amount of effort in case of a power failure."

"While there are still enough panels to completely close the opening, I recommend that when taking apart the ship, the perforated high density plastic flooring be installed at the top to allow some air movement within the caves. We could possibly use the baffles from the engines to create some sort of shutters to close against the wind when necessary."

"Another one of the things we will have to do is to drain all the remaining fuel from the tanks and store it in containers for possible future use. That will also take care of the safety problem of leaving the fuel in the ship's tanks during the storm."

"Finally, we must prepare a way to get down from the plateau. In the future, and in case of emergency, if we need to get down, we must have a way. If nothing else, we need to be able to let Zena and Butkis down to the plain to hunt for meat."

"That's most of it," Drago concluded, then added, "I'm sure there is something I missed, but we'll have to handle that as the need arises."

Everyone sat around in dumbfounded silence. Even Rashad could only shake his head, speechless for the moment. The Captain looked over to Doc and Angelina who just shrugged their shoulders and looked back at him.

"Okay, folks," the Captain said. "We now have a plan, figure out who's going to do what and let's get started. We only have four weeks left until the storms hit. I'm going to go take a nap." With that, he got up and left for his quarters.

The spell was broken, everyone started discussing what to do, and who would do what, as the Captain walked out of the bay. When they asked Drago, he responded saying, "you all have your expertise, and you know which of you is best at what. I'm going to look some more at figuring out how to get up and down from the plateau." With that, he stood up and went outside.

After much discussion, the group decided that Rashad and Maggy would go back and start opening the hole between the two caves. Emir, Matzo, Tani and Angelina would continue dismantling the equipment. Bruce and Molly, along with Choi would continue hooking up the solar panels and power while Doc, the twins, Sophia, and Naomi would go back and help move rocks.

Chapter Thirty Seven

When Bruce and his group finished the power hook up, they would return to the ship to continue dismantling. Hopefully, by that time, the new opening would be done and Rashad's excavating crew would join them. Natasha went looking for Drago.

Rashad's plan of excavating closer to the opening was working out better, so the team was able to move the rocks more quickly and only one time. With Maggy standing there welding the rocks into place as they were being set, they finished closing up the opening in just over an hour.

Upon finishing their project, Doc, the twins, Maggy and Rashad took a small break then went back to the ship to help the others. Sophia and Naomi started to move and set up the kitchen in the waterfall cave. Molly stayed behind to hook up the grill and figure out how to vent it through the hole they had left at the top.

When Natasha found Drago, he was walking up and down the plateau looking for the easiest way to get down.

"Any luck yet?" Natasha asked.

"Not really, I know we can build a cable ladder down to the ground and with the low gravity, it will be easy to get up and down. But that doesn't help us bring supplies up and down. I'm wondering if we can use one of the ships wheels as a pulley. We'd have to be able to hang some sort of cage over the edge with a counter weight that someone in the cage can operate, rather than have someone on top pulling to raise and lower the cage."

"Does your mind ever stop working?" Natasha asked him.

"Not really," Drag replied rather sheepishly. "I've always been this way. I can't help thinking about everything at the same time. I've had to teach myself to try to keep it in some sort of order. Like right now, while I was thinking about that, I thought that with you here, why don't we get some cable, tie it off, and lower ourselves down. We can get Zena and Butkis and allow them to hunt while I'm looking at the plateau from the bottom up."

"You amaze me," Natasha said. "Let's go get the equipment and the cubs and go on down." The two of them headed back to the ship. Drago went to get the cable and equipment while Natasha headed to the kitchen where she was sure she would find the cubs, curled up on their blanket. When she got there, the cubs were exactly where she thought they would be. As she reached down and picked them up, she realized how much they had grown. They would no longer fit in her hand and hung over quite a bit as she lifted them up. They also seemed much heavier. She sent Butkis the thought that they were going to hunt. Zena picked up the thought also. Going to where Drago was with the equipment, she picked up the backpacks and put a cub in each. Drago handed Natasha her equipment, which she fastened on, then put on the backpack while Drago did the same. Going back outside, they set their back packs down as Drago fastened the cable around some rocks at the side of the mountain. Lowering the cable over the side, Drago told Natasha to put on her gloves and follow him down the cable.

Backing up to the edge, Drago faced the mountain and started to lower himself over the edge and down the plateau. It was easy going and in no time, he reached the bottom. Yelling back up to Natasha to do like he did, he watched her start over the edge.

She lost her footing once; then caught herself, finally reaching the bottom.

"That was a challenge," she remarked thankful to have solid ground beneath her feet again.

"Wait till you try to go back up," Drago replied.

Taking off their gloves, they took the cubs out of their back packs and set them down on the ground. Zena immediately took off with Butkis fast on her heels. Drago and Natasha watched them disappear into the grass for a moment then started looking up at the plateau.

"It doesn't look any better from down here," Drago commented as he started walking around the bottom. They continued walking around but didn't see any better way to get up the plateau. Finally, Zena and Butkis came back licking their chops. As Zena sat down and began cleaning herself, Natasha got the backpacks and prepared to put the cubs back in.

"I'd rather walk back up," Zena sent.

"Me to," added Butkis.

"What do you mean?" Natasha asked.

"There is an easier way around the other side," Zena sent the thought back. Natasha passed this information on to Drago.

"Let's follow their lead," Drago suggested in agreement.

"Go ahead and show us," Natasha told Zena. Zena started around to the left with Butkis walking along side and Natasha and Drago following. They had gone about two hundred yards when the plateau made a turn to the left. As they came around the curve, Drago and Natasha were left speechless by the sight. Going away into the distance were a series of mountain ranges, each one towering over the one in front of it.

"Look at how beautiful it is," Natasha said. "It seems to go forever." Their revere was broken when Zena started barking at them. Turning to look at her, they saw she was on a slightly steep slope, but one that certainly could be walked up. Heading up the slope behind the cubs, they eventually came to the top of the plateau. However, they were behind a shoulder on the mountain and could not see the caves. Walking around the shoulder, they eventually came to the caves.

"It is certainly longer," Drago said. "But it's a lot easier than rigging up a pulley and cage."

Upon returning to the ship, Drago and Natasha walked inside to complete chaos. Different groups were taking apart different things and just laying them about the floor.

As Drago and Natasha entered, everyone started asking questions about what they were doing.

"Hold it," Drago commanded. "Everyone needs to stop what you are doing."

Originally, Drago had thought that everyone would be able to figure out how to accomplish their work; he now realized that it was going to take someone to coordinate all the different activities.

"Okay, everyone listen up. We first need to remove all the panels and bulkheads, then take them into the cave and stack them according to size. Put them along the left hand wall next to the stock pile. After that, you will need to remove the seats and consoles, and stack them next to the panels. Then, we will remove the cables marking them as we go, so we know what they were hooked up to."

"We don't have enough tools for all of us to do it that way," Emir stated.

"There were some crates we did not unpack that we already moved into the cave. I believe they were marked tools," Rashad replied.

"Go open them up and see what we have," Drago ordered. "Bring back what you think we can use." Maggy went with Rashad and when they returned a few minutes later, they had the tools everyone would need to remove the panels.

"Now start at the front and work your way back," Drago instructed. "Some of you can haul the panels to the cave while the others are detaching them."

Within a few minutes, things became more organized with everyone following Drago's instructions.

Drago could see that it would take the rest of the day just to remove the panels and carry them to the cave. Seeing everyone working, he headed to the kitchen to see how Sophia and Naomi were doing. When he got there, he noticed everything that could be picked up and carried had been removed. However, the attached equipment like the microwaves had not been touched. Sophia and Naomi were busy taking food and putting it into canisters to move to the cave.

"Hey," Drago said as he and Natasha walked in. "How's the move going?"

"We have moved most of the food into the ice cave and stored some in the waterfall cave," Sophia replied. "Molly is setting up the grill, but we don't have power there yet for the microwaves. So we will be cooking between the ship and the cave until Bruce and Matzo have it hooked up."

"I'll go look in on Molly and Bruce to see how far they have gotten." Drago replied as he headed back out of the ship going to the waterfall cave with Natasha close on his heels. When they got there, they saw Molly using the laser to weld some pipes she had found for the vent on the grill.

"Hey Molly, how's the vent coming?" Drago asked.

"Its coming along okay now—it took me a little while to figure out what material I could use to construct the vent pipe. But that problem was solved when Doc gave me permission to cut some of the piping from the distiller system. He told me that we weren't really using them anymore. Other than adding the cook rocks we brought with us, it should be ready to go. As soon as I finish up here, I'm going to go help Choi with the layout in the main cave."

"Let's check on Bruce and Matzo," Drago told Natasha as they headed back to the main cave. When they got there, they saw Bruce and Matzo were busy hooking up the cables from the solar panels to the battery chargers.

"How's it going?" Drago asked.

"Well, we decided to complete the hook up between the solar panels and the first string of batteries because that was the easiest connections we have to make," Bruce responded as he looked up. "The next step is more difficult because we have to set up a distribution panel. We are just about finished with the initial hook up between the solar panels and the first string of batteries, but these are only half of the batteries, we left the other half installed to run the Captain's quarters, Angelina's controls, and Doc's medical equipment. When we disconnect them and bring the rest of the batteries in, we have to have the main distribution panel set up." Bruce said as he continued to explain. "We really can't do that yet for two reasons. One it will completely black out everything on the ship. And two, it will shut everything down in the cave."

"Besides, until Choi comes up with the final lay-out, we don't know where to set up the power cables and the main panel. When we finish this, were going back to the ship to see what cables we can remove once they have the panels removed," Matzo added.

"Natasha, let's go back to the ship and check on the others." Drago said.

Entering the ship, they saw that everyone was working much more organized. Panels were coming down and being carried into the main cave.

"Make sure after you remove the panels that you remove the struts supporting them as well. We will need them to build and refasten the panels." Drago mentioned to everyone, as he was passing through on their way to Dana and Gerard's testing area. But no one was there.

"Let's go find the Captain and the others first, he told Natasha, then we'll look for Dana and Gerard." Heading to the Captain and Angelina's main control section, they saw that both of them were busy at their computers.

"Excuse me," Drago said upon entering. "We just thought we would check in to see how things are going."

"We are in the process of downloading everything on the ship's computers to disk," the Captain replied. "As I'm sure you already know, downloading and marking the discs takes quite a while. Doc is going through the same process with all the medical information and controls for his systems. We estimate it will take another two days to get all the information downloaded."

"That's one thing I hadn't thought of," Drago stated.

"It's reassuring to know there is something you hadn't thought of," the Captain replied winking at Angelina. "I thought I was becoming a little bit unneeded."

"That will never be the case," Natasha stated earnestly.

"Thank you for that Natasha, how's everything else going?"

"It's going to take a while to get everything removed and then hooked back up," Drago replied. "So far, everyone that we've checked in on seems to be doing fine. After we leave here, we plan to check in on Danna and Gerard to see how they are coming along with their tasks."

"Fine," the Captain responded, "please keep me informed."

"Yes sir," Drago said. With that, Drago and Natasha went looking for Dana and Gerard. Not finding them in the ship, they asked if anyone knew where they were or what they were doing.

"They asked me for tools to remove the cockpit glass and wanted to borrow my laser, then they left," Rashad replied.

"Okay, we'll look for them outside," Drago responded. "Thanks Rashad."

Going outside, they did not see Dana or Gerard.

"Let's climb up the mountain and see if they are up there," Natasha suggested. Drago nodded his assent and they started climbing up the mountain. Both were curious about how it looked from up there; plus, Drago had wanted to check on the solar panels to see how they were fastened.

Climbing up took a little effort, but the mountain provided both hand and foot holds along the way. When they got to where the panels were installed, Drago looked them over and felt they were as secure as could be. He was hopeful that the winds would not knock them loose. Hearing voices, they climbed out of the cut and started making their way around the side of the mountain in the direction of the voices. When they had gone about fifty feet; they saw Dana and Gerard trying to figure out how to install the cockpit glass over the opening into the cave.

When Dana looked up and saw them coming, she said, "I hope one of you can show me how to operate this laser. We have the glass aligned so it covers the hole, but we can't get the laser to work so that we can fasten it in place."

Drago and Natasha stepped over to where Dana and Gerard were working.

"Let me see the laser," Drago requested holding out his hand. Taking the laser, he said, "the safety is still on, and you have to set the level of power." Setting the level to low and disengaging the safety, Drago aimed the laser to where the frames of the glass met the rock. At first, nothing happened; but after adjusting the power setting, Drago was able to melt the rock around the frames, securing the glass.

"That should do it," he said stopping to let them inspect his work.

"Let's hope so," Dana replied. "Now, let's go back down and see how it looks from inside the cave."

When they had climbed back down and gone to the back of the cave, Dana noticed that the light was a little more subdued due to the tinting of the cockpit glass.

"It still gives us enough light to brighten the cave," she said, "but I don't know what we'll do about individual work areas."

"We can remove the LED lighting from the floors and the emergency lighting in the ship to provide some extra lighting," Drago said. "Also, Doc's surgery lights are run by the emergency back up so we can adapt those."

"Good thinking," Dana commented. "Gerard and I will start checking them out right away."

Going back into the ship, Drago and Natasha noticed that quite a bit of the paneling and bulkhead had been removed. They could see that about half way down the ship there was nothing but the support structure and struts filled with the remaining cables and wires.

After inspecting the progress for a few minutes, Drago sighed and came to another conclusion. "I think the best thing to do after they finish removing the panels, is to have Bruce, Matzo, Molly, and Emir start removing the cables and labeling them. That way, we will be able to keep track of them and it should make it easier to hook back up the different pieces of equipment."

Satisfied that he had resolved another piece of the dismantling puzzle, Drago turned to Natasha and said, "we already checked on everyone and they're all doing fine so we might as well help with the panels while we are here." For the rest of the afternoon they removed panels.

Everyone was ready for dinner when Sophia called. Because of all the removal and dismantling that had been going on inside the ship, Sophia and Naomi had moved the table and eating area into the cave. They had then returned to the ship to cook the food. Before taking the steaming platters back to their new eating area in the cave, Sophia had fixed a plate for Emir since they were still afraid to have him go outside. As everyone found their places around the table, they saw that Sophia had made a casserole out of the meat with potatoes and vegetables.

Tani, filled her plate then announced, "I'm going to carry my plate back to the ship and eat with Emir. It's not fair for him to have to eat alone."

"We are going to have and figure out how to get him into the cave eventually," the Captain said as he watched Tani head back to the ship. "We might have to carry him in on a chair or something. I'm afraid once his feet touch the ground that he will go into a trance again—especially now that we are closer to his mountain vision."

Then, changing the subject, he asked, "So, how did everyone do today? I hope you made more progress than Angelina and I did."

"I got the grill hooked up and ready," Molly reported. "Then I went and helped Bruce and Matzo on the power grid."

"We have gone about as far as we can go with that," Bruce stated. "We got the batteries hooked up to the solar panels and charging but we can't hook up the main panel until we disconnect it from the ship."

"What I suggest we do," Drago said "is that everyone but Sophia and Naomi concentrate on removing the rest of the panels from the ship. Bruce, you guys can start marking and removing the cables and wiring from where the panels are already removed. When that's done, a group of us can start removing the struts and supports. We can then stack them in the cave next to the panels. After that, we will need to get all the consoles moved over."

Drago then continued lining out the sequence of events for everyone. "As soon as the Captain, Angelina and Doc complete downloading and backing up all the information off their computers, we will need to start moving their stuff over."

The Captain smiled and noted, "That's still going to take a couple more days—we are talking about a massive amount of information." He then turned to Choi and asked, "How are you doing on the lay out?"

"I think I have it pretty well figured out." Laying some sheets of drawings on the table, he started to point out his design. "Starting at the back, behind the outcrop, I'm leaving all that space for Bruce and Matzo's power grid set up along with the battery charging station." Pointing to the outcrop on the right side, Choi continued with, "Here, I plan on setting up Doc's medical center. Next to Doc, I am putting the Captain's area. As you can see, I've designed both of these areas so that your personal quarters are also within your working quarters. Provided of course you approve?" Choi asked looking at Doc, then the Captain.

"I like that idea," Doc agreed.

The Captain looked at Choi and nodded once in agreement then said, "Please continue."

"I have put Angelina's area next; however, her working area will be on the other side, and these are her personal quarters. After her, I've set up the girl's quarters, then the guys. That still leaves plenty of room on that side for storing the drone and access to the opening for the other cave."

"Going back to the other side, starting about twenty feet from the power room, I created a space for Dana and Gerard's scientific equipment. After their area, I have a general controls area with the majority of the equipment and consoles running down that side ending with Emir's workstation. The rest of the area along the left side is for the stock pile and the additional crates and equipment. I am hoping as we construct the different areas, we will have more room to organize the remaining materials in a structured environment."

As Choi finished up explaining his design, he smiled and said, "I also took time out today to set up some of the tarps along with some benches I made out of the used crates around the hot springs bathing area—to provide for more privacy."

"I'll check that out right after dinner," Maggy chimed in.

"I'm with you," echoed Molly and Natasha.

Cleaning up after dinner took a little longer since they had to carry everything back to the kitchen area in the waterfall cave.

While all this was going on, Tani and Emir were eating alone in the ship.

"This has to be hard on you," Tani said to Emir. "Not being allowed outside or into the caves."

"It is in one sense," Emir replied thoughtfully then continued. "I do feel a stronger compulsion on me to look for the cave since we got here. I have been trying to send mental thoughts back, asking for just a little more time before I'll come. I don't know for sure if it is working or not, but I sort of feel less demand to go."

"What do you think waits for you there?" Tani asked.

"I don't know. I just feel it's my destiny—like this is always what I was meant to do and I'm compelled to go there. How that is possible, I don't have any idea. It is all very confusing; especially when you consider how we ended up here."

"When are you going to go?" Tani asked quietly.

"I don't know that either, but when the time is right, I'll just go."

They finished their meal and Tani said good night and took their dishes back to the cave. When she got there, the Captain asked her how Emir was doing. Tani explained her conversation with him.

"I just hope he lets us know," the Captain responded. "I feel this is the one thing that we don't have any control over. When I try to figure it out, it's as though my mind just slips past it and I am unable to focus or concentrate on it for more than a few seconds at a time. However, there is one thing I do want to do before we dismantle the wings on the drone and that is to take another exploratory flight."

"Captain," Drago interrupted saying, "I suggest the flight go around the shoulder of the mountain. Today, Natasha and I discovered a way up the plateau over that way—or rather Zena and Butkis did. When we got there, we could see a continuing group of mountain ranges heading off in that direction."

"Okay," the Captain replied. "We will have Bruce and Matzo send it in that direction when the time comes. Right now, we have a lot of work to do before we can have another flight."

"I'm off to the hot tub," Maggy stated with a dreamy look of anticipation on her face.

"Why don't all you girls go now?" the Captain suggested. "When you're finished, call us and we'll take our turn."

Agreeing, all the girls including Angelina all headed off to the hot springs. When they got there, they were surprised to see that Choi had done much more than just hang some curtains. He had built a closed in area out of the tarps. Inside, there were two benches and some shelves made from some of the smaller, left over equipment crates for putting clothes in. He had also gone into the ship and brought out soap, some cloths for bathing, and some of the towels that had originally been intended for use by the colony on SBR375.

"We'll have to get something to make hangers out of and we will also need to bring in a container to use for dirty clothes," Molly suggested as she inspected their new bath area. "But all in all, Choi did a great job!"

When the girls were through, they went back and informed the guys, who immediately got up and headed for the hot springs. They too were surprised at what Choi had done and within seconds, they had stripped down and were all in the springs.

"This feels great on old bones," Doc as he slid down into the warm water.

"Yep," the Captain agreed. "All we need now is a massage."

Chapter Thirty Eight

The next morning after breakfast, they all went back to dismantling the ship and downloading the computer programs. By the time lunch was ready, they had taken down all the panels they could. Bruce and Matzo, along with Molly had removed and labeled a bunch of cables and wiring allowing the others to start removing some of the structural supports. After lunch, everyone continued with their work; and by supper time, they had all had enough of removing things from the ship then hauling the dismantled parts and pieces over to the cave.

Sophia and Naomi had grilled some of the meat and made barbeque for dinner. Tani filled her plate then fixed another for Emir and headed back to the ship. After everything had been cleaned up and Tani had returned, the girls repeated their trip to the hot springs. When they returned, the guys slowly got up and headed back for their turn.

While sitting in the hot springs, the Captain asked Drago, "What part do we do next?"

"If we have enough structural material, Choi should be able to start building the areas he described last night." Then Drago continued with, "we have to get enough of the inside removed and out of the way so we can start removing the outside skin to build the enclosure for the cave opening. I'm hoping that Rashad can cut the skin with the structure supporting it intact so we can put the pieces in place and weld them."

"We also need to figure out how to install the door from the ship to enclose the opening when we get the skin panels in place. And, I think we need to use the perforated floor at the top to let fresh air into the cave."

"What about the storm wind?" the Captain asked.

"I thought we could use the flaps from the ship's wings and tail section that move up and down—installing them as baffles so we have the ability to open or close."

"Wow, that's going to take a lot of engineering to set up," Bruce commented.

"I know," Drago replied, "but between you and Matzo, Molly and Choi, I thought you could figure it out."

"Angelina and I should be of some help there," the Captain added. "We had a little bit of training in that area at the Academy."

While the men were enjoying the baths, Maggy and Natasha had taken Zena and Butkis out for their evening hunt.

"What do you think?" Maggy asked. "Will we be able to get it all done before the storm gets here?"

"I think so," Natasha replied earnestly. "We might not have everything set up, but the important part will be to get all the dismantled parts and pieces from the ship moved into the cave and get it closed in."

"What are your feelings on Emir?" Maggy questioned.

"I'm not really sure, I pick up thoughts every once in a while like someone is communicating with him, but I just don't know."

Right then, Zena, and Butkis came back licking their chops. After letting, them play and run around a bit longer so that they had time to do their business, Maggy and Natasha called the cubs so they could head back. Butkis came running up to Natasha and started jumping up and down like he wanted her to pick him up and carry him.

"No way, fat boy," Natasha told him laughing at his antics. "You need to run off some of that fat." Both Natasha and Maggy had noticed how big the cubs were getting. They were now about thirty pounds or so and had lost that puppy look.

As they followed the cubs back up the incline toward the caves, they both continued their discussion as they stopped for a moment to gaze at the mountains in the distance.

"They're going to be big," Maggy commented reading Natasha's thoughts.

"Pretty soon they'll go out hunting without us," Natasha replied.

"I hope not," then as an afterthought added, "Maybe we can go hunting with them for bigger game as they grow."

When they got back, everyone was either sitting around talking or heading for their bunks.

The next morning over breakfast, the group decided that everyone would be involved in completing the stripping of the ship. For the next three days, they fell into a routine of working, eating, getting a hot bath, and then going to bed. Finally, with just three weeks left they were at a point where Rashad and Maggy would start cutting off the skin to make the panels to enclose the cave entrance. At the same time; Bruce and Matzo along with the Captain and Angelina would start removing the flaps and their controls from the ship's wings and tail section.

When Rashad and Maggy crawled under the ship and looked at the skin, Rashad said, "There are like a zillion rivets in these panels."

"We will need to cut right along next to them," Maggy said.

"Have they removed the flooring and the rest of the stuff above us?" Rashad asked Maggy.

"Yeah, I checked in with Bruce and Matzo before we came down here, and they said it was all clear to cut."

"Before we start, I think we should go look at the cave opening again to figure out what size pieces we need," Rashad said.

"Good idea, I'll get a tape and a marker so we can measure and lay it out," Maggy agreed as they crawled back out from underneath the ship.

After measuring and marking out the panel sizes, Rashad looked over at Maggy one last time before they crawled back under the ship to start cutting. Holding the laser at the edge of the rivet line, they were cutting through the skin being careful not to cut the supports. When they got the proper size they wanted, they cut through the structural piece and let it fall to the ground.

Meanwhile, the Captain and Angelina's group had managed to disconnect the flaps and were working on removing the cables and controls.

"We need to go inside and disconnect them from the cockpit controls," the Captain said as they were finishing up. "Then you can pull the cables out."

Going back around the ship, he stopped to check on Maggy and Rashad. Seeing that they were doing fine, the Captain and Angelina headed up the ramp and went to the cockpit. As the Captain entered, he could not help but feel a sense of sadness. Looking around, the glass canopy was missing from the cockpit; there was nothing but support skeletons behind him, and now there were large holes in the floor. Both his and Angelina's seats were gone as well as most of their control panels.

He looked over at Angelina and said. "She was a good ship; she got us here safely and provided us a home." He reached down and patting what was left of his console said a silent thank you and fare well. Coming out of his reverie, he turned to Angelina saying, "Okay, let's take her apart." In a matter of minutes, they had stripped the cables from the dismantled controls. "Okay, you can tell them to pull the cables out now. I'm going to take a walk through what's left of the ship."

Watching out for where Rashad and Maggy were cutting, he walked back into the ship. He could see that the main power panel and grid were still in place. He also noticed that a lot of Sophia's kitchen equipment was still hooked up. When he got to where the cryogenic chambers were, he noticed that they were also still intact. Walking back to the front, he once more turned and looked at the ship. Saluting her one last time, he turned and walked back down the ramp. When he got back to the rear of the ship, he saw that the team had the cables out and lying on the ground next to the flaps.

"All right team," he said, "let's get this stuff into the cave."

Meanwhile Rashad and Maggy had removed quite a few panels and were now working on some of the smaller panels. When they stopped for lunch, they decided they would not cut any more until they saw how the panels were going to be put together. Then they could come back for more as needed. As they walked into the cave, they couldn't help but notice the large amount of panels, wire, and cabling along with all the other equipment that lined the left wall.

"How are we ever going to get that stuff back together?" Maggy questioned.

"That is Choi, Bruce and Molly's problem," Rashad responded; "we're just the grunts that stick it together."

When they sat down to lunch, the Captain started asking Bruce and Matzo about the things left in the ship that needed to be dismantled.

"We can now finish taking apart the kitchen stuff," Matzo replied. "Sophia can cook on the grill until we hook up the power panel."

Then Bruce spoke up reminding the Captain, "As I stated before, we'll have to shut down everything for the day while we relocate the panel and make the hook ups. Once the panel has been energized, we can start running the different leads from the distribution panel to the equipment."

Bruce continued by saying that they had decided not to touch the cryogenic chambers. "Besides, with the chambers being hooked up to that liquid source along with all the other stuff, we thought it would take too much time to figure out. The ice cave pretty much solved our refrigeration problem anyway, so we decided to just leave them hooked up."

The Captain thought a few minutes about what they had just said then responded with, "I hate the thought of leaving anything we can use in the ship to the mercy of the storm, but I see your point. Doc, do you concur?"

"There may be pieces we could use, but we really don't need the chambers as they were designed."

The Captain then concluded with another question. "So, when do we shut down and move the power panel?"

"Well, Matzo and I thought that the rest of today we would start removing what we could. This would also give Rashad and Maggy time to finish what they are doing. Then tomorrow morning, first thing, if every thing is okay, we would start the shutdown. Remove the panel and the convertor generators, relocate them inside, and start the hook up. Once we have made the hook up, everyone can start running cables and power to their stations. With all of us working together hooking up the stations, it should go faster," Bruce replied.

"The problem with that is, I'm no where near finished setting up all the areas yet," Choi told them. "And, I am going to need help with setting up the cubicles in the different areas—that's a huge job. At the same time, Maggy and Rashad need to be installing the enclosure. It's going to take everyone to get this done."

"Okay, okay, everyone chill. We still have almost three weeks to get this done. Let's go one step at a time," the Captain stated. "Matzo, take whoever you need to finish removing the kitchen equipment from the ship. Some of you help Rashad and Maggy with getting the panels moved into the cave and then start setting up for the installation. The rest of you can help Choi setting up the cubicles and workstations."

"I have one problem solved," Sophia piped in, "we have three adult birds left and the three chicks. I plan on having a large thanksgiving dinner after the cave is sealed and before the storm gets here. So, we'll only have the two adults and three chicks to move in. I figure we can move them into the front part of the cave where I have my kitchen. If the storm lasts the three or four days Emir predicted, we should be okay."

"I can live with that," the Captain said. "However, the rest of you will need to hurry up as I am already thinking about a thanksgiving dinner with all the trimmings."

"Thanks Captain for getting us volunteers to help with getting the ship's panels moved into the cave," Rashad said with a grin. "Maggy and I had already decided not to cut anymore until we could determine exactly what was needed, so we are ready to start moving them over. However, if Bruce or one of his group could disconnect the door and the ramp along with the controls, it would be a big help, since we didn't think it would be a good idea to cut them out."

"If Dana and Gerard help us remove the kitchen equipment, we can remove the door," Bruce responded.

"Okay," the Captain said. "It sounds like we have a plan, let's get with it."

As everyone departed, the larger group broke off to go help Choi with the cubicles while the others went with either Rashad or Bruce.

Choi came up to Angelina and asked, "Can you help me with something?"

"Sure," Angelina responded. "What can I do for you?"

"Doc is helping set up his area, since we have most of his cubicles in place. But I would like your help setting up the Captain's area. We have all these consoles and equipment from his quarters and the cockpit, including his pilot's seat. I would like you to help in making it special for him, if you would."

"I'd be delighted and honored to help you Choi. I'm pleased that you thought of this consideration for the Captain."

When they walked in to the cave, they could see that Molly, Tani and Doc had made a lot of headway with Doc's medical area. Tani was going through a container that had nuts and bolts in it while Doc and Molly were standing up and placing the panels. The panel supports had little feet on them—much like cubicles. Inside the medical area, they had already installed the MRI; plus, they had put together Doc's cabinets and working tables, with some of his other medical equipment situated on top. They had also installed his surgical light, even though it would still need to be connected to the power source before it was operational.

His bunk had been placed along the far end wall and there was a small table next to it.

When they saw Choi approach, Doc called out, "We're using a little more space than you had originally laid out Choi, but the panel sizes dictate what we can do." When they had finished installing the panels, Doc had a nice area.

"I need to hang a tarp over the opening," Doc said, "so that I can provide some privacy for my patients."

While Tani went to look for a piece of tarp to hang over the opening, Choi and Angelina started figuring out the Captains area. With Doc and

Molly helping, they went over to the stock pile and started bringing over the Captain's console, tables, and other equipment that would be placed in his area.

"I think we should set it up with a small conference area where you come in, if we put that small table over there, he can meet and have private discussions with people. Along that wall, I would put his computer, console and the rest of his equipment. Then I would install one panel coming out from the wall to give him a private area with a table and chair next to his bunk," Angelina suggested.

"Sounds good to me," Choi agreed. "Let's get started."

Outside, Rashad and Maggy had moved some of the panels to the outside of the cave, while Dana and Gerard were dismantling the kitchen area. As soon as they removed a piece, Sophia and Naomi would take it out and haul it over to the waterfall cave where they were just stacking everything on the floor.

Meanwhile, Bruce, Matzo, and the Captain had been studying how to remove the door and the ramp. Bruce had suggested that they cut the panel the door was already mounted in so that they wouldn't have to figure out how to reattach the hinges and controls.

Dana came out and said, "Can you guys hold up a while? We have a ways to go before the kitchen is completely dismantled. Besides, when we started disconnecting the equipment, we discovered part of it is tied into the water distiller equipment. The good news is that if we can remove the wall mounted toilets, and move them into the hot spring cave, we might be able to figure out how to set them up."

"Humm," the Captain said as he stopped to think for a moment. "Okay Dana, I'll help your group with the kitchen and water distiller equipment." Then he added, "Bruce, this might be a good time for you and Matzo to send the drone out one last time."

"All right," Bruce said with a grin, "let's do it Matzo."

"I want you to send it around the shoulder of this mountain toward the mountain ranges in the distance and get some video," the Captain instructed them.

Got it," Bruce responded with a salute, happy to have the chance to fly the drone again.

CHAPTER THIRTY NINE

BRUCE AND MATZO WENT over to the drone and set up their controls. Within moments, they had the drone in the air.

"We'll have to record everything on the laptop since the computers are pretty much down now," Matzo remarked to Bruce as they adjusted the drone's flight pattern. "Let's maintain altitude just above the mountains but low enough to pick up details. I'll keep all the cameras running. Did you check with Emir about what his cave looked like?"

"Not today," Bruce responded as he continued to concentrate on making the flight programming adjustments. "But when he explained it before, Emir said it was located on a small plateau with a small, door type opening, rather then a large opening.

"Okay, then I'll keep my eyes open," Matzo replied as he refocused his attention on the laptop recording the real time videos.

Back in the cave, Choi's group was busy working on the Captain's quarters. After realizing that they couldn't finish setting up the consoles until the power grid was complete and all the cables had been run to the equipment, they decided to start on Angelina's cubicle. It helped that each cubicle had a common wall with the previous one, reducing the amount of panels to install. The cubicles themselves were all six feet tall, due to the size of the panels. The only problem was that they all had plain openings—without any doors. The group had discussed various ideas for resolving this issue but had decided to wait until all the areas had been completed before they did anything about it.

Meanwhile, Rashad and Maggy had also run into difficulty. While removing the ship's exterior skin, they had realized that the panels and struts were curved and not flat, thereby complicating their installation process. They would have to install them with the curve facing outside.

The other problem they ran into was, with the cave opening being so high, they would have to build some sort of scaffolding to work off of and figure out a way to lift the panels into place.

While they were discussing these issues, Dana came by carrying some more kitchen equipment removed from the ship's galley kitchen. Setting the piece down she said, "Why don't you two help us? That way we can be done faster and then we can help you with the panels. We can't set up most of this equipment in the kitchen until the power is hooked up and the cables have been run anyway." Agreeing with Dana, Rashad and Maggy stopped what they were doing and started helping remove the rest of the kitchen equipment.

Bruce and Matzo meanwhile had been flying the drone for over an hour. They estimated they still had another hour of flying time before they would have to turn the drone around and come back.

"This reminds me of when we flew over the plains," Bruce said. "Nothing but mountains, plains, and forest."

"Have you noticed how it seems to repeat itself?" Matzo questioned. "You have a mountain range, then an open grass area, after that you have another rain forest, some jungle and then another mountain range. Other than each mountain range being a little higher, it keeps repeating itself, almost like it was planned that way."

"That brings up the theory of the planet being in control again," Bruce said. As an afterthought, he added, "I don't know about you, but that makes me nervous." "I don't know about you, but that makes me nervous."

They had continued flying for almost another hour, when Matzo said, "Okay Bruce, swing it around toward the right hand side of the mountains and start bringing it back."

"Roger," Bruce replied.

As the drone swung around the mountain range, Matzo exclaimed, "Bruce, Look! There at the edge of that mountain, do you see it?"

Bruce stopped the drone from circling and flew straight, toward the mountain. There, straight ahead was the small opening and plateau Emir had described to them. They could also see what looked like a trail zigzagging up the side of the mountain to the cave opening. Turning the drone back around, they set it on a course to return with Matzo figuring out the distance to the cave from the ship.

Back at the ship, they had finished removing everything they were going to remove with the exception of the door and the ramp. The group was standing around discussing how best to remove the door and ramp and install them.

"I think if we leave the ramp in place and just remove the door it would work better," the Captain said. "I can't think of anything we need the ramp for anyway."

"I had thought to use it like a draw bridge," Rashad replied. "But Maggy pointed out that we would have to put a step into the opening in order to get it to work, so we decided against it. Also, by leaving it in place, we have something to stand on when we cut out the door. The other thing I decided was that we should cut the door first, put it in place, then attach the panels around it."

"That makes sense," the Captain responded after thinking about it for a couple of minutes. "So, let's get at it."

Rashad and Maggy again inspected around the door to determine the best place to cut.

"We are going to need something to help hold this up as we cut it; otherwise it's going to fall over on us," Maggy stated.

"If we get some cables and tie them to it inside, we can lower it down onto the ramp when you finish cutting it out. Then we can get a couple of the others to help haul it over and set it up in the cave mouth," the Captain directed. With that, Gerard went into the cave to get some cables. Upon returning, Gerard and the Captain along with Emir hooked the cables to the door.

"Okay," the Captain said from inside the ship, "start cutting when you are ready." Checking once again where to cut, Rashad trained his laser beam on the exterior skin and started cutting out around the door, leaving the frame intact.

"All right, get ready," Rashad, said. "I'm cutting the last of it now." As he finished cutting, the Captain along with Emir and Gerard slowly lowered it on to the ramp and let it slide down to the ground.

"All right," the Captain said, "let's get some supports ready and get some of the others to help set this up in the cave."

As they were setting up the supports at the entryway, Bruce and Matzo came up.

"We found the cave," Bruce announced. "It's a ways out, but it matches Emir's description."

"Let's see," the Captain replied. Matzo brought the laptop over and proceeded to run the video of the flight, pausing when he got to the part showing the cave.

"It seems to look like what Emir described," the Captain stated, "let's go show it to Emir."

Going up the ramp through the cut out opening, they found Emir sitting on what was left of the floor. The Captain suddenly realized that they couldn't leave Emir inside the ship anymore and would have to figure out how to get him to the cave without him being frozen.

"Emir," Bruce said excitedly, "I think we found your cave." Matzo, following Bruce into the ship, handed Emir the laptop.

"That's it," Emir said, "how far away is it?"

"A long way," Matzo stated. "Also, if you watch the entire video, you'll notice there are plains, jungles, and rain forest between every mountain range that you would somehow have to go through."

"There must be a way," Emir murmured to himself as he continued studying the video.

"First things first," the Captain stated. "We have to figure a way to get you out of the ship and into the cave. Let's all go back; I want to talk to Drago. Rashad, you, and the others continue setting up the door. Bruce, you and Matzo start breaking down the drone so it will fit into the cave." With that said, he left to go find Drago.

Entering into the cave, he saw activity everywhere. He found Drago with Natasha sorting through panels and bolts to support the others that were setting up the divider panels.

"Can I speak to you a moment?" the Captain asked Drago. "Sure Captain, what's up?"

"We need to come up with a plan to get Emir out of the ship and into the cave without him being frozen or walking off in a trance."

"Let me think," Drago replied. "If we carry him, we may all be frozen, but if we carry him on something without touching him, it might work."

"Let's see what we can use" the Captain replied. "We just can't leave him in the ship any longer."

Finding a small panel, they decided that if they put one person on each corner, they would be able to carry Emir into the cave. Getting Rashad and Gerard to help, they went back to the ship to get Emir.

When they got there, Emir was sitting at the top of the ramp. The Captain explained their plan and the four of them went up into the ship. With Emir sitting on the panel, they then started to work their way down the ramp. About half way down, Gerard slipped and lost his grip on the corner he was holding. With the sudden shift in weight, everyone lost their balance and their grip on the panel carrying Emir. As they fell, Emir was suddenly dropped to the ramp, which he slid down. When he hit the ground, he stood up and told them he was all right. Taking a step forward, he immediately froze in place.

The Captain and the others hurriedly got up and rushed to Emir. They tried to lift him, but just as before, it was if he had been turned into a immobile stone statue. Unable to move him, they had no choice but to stand there watching the multicolored lights move through Emir's body. Then just as suddenly, the lights stopped.

Emir turned and said, "*She* understands and will let me help complete our task before she calls me to the mountain."

The Captain and the others just stood there with their mouths open in shock as Emir started walking toward the cave.

"Who is this '*She*'?" The Captain asked no one in particular, talking mostly to himself.

When Emir entered the cave, everyone started questioning how he was able to do it. All they got was the same answer he had told the others. Finally, everyone started back to work, but the question remained on everyone's mind.

Bruce and Matzo had gone back to the drone and started taking the wings off and disconnecting the controls.

"I feel bad doing this," Bruce said. "It's like someone is taking away your only toy."

"You'd feel a lot worse looking over the cliff at it all smashed up at the bottom," Matzo replied.

"You're right," Bruce said as he continued removing some more screws from the frame.

Back at the cave front, Rashad and his group were putting up supports to hold the door in place so they could set the panels in around it.

Dana and Gerard had gone inside and after meeting with Choi, had started setting up their area on the other side of the cave. Meanwhile, the people working with Choi were setting up bunks in the girls sleeping quarters so they could determine how much room they needed and how many panels it would take to complete the area.

Emir excused himself and went directly to the waterfall cave. Not having been able to bathe while stuck in the ship, no one needed to remind him that he needed a bath as he headed straight for the hot spring.

When Bruce and Matzo had completed dismantling the drone's wings, they pushed the drone into the cave.

Going back to get the wings, Bruce stated, "it looks like the drone body will fit back through the door opening when they get it done."

"It better," Matzo replied. "I don't want to take it completely apart." Putting the wings and drone where Choi had told them to, they decided to go back to the ship and start taking out the power panel and converter generator.

Rashad and his group now had the door and frame supported in the opening and had gone back to measure and pick out what panels they were going to start with.

Coming back with the first panel, they grabbed some supports and mounted them on the panel. Next, they stood the panel up and put it in place against the cave wall with the curved side out.

Looking at it, Maggy noted, "The edge of the cave is uneven leaving gaps along the edges. Do you think we should try melting the rock, then fusing the panel to it so they join?"

"Your guess is as good as mine," Rashad replied. "Let's try it and see. But you might want to get someone else to help you hold it steady while pushing the panel against the wall as I melt it."

Getting Drago and Natasha to help, Rashad started burning the rock. At first it just glowed, then it started to melt. The others started pushing the panel against the melting rock. It wasn't quite working so Rashad decided to burn on the panel also. Finally, after going back and forth between them, Rashad stopped.

"Let it cool now," he said, "then we'll check to see if it holds." While they were waiting, Bruce and Matzo came up.

"We measured the converter and we're going to have to move it and the panels inside before you complete closing the wall," Bruce told them.

"The way this is going, you'll have plenty of time," Maggy responded. "It just took four of us almost an hour to get this one panel in place."

Checking out the panel now that it had cooled, Rashad said, "It seems to be tied in good, pushing on it with his hands. The question now would be, whether we should go across the bottom panels first and then go up, or do we put a couple panels on the bottom then one on the top?"

"It will be easier to weld the panels together than it was welding the rock to the panels," Maggy stated. "Also, if we go across the bottom first, it will hold the door in place, then we can remove those supports and use then somewhere else."

Getting the next couple of panels in place progressed much faster. They were almost ready to start installing the door when it started getting dark and they didn't have enough light to continue.

"It should be getting close to dinner time anyway," Rashad said, putting down the laser. "Let's put everything up and we will start again in the morning."

Meanwhile, Emir had finished his bath. Being pleased not to be locked in the ship by himself any longer, he had checked out the ice cave and was coming back through the waterfall cave when Sophia asked if he could help move some of the equipment that had been brought in so they would have room to set the table for dinner. Emir was more then happy to help, feeling like he was one of the group again. After removing the equipment that had been stacked on the dinner table, he continued to help Sophia and Naomi prepare dinner. Naomi was grilling some of the meat on the grill so he started helping Sophia with the vegetables and mashing some potatoes. They were almost ready when in walked the others.

"Go wash up and come to dinner," Sophia announced.

When they had finished washing and sat down, the Captain looked around. He could tell they were a tired group that had worked hard again that day.

"I see Bruce and Matzo got the drone inside, so that's one more thing off our list. Rashad, how did you and Maggy make out on closing up the cave entrance?"

"We didn't quite make it to the door frame, welding the panels into the side of the cave took a lot longer and was much trickier than we thought."

"How long do you think it will take?" the Captain asked.

"Probably a good week—maybe a couple days more, maybe a couple days less," Rashad responded. "We are going to have to build scaffolding as we go up and we still need to figure out how we are going to hoist the panels up there. Then, we have to install the perforated panels and the baffles at the top."

"That will be cutting it close," the Captain replied.

"Bruce, where do you and Matzo stand on the power panel?"

"We checked it out again today," Bruce answered. "We are going to have to disconnect and relocate the convertor generator and the main electrical panels from the ship before they close up the opening. Otherwise, we won't be able to get them to fit through the door. Matzo and I will need some help tomorrow when we get ready to bring them over. After that, we need to shut down everything and start the hook up. Following that, it will take at least another six to eight hours to get up to capacity."

"Well, right now, other than needing light, we're not using any power," Angelina said. "We can't really complete any of the areas until we get the power cables to them, then we can close them up and put them in place."

"I agree," Dana said. "We still have a lot to of stuff to put together before we're ready to hook up any power."

"Also," Angelina added, "we need to install some of our cameras and other equipment outside on the mountain like we had on the ship."

"All right," the Captain said. "I guess we are not quite as far along as I thought we would be."

"Let's do it this way. Emir, now that it is okay for you to go outside, I want you and Tani to get with Angelina and set up the equipment on the mountain. Rashad, you and your group continue with the enclosure. Drago, you, Natasha, and I will help Bruce and Matzo get the power equipment dismantled and moved inside. Doc, your team should keep installing the panels and setting up as much of the areas that you can. As soon as we get free, we will help with the panels. Hopefully, by that time, Molly and Choi can start running cables to the equipment. Even though you can't hook it up, it will give us a jump start when Bruce and Matzo have the power panel installed. So let's enjoy our dinner, get a hot bath and a good nights rest, then we'll hit it again in the morning."

CHAPTER FORTY

THE NEXT MORNING AFTER a breakfast of meat and eggs with some potato pancakes Sophia had made from the leftovers, they all set out to their work areas.

Angelina, Emir, and Tani gathered up the equipment they needed and went outside to climb the mountain and start their installations.

"Are you going to be okay climbing on the mountain?" Angelina asked Emir.

"I should be," Emir replied. "It feels good to be outside again."

Locating areas to attach the cameras and other equipment to was not easy. It had to be installed high enough to see off the mountain, but not so high that it was exposed to the high winds. After climbing around for about an hour installing the equipment, Angelina again asked Emir if he was doing okay.

"I'm fine, other than wanting to get on to the cave; I don't feel any compulsion to leave."

Three hours later, when they had the equipment in place, they went back down the mountain to gather the cables to run from the equipment.

"We won't be able to find holes to put these cables into the cave, so I suggest we put them under rocks and in cracks then run them through the top of the cave opening," Angelina stated.

Going back up the mountain, they buried and stuck the cables under rocks and in any crevices they could find, finally dropping the cables over the edge at the opening.

When they got down, Rashad asked, "Why are you dropping those cables like that?"

"It's the only way we can get them in the cave," Angelina replied. "We will have to run them though the perforated grating at the top, when you get it installed."

"Okay," Rashad responded looking at the dangling cables, "but I wish you had rolled them up and tied them so they wouldn't hang in our way."

"You're right," Angelina apologized. "We'll go back up and do that. Tani, can you go back to my area and get a couple rolls of that twisty wire? It's in the crate marked miscellaneous supplies."

When Tani returned with the wire, they went back up and tied the cables out of the way. As they got back on the ground, the Captain called to them to see if they could help haul the equipment Bruce and Matzo had finally got disconnected.

It took all of them to drag, lift, and push the equipment out of the ship now that the floor had been removed. When they finally got it all on the ground, the Captain told them to take a break before they hauled it into the cave.

Bruce and Matzo went back into the ship and started gathering up and hauling the remaining cables and piping they had removed back outside.

While they were taking a break, the Captain's group walked over to check on Rashad and his group.

"How's it going?" the Captain asked.

"Okay," Rashad replied. "Right now, I'm dressing up some of the welds where I just tacked it in place. The others are trying to put together some scaffolding so we can start the next level on this side. We decided we would go up two levels, then go do the bottom level on the other side. That way, we have support on both sides as we go up. Are you ready to move in the last of the equipment yet?"

"Yes," the Captain said, "we were just taking a break before we start hauling it into the cave."

"Taking a break?" Maggy exclaimed, "I don't remember us discussing break time this morning."

"It's because I'm old and need to preserve my strength," the Captain replied with a chuckle. "Okay team, let's go back to work, and haul that stuff into the cave. I wouldn't want Maggy to think we weren't doing our part."

The Captain's team then went back and proceeded to carry the equipment in, one piece at a time. It was somewhat easier because they were on level ground, but they still had to set a couple of the pieces down once or twice before they got all the way to the rear of the cave.

When it was all back there, Bruce and Matzo required some more help getting it stood up and fastened in place. Finally, they were done. It was now up to Bruce and Matzo to make the connections and get everything hooked up.

Having finished relocating the power equipment, they split up, going to help the others. The Captain took Choi's place so he could help with spreading out the cables. Tani went with Choi to help remove and mark the cables. Emir stated that he had promised Sophia he would be back to help set up the kitchen so he went off to help her.

Meanwhile, back at the entrance, Rashad and Maggy's group had moved the scaffolding into place.

"It's not very sturdy," Rashad complained. "It shakes and moves."

"We didn't want to permanently fasten it since we will need these supports for the other panels. So, we wired it together, then we took two of the cubicle panels and tied them on top so you would have a place to stand on," Dana explained. "It should hold."

Carefully climbing up onto the scaffolding, Rashad asked, "How are you going to get the next panel up here?"

"You're going to have to come back down. Drago and Gerard will climb up and lift the panel up, they will then move to the side and hold it while you climb back up and weld it," Maggy told him.

"This should be fun," Rashad replied sarcastically.

Drago and Gerard then proceeded to climb up carrying the cables with them. When they got up, they slowly pulled the panel up with those on the bottom helping to lift as high as they could. When the panel was up on the scaffold, Drago and Gerard had to move it in place. Then, with one holding it, the other mounted the supports.

"Okay, we're ready," Drago told Rashad, "climb on up."

Rashad climbed up and steadying himself, started to melt the rock. This piece fit better as the wall was smoother without the large gaps. When he had the rock melting, he then heated up the panel and fused the two together. This time it only took forty five minutes to install the panel.

Rashad looked down and said to Maggy, "See if the other laser has charged up, I've only got a few minutes left on this one."

"Right," Maggy said going off to check. At the same time, Drago and Gerard lowered the cables back down and the rest of the team attached the next panel.

"You'll have to move over to the left," Drago told Rashad, "in order for us to get the next panel up here."

They again maneuvered the next panel into place. Rashad had just enough charge left on the batteries that he was able to tack it in place before the laser needed to be recharged. Maggy showed up just then and suggested, "Why don't you come down and take a break while we swap out the laser?"

"I want to finish welding this piece first," Rashad answered back. "I'll lower this one on the cables then you can tie that one on and I'll pull it back up."

"Okay," Maggy agreed.

Once the swap had been made, Maggy took the other laser back to be recharged. Fortunately, they were charged using the solar batteries so shutting down the power hadn't affected them.

"Let's get these next two panels in place. That way we will have completed this level, and then we can take a break," Rashad said.

The next two panels went up smoothly. Drago and Gerard had returned to the ground when Rashad announced he was done.

"Let's take that break now."

"Seeing it's time for lunch, I wouldn't exactly call it a break," Maggy replied.

When they got to the eating area, everyone was already there. Sophia had fixed a lunch of cold meat sandwiches with a salad. Sitting around talking as they ate lunch, the Captain asked Rashad how it was going.

"Well, we have the second level finished on one side. After lunch, we are going to drop down and do the bottom and second level on the other side." Rashad responded. "When we complete that, we will have to cut a another panel to fit over the door that allows the third level to join—or do parts of each level then complete the installation over the door last. At that point, Bruce and Matzo should be able to install the perforated flooring we planned on modifying to create baffles. Then Angelina can run her cables through and we will be done—about three to four more days, if every thing goes right. However, I'm a little concerned about building the scaffolding any higher, it's pretty shaky now."

"Which reminds me," Maggy interrupted. "We need you guys to hold off on taking any more panels for the cubicles since we may need them for the scaffolding. We are wiring it together temporarily so it can be taken back apart when we're through."

"That is going to slow us down," the Captain said. "We will have to wait for you to finish before we can continue. It's going to take Bruce and Matzo the rest of today and half of tomorrow to get the power up and running. While there are some things that can be done, we're going to have people standing around.

"What if we have two teams installing the panels? Maggy can weld on one side and you on the other?"

"We will have to build another set of scaffolding. Plus, we have been alternating using the lasers. They need to be recharged about half way through the day," Rashad added.

"That means about the time the lasers run out of juice, Bruce and Matzo should have the power up and we can start hooking up the equipment. Therefore, we should not have to lose any time while the lasers are recharging," the Captain stated. "The next day, if you have reached the third level, you can go back to one team. It will take at least a couple more days to hook up all the equipment."

After lunch, Rashad and his group went back to the opening. This time, when Rashad started, he smoothed the wall out first, and then brought in the panel. This seemed to work better than trying to do both at the same time. He laughed to himself, "I'll have this figured out by the time I'm done."

This level went faster. He climbed down and took a break while the rest of the team moved the scaffolding over so they could start the second level. Again, by smoothing the wall first, the panels fit better and faster.

They completed the second level on that side much faster than the other. When they had completed welding the panels together, Drago suggested they go to building the scaffolding for tomorrow for two crews and let the lasers get completely recharged.

With everyone agreeing, they proceeded to build scaffolding. Having the extra time, they were bolting as much as they could to make the scaffolding stronger. By the time dinner was ready, they had the two scaffolds together and erected in place, ready for tomorrow.

When they got to dinner, they found out that Bruce and Matzo had completed the hook up of the power panel, the distribution panel, and the converter generator. Now, it was just a matter of time while they waited for the system to become fully charged.

"So then," the Captain said, "in the morning, the two crews will start welding the panels. The others will continue running the cables from the distribution panel and hooking them up to the equipment."

"Matzo and I can only wait until the power comes up," Bruce said. "I suggest the two of us hook together the perforated flooring to be installed at the top of the door panels. Since it's made from high density plastic, it's much lighter and can be installed in a single piece. With both the scaffolds in place, we can raise it at one time, and then we can start on the baffles. That way, when we take down the scaffolding, we will be done. We can always finish the cubicles during the storm while were stuck inside."

"Good plan," the Captain agreed. We are down to the last five days before the storm. As the guys continued their discussions, the girls excused themselves and headed for the baths.

CHAPTER FORTY ONE

THE NEXT DAY AFTER breakfast, the groups got up and went back to their work areas.

Bruce and Matzo gathered the perforated flooring together and spread it out on the floor so they could start bolting it together. Matzo turned to Bruce and said, "It looks like this panel will be bigger than the opening. But Rashad should be able to put it up and cut it in place easily since it is plastic."

"I agree," Bruce said as he continued bolting.

Meanwhile, the others had started installing the panels. With the two teams working together, they already had the first panel up on each side.

Maggy, having learned from watching Rashad, had smoothed the wall first before fitting the panel. They continued on the side panels, which progressed faster since it involved just welding metal to metal. When both sides had reached the door opening, both Rashad and Maggy got down from the scaffolding and measured out the opening before they proceeded to cut the panel.

After they finished with the cut, their team had it raised up onto the scaffolding. When Rashad and Maggy climbed up onto the scaffolding, they saw that the panel did not quite fit. In moments Rashad had cut it to fit and started welding it. Maggy then returned to her scaffolding and proceeded to prepare the wall for the next panel. Working together, the work progressed much faster with Rashad completing the piece around the door on one side as Maggy did the same on her side. They had installed all the panels on each side except for the last one when their lasers started losing power. Working quickly, both Rashad and Maggy were able to tack weld the remaining pieces together before the lasers quit working altogether.

"Well, it looks like tomorrow is another day," Rashad commented as they stood there for a moment inspecting their work. "At least we got quite a bit done today."

As they were climbing down the scaffold, Maggy said, "Let's go check with the others and see how we can help."

Bruce and Matzo had finished putting together the perforated floor and left to go check on the power panel. When they came back, they told everyone that it would take another two hours or so before the system would be completely charged. Bruce then informed them that he and Matzo planned to go start on the baffles while they were waiting.

Gerard and Dana went to their area to complete putting together their equipment and getting it ready to connect.

Because they couldn't use anymore panels until the scaffolding was dismantled, the rest of the group went to help hook up the cables, put together the kitchen equipment for Sophia, and help Emir set up his area.

When Sophia called them to lunch, Bruce and Matzo went and checked out the power. The rest were eating when they returned and Bruce announced, "The power is at 98%, more than enough to try starting up some of the equipment. By the time everything is hooked up and running, the power should be self sustaining."

"I suggest you start in Doc's area and move down that side since it is more complete. That will give Dana, Gerard, and Emir more time to get their equipment set up," Drago suggested.

After lunch was complete, they all went to Doc's area where the cables and power lines had already been installed and were just waiting to be turned on.

With a solemn gesture, Doc approached the main switch on his console, looking one more time at everyone, he turned and flipped on the switch. His computer screen came up immediately. With a rapid movement, Doc reached over and threw the power switches, for the remaining equipment. When the lights came on over his surgical tables, everyone let out a cheer.

"Okay," the Captain said with some relief. "Let's get the rest of this place up and running." With that, the group cheerfully headed back to what they were working on.

The rest of the day saw much of the equipment up and running. By dinner time, they had completed hooking up everything but Dana and Gerard's area, Emir's area, and Sophia's kitchen equipment.

Sitting down to dinner, they started discussing what tomorrow's activities would be.

"If Rashad and Maggy can complete the enclosure and we can finish Dana's, Emir's and the kitchen, we will have beaten the storm by two days," the Captain said. "Let's get to bed early tonight so that we can get an early start in the morning. If we can get those items finished up, we might be able to get the rest of the cubicles set up before the storm hits."

"I still have to hook up the cables for the outside surveillance equipment after they get the perforated panels in place," Angelina told them.

"With any luck we should have that installed and be ready for the baffles by lunch tomorrow," Rashad replied.

"It will take most of the day to complete Dana and Emir's areas but we should have them done by dinner tomorrow night," Tani stated.

"Good," the Captain said. "Once more, get a hot bath and good nights sleep. We'll hit it early tomorrow, and with any luck we will be ready for the storm."

The next morning, they awoke to a new aroma. The Captain jumped out of his bunk and went to the eating area.

"Is that coffee I smell?" he asked Sophia charging into the kitchen.

"Just a little surprise I brewed up to boost the troupe's energy level. I started grinding it up yesterday, and thought it would help get us through the last push."

"I don't know how many of the kids drink coffee, but Angelina, Doc, and myself will do our share."

"I figure the kids will try it since they have only had water since we have been on the planet."

When the rest of the group showed up, Rashad, Maggy, Tani, and Emir all said, "Is that coffee I smell?" The others who had never had coffee quickly learned from the others, adding honey that Sophia had put out.

When they had finished with breakfast, Rashad and Maggy got up with their group and went to complete the enclosure. Everyone else got up and went back to completing the equipment hook ups.

The group working on the enclosure had by now, got it down to a science. They automatically set up the panels and hoisted them up onto the scaffolding where Rashad and Maggy started welding. They completed the final row just in time for lunch. After eating a quick sandwich and drinking some iced coffee, they went right back to work. While Bruce and Matzo were working on the baffles, the others passed up the perforated panels. With both Rashad and Maggy on separate scaffolds, the perforated panel was installed with in minutes.

When they finished, Rashad asked that someone go let Angelina know that they were ready for her to pull in the cables for the outside equipment. Angelina arrived and started pulling the cables through. She then let them dangle to the floor where she tied them in loops until they could run them back to the equipment.

Maggy's group started taking down the one set of scaffolding so that the pieces could be sent back to the others to be used for installing the cubicles.

Bruce and Matzo climbed up onto the one side of the remaining scaffold, pulling up the flaps they planned to use as the baffles.

The day before, they had attached the flaps on frames and rigged cables to the frame so that they would be able to manually open and close the baffles once they were installed.

Rashad quickly welded the first frame in place. After he finished, they tried the manual controls. Seeing that they worked, everyone climbed down and moved the scaffold to the other side.

After climbing back up, they again performed the same operation. When they were satisfied the manual controls were working properly and they were finished, they climbed down and exchanged high fives with each other.

"Go get Angelina and see if she needs the scaffold to run her cables back into the cave. If not, we will dismantle it and take the parts into the others." Rashad directed.

When Angelina arrived, she was carrying some small metal hooks she had made.

"If you can weld these to the rock Rashad, I'll run the cables through them. This should keep them along the ceiling and off the floor."

For the next hour, Rashad fastened the hooks to the ceiling, with Angelina right beside him pulling the cables through. They would then move the scaffold and do it again, when they finished the last set, they got down and had the crew start to dismantle the scaffolding. They then went into the cave looking for the Captain, when they found him, Rashad announced, "Mission complete," Captain.

"Great," the Captain replied. "I'll tell Sophia to put the bird on. You guys go help the others where you can."

"I can't wait for dinner tonight," Rashad said.

By dinner time, they had completed setting up Dana's and Emir's areas and were in the process of hooking up the cables.

The cubicles and the kitchen area were not quite complete since they had been waiting on the parts and panels used in the scaffolding. Still, a jubilant group sat down for dinner that night.

Even though Sophia did not serve any coffee, they all had a great time. After dinner, they took their customary turns heading to bathe and then to bed knowing they had beat the dead line by one day.

After the girls came back from their bath, Emir delayed going with the guys. Instead, he quietly went to his bunk area, gathered his stuff, and put it into his backpack. He then went and got one of the Sling Around cables and wrapped it around his waist. Making sure no one was watching, he slipped out through the door and headed across the plateau. There was still enough light to see his way around the shoulder. Once he had turned the corner there was a buffeting sound above him. Looking up, he saw Aria landing. Taking the one end of the cable from around his waist, he gave the other end to Aria who took it in her claws then took to the air, carrying Emir with her.

They flew through the night sky for a long time. Emir was not concerned because he knew that Aria was taking him to the cave. When they finally arrived at the small plateau, Aria landed and Emir removed the cable from her claws. Without another thought, Aria flew off into the night sky.

Emir turned and faced the cave, going up to the opening he stepped inside. At once, colors started running up the walls, lighting the cave with multiple lights. Looking around he saw a chair against the far wall. Walking closer, he realized it was more of a throne. It was not man made, but part of the cave itself. Looking at it for a moment, he turned and sat down on it.

"Finally," the voice in his head said, "Welcome."

Chapter Forty Two

The next morning at breakfast, they were all still feeling good. Sophia had again supplied coffee and everyone was discussing what they were going to do that day when Drago asked, "Where's Emir?"

Looking around, everyone noticed that he wasn't there.

"Go check his bunk," the Captain said.

Tani got up and went to his bunk, not only was he not there, but looking further around she noticed his backpack was missing. Running back to the eating area she blurted out, "He's gone and so is his stuff!" Everyone got up and went running through the caves looking for him.

When they all met back at the main cave, the Captain said, "He must have gone out and headed for the cave some time during the night."

"But he'll never get there before the storm comes." Angelina said.

"There's nothing we can do," the Captain stated. "I can't have everyone out searching for him with the storm coming. We have to complete our preparations."

After they had finished with breakfast, Loren went to up Drago. "Drago, we have to try something," she pleaded.

"You heard what the Captain said," Drago responded. "He is correct; we do not know which way Emir went."

"If I get Aria to help, will you go with me?"

"All right," Drago replied hesitantly. "See if you can get in touch with her, then let me know."

Loren went outside and started mentally calling for Aria. Once again, she waited for many minutes. Finally, she heard the flapping of wings, but turning around, she did not see Aria.

"I'm Jar'd, son of Shia. Aria and Shia have other duties right now, but they have sent me to help."

"Wait here," Loren, pleaded. "I need to get Drago." Running back into the cave she got Drago to come outside.

She quickly explained who Jar'd was and asked if he would carry them to the cave. He replied he would. Loren ran back inside and grabbed the canvas carrier they had used before. It wasn't until she went to hook up the harness that she realized that she would not be able to use it as it had originally been designed. Hurriedly making some last minute adjustments, Loren readjusted one of the straps; tied it off and put the one end around Jar'ds neck.

Climbing into the container, she gestured for Drago to join her. After Drago climbed in, Jar'd took to the air flying around the side of the mountain in the same direction that Aria had taken Emir.

"The storm comes," Jar'd warned Loren after they had been flying for a while. They were still far from the cave when the first gust of air hit them. Suddenly, the cable came loose from the container, dropping Loren and Drago into the jungle below. Falling through the trees, they desperately tried to hang on to the container. But both were knocked unconscious as the container finally jammed into some of the lower branches of the tree leaving them wedged in the crumpled heap of the container.

Jar'd with the cable still around his neck, headed back to Aria and Shia.

CHAPTER FORTY-THREE

THEY WERE FRANTIC AT the cave. The fact that three of their people were outside and the storm was upon them was causing both fear and confusion.

"Captain, you must let us try and reach Drago!" Natasha exclaimed.

"Exactly how do you propose to do that?" the Captain questioned. "We have no idea where they are or what happened to them. The only thing we can do is to wait out the storm then try to find them. Right now, my top priority has to be making sure the rest of us survive the storms. Bruce, you and Choi go inspect the baffles and report back to me. Angelina, monitor the cameras. The rest of you settle down back at your cubicles."

The hurricane force winds continued to rise throwing both rain and debris against the panels protecting the caves. Suddenly, there was a large crash against the main cave panels. Using one of the cameras, she had installed outside the cave, Angelina could see that the ship had been thrown against the panels and was blocking the door. "Captain," she shouted above the wind, "the entry is blocked. The wind has blown the remainder of the ship against the front of the cave."

"There's nothing we can do now," the Captain responded. "We will have to wait until the storm is over."

The winds continued to increase; Bruce and Choi had reduced the angle on the baffles to restrict the air blowing into the cave but had left them opened enough so the wind would not blow out the baffles all together. Suddenly there was a loud screeching and grinding noise against the front panels.

Angelina yelled out "Captain, the winds just blew the ship from in front of the cave, over the side of the plateau and down to the ground below."

"That's good news and bad news," the Captain stated, "I hope enough survived so we can use some of the remaining parts."

With that, they all huddled together at the back of the cave by the cubicles; even Sophia came out of the kitchen area to sit tightly surrounded with the others.

Meanwhile, Drago and Loren were still lying unconscious in the jungle canopy. The heavy winds were whipping the trees from side to side. As the rain came blowing across the canopy it brought Loren into semi consciousness. She seemed to see a vague shape reaching for them through the wind and the rain, but passed into unconsciousness again before she could determine what it was.

Morgu, leader of the Ubscanti, had received a calling from Aria, telling him that there were two of the new creatures lying in his domain. Morgu, who was unfamiliar with these creatures, questioned Aria at length. Finally satisfied and with the description, he headed out in the storm to find them. Fortunately, on the ground beneath the canopy, the hurricane force winds were much reduced. Normally, he would have been able to make better time swinging through the canopy, but he stayed on the ground until reaching the area that Aria had shown him. Fighting his way up into the tops of the trees through the storm, he spotted the canvas carrier, described by Aria. Approaching it, he could see the two creatures lying inside. After examining them and the carrier for a moment, he decided to just leave them in the carrier and carry them that way back to his shelter.

Over the generations, the Ubscanti had built shelters in their jungle, much like the pyramids of the Mayans. These were primarily used as shelter when the storms came, but they also served as meeting places among the families. Morgu was the leader of all the families; and as such, had the largest of these pyramids. Right now, only his immediate family occupied it. However, he would have to call the other leaders together after the storm to discuss these new creatures.

When he finally reached his shelter, he was greeted by his mate, Biancu. "Did you find the creatures Aria described to you?" she asked with concern in her voice.

"They are in this sack," he replied. Lowering the sack from his shoulders, he gently opened it to expose Draco and Loren to his mate.

"They are small and look weak," his mate said.

"Yes, we will have to be gentle with them. Tell the others and the young ones that they may look, but not to touch. Please put them in one of the ground nests along with some water and fruit. Then we just have to wait for them to wake up."

Biancu gently lifted them from the carrier and carried them one at a time over to the nest. After putting them in the nest, she got fruit and water and placed it in the nest with them. Looking at them, she decided to take the hollowed out shell holding the water and sprinkle it on the face of the one with the long hair. Loren, feeling the water dip onto her face, once again started to regain consciousness. When she opened her eyes the first thing she saw was a gorilla like creature she had seen in the videos. She immediately sat up and screamed. The creature in front of her jumped back when she screamed and put out her paws gesturing for her to be quite. Loren was backing rapidly to the back of the nest, trying to get as far away as possible. Through her panic, she suddenly heard a voice in her head, like with Aria, saying, "It's all right, be calm, I won't hurt you."

"How do I know that?" she responded.

Suddenly, it was Biancu's turn to be shocked. "You can hear my thoughts?" she questioned.

"Yes" Loren responded.

"Aria called us and sent my mate to find you." Biancu said.

"Aria?" Loren questioned. "She is my friend."

"She is part of the council with my mate." Biancu replied. "She asked him to find you and bring you to safety. She will come to retrieve you and your mate, when the storms pass."

"He is not my mate, but part of my family."

"Wait here, I will go tell my mate Morgu that you are now awake and can talk with us. He will want to speak with you."

Loren sat there, her thoughts running every which way. She looked down at Drago, he was still unconscious, and had a large bruise on his forehead. She couldn't help but marvel that as large as Biancu was and as ferocious as she looked, the voice in her mind was both soft and gentle. Still trying to process all that had happened to them, Loren ripped a piece of her blouse off and was using it to dip in the water and put on Drago's head when Biancu returned with her mate. If she thought Biancu was large and ferocious looking, her mate was a monster.

"This is my mate, Morgu," she said. "He is leader of the Ubscanti."

Loren stood up, and bowed to him saying, "Thank you for rescuing us Morgu, it is a pleasure to meet you."

"She has manners," Morgu commented to his mate. "It is a pleasure to meet you also." he replied to Loren. She was surprised by the deep resonance of his voice; yet, it too was soft and gentle. "Please sit, we have much to discuss."

Loren, sitting down, could not help but notice, that Morgu, while sitting was still taller than her when she was standing up.

"Tell me about your family and how you came to be here." Morgu requested.

"We came from another world," Loren started and proceeded to tell Morgu of all the events that had happened to them up to the point when she and Drago fell through the trees. Many times he stopped her to get further definitions and clarity. She noticed that while they were talking, many of his family had come up and sat down to look at her and listen.

Finally, Morgu said, "that is enough for now, it will take me awhile to understand all you have told me. Eat your fruit now and we will continue this conversation in the morning. We have two more days of this storm and that will give us plenty of time to finish our discussions."

Loren stood up and bowed once again to Morgu as he left. When they were gone, she sat back down and taking some of the fruit began to eat, saying to herself, "Drago, do I have a surprise for you when you wake up."

Back at the cave, the group had settled down and had gone back to doing different chores in the cave. Sophia and Naomi had gone to the kitchen to prepare a meal. Rashad and Maggy had taken over checking on the panels to make sure they were holding. Bruce and Choi were back checking on the power. Dana and Gerard had gone to check on the canopy skylight and make sure it was holding up. The rest had gone back to putting together cubicles and setting up the cave.

"Captain," Angelina reported, "it looks like everything is holding up. The outside cameras show that the solar panels are still in place, and it looks like the panels we used to close up the cave are going to be able to withstand the winds."

"Good, we might make it through this after all," the Captain said. "However, I can't help worrying about Loren, Drago and Emir. I feel Emir is safe only because the planet wants him that way—since it seems to have a special purpose for him. Drago and Loren though may be a different story. I am really concerned about what might have happened to them."

"Why don't we get Natasha and ask her about Drago?" Angelina suggested. "The two of them have a special connection and seem to be able to know what the other one is up to, or where they are."

"Good idea," the Captain agreed. "Go find her and bring her here, we'll ask her."

While Angelina went to find Natasha, the Captain sat down thinking about the affect of losing two members of the party. Drago, he had decided would replace him, if anything happened. His thinking and planning had earned the respect of everyone. On the other hand, Loren had the ability to communicate with the different species on the planet and her loss would affect them dramatically. His training had taught him to expect losses among his people, it was especially more significant being on a strange planet where they had no idea what to expect. However he was not ready to accept their loss yet. As he was sitting there, thinking about this, Angelina showed up with Natasha.

"Natasha, have you been able to communicate with Drago?" the Captain asked.

"I was just telling Angelina, I haven't picked up anything from Drago. But I still get the feeling he's out there some place. I don't have that empty feeling I get when someone is no longer with us." Natasha explained.

"Well that's encouraging; at least, I think so. Thank you Natasha, you can go back to what you were doing."

"I don't think there is much more we can do till the storms are over," Angelina said. "But on my way back with Natasha, I overheard Sophia say that dinner was almost ready."

Walking in to the eating area, they saw that Sophia was already serving the food.

"Beef stew tonight," she announced. "There's nothing better on a windy and rainy night than old fashioned comfort food."

After dinner, everyone headed to their cubicles. Natasha and Maggy went to feed Zena and Butkis some of the left over stew.

"Lets grab a couple of towels on the way," Maggy suggested. "That way we can get a hot bath after feeding the pups."

"Sounds good to me," Natasha replied.

Meanwhile, the Captain, Angelina and Doc headed to the Captain's quarters to discuss the situation. Sitting down at the small conference table Choi had installed, Doc looked at the Captain and asked, "What's the search plan for Drago and Loren after the storms end?"

"First, I want to see if Natasha can contact Drago. If not, I'll have her try to call Aria and see if she knows where they are. I have to be honest with you; never in my life did I expect to call on a bird to help me."

"What if they're gone?" Angelina queried.

"If that turns out to be the case, I'm not sure how we will handle it. I do know that it will be imperative to get to Emir and see if he knows what is happening. The other thing is that we will have to keep the kids active and not let them get weighed down in the loss."

"I think I'd like another shot of that tequila, then I'm going to bed." Doc said.

"Agreed," the Captain said as he stood up to go get the bottle and glasses.

CHAPTER FORTY-FOUR

LOREN HAD AWAKENED AND was checking on Drago when Biancu showed up with some melons for breakfast.

"Good morning Biancu," Loren greeted.

"Fair day to you," Biancu replied. "I have brought you food to eat. Morgu will be here in a moment to continue your talk. How is your friend today?"

"He seemed to rest better last night, I hope he awakes soon." Loren replied. As she was eating the fruit Biancu gave her, Morgu arrived.

"Fair day to you," Loren said standing and bowing to Morgu.

"Fair day to you also little one," he replied. "I have spoken to *She*," Morgu said. "I am told to accept you as one of our own and part of our family. *She* has been talking with the 'Communicator' who is of your group. It seems *She* has talked with the *Mother*, and you are part of her plan."

"I'm confused," Loren responded. "Who is *She*, and who is the *Mother*?"

"I was directed to have that discussion with the one who still sleeps, named Drago." Morgu replied.

"Did *She* say when he would awaken?" Loren asked.

"Today," Morgu replied. "Until then, we will continue our discussion."

"What can you tell me about your family and how you live?" Loren questioned.

"We of the Ubscanti are the protectors of what you call the jungle. We live in the canopy in nests that we make from the tree leaves. We feed off the plants and fruits of the jungle."

"I'm sorry to ask this question," Loren apologized in front of her question. "But if you eat only of fruit and plants, why do you have such large fangs and claws, like a meat eater?"

"*She* told me that you and your people have interesting minds and ask strange questions. But to answer your question, we have them to fight against the Selamiss and the evil they bring with them."

"Who or what are the Selamiss?" Loren asked.

"I will explain it to the one who sleeps, for he will understand," Morgu stated. "Now tell me more of your family."

Drago could feel the cool cloth on his head as he slowly regained consciousness; but when he opened his eyes, everything was out of focus and he was dizzy. Loren who was wiping his forehead with a damp cloth saw his eyes open.

"Lie still a moment and keep the cloth over your eyes," she instructed him. "From what I know, you will be dizzy and unfocused for a moment. Besides, I need to tell you where we're at and what's happening before you open your eyes."

"My head hurts and my mouth is really dry." Drago mumbled.

"Try some of this melon, for your throat," Loren said putting a piece up to his mouth.

"This tastes wonderful," Drago said biting into the melon and feeling the cool juices run down his throat. "Where did you get it?" he questioned.

"Before I answer, tell me what you remember about our fall." Loren asked.

"I remember the cable coming loose and us falling into the trees, I remember trying to catch hold of a branch to stop our fall, then I hit my head and don't remember anything else. I do have a fuzzy memory of being carried by someone or some thing, but that part is still kind of hazy and not very clear to me."

"We were rescued and carried through the jungle to where we are now." Loren told him.

"Who rescued us and where are we?" Drago asked.

"The answer to the second part of your questions is that we are in a large pyramid like shelter, protecting us from the storm," Loren responded. "As to who rescued us, that is what I need to talk to you about. Do you remember the video of the jungle showing that large gorilla like animal?"

"Yes," Drago replied.

"Well, one of them, Morgu to be exact, rescued us and brought us to their shelter,"

"What?" Drago exclaimed. "Do you mean to tell me we're now in a cave with those monsters?"

"They are not monsters; in fact, they're very gentle creatures. Besides, Morgu will be here in a minute. He is supposed to meet with you and discuss the Selamiss."

"Stop. This is too much to take in without being able to see my surroundings. I'm taking the cloth off my eyes right now so that I can see where we are," Drago said removing the cloth from his eyes.

At first, his vision was still blurry, but as his eyes slowly adjusted and came back into focus, he could see he was in a dimly lit enclosure. As he looked around, he could see the large gorilla like animals moving about. Among them, he could see smaller versions of what he took to be their infants and young. Suddenly, one of the largest separated from the group and came toward them. Startled, Drago tried to stand up and back off in fear.

Loren stood and said, "Fair day to you Morgu."

"Fair day to you also Miss Loren," he replied. "I see the one called Drago is awake."

Although Drago had managed to remain standing, he was still more than a little dizzy and disoriented. To his surprise, Drago realized that he could hear Morgu's voice in his head. He could also not help but notice the deep softness of Morgu's voice.

"Do not fear me," Morgu said. "We are destined to work together; *SHE* has determined that you will help lead us in the fight against the Selamiss. But that can wait, eat of the fruit and we will talk of how you came to be here and about my family." Morgu stated sitting down.

As Drago sat down, he felt his head becoming clearer, he also felt less fearful due to both Morgu's and Loren's behavior.

"I am of the family Ubscanti; we are the protectors of what you call the jungle. I am their leader, and sit on the council with the other protectors. You have met Aria, leader of the Tashi, who is also on the council. You, Loren discovered Zentaska, leader of the Wantaso and protector of the plains."

"I don't know any Zentaska," Loren stated.

"You found her remains before she returned to the *Mother*." Morgu replied, "She was killed by one of the tribes of the Selamiss. Her female offspring is to become leader in her place; we are told she resides with your people. Her name is Zena."

"Oh my God," Loren exclaimed. "Maggy will freak when she finds out Zena is to be the leader of the plains."

"*SHE* decided it was a good thing for her to be raised among your tribe." Morgu stated. "Once you get settled in your shelter, you will meet more of the Wantaso."

"We have been paired together by *SHE*. *SHE* has put Loren with Aria. You, Drago are to be teamed with me. Another one of your tribe will be teamed with Chai, leader of the Katorions, protectors of the rainforest."

"Please wait a minute," Drago requested. "This '*SHE*,' you keep referring to, who is *SHE*?"

"SHE is, by the definition in your mind, this planet. *SHE* and all of us were put here by the *MOTHER*, who controls all things." Morgu responded. "Right now, a member of your family—Emir, known to us as the Communicator, is sitting on the throne and all things are being told to him by *SHE*. He will explain all things, when *SHE* is done explaining to him."

"Is he alright?" Loren asked.

"*SHE* takes care of all his needs," Morgu responded.

Drago, becoming his old self had absorbed this information and was now starting to analyze and develop theories about future developments.

"Tell me about the Selamiss, please Morgu." Drago requested.

"Before I tell you of the Selamiss, I must explain what has been told to me," Morgu stated. "*SHE* has told me that the *MOTHER* requires balance in all things. For every positive, there must be a negative; for every strength, there must be a weakness; for every good, there must be evil. Selamiss is the evil.

Morgu paused briefly making sure that Drago and Loren had been able to grasp the importance of his thoughts, then he continued. "There has always been balance here; the Selamiss tribes have always, for the most part stayed to their side of the world. But quietly, over the last few turns, they have started expanding their territory. They have taken over all the water ways, and destroyed the protectors of them."

"We might have met one of them." Drago stated quietly.

"They must have started to move out onto the plains," Morgu said. "For Zentaska was killed by a member of one of their tribes. The *MOTHER* has brought you here to help bring back the balance."

"How does *SHE* expect us to do this? Drago questioned.

"That is up to us, *SHE* cannot interfere; however, the *MOTHER* has stated, should we fail, she will remove *SHE* and all of us from existence."

I don't understand how we are going to accomplish this," Drago stated still trying to grasp what Morgu had been telling him.

"We have another day before the storms cease," Morgu said. "The remainder of that time, you and I will discuss many things. After the storm, you will be taken back to your people so that you can tell them of what you have learned. Then, at the time of the single full moon, we will gather at council. Hopefully, by that time the Communicator will have learned enough to give us direction."

"Do you mean Emir?" Drago asked.

"That is what you call him by."

"What is *SHE* doing with Emir?" Drago questioned.

"SHE attempts to teach him what she knows, so he can then tell us what the Selamiss are doing. *SHE* sees and hears everything; she knows each leaf in the forest, bird in the sky, everything living, why it's here and what it does at all times."

"How is she going to teach all that to Emir? I'm not sure the human brain can handle it." Drago said. "Besides, I thought *SHE* couldn't interfere." He stated.

"I know not how she plans to do it, or whether the *MOTHER* will allow it, I only know she tries," Morgu stated.

"Tell me about the Selamiss," Drago requested.

"First, I will take you to meet the rest of my family, they must get comfortable with you and your kind. They will need to smell you and touch you, so they will recognize others in your family."

As he led Drago into the part of the shelter where the rest of the Ubscanti were, Drago noticed Loren sitting beside a member of the family, and seemed to be grooming her.

"This is my mate, Biancu." Morgu said.

"Fair day to you Drago," Biancu said.

"Fair day to you also," Drago replied.

"They are wonderful and kind creatures, but are really shy, especially the small ones," Loren told Drago.

"What were you doing with Biancu when we walked up?" Drago questioned.

"Grooming," Loren replied. "It is their way of tying together the family."

After Morgu had taken him around to meet the different family members, they went back to where Drago and Loren had been staying. Biancu brought them some more melons and fruit, then went back to join Loren who had stayed behind grooming the youngsters.

"Before we discuss the Selamiss," Drago said, "I would like to ask a somewhat personal question."

"I do not understand what you mean by personal." Morgu responded.

"In our society we have customs where you do not ask questions that would make the other upset or mad." Drago replied.

"I see," Morgu said. "Ask your question, and if it makes me mad I'll let you know."

"The 'let you know' part is what concerns me." Drago replied with a smile. "I noticed not all of your family have large fangs and claws like you do." Drago stated.

"Amongst your family there are also differences," Morgu said. "It is because I was raised in the border lands where battles with the Selamiss occur periodically. We developed with different traits than some of our other tribes. I am of the tribe that defends our borders; I was brought here by *SHE* to strengthen this tribe and I'm also a member of the council. I am not upset by your question."

"Thank you," Drago replied. "Now please tell me of the Selamiss."

"They were once several tribes also, and they had their own council meetings. They had their own protectors of the skies, etc. in their own land. But now, they call themselves conquers of these areas. Malemiss is now their leader. Her older brother used to be leader of their tribe; but somehow, she killed him. Eventually, through deceit and killings, Malemiss took over all the tribes, naming them the Selamiss and making herself queen. Since becoming queen, she has started expanding her territory, and eventually wishes to control all."

"Why hasn't *SHE* stepped in and stopped her?" Drago questioned.

"There are certain rules that the *MOTHER* puts on all her daughters. We are allowed the freedom to behave in many ways, *SHE* does not dictate to us how to live, *SHE* only tells us how we should. Somehow, this move by Malemiss has upset the *MOTHER* to the point that your people were allowed in. Now, we are not sure what rules apply." Morgu reiterated.

"What are these other tribes like? Drago questioned.

"I do not have your knowledge in order to compare or explain how we see them as to how you would see them. That is part of what *SHE* and the Communicator are exchanging, so he can explain it to you."

Drago and Morgu spent the rest of the evening talking. They were joined by Loren and Biancu, who brought more fruit, berries, and melons to eat. Afterwards, Morgu told them to rest, for in the morning the storms would be over and Aria would come to take them back to the cave.

CHAPTER FORTY-FIVE

EMIR HAD NO IDEA how long he had been sitting there. He knew that from time to time he had eaten and drank only to sit back down and resume communicating with *SHE*. She had explained to him that she not only was looking for information from him but also wanted to impart information to him. He had been allowed to ask her questions, which he did frequently. After asking her who she was, she had allowed him to look into the vastness of what he called her mind. She had controlled it, explaining to him that she should she open her mind completely to him, his mind would be destroyed and he would die. Bit by bit, and piece by piece she had been giving him the information. He now knew that he had been picked because of his mental ability to accept the intangible and the spiritual forces as existing, rather than to ignore or classify them. He learned that *SHE* was one of many daughters of the *MOTHER*. He derived that the *MOTHER* was all the universes combined and the many planets were her daughters, each one in control and sentient to themselves. At first, he found it hard to conceive, but when *SHE* had allowed him that peek into what he called her mind, he was overcome with the vastness of it. Therefore, he had accepted the premise of her existence.

SHE was explaining the different tribes that existed when suddenly he was overwhelmed with a tremendous power that knocked him unconscious, losing the mental thoughts they were exchanging.

"You take chances daughter, you were told you could not interfere."

"But I am not interfering *MOTHER*, I am only explaining to one of those you brought here, about us here."

"You split hairs, my daughter. Be careful you do not cross the line by influencing him. For I will call that interference and respond appropriately."

"Yes *MOTHER,* I understand."

Emir awoke with a splitting headache. Rubbing his forehead, he reached down and got one of the water containers that someone or something left every day with his food. As he sat back down on the throne, he felt *SHE* enter his mind once again.

"Are you alright?" *SHE* asked in a concerned tone, then told Emir that his headache would be gone in a moment. "That was *MOTHER*, if I hadn't thrown you out, it would have literally blown your mind. Now where were we, oh yes, I was telling you about the tribes."

CHAPTER FORTY-SIX

BACK AT THE CAVE everybody was just finishing breakfast.

"It would appear that the storms are over," the Captain announced. "However, just to be sure, I think we'll give it a little more time before we open the door and see what it's like outside."

"I checked the different cameras before coming to breakfast, and it seems to be calm outside." Angelina reported.

"I, for one, have to get out," Maggy said using her thumb to point at her chest. "Being cooped up in here listening to the wind howl was driving me nuts. Besides, Natasha and I need to take the pups out and let them hunt. They are totally getting fat and lazy being fed by Sophia all the time."

"We all need to get out," Doc said. "Forced confinement with stress is not good for anybody."

"Alright then, let's clean up the breakfast dishes, and we'll all go outside," the Captain relented.

When they had finished cleaning up, they all headed for the door in the main cave.

"You do the honors Bruce, since you and Choi came up with idea for the hydraulics," the Captain said as he dramatically waved his arm towards the front door.

"Here goes," Bruce stated, grabbing the handle and pulling down on it. There was a little bit of resistance at first, but with Choi helping by pulling on the handle, it finally swung open.

"It looks like when the ship hit, it bent the door. Rashad you'll have to work on it with the laser." Choi said.

Stepping outside, they all took a deep breath of fresh air and enjoyed feeling the sun on their faces.

"It feels good to be outside again," Natasha said.

"We need to check out the equipment and see how it weathered the storm," Angelina said.

"Okay," the Captain said. "Bruce, you go up with Choi and Molly and check out the solar panels. Angelina, grab Dana and Gerard and check out the equipment you and Emir installed. Sophia, you and Naomi can move the birds out and set up their cage. Matzo, you, and Tani go down and check out what's left of the ship. Maggy, you and Natasha take the pups out. See if you can get them to bring us some of those small critters to add to our meat supply. Rashad, start working on the door. Doc, you, and I will air this place out." The Captain ordered.

"Captain, Captain, I just got a message from Drago," Natasha interrupted excitedly. "Aria will be flying him and Loren back sometime later this morning."

"What? How did you get a message?"

"I just was trying to reach him, now that we are outside, and he heard me and replied." Natasha explained.

"Great," the Captain said turning to Doc. "I'll never get use to this telepathy that everyone seems to have on this planet."

Matzo and Tani had come down the slope and were walking around the shoulder when they saw the ship. It lay against the bottom of the plateau. The nose was crushed and what was left of the wing frames were also crumpled.

"Well, it looks like we won't have any problem removing the wheels," Matzo said picking up one of wheels off the ground.

"Let's go inside and see what's left of the chambers." Tani suggested. Going into the ship from the open hole in its side, they worked their way back to where the chambers were located. The glass had been cracked or broken on the first four they looked at.

"Finally!" Tani said. "Here's one that's not broken." Checking out the rest, they found three that didn't seem to be damaged.

"Let's check out the equipment that supplies the fluid and see if it was damaged." Matzo said.

"It seems to be okay," Tani replied.

"I see a small leak at this one fitting," Matzo said, then added "but we should be able to tighten it." Heading back out of the ship they started going around to the slope to tell the Captain.

Meanwhile, Bruce and Choi had made the climb up to the solar panels.

"There's a lot of dust and debris on the panels, but they don't appear to be broken." Bruce informed Choi.

"One of these frames got bent a little—more work for Rashad to straighten out." Choi said.

"Everything else looks fine; I'll just clean the dust off the panels and we will be good to go." Bruce said.

Angelina, Dana, and Gerard were going through the rocks and crevasses checking out the equipment.

"This camera is smashed." Dana reported.

"This one appears to be okay, but it was buried and needs to be reset." Gerard commented.

They finished checking out the equipment and removed the broken camera. Then they started down the mountain to rejoin the others.

Maggy and Natasha had reached the bottom of the slope and were watching as Zena and Butkis ran into the brush hunting.

"So, did Drago say anything else about what happened to him and Loren?" Maggy asked.

"No, all I got was that they were okay and that Aria was going to bring them back."

"I can't wait to hear where they have been and what happened to them."

"Me too," Natasha agreed. Then, their thoughts were interrupted by Zena and Butkis returning. Each had brought one of the small animals back for Maggy and Natasha. The cubs were jumping around their feet; when suddenly Zena stopped, the hackles on her neck and back going up, as she let out a deep throated growl. Butkis immediately imitated her. Maggy and Natasha looked in the direction the cubs were looking. The cubs were slowly moving into the short grass. Neither Maggy nor Natasha could see anything but as the cubs got closer, there was a sudden slithering sound through the grass. Both Maggy and Natasha could see the grass moving as something went away from them. The cubs settled down and began sniffing around the area where whatever it was had been.

"That was spooky." Maggy said.

"Yeah," I agree," Natasha replied. "Let's get out of here." Picking up the small animals the pups had brought back from their hunt in the grass, they headed back to the cave.

Meanwhile, back at the Ubscanti dwelling, Morgu was telling Drago, "Aria will be here shortly. She will take you and Loren back to your family cave."

"I have learned much from you Morgu," Drago stated respectfully. "I will tell the others about you and your family and meet with you at the council."

"You can now contact me the same way Loren does with Aria; it is one of the things *SHE* gives us." Morgu stated.

"Aria comes," Loren said.

"Fair day to you Morgu," Drago said.

"And to you," Morgu replied.

Aria arrived within moments, and Loren ran out to greet her.

"Greetings Aria," Loren said. "I'm really pleased to see you again."

"I too am glad to see you, Loren," Aria replied.

"My people have repaired your carrier," Biancu stated bringing out the carrier.

"Thank you Biancu," Loren said. "I will miss you."

"I too have enjoyed my time with you. Fair day to you Loren."

"Fair day to you also Biancu," Loren replied as she started hooking the carrier to Aria. When she had finished, Drago and Loren climbed in and waved good-bye as Aria took flight.

CHAPTER FORTY-SEVEN

MAGGY AND NATASHA WERE just coming up the slope with Zena and Butkis, when Natasha stopped and said, "Drago and Loren are coming. Hurry, they should be landing any minute now."

Running up the slope to the cave, they got there just in time to see Aria landing the carrier.

"Thank you again Aria," Loren was saying as she and Drago got out of the carrier. They were removing the harness from around Aria's neck when Natasha and Maggy ran up to them.

"Oh Drago, I'm so happy you and Loren are all right." Natasha exclaimed.

"We're glad to be back also," Drago replied. As Maggy and Natasha continued to ask questions, Loren finished freeing Aria from the carrier.

"Thank you again Aria," Loren said. "I hope to see you again soon."

"I will come again, with some of my flock to take you to the council meeting at the time of the single full Moon." Aria replied. With that, Aria took to the sky and headed back to her aerie. Loren watched for a moment then turned to Maggy and Natasha who were pounding Drago with questions. Natasha quickly came up and threw her arms around Loren with a big hug.

"I'm so glad you're back and safe, I don't know what I would have done if we had lost both you and Drago."

"Hold it," Drago shouted. "Let's go inside with the others and we'll tell you all about it. Besides, I need some of Sophia's cooking, I have had nothing but fruits and melons for almost a week now."

Walking into the main cave, both Loren and Drago were surprised to see how much had changed in the short time they were gone. Suddenly, they heard a loud shout.

"They're back," Rashad yelled. At once, they were surrounded by their friends yelling and hugging them.

"Everybody hold up!" the Captain shouted. "Give them room to breathe. Let's all go into the dinning area and they can tell us their story."

"Great," Drago said, I'm starved."

Hearing that, Sophia, who was in the crowd, immediately ran to the kitchen to get food for them. When everybody had sat down, the Captain said, "Alright, start from the beginning and don't leave out anything."

"I'll start," Loren volunteered. "It was my idea that got us into this in the first place." She then proceeded to tell them about her contacting Aria, who sent Shia's son to pick them up and fly them to where Emir was. She explained how in the hurry to get going, she had not secured the carrier properly and consequently it had come loose and the fell over the jungle.

"What happened? How come I couldn't hear you?" Natasha asked Drago.

"When we fell into the trees, I was knocked unconscious," Drago replied.

"He was unconscious for three days." Loren stated.

"I want to take a look at you," Doc said coming around the table. Checking out the bruise on his forehead, he asked if Drago had experienced any dizziness or lack of focus in his sight. Drago replied that he had at first, but was fine now.

"I'll want to take x-rays and check you out as soon as we're finished here." Doc said. "It sounds as if you may have had a concussion."

"Okay," Drago agreed as he gingerly touched the lump on his head.

"Let's get back to the story," the Captain requested.

"I was knocked out also," Loren explained. "I awoke in the carrier as we were being carried through the jungle, then I passed out again. The next time I woke up, we were in the shelter with Biancu taking care of me."

"Oh no, here we go again," the Captain said. "This time I think I'm going to write it down, so I can keep track of the different characters."

Before Loren or Drago could go any further, Sophia arrived with the food.

"I brought you some left over meat, a salad and some bread fresh from the oven," Sophia said. "I can get you more if you want and some melons for desert."

"I've had enough melons over the last few days, but I might have some more of the meat," Drago replied between mouthfuls.

"Okay, back to the story," the Captain said impatiently.

"Biancu is the mate of Morgu, who is the leader of the Ubscanti, he is the one who rescued us from the jungle and took us to their shelter. Aria had contacted him and told him what had happened to us." Loren told them.

"Unbelievable," the Captain remarked shaking his head in amazed disbelief.

"Just wait," Loren said. "This next part is going to freak you out—especially Rashad. You have all seen one of the Ubscanti; in fact, it may have been Morgu himself."

"What?" Rashad exclaimed. "When? I don't remember meeting any Ubscanti."

"You remember that large gorilla like creature in the one video? Well, that's one of the Ubscanti." Loren replied.

"You have got to be kidding me!" Rashad said. "That creature would eat you alive without thinking twice about it!"

"Actually, they're not meat eaters; they eat fruit, melons, and berries. Also, they are a very friendly group or family as they call themselves." Loren stated. Everyone around the table started asking questions about Morgu and his family.

"Why do they have such large fangs and claws if they're not meat eaters?" Maggy asked.

"Okay, I'll take over from here Loren," Drago interjected. "Before we go any further, I have to tell you that Morgu and I spent almost two days discussing everything from his fangs and claws to why we were brought here through the wormhole. It is a long story that will take the rest of the morning and most of the afternoon if I am going to tell you everything. I suggest that I go with Doc now, and then after my checkup, we can meet back here to discuss everything. That should put us close enough to lunch, that we can talk and eat at the same time. Meanwhile, everyone can finish what they were working on or talk to Loren about her experience with the Ubscanti."

"That will work," the Captain agreed. "I'll go with you and Doc to see how the tests come out." With that, the three of them got up and headed to Doc's Med Bay. Everyone else decided to ignore what they had been doing and listened to Loren as she continued to tell them about her experience.

When Drago, the Captain, and Doc got to the medical area, the Captain turned to Drago and remarked, "There seems to be something you didn't want to talk about in front of the others."

"You're staring to know me too well," Drago replied in response. "Like

I said, in my discussions with Morgu, I learned many things. The main thing is the planet, known as *SHE*. *SHE* is experiencing a war between the two major groups of inhabitants. We were brought here to try to rebalance the situation, and fight on the one side. I'm probably not stating this clearly," Drago continued, "but that's the essence of it."

"Doc, check him out to see if there was any brain damage, before we go any further. I'm almost hoping this is something he hallucinated due to the hit on his head, but I'm afraid it's not," the Captain said.

When the Doc had finished taking x-rays and completed his testing he informed the Captain. "He's had a mild concussion but I don't see any permanent damage. If he takes it easy for a few days, he should be fine."

"Then go on with your explanation," the Captain directed. "But first, tell me, were you able to find out anything about Emir?"

"Yes sir, he is with *SHE*. All his needs are being taken care of. He is called the Communicator by the inhabitants of this planet, and *SHE* is giving him the information we will need to help in the fight against the Selamiss."

"The Selamiss are the enemy tribe?" the Captain questioned.

"Actually, what use to be a group of tribes that have been turned into one." Drago replied. "That's just part of the story I have to tell you."

"Let's go back to the others," the Captain said. "You don't want to tell it three or four times." Walking back into the eating area, they saw that the girls were missing.

"Loren said she was dying for a bath, so all the girls went to the other cave to bathe and listen to Loren tell her story. They said to tell you that they would be back in time for lunch." Choi informed them.

"Well, I don't want to wait that long to hear more from Drago," Rashad said in a matter of fact tone. "At least tell us about the Ubscanti."

"I was a little afraid, but I did ask Morgu why he had such large fangs and claws if they didn't eat meat. I had also noticed when he took me to meet his family, that some of them did not have the fangs and claws. He explained to me that he was from the border lands where there is an on-going battle between the Selamiss and the other inhabitants of this planet. Therefore, they had developed the fangs and claws to fight with. He was brought where he is now by *SHE* in order to strengthened his tribe." Drago explained.

"What are the Selamiss?" Bruce questioned.

"Basically they are our enemy; what they are, I'm not sure. Morgu did not have a way to explain them to me; he said Emir would explain it to us when he is finished communicating with *SHE*."

"Hold on," the Captain said, "let's wait till the girls get back before continuing this discussion."

"Yeah, tell me what has been going on here while I was gone." Drago said. The next half hour was spent with the others telling Drago what they had done during the storm, and how the ship had been blown against the door to the cave. Matzo was just telling him about what they had found that was left in the ship, when the girls returned from the baths.

"Sophia said lunch is still ten minutes away and that if we want her to continue fixing our meals, we can't talk about anything until she gets here." Maggy announced with a grin as she delivered Sophia's message.

"Oh that reminds me," Loren said looking at Maggy. "I have some news for you that doesn't need to wait. In our discussions with Morgu, he mentioned that we had met the leader of the Wantaso, Protector of the Plains. When I told him I didn't know what he meant, he told me that the mother of Zena, whose name was Zentaska, was the animal we found the cubs by. Now comes the fun part, the new leader of the Wantaso, is none other then our Zena."

"There'll be no living with her when she hears that." Maggy responded shaking her head and rolling her eyes in mock exasperation.

"Unfortunately, she already knows. She was told to come with us to learn."

"I get the feeling I'm really in for some flack now." Maggy said.

"Not really," Drago commented. "Morgu told me we had already been matched up like Loren and Aria. Maggy has been matched with Zena and I have been matched with Morgu. He also told me that there is another match to be set up in the future. All of us will be going to the council meeting at the first single full moon with our assigned partners."

"What council meeting?" "When's the first single moon?" "What are you talking about?" Came a flood of questions being shouted out from everyone sitting around the table.

"Stop," the Captain said holding up his hands. "Everybody hold on and hush up for a minute! I am not going to risk Sophia following through on her threat of not preparing any more meals for us if we don't include her in our discussions. Drago, please wait till the food comes and then start with the whole story."

At that moment, Naomi and Sophia entered with the food. After serving everyone, they sat down with the others to hear what Drago had to say. Long after lunch was done, they all still sat there listening to what he told them. He explained everything he had learned from Morgu, including what Emir was doing, the Selamiss, and the war that was going on. When he was done, there was complete silence around the table.

Finally, Angelina asked, "What do we do now Captain?"

"I have to think this over; I will need to meet with you and Doc to discuss this in my quarters. The rest of you can talk about everything between yourselves. I'll see you all at breakfast."

Everyone else stayed in the eating area and continued questioning Drago about everything he had told them.

When the Captain, Doc, and Angelina got to the Captain's quarters, the Captain immediately went and got the tequila and glasses.

"If this keeps up, I'm going to have Sophia make us either some corn liquor or rice wine." The Captain stated as he took his seat and poured each of them a drink. "This certainly changes our plans. Up until now, I was just concerned about our survival. But from what Drago has told us, it would appear that we were purposely brought to this planet to be sent into the middle of ongoing confrontation. What is even worse, it looks like we have no choice in the matter."

"What really drives me crazy is that we don't know half of what is going on." Angelina said. "We have to wait for Emir to contact us and tell us; plus, we don't know the time frame or when the first single full moon is supposed to occur."

"I don't like others making our decisions for us, especially when we don't have any input." the Captain said as he took a sip of his tequila.

"I think the important thing is that we secure our position, check out our provisions and weapons and try to be prepared for whatever comes." Doc advised.

"Agreed, we'll need to get everyone into the program in the morning."

CHAPTER FORTY-EIGHT

At breakfast the next morning, they were all still discussing the information Drago had relayed to them from the day before.

"Last night after we went to bed, I thought of a way we might be able to find out when the first single full moon will be." Tani stated. "I worked some with Emir on his weather and astrology programs—at least enough that I should be able to figure out if he recorded or projected the single full moon times."

"Good idea," Drago said. "We already know that he figured out approximately when the double full moon would occur."

"Matzo and I discussed putting the drone back together, so we could make some observational flights," Bruce said changing the subject.

"I think we need to go back and reinstall those weapons we never got around to testing on the drone." Rashad stated.

"We should probably put the other drone together also," Molly suggested. "That way, we're prepared with a back-up if anything happens to the other one."

"I thought Rashad and I would do an inventory of all the weapons and make sure they are on full charge." Maggy stated. "I can go ahead and start, if Rashad is working on the drone."

I'll help you right after we take Zena and Butkis out for their hunt this morning." Natasha volunteered.

"Yeah, that will work. Besides, I can hardly wait to have a discussion with Zena this morning." Maggy agreed grinning.

Walking in and hearing the discussion, Sophia said, "We need to build up our food supplies; also, we could use some more birds, definitely some meat, and we need to start another garden."

"I was talking with Dana and Gerard about strengthening our

perimeter defenses and cameras," Choi stated. "We need to be able to have infrared cameras outside that are able to pick up some of the creatures in the grass, We can also record what is going on at night when we are sleeping." While they were continuing to discus their plans, the Captain, Doc and Angelina walked in.

"Listen up everyone," the Captain said. "I want to talk to you about setting up some plans to be prepared for what Drago told us yesterday." With that, everyone started talking at once, telling him about what they were planning to do.

"Hold on," the Captain shouted, "Obviously you all have been thinking about this, let's go one at a time, and tell me your thoughts." As they proceeded around the table, the Captain was impressed with how they had thought out the problems facing them. When the last one had finished, he added, "Except for thinking about setting up a trauma center for injuries in the med center, I don't think you missed much."

"Actually, I thought about that last night," Doc responded solemnly. "If it's possible, I would like to get one of the undamaged cryogenic chambers out of the ship with the life support equipment, and install it in here. That way, if we need to, we can put an injured person into the chamber and keep them alive until we can do something for their condition." This statement caused a chilling quiet to go around the table. None of the kids had thought about being injured or losing one of their own and remained rather subdued during the rest of the discussions. Upon finishing breakfast, they all quietly carried their plates back to Sophia's Galley and left to start working on their plan.

"Once again they amaze me," the Captain remarked to Doc and Angelina. "They had thought about everything I had and then some."

"They sure hadn't thought about someone getting injured or dying though," Doc said.

"No, that certainly took some of the excitement out of them and made them more serious, which is a good thing," Angelina replied as she got up from the table. "I'm going to get with my group and go over our exterior defenses."

"Doc, why don't you and I go down into what's left of the ship and check out those chambers?" the Captain suggested.

"Good idea," Doc replied.

CHAPTER FORTY-NINE

TANI HAD GONE STRAIGHT to Emir's computer after breakfast and started going through his program files. Within minutes, she had found his research information on the moons. According to what he had determined, the next single full moon would be in about a week. Once she was satisfied that she had found the correct information, Tani shut down Emir's computer and went immediately to tell the Captain and the others.

Maggy and Natasha had the cubs and were heading down the slope to the plains. "They sure have grown," Natasha commented.

Looking at the cubs Maggy replied, "You're right, being with them everyday you don't really notice it. I'd guess they are about a hundred pounds each now, and Zena is as tall as my knees. Which reminds me, Miss Zena, is there something you wanted to tell me?" Maggy asked sarcastically.

"What would that be?" Zena sent back.

"Oh, I don't know, something like Leader and Protector of the Plains."

"Oh that, I thought I would wait till you were older and could handle the information better." Zena replied innocently.

"What!" Maggy exclaimed, "When I'm older?"

With that, Zena and Butkis took off into the high grass.

"Did I hear her laugh at me?" Maggy asked in frustration.

Natasha, who couldn't keep from laughing herself said, "You two make the perfect pair, you both have attitudes."

"Hump!" Maggy responded.

As they waited for the cubs to return, they saw Sophia and Naomi coming down the slope with stuff to plant the garden. Walking over to them, they offered to help, while the cubs were hunting.

"I wonder if the rain will come at night like it did where we were before?" Naomi asked.

"I would think so," Natasha responded confidently, "*SHE* took care of it before, and based upon what Drago said, I'm sure she'll continue to help us."

Maggy and Natasha were poking holes in the ground with some steel rods, while Sophia and Naomi were putting seeds into them. As they were working, Zena and Butkis came back, each one bringing one of the little creatures they hunted with such accuracy.

"Could you get two more please?" Sophia asked them. "That way, I'll have enough to make a stew." Both cubs immediately ran back into the grass, emerging moments later with two more.

"Thank you," Sophia told them. "I'll fix up something special just for the two of you." Both cubs immediately started running around her feet, with tails wagging and making that yipping sound.

"Is that any way for the Leader and Protector of the Plains to act?" Maggy asked Zena with sarcasm.

Zena slowly walked over and sat down in front of Maggy. Looking up at her, Zena sent, "Get over it, you and I are meant to be together, you will always be first with me and I would give my life for you."

Maggy overcome with what Zena had said, bent down and hugged her close saying "I would for you also Zena."

Licking Maggy on the face, Zena replied, "I know."

With that, Maggy, Natasha and the cubs headed back up the slope.

"We'll put the game meat in the kitchen area for you Sophia," Natasha said.

"Thanks, I'll need to come up and clean them pretty soon," Sophia, replied.

Rashad had helped Bruce and Matzo get the drone out of the cave and had gone to check on the weapons. Bruce and Matzo were reinstalling the wings on the drone when Maggy and Natasha returned. Looking up, Bruce noticed they were carrying fresh game and commented his approval, "All right, we'll have meat for dinner tonight."

"How are you guys doing?" Maggy asked.

"We're just installing the wings; then, we will start running the cables and other stuff. Rashad just went in to start checking out the weapons."

"I'll drop these off in the kitchen, then I'll join him, Maggy said. Walking in, they saw Tani coming toward them.

"Were you able to find out about the moon?" Natasha asked.

"Yes," Tani replied, I went to tell the Captain, but he and Doc are down at the ship, so I've been helping Angelina and her group with the outside stuff. According to what I could figure out from Emir's research, we have about a week until the single full moon."

"That gives us some time." Maggy said. Dropping the creatures in the kitchen sink, Maggy went to look for Rashad while Natasha went to look for Drago.

Drago was still in the eating area, sitting at the table, when Natasha came in.

"Hey, Drago, what are you doing?"

"I'm just sitting here thinking about all I learned."

"Did I tell you that I missed you?" Natasha asked.

"I missed you too, especially not having you in my mind." Drago stated.

"Tani just told us that we have about a week until the single full moon occurs."

"Good, I just hope we hear from Emir in enough time to adjust to what we are facing."

"I finished replacing the broken camera," Gerard was telling Angelina. "I replaced it with one of the infrared cameras and aligned it to cover the front and down toward the slope. It's too bad they won't pan back and forth; I was only able to point them in a single direction." Gerard then asked in frustration with a perplexed look on his face, "Do you think we should add another one up higher to watch the top of the mountain?"

"We don't have any more unless we try to adjust one of the helmet cams," Angelina replied. "But I feel we will need those for when people go out into the field."

"Well, I've checked everything else," Dana said, coming to where Gerard and Angelina were. "I even checked out the solar panels and saw where Rashad had already made the repairs. It looks like everything is ready."

"Alright let's go down and see who we can help out," Angelina said. Climbing down and reaching the front of the cave again, they met the Captain and Doc coming up from the ship.

"How did it look Captain?" Angelina asked.

"It will take some work and a lot of effort, but Doc and I think we can remove three of the chambers along with the supporting equipment and bring them to the cave. The question is how much time we have. Let's go see if we can find out if Tani was able to pull any information from Emir's computer research. I am hoping that she will be able to tell us how much time we have before the single full moon," the Captain said going into the cave. When they got inside, they could see Natasha and Drago talking at the table. Looking around they saw Bruce and Matzo had taken the drone outside. As they walked up to Drago and Natasha, Tani came walking in from the other cave.

"Oh, Captain I'm glad I finally found you. The information I got off Emir's computer tells me we have about a week before the single full moon."

"Well, that gives us a little breathing room," the Captain replied. "I just hope we get more information before that time comes. It looks like we have about thirty minutes or so before everyone comes in for lunch. While we are waiting, I'd like to discuss how we are going to remove the chambers and equipment and bring everything into the cave."

As they were discussing the best way to remove the equipment from the ship, the rest of the groups slowly showed up for lunch.

"As soon as Sophia and Naomi serve lunch, we can talk about what everyone has accomplished so far," the Captain stated as everyone took their seats.

Sophia and Naomi arrived with lunch and were setting it on the table when Sophia said, "You're having leftovers today, sandwiches with either bird or meat with a salad. The cubs brought back enough for dinner, but we're going to have to get some more birds and meat. We have vegetables and melons enough, but only about three more meals of the buffalo. Someone is going to have to go out and get us some more game."

"We haven't looked for birds in this area," Maggy said adding, "nor have we looked for the buffalo type animals."

"We should have the drone ready by tomorrow morning," Bruce offered. "We can send it out on a scouting mission to look for game."

"We'll plan on doing that," the Captain said. "Based on Tani's findings, we have about a week to get ourselves set up before the council meeting. After that, there is no telling what we will be doing."

"Maggy and I have finished doing an inventory of our weapons. I suggest we install the stun guns to the drone before it goes out, just so we can test it." Rashad stated

"What other weapons have you found for the drone?" the Captain asked.

"We have both the sonic gun and a laser for it," Rashad replied. "But I'm afraid of even testing the sonic gun due to the recoil."

"Doesn't it have different adjustments?" the Captain asked.

"Yes sir, but I don't know how to test them without destroying the drone," Rashad responded. "If we have the stun gun, we can maybe stun some of the birds,"

"That way some of you guys can just come and pick them up," Bruce said.

"Okay, we will work that out tomorrow after you get the drone up and running," the Captain said. "How many other weapons do we have?"

"We have four laser rifles, two laser guns, two sonic guns, five flash bangs, and five grenades. The flash bangs and grenades won't last long, but the big problem is going to be recharging the rifles and the guns on the drone. We only have two chargers at this time," Rashad explained. "If we get into a long fight, the rifles can easily run out of power. I just wish we knew what we were fighting."

"I'm pretty sure the creature you blasted at the lake was one of them," Drago stated. "Morgu said they had taken over all the water ways."

"If that was one of them, I'm not anxious to meet the others," Rashad responded.

"Okay, let's talk about what we are doing to prepare, enough about the monsters," the Captain said.

"We got all the cameras hooked up, and added the infrareds, Angelina reported. "We're prepared outside as much as we can be."

"We started the garden today," Sophia added.

"Well, Doc and I inspected the chambers and equipment, we believe they can be disconnected and installed in here, but it's going to take a couple of days," the Captain stated. "After lunch, I'd like all the help we can get to start taking them apart and getting them ready to bring inside. The hard part is going to be how to move the vessels containing the liquid and the equipment that supplies it to the chambers."

When the group got down to the ship, they were surprised at how mangled it was. While one person at a time could work their way into it, they could not see how they were going to get the equipment out, let alone get it up to the cave.

"Captain," Choi said, "we have already been discussing this with Dana and Gerard. I think we should get Rashad down here with his laser to cut up the rest of the ship. That should make it easier to remove the cryogenic chambers and the support equipment along with anything else you decide is valuable. Then we should destroy what's left of the ship."

"Doc and I had discussed the same thing," the Captain replied. "I didn't want to, but I think it's the only solution."

With that decision made, everyone headed back up to the cave. After conferring with Rashad, they decided that Doc and the Captain would mark out what they wanted saved and Rashad and Maggy would cut out and destroy the remaining scrap. Doc and the Captain spent the rest of the day tagging salvage items on the ship. Drago also suggested parts to save. Rashad and Maggy, who were with them, realized that there were some areas they could start cutting right away and had gone back to get the lasers. Coming back to the ship, they stopped long enough to discuss with the rest of the group what they were planning to cut. Drago, who had been listening, directed the others where to move and stack the pieces when Rashad and Maggy started cutting.

"Try to cut everything at its joint or connection point so we can maybe reuse the pieces," Rashad told Maggy. With that, they started cutting up what remained of the ships structure. By the time, dinner was ready, they had opened the ship up quite a bit with a large pile of struts, small panels, and pieces stacked on the ground in an orderly fashion. Returning to the cave, Maggy and Rashad went to put the lasers on the chargers while the rest went to clean up for dinner.

At the table that night, they discussed what each group had accomplished. Bruce and Matzo had the wings on the drone and had started reconnecting the cables and controls. Sophia and Naomi had planted more in the garden, and the group that worked on the ship, told the others what they had done.

"Is there any way someone other then Rashad can use the laser tomorrow, so he can start remounting the guns on the drone?" Bruce asked.

"Actually that's a good idea," the Captain said. "We need to have more people familiar with the weapons."

"I could use Molly or Choi's help installing the weapons," Rashad said. "Maggy can teach the others on how to use the lasers and let them take turns cutting up and dismantling the remaining pieces of the ship."

"Okay," the Captain agreed. "Pick one of them, the rest of you I want taking turns with the laser so everyone gets the feel of it. The other thing is, tonight the men will go first to the baths. Doc and I have been crawling around all day in that ship and I need to clean up and soak my tired muscles." This was met with groans and good natured complaints from the girls, but they agreed that maybe this one time the men could go first.

When they got to the waterfall cave, Drago was amazed to see how much had been done to make it into a spa-bathing area. There were enclosed cubicles for undressing in and a separate enclosure where the water went into the ground for a bathroom. He also noticed an area had been set up for washing clothes with a clothes line that had some garments on it.

"Wow," Drago said as he surveyed the bath area. "I can't believe how much this place changed in the few days I was gone."

"Just about everyone contributed," the Captain told him. "We had time on our hands, and everyone had different ideas, so I told them to go ahead and add whatever they wanted. You'll find that there are separate cubicles for the males and the females. Also, Doc and Sophia got together and made some homemade soap for washing. Rashad and Choi made some handrails at the pool to make it easier to get in and out. Molly and Angelina devised some benches and hangers in the cubicles. All in all, it came out quite well."

"The really neat thing is that when we are through, we have to go back through the kitchen area. Sophia has got in the habit of putting out some melons or fruit to eat on your way back." Rashad told him.

After the men had finished and returned to the cave, the girls headed into the bath.

"One good thing about letting the guys go first is we can take as long as we want to soak in the hot springs," Maggy commented as she slid down into the warm water.

"Yes," Sophia agreed. "But I noticed they ate most of the fruit going back."

CHAPTER FIFTY

THE NEXT MORNING AT breakfast, Rashad decided that he would ask Choi to help him install the guns on the drone. All the rest of the groups would go down and take turns learning to use the laser and dismantling the ship.

When they got down to the mangled remains of the ship, Maggy started explaining to Molly and Angelina how to adjust the controls on the laser.

"You adjust it here," she said pointing to the controls. "And this is the safety, which you keep on at all times unless you're cutting. I've set mine for a narrow beam, so I can make cuts that are more precise. Start over here on the outside piece, it will be easier to get at." Maggy instructed.

The rest of the morning, they all took turns cutting and stacking. Inside the ship, the Captain, Doc, and Gerard had been unhooking the chambers and taking apart the piping from the containers.

"These containers holding the liquid are under pressure," Doc informed them. "We will need to keep them as they are, and move them out with the liquid inside them."

"The problem is that even in this lower gravity, they probably weigh about four-hundred pounds a piece," the Captain said. "We'll have to figure a way to get them outside and up to the cave."

"The chambers weigh a couple hundred pounds a piece also," Doc replied. "We'll have to give some serious thought to how we are going to manage transporting them up to the cave without damage to the equipment or persons.

By lunch time, the others had removed all the salvageable material and scrap pieces necessary for them to be able to remove the chambers and supporting equipment.

Meanwhile, Bruce and Matzo had just about finished connecting the wing cables and wires to the internal drone controls. Rashad and Choi had mounted the guns and were reading the manual to see how to hook up the controls.

"Matzo," Rashad called out, "I think you need to look at this to figure out how it hooks into the computer control panel."

"We're almost finished here," Matzo replied, "give me a couple more minutes and then I'll look at it."

"Okay, I just wanted to get everything done before lunch so we could try it out this afternoon." Rashad responded.

"We'll stay and get it done, because we want to fly it after lunch too." Bruce said.

With Matzo helping, they soon had the guns set up. Bruce had finished the other connections and the drone was complete.

"Look at this," Matzo said. "The computer shows an actual gun site on it when you call up weapons."

"Oh man," Bruce exclaimed. "That looks just like a computer game. Let's trade! You fly and I'll run the computer."

"No way," Matzo replied. "Let's go get lunch so we can get back and fly it."

When they got back to the cave, everyone was all ready eating.

"I was about to give up on you guys," the Captain told them. "Did you get the drone put back together?"

Sitting down, Bruce replied, "Ready to fly Captain. That's why we were late, we wanted to complete all the installations and hook-ups, so we can fly it right after lunch."

"Rashad, did you and Choi get the guns mounted?" the Captain asked.

"Yes sir," he replied. "We want to try them after lunch also."

"What I'd like to have you boys do is fly the drone out over the plains and along the tree line to see if you can spot any birds." the Captain said. Then he continued with, "If you do spot some, we can send out a group to gather them up.

"Which reminds me," the Captain said in a no-nonsense tone of voice. "From now on when anybody goes out, I want an extra team with weapons to go along as guards. Based on what Drago has told us, we have to be on high alert from now on."

After making sure that they had absorbed the seriousness of what he had just said, the Captain continued. "Our salvage team completed cutting up the ship before we broke for lunch. We still have some more disconnecting to do on the equipment; however, we should be ready to remove the chambers and equipment from the ship today. The only problem is that the chambers and the supporting equipment pieces are too big and heavy to move. We may get it to the ground, but I don't know how to get it in the cave. Drago I'd like you to look at it after lunch and see what you can come up with."

"All right Captain, I had been trying to figure out a lifting system before we found the slope up the plateau." Drago said. Finishing their lunch, part of the group went with the Captain and Doc back down to the ship while the rest went to watch Bruce and Matzo launch the drone.

"One thing that works in our favor is that this plateau gives us plenty of take off room," Bruce was telling Matzo. "Although, with the added weight from the guns, I'm not sure what affect that will have on the maneuverability or flying time."

"Come on, you guys, launch it," Rashad interjected impatiently. Bruce and Matzo turned on the controls and launched the drone.

"It feels a little different," Bruce noted.

"Try some maneuvers with it," Matzo suggested.

Bruce completed a couple of maneuvers with the drone until he felt more comfortable with it.

"Alright, let's head for the plains and the tree line, to see what's out there."

Flying out across the plains, Matzo had all the cameras on record. When they got to the edge of the tree line, he instructed Bruce to fly the drone back and forth along the edge.

"It looks like there are some birds by those berry bushes," Matzo exclaimed.

"Should I go down and try to stun them?" Bruce asked.

"No wait, lets get some of our group out there, so when you stun them they can pick them up." Matzo said. "Rashad, you, and Maggy go get your gear on, remember what the Captain said. Natasha, you and Sophia and Naomi get some sacks to put the birds in. Get Molly to go with you so you can all do the sling around, the birds are about thirty minutes out."

As everyone was getting ready, Bruce kept the drone circling high enough not to disturb the birds. When everyone got back, and were ready, Matzo told them what direction to go in. They all went down the slope and when they got to the bottom, they hooked up to start the sling around.

"Maggy, you follow at the rear, I'll go out first," Rashad commanded. "That way we have protection both front and rear."

Maggy was tied with Natasha, and Molly and Rashad were together, with Sophia and Naomi connected to each other in the middle. Rashad and Molly started out slowly in the direction Matzo had indicated. After seeing the others were coming along fine, they quickly picked up the pace.

When they reached the edge of the tree line, Matzo's voice came over their ear bugs saying, "You need to go about a hundred yards to your left."

Moving that way, Matzo called them to a halt about halfway there and told them to wait where they were.

"Okay Bruce, see if you can fly down and use the stun gun on them." Matzo instructed. Bruce brought the drone around so he could fly over the largest group of birds.

"Here goes," he announced grinning. On the first pass, he managed to stun two birds but not the rest.

"Matzo, widen the beam on the stunner so I can hit more of the birds with one shot," Bruce instructed as he circled the drone around to make another pass. This time he got five more birds.

"Okay everyone, go gather up the birds and put them in the sacks," Matzo shouted. Unhooking their cables, everyone ran up and started putting birds in the sacks.

"I'm going to check for babies," Naomi informed them as they were gathering up the birds.

Sophia said, "We don't have a pen big enough to hold all these birds and we are also going to need to pick some of the berries to feed them with."

"Okay, lets carry the birds back, then Maggy and I along with Sophia and Naomi will come back here to gather berries. The rest of you can get material to enlarge the pen." Rashad directed the group.

About that time, Naomi returned empty handed saying, "I couldn't fine any babies."

"All right then let's head back," Rashad directed.

When they got back to the cave, Maggy hooked herself up to Rashad for the return trip while Molly went to gather materials. Natasha stayed with the birds in case they needed to be stunned again. When Molly got to the cave, she went to where the material was stacked up. She found a few pieces she could use but not enough. Going back outside, she went down to the ship where they had stacked the left-over salvage pieces. Coming up to the group she asked, "Can I have some help? We got a lot of birds and I need to increase the size of the pen to hold them. We are going to need some of these pieces to complete it."

Both Dana and Gerard volunteered to help, and grabbing up the pieces Molly pointed out, headed back up the slope, to where Natasha was waiting with the captured birds.

When they got there, Natasha told them, "Some of them started moving around in the sacks a little so I just stunned them all again."

"Let's get this stuff over to the other pen, and start putting it together," Molly instructed.

Back at the ship, Drago had suggested that they try to slide the equipment out to the ground, then worry about how to get it up the plateau. They had laid some panels out, tied cables around the first chamber, and were attempting to pull it out.

"We are going to need more people," the Captain said. "Choi go see who you can round up to help us."

When Choi got up to the cave, Rashad, Maggy, Sophia, and Naomi were just returning.

"We need help down at the ship," Choi said. "Can any of you guys help us?"

"Maggy and I can," Rashad said.

"I will go with you;" Natasha volunteered. "Molly and her group can finish the pen."

"Well, if you want roasted bird with potatoes, Naomi and I need to start cooking," Sophia stated.

"No, you go cook," two or three replied at the same time.

When they got down to the ship, they could see everyone was taking a break.

"We got the first one moved about halfway out," the Captain explained. "But we need extra help."

Drago, who had been looking through the discard pile said, "There are some pipes here, if we can get them under the chamber we can roll them out. We just have to keep picking them up and putting them back under when they come out the back side. Rashad, get something we can use as a pry bar to lift the chamber up, and put the pipes underneath."

Gathering up a large flat bar, Rashad slid it under the chamber and lifted. Drago was able to get the first pipe underneath, after that, the other pipes were easier to put under the chamber. Pulling on the cables and reinstalling the pipes as they came out, they soon had the first chamber on the ground.

"That's one," the Captain said. "Only two more chambers and the pressurized containers to go."

With a groan they all went back into what was left of the ship and got set up to move the next chamber. It had been a struggle, but they had managed to get all of the equipment out by supper time. Exhausted from their efforts, they slowly headed back to the cave.

Back up on the plateau, they had finished the pens and were putting the birds into it when Sophia said, "Don't put those last two in; they're going to be supper tonight." Reaching into the sack, she pulled out the last two birds and swiftly broke their necks. Lifting them up, she headed back to the kitchen area.

"I don't know how she does that so easily." Naomi remarked shivering.

"She's been doing it for years," Molly replied, "it doesn't even faze her."

Bruce and Matzo were just bringing the drone in for a landing when the group from the ship walked up.

"You guys look beat," Bruce said.

"You should try spending all day moving hundreds of pounds of equipment around," Angelina responded.

"I understand you found some more turkey-birds," the Captain said. "Did you have any luck locating the buffalo animals?"

"We started flying out over the plains after we got the birds," Bruce replied, "but we didn't see any of the buffalo. We'll try again tomorrow."

Walking into the cave, the Captain went into the kitchen area.

"How long till supper?" he asked Sophia.

"About an hour or so, long enough for you to go to the waterfall cave and take a bath."

"I'm on my way," the Captain said. Going by Doc, he whispered to him, "We have enough time to take a bath, if we sneak in and don't tell anybody."

"I'm with you," Doc said grinning as the two of them snuck off and headed to the bath.

Everyone else was sitting down at the table and talking about the day's events.

"How long till supper? Rashad asked. "Can someone ask Sophia for me? I'm too tired to get back up."

Molly, who hadn't sat down yet, said, "I'll ask her." When Molly came back, she let them know, "Sophia said it would be about an hour or so before everything would be ready."

"That gives us enough time for a bath," Maggy said cheerfully.

"I thought the same thing," Molly replied. "But Sophia told me that the Captain and Doc had already beaten us to it."

"That means the guys can go," Rashad replied getting up and heading for the bath.

"We might as well take Zena and Butkis out for their evening hunt," Natasha told Maggy.

"Okay," Maggy agreed getting back up. "If it means we can lie in the tub for as long as we want after supper."

The men returned from the bath just as Sophia was serving dinner. Maggy and Natasha had returned with Zena and Butkis who were curled up comfortably at their feet.

"The smells are killing me," the Captain remarked to no one in particular as he sat down at the table. The next hour was very quiet as everyone concentrated on eating. As they were finishing up, the Captain looked over at Bruce and said, "Tomorrow, I want you and Matzo to fly over the plains again and see if you can spot any of the buffalo. If you do, we can try stunning a couple of them like you did today with the birds. That would make it much safer and easier for Rashad and Maggy to move in for the kill. We will still have to be careful about Zena's relatives though."

"Not so," Zena sent to Maggy.

"What do you mean?" Maggy asked Zena.

"I can just tell them you're coming; better yet, I'll go with you. It's time you met my clan anyway."

"Excuse me Captain," Maggy interrupted. "But Zena just informed me, she can communicate with her clan and let them know we're coming and who we are."

"I don't suppose she can tell us where the buffalo are?" the Captain questioned.

"I asked her and she said of course," Maggy replied. "She is leader of the Wantaso, after all."

"I'll never get use to this," the Captain replied shaking his head. "Now if you'll excuse me I'm going to bed, we can figure this out in the morning."

"And we're going to the bath," replied the girls in unison.

CHAPTER FIFTY-ONE

THE NEXT MORNING, NATASHA and Maggy took the cubs out before breakfast. When they came back from their hunt, Zena informed Maggy she had communicated with her clan and knew where the big animals were grazing. Returning to the cave, they went into the eating area and sat down. When the Captain arrived and sat down, Maggy told him what Zena had said.

"Can you describe their location?" the Captain asked.

"I have a visual but I'm not sure about the distance." Maggy replied.

"We can send the drone out in the right direction and spot them." Bruce said.

"Okay, after breakfast we'll send the drone out, once you have confirmed the location, Rashad's team can head out," the Captain said.

"Zena says she and Butkis will go with us," Maggy stated. "She'll be able to contact her clan to help us."

"Which of you will be going?" the Captain asked.

"I think myself, Maggy, Natasha, and Loren, along with Sophia and Naomi to butcher the meat," Rashad replied. "I was thinking, if we can get Zena's clan to separate some of them, Bruce can fly the drone in and stun them. Then, we can go in and finish them off."

"Let's hope it works," the Captain said as he turned to Drago and asked, "Now, Drago have you figured out how we are going to get the equipment up to the cave?"

"I thought about rigging up some type of pulley, but we still have the weight of the equipment to consider and how to get it into the cave." Drago responded. "I was thinking about trying Loren's way."

"What's Loren's way?" the Captain asked.

"I was thinking about trying to contact Morgu, and see if he would carry them up."

"What, you're going to ask that monster to come here?" Rashad exclaimed.

"He is not a monster; plus, we're going to be working with the Ubscanti, so we might as well get comfortable with them." Drago replied.

"In that case I'll stay back," Loren announced.

"Molly can take your place," Drago said.

"So, how are you going to do this?" the Captain asked.

"After breakfast, I'll go outside and try to contact him."

"Well this is going to be a pretty interesting morning and day," the Captain said.

After finishing up with breakfast, Bruce and Matzo went out to launch the drone. Maggy followed along behind with Zena to give what directions she could while Drago went out to try to contact Morgu.

"I find that if I send out to Aria, and then think about what I want, she seems to understand." Loren stated. Drago went over and stood by himself as he concentrated on sending his thoughts to Morgu. He was surprised by the ease and clarity of the responses back and forth between the two of them as he communicated his request for Morgu's help. Drago stood there for a few more minutes, then turned and walked back to the cave. When he got back inside, Drago found the Captain still sitting at the breakfast table talking with Doc and Angelina.

"Morgu is coming. I was able to get in touch with him and explain that we needed his help. He agreed and told me that he would bring three others of his family with him."

Loren, who had followed Drago into the cave said, "I'll go help Sophia prepare some melons and berries for them to eat when they get here."

"Did he say how long it was going to take for them to get here?" the Captain asked.

"He said it would take them till the suns were almost straight up." Drago replied.

"That's roughly three hours or more from now," the Captain remarked. "That should give us enough time to send the drone out, locate the buffalo herd and send in Rashad's group." Going outside, they went over to where Bruce and Matzo were sitting with their lap tops.

"How are you doing?" the Captain asked.

"Were heading toward the place Zena and Maggy instructed us to go," Bruce replied.

"I see them," Matzo said, "turn more to your left. There they are. Rashad's group should be able to get there in about forty-five minutes using the sling arounds."

Following the directions given by Matzo, the group headed out toward the buffalo herd. Zena and Butkis had no difficulty keeping up with the others, and got ahead of them more than once.

"Zena says to move over to the left and wait by that bush," Maggy instructed. "Her clan is coming over that way behind the animals. Bruce, get ready. Zena tells me that they are going to cut five out of the group and drive them towards us."

"I see them," Bruce said looking at his hand held control. As Zena's clan cut the animals out about twenty yards from the herd, Bruce's voice came over their ear bugs with new instructions. "Maggy, tell your clan to drop back, I'm going to use the stun gun."

Bruce flew the drone low over the animals, having set the stun gun on wide, he fired at the running animals. His first shot got four of them with a fifth one only partially affected. As he was circling the drone around for another pass, Rashad's group watched from a safe distance as Zena's clan ran in and brought the dazed animal down. Rushing in with their lasers drawn, Rashad and Maggie quickly dispatched the four animals that were stunned. Looking around, Rashad signaled the all safe sign when he realized that Zena's clan had already finished off the fifth animal. As Sophia and Naomi moved forward to start cutting up the meat, Zena's clan came forward.

Maggy clearly heard their leader saying with respect, "Fair day and good hunt to you Zena, Leader of the Clan."

"And to you," Zena replied. "These are the ones I told you about."

As the clan moved in closer to smell the others, Natasha said, "Fair day and good hunt to you." The other members of the clan were shocked to hear her in their minds.

"She speaks to us," said the leader of the group with surprise.

"Yes, there are others who also speak to us." Zena replied. "We will be spending much time with them, and they are going to the council meeting." Then she turned to Natasha and asked, "How do we split the food?"

"We wish for two," Natasha replied. "The rest belong to the clan." With that, some cubs ran out of the grass and started to feed on the animals. Natasha bent down and was talking to the cubs and petting them.

"She cares for our cubs," the group leader noted. "This is a good sign."

"They have many who care," Zena said. As Sophia and Naomi finished butchering the animals, the rest of the group was busy loading the meat into the carry-sacks.

Back at the cave, the Captain had watched the progress of the hunt on the computer with Matzo.

"They'll be coming back now," the Captain said. "Let's see if Morgu has arrived yet." Going up to Drago and the others he asked, "Anything on Morgu and his group?"

"He contacted me a few minutes ago to say they were at the edge of the plains and were getting some water before coming on." Drago replied. "They should be here any time now." As they looked down off the plateau, they could see some creatures in the distance. They moved across the ground very swiftly on all fours using a galloping motion, which rapidly covered ground. Within minutes, Morgu and his group were on the plateau.

"Fair day to you Morgu," Drago said. "Thank you for coming to our aid."

"Fair day to you also," Morgu replied. "I was looking for a way our people could get together before the council meeting, this works out well. Let me introduce the members of my family who came with me. You already know Biancu my mate; this is her sister, Beebe and her mate Gordo."

"Fair day to you also and thank you for coming to our aid." Drago said bowing respectfully.

"Fair day to you also," they replied.

"We have fruit and berries for you to eat, since you have traveled a long time to get here," Drago said.

"That is welcome," Morgu said. As Drago lead them into the cave, he explained their living conditions.

When they arrived at the eating area, Loren walked in and said, "We have lots of food for you. Please make yourself comfortable and I will serve you."

As Loren started passing out the food, Biancu said, "This is quite polite and hospitable."

"Trust me," Loren said smiling as she walked up and embraced Biancu. "Sophia, our cook, only lives to cook and feed others. She prepared this for you." While they were eating, Drago explained their problem to Morgu.

"I understood that you had some heavy things to move when you contacted me," Morgu replied. "When we have finished eating, we will look at this problem."

"Let me introduce you to the rest of my family while you eat," Drago said. After introducing the rest of his group to Morgu's family, they finished eating and went outside.

As they made their way down the slope to the ship, Drago explained. "Our problem is that we need to move this equipment into the cave but it is too heavy for us to carry up."

When they got to the ship, Drago showed Morgu the equipment. Morgu reached down and grabbed one of the chambers and lifting it up, he said, "Gordo, grab the other one, Biancu you and Beebe can carry the last one." Throwing the chamber on his shoulder, Morgu walked back around to the slope and carried the chamber up to the cave.

"Where would you like this placed?" he asked.

"Over here please," Doc said pointing to a spot just outside his medical area. Gordo, Beebe, and Biancu came in right after that and Doc showed them where to place them.

When they got back down to the ship, Morgu looked at the containers holding the liquid. Lifting one up to test the weight as he had done with the chambers, he informed Gordo. "These are much heavier, you take one and I'll take one. We will have to make two trips, as I do not want our mates to carry them." After they had completed taking the containers into the cave and placing them in the locations Doc had directed, they returned with Drago to the eating area.

"If I may," the Captain asked politely. "Have you received any more information about Emir?"

"No, I have not," Morgu replied. "But I believe he will return to you next week. We must go now if we are to get back to our family tonight. It has been very informative meeting all of you." As they were walking out of the cave to begin their journey back, Rashad and his group returned with the meat.

"Whoa," Rashad said, pulling up his rifle. "It looks like the monsters are here."

"Put the rifle down," Drago said. "These are our friends." Lowering his rifle, Rashad said, "I'm sorry, but they're pretty scary."

"Who are you to say?" Gordo asked. Rashad was surprised to hear Gordo in his mind.

"It seems we have another connection," Morgu said.

"He does not trust us," Gordo said.

"Nor do you trust him," Morgu stated. "However you and he are tied, like Drago and me, and Loren and Aria."

"I could crush him like a bug," Gordo sent in response.

"And I could blow you to smithereens before you even had the chance," Rashad said aloud so that everyone could hear.

"You two are to be our leaders of war," Morgu stated. "Our success depends on the two of you working together. I suggest you spend some time together and get to know one another."

"Consider that an order," the Captain said looking sternly at Rashad.

"Yes, sir," Rashad responded as he mentally heard Gordo replying in the affirmative to Morgu.

"We could use more melons," Sophia suggested breaking the tension.

"Good idea," Morgu responded with a chuckle. "Tomorrow, the two of you can get together and gather melons, for Rashad's clan. I'll have Gordo meet you at the edge of the rain forest tomorrow morning."

"Till then, fair day to you all." With that, Morgu and his family left, headed home to the rain forest and jungle.

"Thanks Sophia," Rashad said sarcastically. "I can hardly wait to go melon picking with him."

"Get over it," the Captain ordered. "It's important to our success that you and Gordo get along."

"Yes sir, I'll try, but he is really scary looking," Rashad replied.

They stood there for a few minutes longer watching as Morgu and his family disappeared in the distance. When they returned to the cave, everyone went back to see if they could help Doc set up the chambers.

Meanwhile the others were returning to the cave with the meat they had. Coming up the slope, they had to glide since there wasn't enough room to execute their sling-around maneuver. Suddenly, both Zena and Butkis were growling and their hackles were up. Both were walking stiff legged toward the tall grass. As everyone stopped and looked, there was a rapid moving of the grass away from them. Zena and Butkis went immediately to the area and started sniffing around.

"Whatever it was, it seems to be gone now," Natasha said.

"Selamiss," Zena sent to Maggy and Natasha.

"Let's get up to the cave, now," Maggy ordered. With that, they all grabbed their sacks and hurried up to the cave.

Coming into the cave, they were greeted by Loren. "I see your hunt was successful."

"Yes, it really went a lot easier with the help of Zena's clan," Maggy replied.

"Don't forget our part," Bruce stated. "I was pretty good with the drone's stun gun."

"Yes you were," Sophia said. "Now, help us get this meat into the ice cave."

At dinner that night, they were all discussing the day's adventures. Natasha and Maggy had informed them about Zena smelling the Selamiss and the movement in the grass. Bruce was telling everyone about the hunt when Molly interrupted.

"So Rashad, when are you going melon hunting?"

"He goes out in the morning," the Captain replied, as soon as Drago gets the information from Morgu, he will go meet Gordo."

"I can hardly wait." Rashad replied.

CHAPTER FIFTY-TWO

THE NEXT MORNING AT breakfast, they were discussing what duties they would be performing that day, when Drago entered and said, "I have heard from Morgu. Gordo will meet you at the edge of the rain forest in an hour, Rashad."

"Great," Rashad replied sarcastically. "I can hardly wait to take the laser rifle and some sacks and go on the big melon hunt."

"We can use the fruit," Sophia said.

"It is important that you and Gordo bond," the Captain said. "But before you go out, you have to select a team to go along with you on your melon hunting adventure. You will need someone to help carry melons back if nothing else. More importantly, I don't want anyone going out without a team to protect each other."

"Today, Dana, Gerard, and anyone else I can get, will be working on setting up and connecting the chambers," Doc informed the Captain.

"I need to work in the garden," Naomi stated.

"We could fly scout for the party going out," Bruce stated.

"That's not a bad idea," the Captain agreed.

"I need to check out the videos from last night, and I want to make sure our surveillance is working," Angelina said. "I could use some help with that."

"Okay, it sounds like we need to get organized, let's start over and get organized. Rashad, who do you want for your team?"

"I'll like for Maggy, Natasha, and Molly to be on my team. That gives me someone to sling around with, plus security and help bringing the melons back."

"I'll take Tani and Loren," Angelina said. "Bruce, if you and Matzo will activate the infrared scanners while you are scouting with the drone, we will try to determine if any of the creatures are part of the Selamiss. Tani and Loren can also help me review the security videos from last night."

"I'll work with Dana and Gerard, hooking up the chambers," Choi volunteered.

"I'll take Zena and Butkis out for their hunt, and then help Naomi in the garden." Sophia replied.

"Sounds good to me," the Captain replied in agreement. "I'll work with Doc and his team setting up the chambers. Rashad get your team ready, and head out to meet with Gordo."

As the different teams headed off to their various assignments, Rashad gathered up his group and started passing out equipment.

"Do you think we should take the sonic gun?" Maggy asked.

"I've been thinking about that," Rashad replied. Even though it has a big kick, I think I would feel better if we had it along."

"I'll carry it." Maggy volunteered slinging it over her shoulder.

"All right then, lets get the sacks and head for the meeting at the rain forest." Rashad stated. Going out of the cave they got off the plateau and started slinging toward the edge of the rain forest. When they reached the edge, they stopped and disconnected themselves from the cables.

"How do you want to work this?" Maggy asked.

"You three stay here," Rashad replied. "I'll go in and meet Gordo. When we have enough melons I'll call you in, we'll pick up the melons, and head back to the cave."

Rashad then left the three of them there and headed into the rain forest. When he had gone in about a hundred yards, he called out, "Are you here Gordo?"

"Yes little one, I am here." Gordo replied. "I'm up here in the trees, where the melons are."

"How do you want to do this Big Guy?" Rashad asked.

"I'll throw them down and you pick them up."

Great, thought Rashad to himself—true bonding. But with Gordo already dropping melons from the tree, Rashad had to scramble to catch the melons and put them in a pile.

"Hey watch it," Rashad yelled, "You almost hit me with that one."

"Pay attention and keep your head up." Gordo replied chuckling. Suddenly there was a great crashing in the trees, and loud growling from Gordo.

"What's going on?" Rashad yelled. But the crashing and thrashing sound continued as Gordo fell to the ground wrapped up by a huge snake.

"Holy Crap!" Rashad yelled. Pulling his rifle around, Rashad could see that the snake had totally wrapped Gordo up in its coils. It was about twenty feet long with a huge head that had large teeth and fangs. Gordo wrapped in the coils was having trouble using his claws and teeth to fight it off. Rashad moved in closer, pointing his laser and yelling for Gordo to hang on until he could get a clear shot. As Gordo struggled to hold the snake's head, Rashad pointed his laser and proceeded to cut it off just above Gordo's grip. Even without its head, Gordo was still trapped in the coils.

"Hold still," Rashad yelled, "I'll cut these coils away, but I'm afraid of hitting you."

The rest of the group, hearing Rashad yell had came in running with their weapons drawn.

"Don't shoot. You might hit Gordo." Finally, Rashad had cut enough away, so that Gordo could remove himself from the coils. As he struggled loose, Rashad said. "Well Big Guy, I guess there's a use for us little people after all."

Gordo stood up and coming over to Rashad sent the mental thought, "Thank you, I wasn't paying attention and it coiled around me before I could use my claws. Maybe we can work together after all." The others gathered around the large snake staring at its size.

"This thing is a monster!" Maggy exclaimed.

"Be careful," Gordo warned. "They always travel in pairs."

"Give me the sonic blaster," Rashad told to Maggy. "I'll take care of the other one."

"If you shoot up in the trees at one of those, the gun will drive you into the ground," Maggy stated. Just then they saw movement in the trees and a large snake head appeared.

"I've got an idea," Rashad said. "Gordo; put your back against mine. You're big enough that it might stop me from getting blown into the ground or some trees."

"Hurry," Maggy yelled, "It's coming out of the trees." Gordo quickly positioned himself where Rashad directed.

"Get ready, here we go," Rashad shouted. With that, Rashad pulled the trigger. The snake blew into a hundred pieces, splattering all of them with snake parts. Gordo and Rashad were still knocked back about ten feet from the recoil.

"We'll have to practice that," Gordo stated. "It was stronger than I thought."

"Let's gather these melons and get out of here," Natasha said. Quickly gathering the melons and putting them in sacks, the group ran out of the rain forest.

When they got back to the plains, Gordo walked up to Rashad and said. "You saved my life little one, we are now brothers." Extending his paw he reached out to Rashad and gripped his arm clasping his claw about Rashad's arm. Rashad returned the gesture gripping Gordo about his arm.

"We will practice working with this gun, together we will be invincible," Gordo said. "We will get together again and we will work it out. I now return to my tribe to tell them of today's events, fair day to you."

"Fair day to you also," Rashad replied; then added, "Safe journey." Gathering up their carry-sacks, the group started their return to the cave.

"I about peed my pants when I saw that snake," Maggy said.

"You! I think I was too scared to even do that," Rashad replied.

"Let's move a little faster," Natasha, suggested. "Molly and I want to get back before any more show up." With that, they hooked up their sling-around belts and took off at top speed heading back.

Meanwhile, Bruce and Matzo had been flying the drone around the plains area.

Looking at his computer screen, Matzo said, "It looks like the infrared scanner picked up quite a few different creatures. I hope Angelina and Loren can match them up to what we know about the different animals."

Flying back along the edge of the rain forest, the drone cameras picked up Rashad's group returning.

"I can see Rashad's group returning," Matzo stated. "It looks like they are really hotfooting it back to the cave."

"Let's take the drone back too," Bruce said. "It's almost time for lunch anyway. Besides, I want to hear their story and see how Rashad got along with Gordo."

"Probably not too well," Matzo remarked.

Back at the cave, the group working on the chambers had also decided to break for lunch.

"Another few hours and we should have it complete." Doc was telling the Captain.

"I hope so," the Captain remarked. "I don't know why, but I'll feel better knowing the chambers are working."

"I know what you mean, I feel the same way." Doc stated in agreement.

They arrived at the eating area just as Rashad and his team was coming in.

"How did it go with you and Gordo?" the Captain asked Rashad.

"Great," Rashad replied, "we're now brothers."

"Right," the Captain replied skeptically. "I can't wait to hear this story." With that, they all started talking at once, telling about the huge snake.

"Hold it," the Captain yelled loudly. "One at a time, please."

Rashad was just starting to tell the story and had got to the part about Gordo falling from the tree wrapped up by the snake, when Bruce and Matzo walked in.

"What snake?" Bruce asked. "Start at the beginning."

"Wait," the Captain said. "We might as well wait till the others get here so that they can tell everyone at the same time."

Sitting down at the table, they were still asking questions when Sophia and Naomi entered with lunch. Angelina and Loren came in about the same time.

Angelina immediately said, "I can't believe the size of that snake you killed."

"How did you know about that?" Maggy asked.

"We saw it on the head cam videos," Angelina replied.

"I'm so use to wearing them, I forgot we had them on," Maggy responded.

"That's the way it is supposed to be." Angelina said in a matter of fact tone.

"Let's pass out the food, then you can tell your story." the Captain said.

"Where's Drago?" Natasha asked.

"I haven't seen him all day," Angelina replied.

"Nor have I. Natasha, go outside and use your talent to find him," the Captain suggested.

Natasha went outside, and a few minutes later returned with Drago.

"Where have you been all morning?" the Captain asked.

"I have been sitting up by the solar panels, talking with Morgu. He has been explaining many things to me about the planet and what's going on. He was just telling me about Gordo returning and his experience when Natasha found me."

"Well, you're just in time to hear the story with the rest of us," the Captain said. With that, Rashad started from the beginning and told about his experience with Gordo and the snakes. After Maggy and the rest had joined in with their versions, everyone sat there discussing the situation.

"Well that's one creature we have a good computer reading on," Angelina stated. "We will now be able to recognize it from its computer footprint, even with infrared. After lunch Loren and I will continue trying to establish the different footprints; from there, it's just a matter of identifying which creatures are what."

"According to Morgu, all these creatures are reptilian in form." Drago responded. "There is the alligator-like creature Rashad killed, there are snakes of all sizes and some types of lizards. There's also a flying type reptile, I'm calling it a phorushacos or terror bird. I read about it in a Prehistoric Bird book."

"Why would you read about prehistoric birds?" Maggy asked.

"I was reading about dinosaurs and other prehistoric animals for a report I had to do in school. This bird's skull showed a large head with teeth and a wing span about eight feet, the scientists figured."   "Great," Rashad said. "It's not enough that we have giant alligators and snakes. We have to have giant man eating birds also."

"That's the best I could figure out, based upon what Morgu tried to explain to me. We discussed me going with him to the border lands to see for myself."

"That's not going to happen," the Captain said. "There is no way you're taking a side trip by yourself with Morgu."

"We'll have to wait and see Captain; according to Morgu, I won't be the only one going on a side trip."

"Who's making these decisions anyway?" the Captain asked.

"We're supposed to find out more from Emir when he returns and then at the council meeting." Drago responded.

"We should be able to complete hooking up the chambers before dinner," Doc interjected to change the subject.

After lunch, Doc and his group went back to work on the chambers, while Rashad and Maggy went to clean their weapons and put them on the chargers.

"Choi, have you finished making the piping connections?" Doc asked.

"I'm finishing up with the last two," Choi responded. "As soon as I'm done, I'm going to see if Bruce is around and can help hook up the power and computer wiring."

"Dana, how are you and Gerard doing?"

"We're done, we have completed setting up the chambers and have the fluid tanks ready. What's left will have to be completed by Choi and Bruce."

"Okay then, you and Gerard come with me and we'll start setting up the triage area in the Med Center." Doc ordered.

Choi found Bruce with Matzo working on the drone. After explaining to him what he needed, Bruce returned with him to finish the chambers.

When Doc, Dana, and Gerard got to the Med Center, Doc explained, "We need to review all the anti-venom serums we have plus poison remedies. We will also need to set up an area to make our own anti-venom. Based on what Drago said, we will be dealing with snakes and reptiles. I wonder if we can get Rashad or Maggy to go into the high grass and try to stun some snakes so we can make the anti-venom?"

"We should check with Angelina and her group, they have been compiling information based on the infrared images of the animals in the grass." Dana informed him.

"We will also need some type of containers to keep them in," Doc stated. "We'll discuss it with the others at dinner tonight and see what we can work out."

Meanwhile, Choi had finished with the connections and went over to see how Bruce was doing.

"Hey Bruce, how goes the hook up?"

"I've finished making all the connections between the tanks and the chambers, I'm now going to run the cables over to the power panel then run the computer cables and hook them up in Doc's office to his computer, give me a hand here, will you?"

As Choi helped pull the cables, Bruce made the connection to the power panel. Once completed with that, they started running the computer cables to Doc's computer.

"Make sure we keep the cables behind the panels so they are not lying out on the floor creating tripping hazards." Bruce instructed Choi.

Doc and his group were working in the same area, so when Bruce finished with the computer hook-ups, he called over to Doc. "Hey Doc, we're all set up. Is there a way you can run a test?"

Doc came walking over and said, "I want to go ahead and start one up to ensure everything works, I can program it, then shut it down after verifying it is running properly."

"How long will that take?" Bruce asked. "We have about three hours till dinner."

"That should give us just about enough time," Doc responded. "We will need to run it though the initial start up procedures then stop the sequence before it causes any problems."

"Alright, let's start it up." Bruce said.

"Okay," Doc said. "Let me sit down at the computer and start the sequence."

Outside, Maggy and Natasha were letting Zena and Butkis run while Naomi was working in the garden.

"How do you feel about what Drago said?" Maggy asked Natasha.

"I don't know, I'm too scared to think what it could really mean to us."

"I know what you mean. The thought that we could be fighting for our lives and someone could be seriously injured or killed really messes with my mind."

"It just doesn't seem fair, first we end up on a strange planet, and now we have to fight to survive," Natasha complained.

"I had a counselor at the orphanage that always said, "Nobody said it was supposed to be fair," Maggy replied.

Suddenly Zena and Butkis started growling and barking. When Maggy looked over, they were walking stiff legged, with their hackles up toward the garden and Naomi.

"What's up Zena?" Maggy asked running toward the cubs.

"Danger, enemies" Zena sent.

Naomi, who was closer, left the garden and started walking toward the cubs.

"What's wrong babies?" she asked. "Ouch!" she yelled. "Ow, Ow, something's bit me!" she yelled.

Butkis jumped in and was barking, biting and growling. There was a lot of trashing in the tall grass as Butkis fought with something.

"What is it?" shouted Maggy. "I can't see anything."

"Naomi, are you alright?" Natasha shouted running up.

As Natasha got next to her, Naomi suddenly collapsed and fell to the ground. At the same time, Butkis came into view. He had his teeth clamped around a snake like animal and was biting it in half. As Maggy and Zena got to Butkis, Maggy noticed that the snake had buried its fangs into Butkis's neck, and even though Butkis had bit it in half the head was still attached to his neck.

Matzo, who had been working on the drone, came running over when he heard all the commotion.

"Go get Doc!" Natasha shouted, "Naomi has been bitten by a snake."

Matzo immediately turned and ran to the cave. Running into the cave he started shouting, "Doc, we need help. Naomi has been bitten by a snake."

Doc, who was watching the computer to see how the chamber was working, jumped up and said, "What's that, what did you say?"

Matzo, running up to him exclaimed, "Naomi's been bitten by a snake and is on the ground, come quick!"

"Dana, get all those anti-venom serums ready. Gerard, you and Matzo come with me. Matzo pick up a stun gun on the way, lets go," Doc commanded. "Bruce, stop the sequence started on the chamber, just hit delete on my computer."

The others working in the cave heard the commotion and came running.

"What's going on?" the Captain yelled.

"Naomi's been bitten by a snake, we're going out there now," Doc responded.

Running outside and over to the garden, they could see Natasha and Maggy bending over Naomi on the ground.

"Get back," Doc commanded. "Give me some room."

"She's been bitten on the leg, I took my shoe lace and made a tourniquet," Maggy informed him quickly as she moved out of the way.

Doc, bending over Naomi, immediately started sucking on the bite and spitting out the venom.

"All right, let's get her back to the Med Center," Doc said.

Reaching down and picking her up, they carried her back to the Med Center. "Set her there on the table," Doc instructed. "Dana give me those serums."

"How do you know which one to use?" the Captain asked.

"Naomi, how do you feel? Are you in pain?" Doc asked. As Naomi started to answer, her eyes rolled back and she suddenly went into convulsions.

"Dana, start checking her blood pressure and heart rate," Doc ordered.

Again, the Captain asked, "How do you know which anti- venom to use Doc?"

"I am still trying to determine her symptoms," Doc responded. "Some snake bites affect the nervous system, some cause convolutions, and shock. Others can cause high blood pressure and with the case of the coral snake, symptoms may not show up for two days."

"Her blood pressure is elevated," Dana announced.

"Okay, I'm going to start with the Cobra anti-venom first," Doc said. "We will have to wait and keep an eye on her before we try anything else. Meanwhile, Bruce make sure the chamber is ready, if we don't see any improvement by the morning, I want to put her in the chamber. We will have to set up the chamber so we can give her drip feedings of anti-venom along with the other chemicals provided."

"Can you do that?" the Captain asked.

"Yes," Doc replied. "The chambers were set up to provide different medications in case of something going wrong with the person in the chamber. You can help out by getting me one of the snakes to test—still alive preferably so that we can milk the venom. Her life may depend on my ability to make an anti-venom serum from the snake that bit her."

"I'll get right on it," the Captain replied. Turning to look at the group that had gathered around them he ordered, "Rashad, get with Maggy and see if you can stun any snakes in the grass. Then I want you to take the lasers and burn or melt all the grass on the plateau so nothing can sneak up on us."

"Aye, aye sir," Rashad responded.

"Sir, I have one of the stun guns with me," Matzo said. "I'll go out with Rashad, that way Maggy can use the laser right behind us."

"Okay," the Captain said, "but be extremely careful, I don't want anyone else to get bitten."

"Gerard, you and Bruce start looking for containers to put any snakes in they bring back," Doc ordered. "Angelina, you and Dana stay with me and keep checking her vital signs."

Going outside, Rashad and Matzo went looking for Maggy. They had stopped and picked up another rifle for her to use. When they got close to the garden, they noticed Maggy kneeling, close to Natasha. She was holding Zena close in one arm with the other around Natasha's shoulder who was sitting on the ground sobbing.

Walking up to them, Rashad asked, "What's going on?"

"Butkis is dead," Maggy, replied. "He was killed by the snake while defending Naomi."

Both Rashad and Matzo started offering their condolences to both Zena and Natasha.

"He fought well and has gone back to the mother," Zena sent. Natasha was too heart broken to reply anything. She just held Butkis in her arms and continued to rock back and forth as the tears streamed down her face.

"Hold it," Rashad said. "Is that the snake's head I see stuck in Butkis's neck? We need to take that into Doc. Besides, I read somewhere that a snake's head can still kill you if the fangs hit you even after its dead."

"Natasha, let go of Butkis so we can remove the snake head," Maggy said softly as she gently lifted Butkis up from her lap.

Setting Butkis on the ground Natasha turned to Maggy, who took her in her arms and stood up moving away from Butkis. When Rashad and Matzo leaned down, they gently turned Butkis over until the snake head was exposed.

"Be careful," Matzo warned Rashad.

Slowly, Rashad grabbed the snake head just behind its jaws and pulled it from Butkis's neck. Holding it so the head hung down, Rashad carefully handed it over to Matzo. "Take this back to Doc, then return here and we'll do what the Captain ordered." Carefully holding the snake head away from him, Matzo handed the laser rifle to Rashad and returned to the cave to give it to Doc.

"What did the Captain say to do?" Maggy asked.

"He wants us to see if we can stun any snakes for testing and then to take the lasers and burn or melt all the grass off the plateau."

Maggy, still holding the crying Natasha said, "Natasha, we have to do what the Captain asked. Why don't you take Zena back to the cave and I'll help Rashad and Matzo."

"No," Natasha replied as she pulled herself from Maggy's arms and wiped the tears from her cheeks. "You take Zena and see if she can tell if there are any more snakes hiding in the grass. I'll take the laser and burn everything once you have passed that area. Maybe I'll get lucky and find one you missed so I can cut it into pieces."

"Okay Zena, can you find any more Selamiss in the grass?" Maggy asked, sending Zena thoughts on what they wanted to do.

"None close," Zena sent back, as she started moving down the plateau through the high grass. Natasha immediately took the laser and started burning and melting the grass. Starting close to the garden, she began to work her way across the plateau and down the slope. Suddenly Zena froze and the hackles on her neck went up.

"There are some ahead," she sent. "I smell two of one kind and one of another. They are laying in wait just ahead of us."

"Can you show what direction?" Maggy asked.

"I am pointing at them now," Zena replied.

"Rashad, Zena is pointing to where there are at least three of them ahead. How do you want to do this?" Maggy asked.

"Let's just spray from in front of Zena outward, covering both sides and the middle. Then she can tell us if we got them," Rashad replied. With that, they started spraying the stun guns moving forward slowly.

"There is one just ahead," Zena sent.

Maggy told Rashad and they both concentrated their stun guns where Zena pointed. Zena walked up slowly ready to attack at a moment's notice. "It does not move," she sent back to Maggy.

"It looks like we got one," Maggy told Rashad. "What do we do now?"

"Hold it there, tell Zena not to get too close. Didn't Naomi have a sack with her at the garden?" Rashad questioned.

"Yes," Maggy said turning to find Natasha. "Natasha, will you go get that sack that Naomi had and bring it here?"

Natasha, who was burning everything insight, with a vengeance, look up and said, "What?"

"Get Naomi's vegetable sack and bring it here," Maggy repeated.

Natasha stopped and walked back to the garden returning with the sack. "What do you want this for?" she asked.

"To put the snakes in," Maggy responded.

"If it weren't for saving Naomi, I'd just as soon burn them up." Natasha said.

"Okay, let's go real slow. Remember, there are still snakes in the area," Rashad warned. Going slowly forward, both Maggy and Rashad continued to spray the guns in the grass around them. When they got to where Zena stood, they looked down in front of her and could see the snake. It was about three feet long and was a brown and green mottled color.

Rashad stunned it again for safety as he instructed Maggie to hand him the sack without taking his eyes off the creature. Grabbing a hold of the sack, Rashad proceeded to use his foot to push the snake about halfway inside, then finally grabbed it by the tail and dropped it in. "That was scary," he said quickly knotting the material to prevent any escape.

"The other two are over there," Zena sent, pointing to the right of them. Rashad and Maggy immediately started to spray the area with their stun guns, moving slowly forward in the direction that Zena indicated.

"They no longer move," Zena stated walking in toward them. When Maggy and Rashad got close to Zena, they could see one snake but not the other.

"Where's the other?" Maggy asked.

"There," Zena pointed a little farther to their right.

Rashad fired the stun gun in that direction then walked forward with Zena. Maggy had fired her stun gun again at the second snake and was using her rifle to push it into the sack, when Rashad yelled back to her, "This is not a snake—it's some kind of lizard."

Maggy finally got the snake into the sack and carried it over to Rashad, who was standing there, looking down at a three foot lizard.

As soon as Maggy got there, he instructed her to hold the sack open as he reached down, grabbed the lizard by the tail, and dropped it inside.

Quickly retying the knot, and holding it out away from his body, Rashad told Maggy, "I don't care if there's more. This should be enough for Doc." Rashad then turned to Natasha and said, "Burn everything to your heart's content, including any other snakes you find. Maggy, you and Zena stay with Natasha. I am headed back to the cave to give the snakes to Doc."

Meanwhile, when Matzo got back to the cave, he went directly to the Med Bay holding the snake's head at arms length. When the others saw him, they just stood back and let him pass following him to the Med Bay. When he got there he announced, "Doc, I've got the snake head for you," holding it out for Doc to take.

"How did you get this?" Doc asked, gingerly taking the snake's head from him.

"It was still in Butkis's neck. Rashad pulled it out, but Butkis is dead."

This brought a solemn quiet to everyone gathered around. This was the first casualty of their group. Sophia started crying softly and there were tears in the eyes of others.

"How's Natasha taking this?" Sophia asked.

"Not good," Matzo replied shaking his head. "She's pretty shook up."

"Gerard did you and Bruce locate any containers?" Doc asked.

"We found some large glass vessels with cork tops and two metal boxes. We will have to put holes in the tops for breathing though," Gerard responded.

"Good," Doc said. "Let's hope Rashad and Maggy are able to capture some live ones." Still holding the snake head, he turned toward one of the work counters. "I'll going to put this head into one of those small containers over there. Hopefully, I'll be able to get some venom from it later."

"Okay everyone, let's leave Doc and Dana alone and go back to what you were doing." the Captain ordered.

As they all were going back, they were discussing the loss of Butkis and how it affected them.

Sophia announced, "I'm going to the kitchen and get started making supper. I don't have Naomi to help, but I have to do something."

"I'll help you," both Molly and Tani volunteered at the same time following her into the kitchen.

A few minutes later, Rashad showed up with the snakes and the lizard in the sack. Walking in, the first person he saw was the Captain.

"Did you have any success?" the Captain asked.

"Yes sir," Rashad responded. "I've got two snakes and a lizard."

"Great, let's get them to Doc right away."

My plan exactly," Rashad said holding the sack as far away from himself as possible. "The sooner the better; I stunned them again just before I entered the cave…just to make sure."

When they got back to Doc's Med Bay, the rest of the group had followed them in waiting to see what the snakes looked like.

"Doc, I've got two snakes and a lizard for you," Rashad announced.

"Gerard get those containers over here," Doc commanded. "Let's see what you've got," Doc said taking the sack from Rashad. "Are you sure they are completely knocked out?" Doc questioned before dumping the sack.

"I stunned them again before entering the cave," Rashad answered.

Getting all the containers lined up before opening the sack, Doc proceeded to slowly dump them out on the table. He immediately took the two snakes and dropped them into the large glass containers. Looking at the lizard, he saw it wouldn't fit into any of the containers. He slid the large metal container over and it was still too small by about three inches. Reaching up on the table to his instruments, he took down one of his scalpels and proceeded to cut the tail off the lizard.

"If it is anything like lizards on earth, it will grow its tail back; if not, it won't matter," Doc informed everyone. "Gerard, poke some holes in the metal top, and put one hole only in the cork tops on the glass," he instructed.

Everyone was gathered around the glass containers looking at the snakes when the Captain asked, "Where's Natasha and Maggy?"

"The last I saw of Natasha, she was burning everything in sight on the plateau. I left Maggy and Zena with her for protection, then came here." Rashad responded. "Natasha was pretty upset and it seemed to make her feel better burning off the grass in hopes of maybe burning up a snake."

"It might be good therapy," the Captain agreed. "Let's leave Doc and Dana alone now so they can continue their work. Besides, I want to get an update from Angelina on Naomi's condition.

It was almost time for supper when Maggy, Zena, and Natasha returned. As they came into the cave, people started going over to Natasha and Zena to tell them how sorry they felt. When Sophia heard they were back, she came running out of the kitchen and wrapped her arms around Zena saying, "I'm so sorry baby, I'll miss my other baby lots and lots."

Zena looked up at Sophia and for the first time communicated with her directly saying, "He has returned to the MOTHER. While his bones go to *She,* his spirit goes to the Mother and she will return him to us once again."

Sophia, with tears spilling down her cheeks was stunned into silence. "She spoke to me," she said in amazement. "I actually heard what she said." Wrapping her arms around Zena even more tightly, she said, "Thank you Zena for telling me." Looking up, she saw Natasha standing there. Sophia immediately stood up and up took her in her arms saying, "I'm so sorry Natasha, I know how much he meant to you." They both stood there hugging each other with Natasha sobbing quietly on her shoulder.

After a few moments, the Captain interrupted. "You mean you actually heard Zena then, Sophia?"

"Yes," Sophia replied with her arm still protectively around Natasha's shoulders.

The Captain then looked down at Zena and asked her directly, "Zena, can you talk to anyone you want like that?"

Zena, looking at the Captain with that look Maggy described as "superior" replied, "Yes we can choose who we want to communicate with. But it also depends on whether that person is receptive to the idea, like now I'm talking to you."

The Captain stood there with his mouth open and a funny look on his face as he clearly heard Zena in his mind for the first time. The only thing he could say was, "But, but…"

"Once one of us has communicated with one of you, that one can communicate with any of us if they so choose," Zena finished.

"Why don't you all just sit down here," Sophia said. "I'll go finish dinner; it should be ready in a few minutes." As Sophia turned to head back to the kitchen, the rest of the group sat down and quietly continued their discussion of what had happened.

Natasha said, "I want to have a funeral for Butkis and bury him here on the plateau, is that okay with you Zena?"

"I do not understand what you mean," Zena replied. After Natasha explained it to her, Zena replied, "His spirit is already with the Mother, putting him beneath the dirt is no different than leaving him above, his bones will return to *She.*"

Just then, Sophia, Molly, and Tani came from the kitchen bearing platters of left-over's with melon slices for dinner. As they sat down around the table nibbling, they continued their funeral plan discussion for Butkis. While they were talking, Doc, Gerard, and Dana came in from the Med Center.

"How's Naomi?" the Captain asked.

"Her blood pressure is still high, and her breathing is erratic. She's almost in a coma like state," Doc replied in a concerned tone of voice. "Angelina is still sitting with her."

"How is the testing or making the anti-venom coming?" the Captain asked.

"I haven't started yet," Doc, replied. "I need to set up some other equipment first, then I have to be able to milk the snakes. I've asked Angelina to set up some additional equipment, since I'm not sure yet how to do the lizard. Also, I have to keep a close eye on Naomi. I'm going to try another anti-venom tomorrow, if she doesn't respond within two days, we need to discuss putting her into the chamber."

"Speaking of the next two days," Drago interrupted. "Morgu contacted me and wants a select group to meet with him to visit both the rain forest and the border lands."

"Here we go again. Why are the decisions being made always out of my hands?" the Captain said in exasperation. "Exactly what did Morgu say, and just who is supposed to be going?"

"He will be here in the morning with Gordo. Me and Rashad, Maggy, Zena, and Natasha will be going with them. Maggy, Zena, and Natasha will only go as far as the rain forest; the rest of us will go to the edge of the border lands." Drago responded.

"I don't like this," the Captain responded, "Why are Maggy and Natasha going to the rain forest? What are you and Rashad going to do at the border lands?"

"I won't know till we meet with Morgu tomorrow," Drago answered.

"I repeat, I don't like it," the Captain stated.

"Why am I going?" Natasha asked.

"I don't know, all I know is that Morgu said you had to be the one," Drago answered.

"Well, we're not going to send anyone anywhere in the morning, until we have the funeral for Butkis," Sophia stated putting her arms protectively around Natasha.

"I still don't like any of this," the Captain repeated.

After dinner Doc and Dana went back to check on Naomi and relieve Angelina while the rest went to their cubicles.

CHAPTER FIFTY-THREE

THE NEXT MORNING RIGHT after breakfast, they all went out to the plateau for Butkis's funeral. Choi had dug a hole and someone had made a headstone out of metal with Butkis's named burned in it. Standing there with their heads bowed, Natasha finally said, "He was a good companion and a great hunter. He gave his life for one of us. Please take him back as one of yours, Mother." Then Choi and Matzo slowly lowered Butkis into the hole and filled it with dirt.

"Interesting," Zena sent, "but I feel the respect you give him."

As they were standing there, Morgu and Gordo came walking up the plateau.

"Fair day Morgu," Drago stated.

"Fair day to you also," Morgu replied, "and to you also Zena, Leader of the Plains."

Fair day to you Morgu, Leader of the Jungle and your companion Gordo," Zena replied.

"What is going on here?" Gordo questioned.

"It is a way these people honor their dead," Zena replied.

"Who has died?" Morgu questioned.

"It is my brother Butkis, he was killed by one of the Salamis,"

"They have their scouts this far then. We will have to be more alert." Morgu said. "Now, is the group ready to go with us?"

"Hold on there, I'm not ready to let anyone go anywhere until I know more about what's going on," the Captain said with authority. But before he could say anything else, he was frozen in place.

"I believe *She* has ended the discussion," Morgu remarked. "I ask again, is the group ready to go?"

"Let us get some equipment first," Drago said. "Rashad, please get the sonic gun and a laser for me. Maggy, get a laser and stun gun for you and Natasha."

When they returned, Drago said, "Maggy, you and Natasha use the sling-around and I'll do the same with Rashad, that way we can keep up with Morgu and Gordo."

As they were gearing up, Sophia came out and handed Maggy and Natasha back packs saying, "I've put some food into the back packs and your water bottles in case you need it. You make sure you come back now." She then gave each a hug and went back to the cave.

"Is everyone ready now?" Morgu asked. "If so, let's go. Zena, when we get to the rain forest, you will lead Maggy and Natasha to where they must go while we go on to the border lands."

With that, Morgu led off using that galloping gate that he and Gordo used to cover the ground quickly. Drago's group quickly followed using the sling-around. When they reached the rain forest, Morgu turned to Zena and said, "You know where to take them. We will return at sundown tomorrow and meet you here." He then turned to Drago and instructed him and Rashad to unfasten their cables. "From here on, we will travel through the trees. You will need to figure out how to fasten the cables to us, for we will be carrying you from here on."

Drago and Rashad came up with a way to modify their sling-arounds that allowed them to sit comfortably on Morgu and Gordo's backs. As soon as they were in the slings, Morgu and Gordo climbed up into the trees and began to swing through quite rapidly. Even when they had to go to the ground, they quite easily carried the two on their backs.

As Maggy and Natasha watched them swing up and out of sight, Zena sent, "Undo your slings from each other and follow me,"

Meanwhile, back at the cave, as soon as Drago's group was out of eyesight, the Captain came out of his frozen state.

Doc was standing at his side when he became unfrozen and asked, "Are you alright? Talk to me."

I'm all right," the Captain replied. "I was just told not to interfere and was locked in place till they left." Then added, "I really hate that."

"You're going to have to get used to not being in control on some things," Doc said.

"I'm not sure; *She* did say that Emir would make it much clearer for me when he got here."

"Did *She* say when Emir would return?"

"Soon, was all she said," the Captain replied.

"Let's go back to the cave and get everyone to settle down. There's nothing we can do but wait now." Doc said.

"Slow down Zena, Maggy said. "It's not easy going through all these bushes."

"It's not that hard down here," Zena replied. "Be patient my friend. We will get to an easier place soon." After struggling for a few more minutes, they came to a small hill. Zena started up the hill then turned suddenly into a cave. When they entered the cave, Natasha dropped to her knees.

"What's happening?" Maggy asked nervously.

"This is necessary," Zena replied.

Standing there, Maggy continued to watch as Natasha suddenly started shaking and began crying again. Then, out of the corner of her eye, Maggy noticed something coming out of the shadows in the back of the cave. Looking closer, it appeared to be a large cat that changed colors, chameleon-like as it moved through the different shades of light streaming through the cave opening. When it reached Natasha, it stopped and sat down on its haunches directly in front of her, then slowly rubbed its head against her. Natasha who's head was down, reached up and put her arms around the cat burying her face in its neck.

After a few moments, Natasha stood up and faced Maggy saying proudly, "This is Chai, Leader of the Katorions and protector of the rain forest. She is to be my companion."

"Fair day to you Chai," Maggy said. "Welcome to our group."

"Fair day to you also. Please sit, Zena and I have much to discuss with you."

Sitting down, Maggy and Natasha took food and water from their back packs. Sharing with Zena and Chai, they settled in to hear what Chai had to tell them.

"We are close now," Morgu sent as he looked over his shoulder at Drago. The Selamiss cannot hear our inter-thoughts; however, they can see, hear, and smell us so we must move quietly. Slowing down, Morgu climbed to the top of a tall tree. Gordo joined him telling Rashad he could get out of the sling. When they were both out of their slings, Morgu pointed toward an area to their left.

"That area is now controlled by the Selamiss. Their land used to be on the other side of a river that is quite away beyond here. But they have increased their area by quite a few miles."

"How do you know where they are?" Rashad asked.

"See that mound to the right of those trees? That is what the large snakes make and burrow into." Morgu replied pointing. "My tribe watches and tries to attack them when they leave their mounds."

"Look above you," Gordo said. "Do you see the large birds circling? They act as spotters, and attack our people when we defend our territory."

"If you look closely, you can see some of our tribe in the trees waiting for them to appear." Morgu sent quietly.

"I've got an idea," Rashad said. "What if I shoot the sonic gun at the burrow while Drago uses the laser on the birds?"

"I like the idea," Gordo replied. "It will give us a chance to see how these weapons work. Knowing that, we can plan our attacks better."

"We were only to observe," Morgu cautioned. "I will need to check with our people and *SHE* to see how they feel." He sat there a minute concentrating on communicating. Finally, he said, "Our people are moving back. *SHE* replied it was none of her business, so let's set up and give it a try."

"Okay Gordo, brace yourself against the tree and I'll back against you like we did on the melon hunt," Rashad instructed.

"Do we need to get closer?" Gordo asked.

"I don't know. Maybe we should go down on the ground and try to get a bit closer. I haven't tried shooting anything long range with the sonic gun."

Gordo picked up Rashad and climbed to the ground. Drago stayed up in the tree with Morgu, keeping watch on the birds above them as Gordo and Rashad made their way through the brush below. When they were about fifty yards out from the mound, Gordo stopped and informed Rashad, "The Selamiss have seen us. We have to do it now, if we are going to."

"Okay, get behind me and brace yourself," Rashad said.

Putting himself against Gordo's back, Rashad aimed the gun at the mound and pulled the trigger. Rashad and Gordo were moved back about three feet, but the mound was totally destroyed leaving a hole about twenty feet deep and animal parts flying everywhere.

"Wow, did you see that?" Rashad exclaimed. "We blew the crap out of that mound and all the snakes in it!"

"That was truly amazing," Gordo sent. "You killed more in that one moment than we have over a long time." Then cautioned, "please contain your excitement little one. They cannot hear your thoughts but they can hear your words. Do not forget that we are in enemy territory."

Just as soon as Gordo finished relaying his thoughts to Rashad there was a sudden crashing in the trees. Both looked up to see one of the birds falling through the trees with its wings cut off. Looking back to where they had left Drago and Morgu hiding, they could see Drago firing at three or four of the birds that had come to attack Rashad and Gordo.

"Let's get back to Morgu and Drago and get out of here," Gordo said as Rashad quickly climbed into the sling on Gordo's back and they started moving back through the brush. When they got to the bottom of the tree, they saw that Drago had shot down three of the attack birds.

Morgu sent out, "We need to get out of here, there are Selamiss coming from everywhere to see what happened."

With that, both Drago and Rashad got back into the slings on the backs of Gordo and Morgu, and took off swinging through the trees toward safety. After they had gotten quite a distance away, Morgu motioned for them to stop. He then dropped down to the ground along with Gordo so that they could take a moment to discuss what happened.

"My tribe tells me the Selamiss are out everywhere in that area. The tribe has pulled back to one of our safety areas."

"That was certainly impressive," Gordo said.

"The problem is that now they are aware of our powers," Morgu said. "Let's get back to the others and we will discuss further how we will use these powers."

Drago and Rashad climbed back into their slings and Morgu and Gordo took to the trees once again as they headed back to meet the others.

Maggy and Natasha were still in the cave with Chai when Zena announced, "We need to go meet the others. They are returning."

As they prepared to go, Zena informed Maggy, "Natasha will be staying. We will see her again at the council meeting. Until then she needs to stay with Chai."

Maggy who had gotten used to these changes did not question the statement but went over to Natasha and said, "Take care my sister, I will see you at the council meeting."

"I will be fine, Chai and I have much to discuss and plan."

With that, Maggy and Zena left to go meet up with the others. When they got to the meeting place, Drago and the others were already there waiting for them.

"Where's Natasha?" Drago asked.

"She remains with Chai and will meet us at the council meeting," Maggy replied.

Drago, who had also become used to these decisions responded with, "Okay, let's go back to the cave. Maggy you get into one of the slings and Rashad and I will do the sling-around."

When they got back to the cave, Matzo, who was working outside, called out to the others letting them know that Drago and the others were returning. The rest of the group coming outside noticed that Natasha was not with them.

"Where's Natasha?" Sophia asked.

"She had to stay with Chai," Maggy responded.

"Who's Chai?" Sophia continued.

"Natasha's new companion," Maggy answered. But before she had time to explain any further, Morgu's mind-speak thought interrupted them.

"Gordo and I must now return to our people. We will see you at the council meeting. Fair day to you all."

"Oh," Sophia said somewhat disappointed. "I was hoping that you could stay long enough to share some fruit and bread with us. You must be hungry and thirsty after your journey."

Looking directly back at Sophia, Morgu responded with, "That is most kind and hospitable of you but we still have a ways to go before the day ends."

As they stood there watching Morgu and Gordo make their way down the plateau and back across the plain to their people, Loren suddenly announced, "Aria is coming. She is bringing Emir home."

With that, they all looked to the skies trying to spot Aria. She finally came into view carrying Emir. When she landed, Loren went up to her and said, "It's so good to see you again Aria."

"It's good to see you also. But I must return, I will see you at the council meeting."

Tani went up to Emir and putting her arms around him said, "Welcome back Emir, we have missed you."

"I have missed all of you also." Emir replied.

"Okay, everybody, we have a lot to talk about. Let's all go inside and discuss what has happened and what we need to do next," the Captain ordered.

When they got inside, they all gathered round and sat down in the eating area. Sophia immediately called everyone to a halt saying, "If everyone will wait a few minutes, I can throw some munchies together, then we can talk."

Sitting around waiting for the food, Rashad and Drago told them of their experience in the borderlands with the Selamiss. When Sophia showed up a few minutes later with a platter of munchies, the Captain began with, "Emir, we are so glad you're back. Let's start with you. Tell us what you have experienced and what we are to do."

"Let me start by saying that *SHE* has given me much information to share. First, is the fact that not all of our companions totally accept us. Secondly, the results of the council meeting will determine how we go forward. More importantly, before we get into a deep discussion of what I learned, you must know that we may not succeed—in which case, we will be eliminated from this planet. So now let me tell you what I have learned."

The saga continues in *The Council.*

EPILOGUE

WHILE EMIR IS RECOUNTING all the information he received from *She* and preparing the group for the council meeting, another meeting is taking place.

Malemiss had called her tribes around her after she had been informed of the attack on the mound and the killing of the birds. In her initial anger, she had struck out and killed the messengers. Now she lay coiled, seething with anger, planning her retaliation.

The story continues in Book Two
The Council

LIST OF CHARACTERS

DRAGO - 11 YEAR OLD AND YOUNGEST OF GROUP

From orphanage in Puerto Rico.

NIPSA Evaluation Report; Short Form. Complete
analysis sent to planet facility.

Personality Profile:

- Quite and unassuming. Gets along well with others but keeps his opinion to self.
- Daydreamer.
- High test scores; total of scores 680
- Score of 430 on Physic evaluation
- More of a poet than rational scientist. Mind does not function in a strictly logical, linear fashion.
- Ability to think in highly abstract and symbolic terms.
- Can be come immersed in own thoughts and overlook immediate environment.
- Strongest assets; imagination and understanding of other people.

RASHAD- 13 YEAR OLD AFRICAN AMERICAN

From orphanage in Brooklyn, New York

NIPSA Evaluation Report; Short Form. Complete
analysis sent to planet facility.

Personality Profile:

- Street smart, physically and mentally tough. Leadership capabilities.
- High test scores; total of scores 465
- Highest score on physical coordination and reflexes
- Sees the world in black and white. Does not consider gray areas.
- He thinks and moves simultaneously.
- Strong sense of loyalty
- Strongest assets; immediate understanding of environment and reaction to it.

EMIR -14 YEAR OLD INDIAN

From orphanage in India

NIPSA Evaluation Report; Short Form. Complete
analysis sent to planet facility.

Personality Profile:

- Quite, unassuming, tends to stay in background
- High test scores; total of scores 525
- Highest scores in abstract scientific matrixs.720
- Intangible or spiritual forces are as real to him as anything in the concrete world.
- Does not appear to be intensely emotional or sentimental person
- Would rather talk things out reasonably or rationally.
- Strongest assets mental equity.

BRUCE-15 YEAR OLD FROM CALIFORNIA

From orphanage in San Francisco, California

NIPSA Evaluation Report; Short Form. Complete
analysis sent to planet facility.

Personality Profile:

- Lively, active, highly emotional
- High test scores; total of 489
- Highest scores; computer sciences. 967
- Out going personality, can be highly vocal.
- When at computer goes into own world. Talks to himself.
- Can function for days without food when at computer controls.
- Strongest assets; computer sciences.

NOTE: Suspected of hacking government systems. Not proved. investigation continues.

GERARD - 14 YEARS OLD.
TWIN OF DANA FROM GERMANY

From multiple orphanages in Europe

NIPSA Evaluation Report; Short Form. Complete
analysis sent to planet facility.

Personality Profile:

- Well spoken, thinks before talking. Can be dogmatic, but is open to ideas based upon sound logical premises.
- High Test scores; Total of scores 458
- Highest score; intangible study of concepts and evaluations 843
- Strong personality. Can be overbearing at times. However listens well.
- Defers to his sister on opinions.
- Strongest assets; Intellectual and scientific research

NOTE- GERARD WITH SISTER Dana scored extremely high on ESP with each other. Communicate nonverbally.

MATZO-12 YEARS OLD FROM CHINA

From orphanage in Beijing, China

NIPSA Evaluation Report; Short Form. Complete analysis sent to planet facility.

Personality Profile:

- Soft spoken, articulate, strong command of language. Intense in his studies.
- Works well in a group.
- Highest test scores; Total of scores 521
- Highest scores; Engineering sciences 890
- Extremely serious in his study of sciences. Communicates well with others,
- Strong work ethic.
- Strongest assets; Engineering sciences.

CHOI- 14 YEARS OLD FROM KIYOKO JAPAN

Multiple orphanages in Japan

NIPSA Evaluation Report; Short Form. Complete analysis sent to planet facility.

Personality Profile:

- Outspoken, polite, gregarious, deep belief in spiritual influence in life and universe.
- Works well with others. Likes to share knowledge
- Highest test scores; Total scores 564
- Highest scores; Engineering Sciences 890
- High degree of study habits. Soft spoken and serious but can be funny and entertaining.
- 2nd degree black belt in Kung fu
- Strongest assets; Engineering sciences.

DANA - 14 YEAR OLD. TWIN OF GERARD FROM GERMANY

Multiple orphanages in Europe.

NIPSA Evaluation Report; Short Form. Complete analysis sent to planet facility.

Personality Profile:

- Well spoken. Works well with others, all though can be domineering.
- Not as dogmatic as brother and has better social skills.
- Highest Test Scores; Total Scores 460
- Highest score; intangible study of concepts and evaluations 850
- Strong scientific diagnostic and analytical mind.
- Not as dogmatic as brother.
- Has control over brother
- Low emotional qualities uncomfortable with tears and tantrums.
- Pervasive in discussions.
- Strong ESP connection with brother.
- Strongest assets; Intellectual and scientific research

NAOMI-16 YAEARS OLD. OLDEST IN GROUP FROM HAITI

From orphanage in Port Au Prince

NIPSA Evaluation Report; Short Form. Complete analysis sent to planet facility.

Personality Profile:

- Out spoken, Strong Maternal complex. Tends to try and lead groups by strength of personality.
- Highest test scores; Total test score 400
- Highest Score; Empathy 723
- Compensates for insecurities and feelings by being bossy.
- Has strong empathy and compassion for others.
- A worrier
- Strongest asset; Empathy and maternal instinct.

LOREN- 15 YEARS OLD FROM ALABAMA

Multiple foster homes in Birmingham, Alabama

<u>NIPSA Evaluation Report; Short Form. Complete analysis sent to planet facility.</u>

Personality Profile:

- Quite, soft-spoken. Speaks only when spoken to. Works well in a group
- Highest test Scores; total test score 515
- Highest test score; Environmental, agriculture and animal husbandry 830
- While seeming to be shy can get quite conversant and outspoken when talking about plants or animals.
- Seems to communicate directly with animals.
- Strongest assets; Environmental, agricultural, animal husbandry.

NATASHA - 14 YEARS OLD FROM RUSSIA

From orphanage in Moscow

<u>NIPSA Evaluation Report; Short Form. Complete analysis sent to planet facility.</u>

Personality Profile:

- Strong but silent type. Gets along well in a group.
- Highest Test scores; total test score 612
- Highest test Score; Physic ability 430
- Strong work ethic. Give her a project and it will get done.
- Strong empathy for others
- Artistic training in ballet and dance
- Possible leadership qualities.

NOTE: Her testing showed extremely high in some areas, lower in others somewhat fluctuating on her mood. Evaluation unsure.

TANI- 13 YEARS OLD FROM INDIA

From orphanage in Delhi

<u>NIPSA Evaluation Report; Short Form. Complete
analysis sent to planet facility.</u>

Personality Profile:

- Quite spoken, shy, well mannered. Gets along well in a group
- Highest Test Scores; total test score 613
- Highest Test Score; Computer sciences 980
- Quite but friendly.
- Has tendency to back off her opinions if challenged.
- Lacks strong self esteem.
- Strongest asset; Computer sciences.

MOLLY -13 YEARS OLD FROM JAPAN

From orphanage in Tokyo

<u>NIPSA Evaluation Report; Short Form. Complete
analysis sent to planet facility.</u>

Personality Profile:

- Well spoken but shy. Friendly, works well in a group.
- Highest test scores; total test score 580
- Highest test score; Engineering sciences 943
- While being friendly and outgoing. She is extremely shy.
- Old school Japanese. Has tendency to take second seat to men
- Multiple martial arts training
- Strongest asset; Engineering sciences.

MARGARUITE (MAGGY)
-15 YEARS OLD FROM LOS ANGELES, CA.

Multiple foster homes in Los Angeles, California.

NIPSA Evaluation Report; Short Form. Complete
analysis sent to planet facility.

Personality Profile:

- Highest test scores; total test scores 560
- Highest test score; survival sciences 956
- Strong, tough. Dislikes authority.
- Does not take direction well.
- Quick to judge environment and react to it.
- Leadership possibilities.
- Strong willed, tough, a loner.
- Does not work well in groups that restrict personal input.
- Strongest asset; Survival sciences.

NOTE: Possibility of abuse in foster homes.

SOPHIA (SOPHIE) -
15 YEARS OLD FROM MISSISSIPPI

From orphanage in Columbus, Mississippi

NIPSA Evaluation Report; Short Form. Complete
analysis sent to planet facility.

Personality Profile:

- Highest test scores; total test scores 480
- Highest test score; culinary sciences 732
- Self assured.
- Well organized.
- Outgoing and friendly.
- Open to new ideas, gets along well with others.
- A leader within her environment.
- Strongest asset; culinary sciences.

**NOTE: Evaluator added special comment to file. While
at space station, worked in kitchen and made amazing
changes to food. Sophia will be sorely missed.**